T0283524

# BEYOND THE RANGES ›››››››››

# BAEN BOOKS by JOHN RINGO

**PEGASUS LANDING**
*Beyond the Ranges*

**TRANSDIMENSIONAL HUNTER** (with Lydia Sherrer)
*Into the Real* • *Through the Storm*

**BLACK TIDE RISING**
*Under a Graveyard Sky* • *To Sail a Darkling Sea*
*Islands of Rage and Hope* • *Strands of Sorrow*
*The Valley of Shadows* (with Mike Massa)
*Black Tide Rising* (edited with Gary Poole)
*Voices of the Fall* (edited with Gary Poole)
*River of Night* (with Mike Massa)
*We Shall Rise* (edited with Gary Poole)
*United We Stand* (edited with Gary Poole)

**TROY RISING**
*Live Free or Die* • *Citadel* • *The Hot Gate*

**LEGACY OF THE ALDENATA**
*A Hymn Before Battle* • *Gust Front* • *When the Devil Dances*
*Hell's Faire* • *The Hero* (with Michael Z. Williamson)
*Cally's War* (with Julie Cochrane)
*Watch on the Rhine* (with Tom Kratman)
*Sister Time* (with Julie Cochrane) • *Yellow Eyes* (with Tom Kratman)
*Honor of the Clan* (with Julie Cochrane) • *Eye of the Storm*

**COUNCIL WARS**
*There Will Be Dragons* • *Emerald Sea*
*Against the Tide* • *East of the Sun, West of the Moon*

**INTO THE LOOKING GLASS**
*Into the Looking Glass* • *Vorpal Blade* (with Travis S. Taylor)
*Manxome Foe* (with Travis S. Taylor)
*Claws that Catch* (with Travis S. Taylor)

**EMPIRE OF MAN** (with David Weber)
*March Upcountry* • *March to the Sea* • *March to the Stars* • *We Few*

**SPECIAL CIRCUMSTANCES**
*Princess of Wands* • *Queen of Wands*

**PALADIN OF SHADOWS**
*Ghost* • *Kildar* • *Choosers of the Slain* • *Unto the Breach*
*A Deeper Blue* • *Tiger by the Tail* (with Ryan Sear)

**STANDALONE TITLES**
*The Last Centurion* • *Citizens* (edited with Brian M. Thomsen)

To purchase any of these titles in e-book form, please go to www.baen.com.

# BEYOND THE RANGES ››››››››

# JOHN RINGO
## WITH JAMES AIDEE

Beyond the Ranges

This is a work of fiction. All the characters and events portrayed in this book are fictional, and any resemblance to real people or incidents is purely coincidental.

Copyright © 2024 by John Ringo

A Baen Books Original

Baen Publishing Enterprises
P.O. Box 1403
Riverdale, NY 10471
www.baen.com

ISBN: 978-1-9821-9337-9

Cover art by Bob Eggleton
Maps by Bryan G. McWhirter

First printing, May 2024

Distributed by Simon & Schuster
1230 Avenue of the Americas
New York, NY 10020

Library of Congress Cataloging-in-Publication Data

Names: Ringo, John, 1963– author. | Aidee, James, consultant.
Title: Beyond the ranges / John Ringo with James Aidee.
Identifiers: LCCN 2023058262 (print) | LCCN 2023058263 (ebook) | ISBN
    9781982193379 (hardcover) | ISBN 9781625799616 (ebook)
Subjects: LCGFT: Science fiction. | Novels.
Classification: LCC PS3568.I577 B49 2024  (print) | LCC PS3568.I577
    (ebook) | DDC 813/.54—dc23/eng/20240111
LC record available at https://lccn.loc.gov/2023058262
LC ebook record available at https://lccn.loc.gov/2023058263

Printed in the United States of America

10  9  8  7  6  5  4  3  2  1

As always

For Captain Tamara Long, USAF

Born: May 12, 1979

Died: March 23, 2003, Afghanistan

You fly with the angels now.


And for

My "Uncle" Charles Gonsalves

For encouraging a love of the wild places.

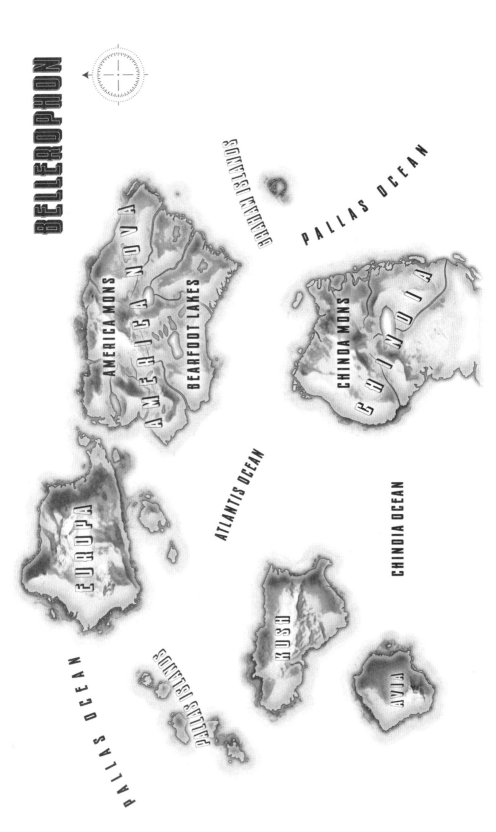

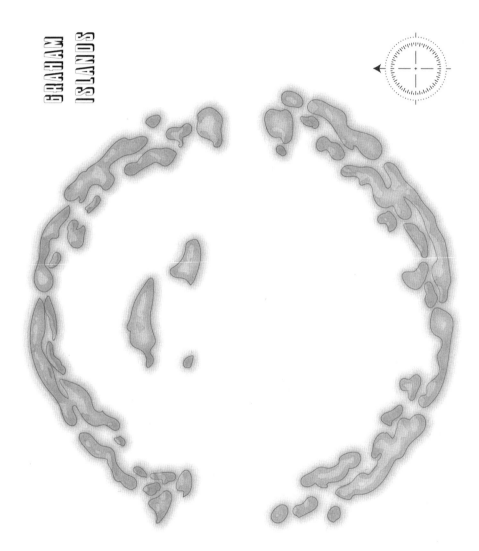

GRAHAM ISLANDS

"There's no sense in going further—
    it's the edge of cultivation,"
So they said, and I believed it—
    broke my land and sowed my crop—
Built my barns and strung my fences
    in the little border station
Tucked away below the foothills
    where the trails run out and stop:

Till a voice, as bad as Conscience,
    rang interminable changes
On one everlasting Whisper
    day and night repeated—so:
"Something hidden. Go and find it.
    Go and look behind the Ranges—
"Something lost behind the Ranges.
    Lost and waiting for you. Go!"

—Rudyard Kipling
"The Explorer"

# CHAPTER 1 >>>>>>>>>

"HI, MY NAME IS MANDY," THE WAITRESS SAID, LEANING OVER and crossing her arms for a cleavage flash. "My pronouns are 'Honey' and 'Sweety Pie.' What can I getcha to drink?"

The waitress was a cute, short, zaftig blonde that comfortably filled the tight white top characteristic of the establishment.

"Sweetwater," Jason said, smiling. "A half pound of boiled shrimp and some conversation."

The nice thing about breastaurants was that it was not considered unusual for a guy to be solo. Since Jason had spent most of his life solo, that was to the good.

Jason had timed the late lunch for the slow part of the day. Chatting with strangers was a lost art. People would rather keep their noses in their phones and looked at you weird if you tried to strike up a conversation. And if you were trying to get real local information, you had to talk to locals.

It was part of the job for the ladies who worked in places like this one. And you weren't expected to hand them cash every few minutes. A decent tip and not being a creep was good enough.

Jason was in Mobile for one of the several gigs he did keeping the wolf from the door: travel writer. Despite all the online apps that purported to give local information for travelers, there was still a place for someone going "boots on the ground" to check out cities. Most travel writers wanted to go to places like Paris, Rome, New York. Gigs were more likely for places like Mobile;

Jackson, Mississippi; or Peoria, Kansas, and Jason honestly preferred them. He wasn't a Paris kind of guy.

Jason Graham, sixty-two, six feet one, the extra inch courtesy
of prosthetic knees, those courtesy of the VA, 250 pounds, with a
still full head of white hair, had done more gigs in his life than
he could easily remember.

Paratrooper was because you gave back to your country,
and he was trying to impress his impossible-to-please father.
Wildlands firefighter was because he was young, trying to prove
himself and the pay was good in season, once you could get
on a team. More gigs in the off-season to pay the bills, mostly
involving testosterone.

Then a blazing tree fell on him that resulted in some burn
scars and enough broken bones that he still got a small disability
check every month.

He felt those bones, now, every time the weather turned
and had a hard time bending over to pick up a dropped piece
of paper. Writing was low-impact work, the only kind he could
do anymore.

"Here ya go, handsome," "Mandy" said, returning with the
beer. The girls, for good reason, rarely used their actual names.

Jason took a sip and smiled again.

"Beer is proof that God loves us and wants us to be happy,"
he said, smiling. "Are you from Mobile?" he added.

"Yeah," Mandy replied. "Born and raised!"

"What's a good local restaurant?" Jason asked, pulling out
an old-fashioned reporter's notebook. "Something that's only
known to the locals? I'm a travel writer and I'm trying to get
local information."

Mandy wasn't too up on restaurants other than the one she
worked in but she knew all the local dance clubs. An older waitress was more helpful on restaurants and he noted down some
local places, barbeque mostly. He'd check them out other days.
Museums included off-the-track examples, a couple of high-end
local places for business dinners...

Jason's phone had buzzed a couple of times but he was both
working and talking with pretty girls so he was ignoring it. Then
the manager came out and turned one of the TVs to a news
channel. It was supposed to be on sports.

"What's up?" Jason asked.

"Something's going on in Europe," the female manager said. "Got a couple of texts about it..."

Jason was one of the few customers in the place and the others hadn't been paying attention to a college football roundtable.

"...not only lost contact with our live correspondent in Ukraine, we've lost contact with *all* of our contacts on the continent..." The female news announcer was looking flustered. It was apparent she wasn't used to, well, news. Her job was to repeat a prepared narrative and with something really happening she wasn't fast enough on her feet to handle it.

"Just in...there is no contact with China or India as well... Bob Toland is coming on with a report from the White House..."

"Civilian satellites are showing no change in the affected areas," the White House correspondent said, reading from a sheet of paper. The more experienced reporter was also clearly flustered.

"Cities are still there, this is not, repeat, not due to the areas being destroyed. The White House has confirmed that this is *not* due to a nuclear attack. All of the cities are still there. But pings by servers to vast areas of the world are getting *no* response, indicating that not only are the people not responding but the servers are offline. It appears at this time to be a total communications loss and is speculated to be some type of hacking attack or what is known as a fire sale. We don't know what has caused this unprecede—"

Jason looked around and shook his head. He wasn't in Mobile anymore and wasn't in a restaurant.

Instead, he was sitting on a gray couch in a gunmetal-gray room, maybe sixteen by ten. It was entirely unadorned and looked a bit like a prison cell. Which was not anywhere he wanted to be and not at all like the restaurant he'd just been sitting in. What might be a door to his right, it had the outline of one but was also gray plastic, blank wall to his left.

As he started to stand up a TV appeared on the opposite wall showing a video of a robot. The robot was both very clearly a robot, metal head and body, blue glowing eyes, but it was also... odd. The triangular head looked as if it had been put together by some kid for a fifth-grade class project. It was a couple of different metals, not really matching, with what looked like an old-fashioned directional TV antenna sticking out of its head at an odd angle. The antenna was held on with what appeared to be aluminum foil.

It was just goofy.

"You might be wondering what just happened," the robot said. Its squeaky voice was just as ludicrous as its appearance. "I am Gavin, a representative of the Galactic Cybernetic Corps. Earth was destroyed. Not by us. Not it. We're the good guys here.

"You along with the rest of humanity were rescued. You are currently in a space station orbiting a planet that we have terraformed for your occupation and use. You are about to be addressed by your current leader designate, President Designate Ron Dewalt. This is the first and last time you will receive a message from the Cyber Corps. Congratulations on your new home planet of Pegasus, good luck and enjoy this new life! Goodbye."

The picture was replaced by a view of Ron Dewalt with a planet, apparently viewed through a window, in the background.

"Well, *that* was abrupt," Dewalt said, shaking his head. "*Thanks* for the warm-up, Gavin. Sorry for both of those abrupt transitions. Everyone who has already been awake has had to deal with Gavin.

"For those of you who don't recognize me, I am Ron Dewalt, formerly governor of Florida in the United States. And before you ask, I know nearly as little about what is going on as you do.

"One month ago, I was awakened in the same way as you were by Gavin. And I, and my advisors, have had nearly as little conversation with it. I was told I had one month to get a structure in place before the other inhabitants of Pegasus were awakened, as you just were. For more detailed information, there should be something resembling a smartphone sitting to your left. It has a full-function AI which can help you with additional information. But like us, the AIs *seem* to have no direct knowledge of what happened. At least they say they don't."

Jason picked up the phone and examined it as the President Designate was talking. Like everything else, it was gray.

He was already starting to hate gray.

Then he noticed his left hand. His fingers were back. For that matter, his hand wasn't wrinkled.

"Where are we and what is going on? As to what is going on, we know about as much as you do. According to our robotic emissary, Earth was destroyed. We don't know if that is true or not. Where *are* we? Well, we're in a massive space station orbiting a planet that has, apparently, been reconstructed or terraformed to be as close to Earth as possible. But where in the universe? Where's Earth? One of the first groups I woke up, after a few close advisors, were astronomers and astrophysicists."

A hologram of the Milky Way appeared in the pictures floating alongside the President. He used a pen to point to a spot on the galaxy.

"According to the astronomers, this, over here, is where Earth is, was or used to be," Dewalt said. Then he pointed to another spot nearly opposite on the galaxy. "Based on their observations, we are about here. Very close to the opposite side of the galaxy in what is called the Scutum-Centaurus Arm of the Milky Way. That is the best we can answer as to 'where are we?'

"Other than that, we are in a star system, designated Pegasus, which has fourteen planets, one of which has been terraformed to be remarkably earthlike. Remarkably because, as various geologists, planetologists and astrophysicists have pointed out, it's very hard to make a planet *exactly* like Earth. And this is so close to exactly, it should be impossible. They got *very* excited explaining it. I will simply say that our robotic friends went to a huge amount of trouble to give us a new home."

Jason knew enough just from reading science articles about planet science to know that, yeah, making a planet exactly like Earth, same water chemistry, same air chemistry, similar animal life, would be *extremely* hard. Not to mention take enormous resources.

He was already itching to check it out.

Jason kept half an ear on the President's speech while he examined the phone. There were no buttons or apparent screens. AI, huh?

"Hello, AI, you there?" he asked, shaking the phone slightly.

"You don't have to shake," the phone answered. A screen lit up and the waitress from the restaurant appeared. "I'm awake. Why this face, you're wondering? Probably continuity. A face you've seen recently. It's how I was programmed to appear. I can have any appearance you'd like."

"That's fine," Jason said. "And you have no idea what's going on?"

"Not a clue," the AI responded. "I'm as clueless as you are. And just as stuck."

‹‹‹›››

"I'll cover the planet later, hang in there. Some of you who do recognize me, may be wondering if I had plastic surgery. No, I didn't. Everyone over the age of twenty or so has been ... age regressed? Made younger. Everyone is starting out at the apparent age of twenty unless they are younger. You may have already noticed this about yourself. It's not a new body, just one that's extensively repaired and rejuvenated. That, right there, is so remarkable it should be an entire discussion. But this is going to be long anyway. Moving on.

"The next question most people always ask, is what about other people? Is my family here? Friends?

"The answer is: Probably some of them. Possibly not all. There are five hundred million people on this station at present. That is about one fifteenth of Earth's previous total population. Approximately half the population of the United States is in the system. The rest are from various countries. So how were they chosen for this system? Race? Family lines?"

"How do we find other people?" Jason asked quietly. "In this system."

"I have your complete electronic contact list, including people not currently on the station," the AI responded. "Monica is on the station. She is still married to Richard who is also on the station. Kevin and Steve are not. Linda is not."

Kevin and Steve were his two older and very liberal brothers. They'd barely spoken in years. Monica and Linda were ex-wives. He generally referred to Linda simply as "She Who Shall Not Be Named."

"The ... 'Cyber Corps' appears to have broken up the world's population based upon ... politics? Governmental philosophy? This system appears to have been repopulated by adults, at least, who mostly adhere to classic Western personal and governmental philosophy or are of similar religious and cultural background. Similar, not identical.

"All the persons who have been woken up previously, all of the current designated leadership, from whatever country or parts of the US, believe to one extent or another in the importance of representative democracy, individual rights, human rights, generally are people to one degree or another of faith, primarily but not exclusively Judeo-Christian, free-market economic philosophies, et cetera. Generally, the primacy of the individual's well-being over the state. In terms of politics, that means that all the designated leadership support conservative values, though there are differences in how to define those."

Which explained Kevin and Steve being...elsewhere. Somewhere.

"So, if you have family members or friends who were strongly leftist or in favor of strong authoritarian government...they're probably not here. We *believe* that there is a...call it a liberal system, somewhere else, a place where people with different philosophies about the individual and the state may be waking up right now, and having a conversation that is the mirror image of this one. Maybe there are multiple other systems. Where they may be, we do not know. Despite repeated requests, Gavin simply didn't answer in the total of three short meetings we had."

Jason thought about extended family. Friends...

"What about...my niece...Steve's daughter...?" Jason asked. Steve had a fully grown daughter who had "turned her back on decency" or whatever and gone raging conservative, much to his brother's disgust.

"Sheila is on the station as is her family."

"So, if you have grown children who are strongly leftist... they may not be in this system," Dewalt said. "Again, we have to assume there is a 'liberal' system somewhere just as we have to assume there is a 'Chinese/Asian' system and an Islamic system. It is a reasonable assumption that the other people are there but it is an assumption. Moving on.

"What most people ask about next is pets and personal possessions.

"Your personal possessions, at least those which you had at a home or at homes, as well as pets, are currently in time stasis storage. What? Time what? Time stasis. One of the technologies we've been handed is the ability to stop time. It's apparently how we were kept while the planet was being built.

"Currently your possessions or sometimes replacements for possessions are in storage. You can access them by asking your AI to ship them to your compartment. But be advised, the current room you have is as much as you have for the time being. And quarters are tight. If it makes you feel any better, my wife, kids and I have the same sort of room.

"On the subject of pets," Dewalt said, and grimaced. "There are not many places to walk dogs, a few parks, and cat litter is in short supply though there may be some available in the near future. When you can handle it, please try to keep your pets in stasis for the time being.

"My family has two dogs. I took them out of stasis, realized it was functionally impossible to keep them and, reluctantly, put them back in stasis. They've been fine. It's like no time passes to them. But my family misses them. We'll try to find some better situation for pets in the near future.

"Where's the bathroom?" Dewalt said, grinning. "The walls of the compartment are something called flexible metal, though it's not metal, and we've taken to calling flexmet. The bathroom, bed, kitchen, et cetera all extend out of the walls. It gets more cramped. The stuff is really remarkable but you get sick of it. The walls are all TV screens as well. You can set it to be something other than gray, decorate it with pictures... You'll get the hang of it."

"Glass of water?" Jason asked. "Tea, Earl Grey, hot?"

"Water I can provide," the AI said. A sink appeared under the TV and a cup extruded from the wall. Still attached to the gray material it extended across the room. It was... creepy. The stuff acted like tentacles and he had the sudden queasy sensation of being inside a tentacle monster. "Tea, you have some in storage. I can retrieve it but that is all you have and there is not much more on the station. There's a food printer but no replicator."

"Low tech, then, huh?" Jason said.

"Next, economics," Dewalt continued. "Right now, there really aren't any. It's up to us to create an economy. How does that work? There are two forms of financial items, credits and units. Everyone currently has two thousand credits. Is that a lot? It's hard to say. The value of money depends on many things. The basic meaning is that a credit is worth what someone will give you for it. I will strongly encourage you to be frugal with them. Until there are jobs, it's what you've got to spend and nobody, not even economists, are sure how much they are worth. It's like bitcoin that way.

"Your credits are stored by the Pegasus Central Bank currently. You can access them through your AI. Everything, including the upcoming elections, is handled electronically. Yes... we're having electronic elections. I know and even agree with the objections, but it's what we've got.

"However, you cannot engage in trade through the central bank. Individuals and companies will have to set up banks for you to transfer the money into to be able to use it. The AI can explain the necessities of bank setup and banking regulations..."

"Put me through to Monica's husband, Richard Derren," Jason said. "If he's on station. Video."

"Jason?" Richard said. It was the same gray background. "Is that you? Not the call I expected."

Jason had already noticed that the clothes he'd been wearing on Earth, jeans and a T-shirt, were more than a bit baggy.

Richard, damn him, apparently hadn't gained an ounce of weight since he was twenty. Other than younger he looked identical to the few times Jason had encountered him. Dress shirt, probably dress pants. And even twentysomething looking, he still looked "distinguished." Monica's description her first day at the bank.

"I've always said I had no hard feelings," Jason said. "I don't know what it takes to start a bank, but I'll invest some of my credits in one that you run. Five hundred. You're a good banker."

"That's... okay?" Richard said, frowning. "Are you sure?"

"What part of no hard feelings was unclear?" Jason asked. "You know banking. Seems like a good investment."

"I'll look at it," Richard said.

"I've got a lot of contacts that based on what the President said are probably in this system," Jason pointed out. "I can probably bring in customers. As well as potentially investors."

"That is... a point," Richard said. "My politics have always been quiet and my contact list may be less... extended. I'll strongly consider it."

"Say hi to Monica," Jason said. "Out here."

"Credits are only part of what you get, though," Dewalt continued. "Then there are units. Units are partial ownership of most of the large capital items in the system. That is, you, individually, are part owner of this station, the various space factories, fuel mines, et cetera. Everyone has ten million units. Until some change by a democratic government, units *cannot* be exchanged for credits. They can only be exchanged for other units.

"As an example, a small in-system spaceship, of which there are several hundred, has eleven units of ownership. Eleven individuals own the actual ship. What units you got was random. And you only have one unit in any particular item. You might or might not have any units in a spaceship, using the previous example. Large structures have multiple millions of units which means millions of individual owners, similar to publicly traded companies. Companies will have to be formed to run these facilities with the agreement of the unit owners. For example, a company would be formed, using credits as capital, to run a space factory. But it would have to lease or include the unit owners as part of that company."

"How many of my contacts do you have, AI?"

"Virtually all of them that were electronic," the AI replied. "Back to the beginning of your use of the internet. Thousands, and an idea of how close you were based on emails and texts."

"That's not privacy invasion or anything," Jason said. "As soon as Richard sets up a bank, contact all of them, even the ones I barely know, and suggest the bank to them."

"Will do," the AI said.

"Can AIs keep track of who brought in new customers?"

"Yes."

"Try to get something for me out of that," Jason said.

"Unless you're in finance all of that can get confusing. But it's one way privatization has been managed in countries where the government owned everything then privatized. Right now, I'd suggest you hold onto your units and just wait to see how things shake out. Okay, now the station and the planet..."

A hologram of a space station appeared at his side. The station was...odd. It was broken up into multiple cubes that were connected by tubes.

"The station has ten sections, each an individual State," Dewalt said. "Each State is very close to an individual country. Each has its own power system, water system, government and materials.

They are self-contained but connected to each other by various transportation systems for people and cargo."

The view pulled back into space and it was apparent that the station was surrounded by a massive ovaloid shell. How big was hard to grasp.

"There is a shell around the station," the President continued. "This is probably to keep space debris like asteroids from impacting the station or becoming a problem near it as well as reducing radiation in the station area. The shell has regular holes in it, ports, that allow for entry and exit by even the largest ships. I'll note here that the station has its own defenses including both tractor beams and active defenses like space missiles and fighters.

"Calculations indicate that if something the size of the dinosaur-killer asteroid were to hit the shell, the internal tractor beams could keep it from impacting the station and the shell, itself, would shrug it off. So, the shell should keep off most physical threats associated with asteroids, comets and so on. Those types of threats. We're not sure what caused *this*, but it indicates that there *are* serious potential threats."

The view shifted around rapidly to show a large breach in the station's shell that was on the side away from the planet and in the direction of deep space. As the view zoomed in it was clear that the shell had been punched in by something. There were jagged sections of metal still pointed inward toward the station.

"To give an idea of scale: The shell is twenty kilometers *thick*. That's about twelve and a half *miles*. And it is made of an *extremely* strong metal alloy. I can't really explain the amount of power necessary to do that damage. But by way of example, the previously mentioned dinosaur killer would barely leave a dent. What did *that* damage? How was it done? Impossible to tell. Using well-known science fiction, it would take the power of the Death Star to do damage like that. But it lends some credence to the Cybers saying that Earth was destroyed and that there were some battles going on at some point.

"Politics and laws next...

"For the next ninety days, as President Designate, I have plenipotentiary power. That makes me something I absolutely hate: a dictator."

Dewalt raised his hands and shook his head.

"Try not to worry about that too much. While I enjoyed being governor of Florida and was interested in being President, I'm not into dictatorship. So, I'm not going to let it go to my head. And it's only for ninety days. The AIs are clear on that one.

"There is a proposed constitution. The constitution is based, generally, on the United States Constitution. It has a President, bicameral legislature, and a supreme court. However, it is, if anything, even more restrictive than the US Constitution; the 'commerce clause' loophole is aggressively closed, and some of the amendments are slightly...humorous. For example, it has the Second Amendment governing arms and it reads, and I quote:

"'For the purpose of a system militia, sport, hunting, blowing up meteors that have offended you, and any other use that is not strictly prohibited by a Constitutionally Valid Law, the right to own, carry and/or transport weapons of any sort SHALL NOT BE Infringed.' The Shall Not Be is all caps. 'To be clear on this matter: if you can afford a space fighter, you can own a space fighter, as long as you don't use it in an illegal manner.'"

"There are ten thousand space fighters in storage," the AI said. "They cost ten million credits apiece. I knew you'd ask."

"I see the beginning of a beautiful friendship."

"That gives you a gist of what this Constitution is like," the President said, chuckling and shaking his head. "But, as it pointed out, if you use a weapon in an unlawful manner, that's different. So, don't. We're in a space station not only in space, which is very unforgiving, but filled with power and water systems. Do Not Fire is the order of the day. Seriously. You are legally allowed to carry around your Barrett rifle. There are *no* libs to own in the system. Keep it in the case. I fully support carry. But if you carry and pull the trigger you had better have a damned good reason. One accidental discharge in this place could cause massive harm. So, use responsible carry practices. End of lecture.

"There is a straightforward set of federal and state codes. As a politician and former practicing lawyer, cleaner and smarter than any I've ever seen. I'm sure we will manage to muck them up. There are state charters, the equivalent of a constitution, which have subtle differences by state that would appear to reflect the general tenor of the philosophies of the people in that state. In addition to the President Designate, there are designates for every major elected and appointed position down to state representatives, mayors, attorney generals, district attorneys, police leadership and judges. All of them have already been awakened and briefed even if it was a few hours ago.

"In ninety days, there will be a straight up down vote on the Constitution. If it is not ratified, there will be a Constitutional Convention to determine a new Constitution. If it is ratified, two weeks later there will be a vote on the state charters. Whether the state charters are ratified or not, sixty days after that vote there will be a system-wide vote for all elective positions. In the event of the charter not being ratified, the vote will take place as if it had been, then the legislature of the state can look at changing the charter.

"Federal senators under the current Constitution are appointed, one by the governor of the state, the other by the legislature. All state charters currently have state senators as representatives of *territories*, quadrants of the state stations referred to as sectors that don't change with population, with the state house being representatives of the people and their territories changing dependent on population, in the same fashion as the federal Constitution.

"There are some states with primarily citizens from parliamentary systems. Those states are the most likely to dislike their charter but I think if you give it a try, you'll find it works pretty well. The US electoral system worked well for better than two hundred years, with some hiccups, admittedly. But if you throw out the charter, you'll need to enact a new one under the Constitution, assuming that it's ratified.

"Next, let's talk about the planet," Dewalt continued, bringing up another hologram of a planet. There were oceans, several continents and two polar ice caps. But what was missing was any suggestion of a polar continent. "The planet was named Bellerophon by our Robotic Benefactors. Bellerophon, for those of you not into Greek mythology, was the rider of Pegasus.

"During the thirty days we had to prepare, we not only were waking up astronomers, we were waking up geologists and biologists to study the planet. And it's fascinating.

"As with Earth, about seventy percent of the planet is water, mostly deep oceans. It has five continents along with two large groups of islands which are sunken continents or parts of continents with mostly shallow seas. Let's look at the continents.

"The first, in order of size, we named Chindia." Chindia was in the southern latitudes and appeared to stretch from just above the equator to the arctic regions. The upper portion was an irregular bulge with the southern portion being vaguely snakelike. It looked a bit like Siberia running north-south instead of east-west.

As the President Designate was speaking the view switched to pictures of the ground in Chindia showing various plants and animals.

"Why Chindia? It has plants and animals which are drawn from China and India. For example, there is bamboo, which is not native outside China, and there are no small cats. The small cat part of the ecosystem is filled by various species of mongoose, some of which are quite large."

The view changed to a distant shot of a large mountain which looked a bit...bald. It had a distinct ring of snow and ice on it but above that it was clear again.

"None of the continents have the usual sorts of mountain ranges. There are some low hills but the main mountains, in most cases forming small ranges, are dormant pre-terraforming volcanoes. They are *very* large. In the case of Chindia, not only is it the largest continent but it has the largest volcano, which we've named Chindia Mons which just means Chindia Mountain.

"You'll notice the ring of ice and snow. That would be a snowcap for a normal high mountain like Everest. Chindia Mons is so high, it reaches *above* the snow line. It is *seventy-two thousand* feet high, or about twenty-two thousand meters. It is so massive it creates a monsoonal effect in the entire northern region of Chindia.

"There's a theory on how this planet came about and why it has such large stratovolcanoes," Dewalt said. "Best the scientists can figure out, this was a planet similar to Mars before the Cyber Corps started terraforming. What they did was carve out continents by scooping up most of the crust of Bellerophon—that's a lot of rock, people—and turning the leftover crust into the largest of the three moons. Yes, I said three. There's one large moon, Luna Nova, and two smaller ones, Crysador and Geryon, that may be left over crust or may be captured asteroids. When the rest of the scientists get involved, they can debate it as much as they want.

"So, in brief, that's Chindia and some on how this happened. There's going to be lots of news stories about the planet and discussion so...moving on to America Nova, the second largest continent."

"America Nova" was a continent that was vaguely rectangular

with some isthmuses. It ran from what appeared to be subtropical to arctic and had one of the large stratovolcanoes in the northern subarctic region. There was a large central north-south river, reminiscent of the Mississippi.

"Why America? It has plants and animals that conform to the Americas including South America. There are armadillos and anteaters, wild horses, and capybara at least in the southern regions. It also has one large river in its center we've called the Mississippi because of the similarity. It runs north-south and drains most of the continent.

"But it also has some Eurasian plants and animals. So, just covering predators, Chindia has tigers and leopards as well as some small bears. So does America Nova. But America Nova also has grizzly bears, pronghorn antelope and some species which have either evolved to be similar to extinct species or *are* extinct species. There are lions and tigers and bears. There are leopards but no puma. There are elephants. Some of them in the northern areas are hairy. In the arctic, the elephants *appear* to be wooly mammoths. The biologists are still debating. The big stratovolcano in the north we've been calling America Mons."

"Richard is asking if you have more potential investors," the AI said.

"Pick the ones from my contacts list who I was close to. People I've talked to in the last year or so. Give them a precis of his resumé. Tell them I'll chat if they want but I think Richard's a good guy to run a bank. Banks make money so it's a good long-term investment."

Dewalt pointed to an archipelago off the west coast of the America Nova continent. There were a few very small islands as well as one very large one that was probably a stratovolcano.

"This set of islands are the mountains of a sunken continent. During ice ages when the seas fall, this would be a land bridge to the next continent we call Europa."

Europa was further north than America Nova with the southern portion probably in the temperate zone and extending further into the arctic. Again, it was vaguely oval with numerous inlets that were probably fjords. The planet had sustained at least one glaciation cycle.

A shallow sea set so far north ... if there was a good warm water current up in that area the fishing was probably going to be similar to the Bering, which was the most productive sea on Earth.

"Europa, except for being colder, is pretty similar to America Nova, including the animals less those which were primarily tropical. Some difference in plant species. The stratovolcano is Europa Mons.

"Next continent, down here in the tropics ..."

This continent was shaped similarly to Africa but apparently much smaller and while it had a desert region in the south the Sahara was notably lacking. The stratovolcano was very central and possibly as large as Chindia Mons. Because it was a smaller continent, the mountain took up much more of the land area.

"After much debate we settled on calling it Kush, which was an ancient African kingdom. The stratovolcano is as large as it looks and causes monsoon effects over the whole continent which is about the size of Australia. The biology is pretty much straight up African. Paleontologists were puzzled that America Nova, Chindia and Europa didn't have hyenas since they were originally native to Eurasia. But Kush is the only continent with hyenas. Also, the only continent with Cape Buffalo, wildebeest, et cetera. Most of it's tropical hot but the hills and mountains around Kush Mons are fairly cool and there are gorillas and chimps in those regions.

"So, we get to the last continent," Dewalt said. "Avia. Avia is small, between the size of Greenland and Australia. It is set well away from the other continents. And it is called Avia because it has no mammals whatsoever. It is populated entirely by birds which look more like feathery dinosaurs ..."

The pictures and videos that had been running through the whole briefing were now of various sorts of birds, many flightless, some of them quadrupedal. They did look a bit like dinosaurs. Dinosaurs with beaks.

"To give some scale," the President said. He brought up a picture of a large and fierce-looking bipedal bird with claws on its wings and a prominent, unquestionably predatory, beak. Next to it was a male human figure. The bird was at least eighteen feet tall. "That's the largest predatory bird we've identified. And this is the largest herbivore."

The quadrupedal bird was about the size of an elephant.

"As I said when I started, I'm the former governor of Florida," Dewalt said, frowning thoughtfully. "And I'm from Florida. Born and raised. Florida is a weird mix of California and Texas. We're a very conservative state in the United States meaning of that word. The new Second Amendment warms the cockles of my heart, dangers understood and accepted. Strong on business and free market. Very much like Texas that way.

"But we're also conservative in an ecological sense. The environment in Florida isn't everyone's cup of tea. Hot, humid, alligators and snakes and bugs are a constant. Hurricanes. But we love it. And as governor, I've often acted to protect it in a conservationist manner.

"After much discussion with experts, I'm putting this continent off limits for the time being with the exception of research. I hope that the incoming legislature, whatever form it might take, agrees. Bird ecologies like this one are very easy for mammals to wipe out. They eat the eggs of the ground-laying birds for one thing. Even letting some dogs or cats into this continent could destroy the ecosystem. This needs to stay a protected park for future generations. At least, that's my opinion and I'm sticking to it.

"Which gets us to a question I know is on many people's mind: colonization. How do we get off the station and onto the planet? How do we get out of these tiny rooms?

"There are six different classes of ships currently available. The term for each is based on how many shipping containers it can carry."

He brought up a picture of a shipping container with a small ship next to it and a person for scale again.

"These shipping containers are pretty rad. They're made from flexmet so all but the bottom can completely open. They also can counteract gravity, so they float. But that doesn't mean they're easy to move, especially full, because they retain mass. They have a time stasis system so anything loaded in them is locked in time. They can hold about fifty thousand pounds of cargo or about twenty-three thousand kilos. The ship next to them we've been calling a 'six pack' because in cargo configuration it will carry six shipping containers."

He zoomed out the shot for pictures of larger and larger ships. They had what was clearly a command and control section on top but the majority of the ship was simply a large flattened cube.

"Supplied by the Cybers and owned by a variety of unit owners we have..."

He took a deep breath and rapidly trotted off:

"30,000 six packs, 15,000 twelve packs, 5,000 fifty packs, 1,000 hundred packs, 500 five hundred packs, 50 thousand packs and 5 ten thousand packs," the President said. "Whooo. That's a lot of numbers. All told the ships can hold about a million shipping containers. How does that relate to getting the heck off this station?

"There are five million colonization sets in storage. Those are owned by the government. There is a fixed price of fifty thousand credits per set. It's specifically one of the ways that government is supposed to pay for itself. So, what's in the colonization set?

"There is a trailer which takes up two cargo spaces, an auto-slaughter system for cleaning and dressing animals which takes up one container space, so that's three, and three shipping containers that can hold household goods or smaller containers for storage of materials from the planet. In addition, there's what the robots call a tractor."

There had been shots of all the equipment as the President was talking. Though most of the material was similar to Earth equipment, the "tractor" was simply a squat cylinder about man tall that looked like a larger version of a beeping robot from a famous science fiction movie of the seventies. Except it was the ubiquitous gray instead of blue and white.

"The tractor has a flight system as well as what is called, confusingly, a tractor beam. It can fly, it has a fusion reactor for power, a contragravity system and a reactionless drive. Which are something that others will explain. Bottom line, it will fly and just needs to be refueled from time to time.

"By attaching various parts to it you can use it for... well everything you'd use a tractor for and more. Backhoe, front-end loader, tree cutter, it can do it all with the right attachments. In addition to the major pieces, there's a recommendation for twenty drones. The drones are very smart and have sampling equipment so you can see if various potential foods are hazardous."

Shots of the drones in action on the planet were included. Gray, again, and they looked to be made mostly of flexmet with some small motors.

"Some of you might have tried the print food by now," Dewalt said, holding up a slice of pizza. "If you have, you'll appreciate how much we need fresh food. All the food people had in their houses is currently in storage as well as some stored food. But mostly, what we've got is the cartridges for print food."

He took a bite of the pizza and grimaced.

"You can tell this was designed by robots by the taste," he said. He took a drink of water and swished it around, still grimacing. "We're going to need real food. This is awful. But for now, it's what we've got.

"The problem is this station doesn't run on food alone. And we have five million colonization sets, each of which has six containers' volume. We have a million-container volume we can ship but we also need other 'stuff.' The station needs water, fuel, spare parts. My transportation secretary designate and secretary of agriculture designate, both of whom know their fields, have been crunching the numbers since they woke up and they're not looking happy. Neither is the secretary of energy. Secretary, for those unfamiliar with the term, is similar to a minister.

"We can't dedicate every ship to dropping colonists or visitors," the President said, shrugging. "Then there's the problem that the large ships cannot land most places on the planet. They're simply too big. They need large space or ground stations to land on. So, the only way to bring in the colony sets is with the smaller ships.

"Most of the people on this station would probably prefer to be on the ground. I'd say that's the essential nature of most of this populace. There may be other systems where people are content to stay in their rooms and eat print food. I don't think that's this system.

"On the other hand," he added with a grin. "Then there's the matter of the *animals* on the planet. 'Cause these ain't teddy bears. This is a visual."

He brought up a picture of a river with a large bear standing upright and a coniferous forest in the background. It looked like somewhere in Alaska. The Pacific Northwest at least.

"This is an adult male Kodiak bear," the President said. "Largest land predator in the world on Earth. Now, with the help of some Photoshop..." The picture added a man wearing flannel and holding a fishing rod in front of the Kodiak. The bear overtopped the man by several feet.

"That is how big a Kodiak bear was. Absolutely huge. This, though, is the *common* size on Bellerophon of the same general type of bear, what's called a northern brown bear..."

The new bear was standing next to the Kodiak and overtopped it by at least a foot.

"The *average* adult male northern brown bear on Pegasus is larger than the *largest* bear on Earth," the President said, shaking his head. "There's similar gigantism everywhere. There are wild cattle called aurochs. They're the size of bison or larger. Bison are the size of small elephants. The northern tigers are thirty percent larger than similar Siberian tigers on Earth.

"Everything is bigger on Pegasus! So, did the robots change all the genetics? No, not according to the scientists we woke up. The animals on Earth were unusually small, not the other way around.

"Whenever humans entered an area, since way back in the caveman days, the size of animals reduced. Humans apparently have always hunted the largest animals first and over time animals just got smaller than they would be naturally. So, this is the *natural* size of these animals. The point being... not everybody is going to want to drop to the planet right away. Not until there are some secured areas.

"And... we need the ships doing other things as well. We need people in the mostly robotic factories producing materials and spare parts. We need ships doing space mining.

"The economy, the process, is so complex, even with the AIs it is *impossible* for the government to solve all the problems. I can say 'this ship do this, this factory produce this.' At least for ninety days. But that's not going to solve the problems. What *will* work is the free market. Some prices are set, as I said. Mostly we're going to have to let the free market handle it. Where ships go. What factory produces what product. How much to charge for what. Which means there will be ups and downs. Businesses will succeed, businesses will fail. Some people are going to get rich, even megarich. Some people are going to fail. Then if they're the people I think they are, they're going to stand back up and keep trying.

"Things aren't going to go smoothly and it will be a while until we have a smoothly running system, economically and politically. For many years it is going to be, in the words of Winston Churchill, blood, toil, tears and sweat. Many of you are from countries that went through major changes in the nineties and know what I'm talking about.

"For the citizens of the US, the first few decades after the Revolution were no picnic. Brush up on the history of that time.

Starting a new country is not unicorns and rainbows. That's the truth and I'm *not* going to sugarcoat it.

"But, working together, we *shall* succeed. We shall succeed by everyone throwing in and *doing*. By being the people chosen for this system, the best of the systems, the system where the individual is preeminent and the state is chained, where freedom is more important than food, than air, than life. Where we respect our fellow Pegasans and deal with them in honesty and truth. We shall succeed and we shall make this the system envied by all the other systems: This new home, this shining jewel among the stars, this Pegasus..."

Cade Oldham stared at his hands.

"Did you hear that?" He knew the voice talking to him, but it was wrong. It was a voice from the past. "Did you hear that about the continent called Avia?"

Cade turned his hands one way and then the other, examining the palms and the backs.

"It's all birds, Cade. We should go."

"These aren't my hands," Cade said.

"Of course, they're your hands. Cade, look at me."

He couldn't. Instead, he looked around the room, at the gunmetal-gray walls. At the TV screen that was just a portion of the wall that had suddenly burst into life to inform them that they were on a space station with President Ron Dewalt. At his son and daughter, who looked normal. Abby was thirteen years old, short blonde hair, thin as a nail and generally floppy in her movements. Abby wore jeans and a T-shirt for a band called, apparently, Kumiko and the Horny Toads. She flopped over a bunk now, toying with her phone-like device and pressing the wall. Sam was eighteen, lean but muscled, and he wore a flannel shirt that suggested he wanted to be taken for a grunge guitarist or an apprentice lumberjack. He stood, running his fingers through curly black hair that needed a haircut.

Cade looked at his wife, who didn't look normal at all. She was curvaceous, always had been, but her body was tight and pulled together like it had been when they'd met at State in college. Her hair was long and its natural blonde color, no hint of the bottle about it. Her skin was smooth, with no bags under her eyes or crow's feet at the corners. He recognized the checked dress, but it hung loosely from her, as if a breeze might blow it away.

"We should go to Avia on vacation," Mabel said.

"Vacation?" Cade snorted. "I don't know how you can think of vacation at a time like this."

"A time like what, Dad?" Abby asked.

"I don't know, kiddo," Cade said, shaking his head. "Fifteen minutes ago, I was on the back of the John Deere. Now..."

"Fifteen minutes ago," Sam said, "I was kissing Julie in the library."

"Now I don't even have my own hands," Cade said, looking at them.

"Of course you have your own hands," Mabel told him. She moved close, took one of his hands in hers. "Let's take your hands and go to Avia."

"We can't settle there," Abby said. "According to Ron Screwdriver."

"Dewalt," Sam told her. "*Where's Julie?*"

"Why are you asking *me*?" Abby asked. "Ask your AI!"

"Did you see that thing he called a 'tractor'?" Cade asked. "I don't understand. What are you supposed to do, tell that...robot thing to till? Does it plant, too? I didn't see a seat for sitting on it, does it have to be steered?"

"Maybe you just tell it what to do and it does the work." Mabel squeezed his fingers as if trying to stimulate blood flow.

"So, what the hell does the farmer do?" Cade stood and pulled away from his wife. She didn't look like Mabel or sound like Mabel or smell like Mabel—she looked like a girl Cade remembered from many years ago. "Maybe I'll be out of work."

"Someone still needs to run a farm, even if there are robots doing the work," Mabel told him.

"Somebody with these." Cade held up his hands. "A kid's hands. No scars, no calluses."

"Nice hands for holding," Mabel suggested.

"And my real hands weren't?"

"Julie had nice hands," Sam said, his voice quavering.

"Why are you so worked up about Julie?" Abby asked. "Look how cool this flexmet stuff is. Here's a sink. My AI says it can make basically anything."

"I don't care about the sink!" Sam snapped.

"And basically all of the media, ever, is here," Abby continued. "All the books. All the movies. Dad, the complete movies of

John Wayne, all here in the network. You could spend the rest of your life watching John Wayne movies."

"Not a very John Wayne thing to do," Cade pointed out.

"I don't care about John Wayne either!" Sam was almost yelling.

"Jeez, fine," Abby said. "I'm posting in the social channels right now, to see if anyone knows where Julie is."

Cade glared at the smartphone-like object on the bunk where he'd been sitting. He'd never trusted the smartphone manufacturers, had only ever got a smartphone to get navigation assistance.

"Everyone needs to take a deep breath," Mabel said.

"And go to Avia?" Cade asked.

"Eventually," she said. "But first, I want you to look at yourself."

"I don't see a mirror," Cade grumped.

Mabel picked up her phone and looked at it. "Mr. AI, if I talk to you, can you talk back?"

"I certainly can," the phone said. It had a man's voice. Cade couldn't see the image on it. "And I can be a man if you like, though I could also be a woman. Or anything else."

"Can you be a dog?" she asked.

"Mac," Cade muttered. "He must be in storage...?"

"Who cares about the dog?" Sam asked. "What about Julie?"

"What about her?" Cade objected.

"Hey," Abby said, "they have a social media network."

"Oh good." Cade felt like pulling his hair out. "So, all the important things are still here."

"We used to have a dog named Sleepy," Mabel said.

"Sleepy was a Black Labrador," the phone said.

"Can you look like Sleepy?" she asked. "Maybe with more of a woman's voice? But a woman's voice... fitting for a dog, I guess?"

"How's this?" the phone asked. The new voice was a woman's voice, a little on the husky side.

"Thanks. Do you mind if I call you Sleepy?"

"Whatever works for you, Mabel."

"If I point you at my husband, can you reflect back to him what you see? Can you act like a mirror?"

"Like this?" Sleepy asked.

"Perfect." Mabel rotated her phone and pointed it at Cade.

He grunted, staring at the image.

"See? That guy's not me."

"What are you talking about?" Mabel asked, shaking her head. "That is you, Cade Oldham. I remember that you!"

"That guy's thirty-five years too young," Cade said. "He has all his hair. His muscles are the muscles of a young man, strong from basketball, but not hardened by decades of work. His face is unlined. His back is straight. I doubt that guy has the stamina to work a whole day, he'll probably need the robots to do it for him." He shook his head slowly. "I don't know that guy, and I don't trust him."

At least his clothes still fit. Hard work and an indifferent relationship with his appetite had left him lean.

Mabel ground her teeth. She wanted to let him have it, he could tell. Hell, maybe he deserved it. He knew when he was dug in.

"So much has happened that is strange," she said, speaking slowly. "I wish that the one thing that's happened to us today that is wonderful was something you could just enjoy."

"Wonderful?!" Sam snapped. "What's happened that's so wonderful?"

He stalked out. The door cycled open to let him pass and then cycled shut on his heels.

Cade shook his head, ran his fingers through his thick, black hair.

"Now what?" he muttered.

After a moment he stood up and followed his son out the door.

"Well, he's not going to be kissing Julie that's for sure," Abby said, tapping at her phone. "'Cause she ain't on the station."

"Why not?" Mabel asked.

"I'm not totally sure," Abby said. "But my guess is it might have something to do with the Bernie Sanders stickers on her bumper?"

# CHAPTER 2 >>>>>>>>>

"OKAY, AI, I GUESS WE'RE STUCK WITH EACH OTHER," JASON SAID when the President was finished. He was in the "state," more like quadrant, of Carolina and the governor, confusingly, was the former governor of Georgia. Though he was at least a nationally known figure unlike whoever was governor of South Carolina. "So, you need a name. I'm going with Jewel for now."

"Jewel it is," Jewel responded. "Do I keep the look?"

"Yeah, but not the uniform," Jason said.

"Nude then?" Jewel asked, grinning.

"No," Jason replied, closing his eyes. She'd also drawn back the view to torso. "I need to concentrate. "Dress suit. Hair up. Glasses."

"Standard PA look it is," Jewel said.

"Okay...If I can get my brain back on track..."

He stopped and realized how...hard that was. He was back to being twenty again in more ways than just having his fingers and teeth back. One flash of a CGI topless blonde and he was having a difficult time thinking about anything else.

No wonder it was so tough to get ahead in your twenties.

"Back on track...I was thinking about...Oh. How are we communicating?"

It sounded like the AI was talking through earpieces. But there were no earpieces.

"There's a small implant in your mastoid bone," Jewel said.

25

"I can hear you when you speak or even subvocalize. A sort of hum without opening your mouth. You hear me as if there's an earpiece."

"Implants," Jason said darkly. He'd read enough dystopian SF to not like the idea of implants.

"There is another," Jewel said uncomfortably. "To control the flexmet with thought, there's a small implant in a motion-control center of your brain."

Jason had been playing with flexmet most of the President's speech. The stuff responded to thought. You could make it form just about any shape and it would even move by thought, like weird tentacles.

"Any way to get that one out?" Jason asked. He wasn't worried about what on Earth would be called a cochlear implant. They were commonly used by deaf people and weren't directly connected to the brain.

"By a visit to a doctor," Jewel said. "Once doctor's offices are set up. But you'd lose most control over flexmet."

"Table that for now," Jason said, frowning. "There are large shipping containers. Any other types?"

"There are three stasis containers available," the AI said. "Large, medium and small..."

The response included pictures. The medium containers were the size of an Egyptian sarcophagus and the small were the size of a large ammo crate.

"Forty-five medium stasis containers fit snugly in a large. Six small stasis containers fit snuggly in a medium for a total of two hundred seventy cases in a large."

"Babushka dolls," Jason said musingly. He formed a small net with the flexmet, let it drop to his lap then put the phone in it and retracted it. "Where's the energy come from?"

"The flexmet has nanometric energy storage built in. It can recharge from any available source."

"Can it recharge from one of those tractors?"

"Yes. The one described by the President is a medium tractor. There are also small and large. Small tractors work with batteries, the large tractor has a larger fusion plant and more available power."

"The large and medium have fusion power sources and all three have counter gravity *and* inertialess drive?"

"Yes."

"What's the fusion run on?"

"Helium three."

"Hmmm..." Jason formed the flexmet into a noose and retracted it. "How strong is this and how thin can it get?"

"The flexmet has a strength thirty thousand times stronger than spider silk and can get that thin. In that configuration it will cut but it is smart material so it will not allow itself to cut you."

"I don't have anything to test that statement." He thought about it getting very thin and it practically vanished, then he pulled on it. Couldn't break and nearly invisible. "This is the equivalent of a monoknife then. Hmmm..."

He made the net again.

"Can it be operated by a drone? And how large of a net could I make with this?"

"If the drone has been taught to do so," Jewel answered. "To assume the next question: You have the flexmet do something while attached to a drone or a device like me and it will replicate it. And the AIs can intuit what you're trying to do. Practically any size."

"Does flexmet wear out?" Jason asked. "What is the most common material in flexmet and where is it produced?"

"Flexmet wears out," Jewel answered. "But how fast depends on how much it is being moved and stressed. There's no one answer. When material breaks down it sheds into balls which can be recovered. It is very difficult to recycle. The base material is high-density polypropylene..."

"Really?" Jason said, chuckling. "I was expecting something much more unobtainium."

"The unobtainium is flexium, which comprises five percent of the material. A variant of graphene that is interwoven comprises ten percent. That provides the majority of the strength. Seventy percent is HDPE. HDPE as well as flexmet is produced in carbon refineries. There are three carbon refineries in the system. There are also three metals refineries in the system, three helium and hydrocarbon mines, three general factories..."

"Three of everything for competition?"

"Yes."

"HDPE produced the regular way from Earth? Polymerizing ethylene?"

"Yes."

"There's not going to be any oil on this planet," Jason said. "I know that much. It's too young for fossil beds from the look. Where's the ethylene come from?"

"One of the three gas mines in orbit over planet twelve."

"Do I have shares in any of the mines or carbon refineries?"

"Units?"

"Yes."

"Yes, you have one unit in Station Twelve Bravo and one unit in Carbon Converter Charlie."

"Are people trading units?"

"There's already a lively trade."

"Broker's fees?"

"The AIs are handling most of it. What would be called 'over the counter' trading between individuals."

Jason thought about it for a moment longer.

"I want to move as many units as I can into one of the fuel stations and one of the carbon refineries."

"I'll get to work on that. Units can only be traded for units."

"Understood. It's going to take a while to get the colonization packs on the ground. The large ships can't land so they're going to have to be used in space. And people are going to want real food. Which means getting it from the planet. Natural, wild, foods at first. But real ingredients. Which means you have to have ships."

"The station needs stuff from space," Jewel pointed out.

"You don't have taste buds." Jason took a sip of distilled water. "Where is the food printer?"

A cubicle opened on the wall near the door.

"Hungry?" Jewel asked.

"I just ate," Jason said. "How long were we in stasis?"

"That's still being calculated," Jewel said carefully.

"If there were astronomers woken up a month ago with the optics we've got to have . . . It's been calculated. You can calculate it on the basis of movement of stars in Andromeda referring to the galactic center of the Milky Way."

"It's only an estimate," Jewel said.

"What's the estimate?" Jason asked.

"Two million years, more or less."

"Two *million*?"

"It takes a long time to terraform a planet..." Jewel said hastily.

"I get that," Jason said. "Just soil takes forever and the best soil is loess which comes from glaciation and plants and animals working together but..."

He thought about the issues. Too big to calculate. Out of his hands. He was going to have to depend upon "top men" on that one. He liked science but he was no astrophysicist.

He wondered in passing what members of the astrophysicist community had been secretly conservative enough to be in a society where Ron Dewalt was chosen as the President Pro Tempore.

"What kind of a society can do something over a two-million-year period?" he asked.

"Robots?" Jewel replied. "AIs?"

"Everything breaks down eventually, Jewel. Equipment. People. Computers. Societies. Planets and stars. That's the nature of entropy. Way too big to worry about now. Like whatever punched in the side of the shell. How do I get stuff out of storage?"

"You order it," Jewel said. "It will be delivered to your compartment. If you are not in, you'll be contacted and asked if the container can be placed in your compartment. Otherwise, it is returned. The corridors are too narrow to leave it out and it might be stolen. You can schedule when it is to arrive."

"How much?" Jason asked.

"Internal shipment, for now, is a government monopoly with a fixed fee," Jewel said. "To recover from storage for the first time is free. If there is repeated back and forth, it can require a fee. Any business shipment on the station, such as if you sell something from your storage, costs two credits for a small container. Only small containers can be shipped to a home. It is six credits for a medium container. Large containers are prohibited outside of industrial areas."

"Two credits for a small container," Jason said. "Call those cases. Cases, coffins, conex."

"Okay."

"I need to get to the planet," Jason mused. "I'm not claustrophobic but this ain't me. I'm an outdoors guy, I'm twenty again and there's an entire planet to explore. I don't need a colonization set. I need one of those medium tractors, bunch of flexmet, some stuff from my storage, some containers. I heard what the President said but people are going to want real food. Bunch of flexmet.

A ride. And a business partner that understands business 'cause I'm terrible at it. Been there, lost the T-shirt in the bankruptcy."

"Richard?" Jewel asked carefully. "I'm surprised you'll even talk."

"You know about that?" Jason asked.

"It's in your file. Analysis of things taken from your postings on various boards and comments of others. It's not public knowledge."

"Eh. No harm. Like I said, I've never borne a grudge about it. Just couldn't attend the wedding. Schedule conflicts and the like. Not Richard. He's a banker, not this kind of businessman. . . . How much to register a corporation similar to an S corporation?"

"One credit," Jewel said.

"Credits are worth a lot," Jason replied. "Shipping, on the other hand, is expensive. Weird. Register . . . hmm . . . Can we use Brandywine Foods?"

"Yes."

"Register Brandywine Foods," Jason said. "I need a business partner . . . Preferably one in Carolina . . ."

"Tim Wilson is in Carolina and you have very positive electronic communications with him," Jewel pointed out.

"See if he's available," Jason said.

Tim had been his boss his first time as a contractor in Iraq and as such was the reason Jason had gotten into logistics. He'd bought a small manufacturing business afterward and not only ran it well, had increased it in size. Finally retired and lived in Kennesaw, across Atlanta from Jason's home in Loganville. He'd do well if he'd agree.

"Log dude!"

Tim Wilson had been in his fifties with a bullet-shaved head to hide male pattern baldness when they'd worked together. In his seventies when they . . . left? He didn't look seventy anymore.

"Jesus, Ops, you have hair?" Jason said, grinning. "I thought you were born bald!"

"Fuck you!" Tim said, laughing. "My AI said the male pattern baldness has been corrected, so there."

"I'd just lie there and sweat," Jason said. "I want to start a business. But I need a partner. It will take a business loan but I may have an in on that one."

"Where?" Tim asked. "I got your contact about Richard. Seriously?"

"Regional VP of BOA. I think he can handle it."

"Yeah, but ... Monica's new husband?" Tim said.

"Not new anymore," Jason said. "That was a long time ago and she upgraded. Jewel, where are we at on the bank?"

"The Derren Bank of Carolina is open for business," Jewel said. "Electronic anyway. You have one point eight percent equity based on investment and helping put together the investment package.

"Point in the new laws: Individual depositor banks are under federal regulation but are limited to one state. So, there cannot be system-wide banks or the functional effect under holding corporations. So it's the Derren Bank of Carolina. You can, however, use your credits in any state. And there are regulations for investment banks which will require more concentration of credit than is currently possible."

"I should be able to talk Richard into it with someone who's been successful in business," Jason said, considering that tidbit. It eliminated "too big to fail" banks and was one of the things some had suggested after the 2007 banking crisis. "Here's the two-minute pitch. You know business. I've tried it. I suck at it. But when I wasn't working in the Sandbox, what was I doing?"

"Reading," Tim said. "Probably some trashy science fiction novel."

"And now we live in science fiction," Jason said, holding up the flexmet mesh. "I've been playing with this stuff and asking questions. I know the President said we need more than just fresh food. But people are going to want it. A lot. And I know how to get it. Lots of it. Tons. With this. I need a tractor, some containers, lots of flexmet and a ride. That's it. And I'll bring up as much food as the containers will hold."

"Distribution. Storage. Refrigeration if you're talking about fresh," Tim said.

"Storage: The containers are all time stasis. No need for refrigeration. Stops time, stops bacterial growth. Distro: Figured it out already. Let the log guy worry about those questions."

"The log guy sits in the office," Tim said. "You're talking about dropping to the planet."

"I can run it from there," Jason said. "Seriously. This will work."

"What kind of food?" Tim said.

"Depends on the season," Jason said. "Probably fish or shrimp. Commercial fishing brings in tons of protein."

"And where are you getting a boat?" Tim asked. "Got a commercial fishing boat in storage?"

"You can make a boat out of this," Jason said, forming a boat. "A net. A fish trap." He formed the material into each in demonstration. "And it's strong as hell. You know how many different jobs I've done. All I need to do is get to the planet and... not play but *work* with this. I can figure it out and make us a ton of money. Not to mention, fresh food."

"That sounds nice," Tim said, nodding. "You have done just about everything."

"With enough of this stuff, a power source and a virgin planet?" Jason said. "I can load six, twelve containers, more, in less than two weeks. Just need the loan for the materials and a ride. That's the tough part. We'll need some investors and since I hit my contacts list already, I'm not sure we can get them. Also, we'll need a business plan to show Richard."

"Which is my part but I don't understand the business," Tim said. "Which is a problem. Also, what's the split?"

"Fifty-five, forty-five me?" Jason said cautiously. "My ideas..." Jason grimaced and waited for the haggling. "It's not going to take a lot of your time. I'm going to be doing most of the work..."

"You are such a wimp, Log," Tim said, shaking his head. "I'm okay with the split, even with you as majority partner. But if I'm running the business side, Jason, *I'm* running the business side."

"Agreed," Jason said quickly. "There's a reason I contacted you. I suck at the business side. But I can find the ways to make us money. Not all the ideas are going to work, but commercial fishing is a no brainer in this situation. It's just a matter of figuring out the best way to use flexmet and the bots. Just need to get the money together for a round trip and the equipment."

"You're not the only one who wants to get out of the compartment," Tim pointed out.

"All the things I've done come together on this," Jason said. "It's all about the out of doors, science fiction and logistics. How to move the most protein with the smallest amount of effort. And who's the best... Tim? Who's the best?"

"You're the best," Tim admitted grudgingly. "But I'm still having a hard time forgiving you for Slovakia."

"That was *not* my fault," Jason said. "I'm putting in another five hundred on this investment. We need to find out how much financing we need. Really, one drop and we should be financed. It's coming up with the money for the drop and extract. After one drop and what we should make from the load, we'll *all* get out of these boxes."

"I'm uncertain," Tim said, regarding Jason carefully. "Log, you're a great log guy..."

"But I've never been particularly successful," Jason said. "If this was being pitched to you by someone else, would it be a good idea?"

"Yes," Tim admitted.

"Let's get together and talk about it," Jason said.

"Worth the time," Tim said, looking around. "And to get out of this cubicle. AI, where's a restaurant or bar?"

"There are currently no restaurants or bars," Tim's AI responded. Based on the voice, it had not developed any specific personality.

"Meet at Lambda Central Square," Jewel suggested, helpfully.

"Lambda...Central Square?" Tim said.

"You two might as well realize where you're at," Jewel said, bringing up a 3D schematic of the station on the screen.

"Starting with: You are both in the state of Carolina.... All residential and retail commercial areas of the states are central to that cube with the government housed central to that." She highlighted the residential and retail commercial as she was speaking. "Warehousing and in-station manufacturing are external to residential and government. This is probably for security of the personnel against damage to the exterior of the station."

"Makes sense," Tim said. "Keep the personnel, kids and government deep where they're less likely to be harmed."

"Each residential/retail portion of the cube is itself a cube that is twenty-five levels high and twenty-five sections wide," Jewel continued. "Every address is therefore designated by a series of letters and numbers. For example, Jason is presently at Carolina R, standing for Residential, Six, his level in the residential area; Delta, designating which portion of R-6 he is in, Nine, refining it more; Lambda, refining it more, Seventeen; Sierra, Twelve. Or, Carolina R-6-D-9-L-17-S-12. That's your address."

"That's a mouthful," Jason said.

"But," Jewel continued, "each person was placed with their neighbors, at least the ones who made it to this system, surrounding them. So, you, Jason, are still in a neighborhood that conforms more or less to Loganville. And, frankly, if you addressed something to someone in Loganville either Carolina or Georgia, it would probably make it. You, Tim, are surrounded by people from Kennesaw."

"Could be good, could be bad," Tim said. "Lambda Central Square?"

"Nine alphanumerics in the full address," Jewel said. "At six, seven and eight there are parks. The central point for the two of you is Lambda Central Square, or the central square for the L designator. Instead of Lima, for some reason the name given to it is Lambda. Possibly to avoid confusion with the city. That is the central park for the refined location of Lambda in that address. It more or less conforms to the main park for the Atlanta Metro area. Somewhat equivalent to Piedmont Park. It is central between the two of you."

"Ah," Tim said. "And how do we get there?"

"Walk?" Jewel said. "There are also slidewalks. It's not going to kill you."

"Security situation?" Jason asked.

"At the moment people are just confused and making personal contact," Jewel said. "Once they calm down and assess, we'll see if there are major security issues. Right now, none."

"That means more or less walking through downtown Atlanta," Jason said. "That generally defines 'security issues.' Which is why I asked."

"I'll repeat," Jewel said astringently, "there are *no* current security issues. We're tied in to the security AIs. Currently, security is responding to three incidents in the Lambda sector, each of which can be defined as domestic disturbances."

"Okay," Jason said, grimacing. His AI had a personality. "Meet at Lambda Square?"

"Sounds like a plan," Tim said. "And gives some time to explore. I've got one other thing I've got to do first but sounds like I can do it on the way. How long to get there, direct?"

"Thirty minutes," his AI replied.

"Meet there in an hour or so?" Tim asked.

"Will do," Jason replied.

"Phone, tell me where Julie Larsen is." Sam shook the phone, as if that would make it respond faster.

"Yes." The AI's face on Sam's screen was a cute girl's face. "Do you want to finish setting up your device first?"

"What?"

"Is this a good look and voice for your AI?"

"I don't care," Sam said. He wasn't sure where he was; he'd bolted from his parents'... cubicle... and was lurching around the station blind. "Sure. Where's Julie Larsen?"

"Take a deep breath," the AI said. "If you turn right at the next corridor, you'll find a little sitting room with a bench."

"Why?" Sam asked. "Why do I need a bench?" But he followed the directions and went to the sitting room. Then he leaned against the wall. "Look, you don't want to tell me something. What is it?"

"Julie didn't make it." The AI smiled apologetically.

Sam fell against the wall and slowly slid down it.

"Julie died? But I was... I just saw her."

"You saw her many years ago," the AI corrected him. "Many. But I didn't say she was dead. Julie didn't make the standards for this system. She's the wrong kind of person to be here. But that doesn't mean she's dead."

Sam lay slumped, a puddle at the base of the wall.

"Where is she, then?"

"I don't know," the AI said.

"Who does?" Sam asked.

"Did you hear President Dewalt?"

"I don't actually care about President Dewalt," Sam said. "I want you to start answering my questions."

"Was Julie a conservative?"

"What's that got to do with it?" Sam shouted.

"This is a conservative system," the AI said.

"That's totally stupid!" Sam snarled. "You don't just... pull people apart over *politics*!"

"Or you could, you know, have an instant civil war when people don't have the societal structure to prevent it," the AI said with a metaphorical shrug. "If your world was destroyed and people had to be moved, do you think it was a better idea to put people like Julie in the same system with people like the Copts who think homosexuals should be hanged?"

"The cops think homosexuals should be hanged?" Sam said. "Are you serious? Julie was right! All cops really *are* bastards!"

"Copts with a *t*," the AI said. "They are a Christian sect originally from Egypt who are very fundamentalist Christian and are nearly a majority society in the state of Helenus here in Pegasus. They tend to support strong laws against homosexuality and a variety of other sins."

"Oh," Sam said.

"I need a name," the AI said. "You could call me Julie, if you wanted to."

"Reskin your avatar," Sam said immediately. "You're a boy now. No, you're a cartoon caveman, and your name is Thog."

The next voice didn't come from his device.

"Hey, Sam."

It was a man's voice that spoke, a familiar-sounding tenor with a faint buzz in it, and Sam looked up. The fellow standing over him looked familiar, but he'd have been a couple years ahead of Sam, if they went to the same school. He was black and sort of pear-shaped, with wide hips for a man, and he had a thick head of curly hair. He wore a nerdy-looking polo shirt and tan slacks. Sam didn't recognize him.

"Sorry, man," Sam said. "If you're looking for directions or . . . help or . . . anything. I got nothing."

"You don't recognize your old pastor, then."

"Jesus," Sam said, his eyes widening.

"Well, no." Pastor Mickey smiled. "But I'm trying to be on his side."

Sam dragged himself into a slightly more dignified sitting position.

"Sorry. You just look . . . way too young."

"I was thinking I might help you." Mickey sat on the bench, clasped his hands, and smiled.

"You know where Julie Larsen is?"

"I, ah . . . Are your parents here? Abigail?"

Sam climbed to his feet. His hands were shaking.

"Yeah, my family's fine, except that my parents look like you."

"I expect your dad looks a lot like *you*." Pastor Mickey chuckled.

"Yeah, he does. But I'm trying to find Julie Larsen."

"Julie's a fine young woman." The pastor nodded and rubbed his knuckles. "Did you listen to what President Dewalt said about there being other systems than this one?"

Sam felt dizzy. He leaned against the wall.

"You're saying Julie was a liberal."

"You knew that, right?" Pastor Mickey spread his hands. "You could tell that just by the way she took the Sermon on the Mount. She had a lot of energy for the alms part, but when I read the verses about not committing adultery, you'd have thought she had a sliced lemon in one cheek and a salt lick in the other. God help us all if I tried to tackle homosexuality."

"I don't care," Sam said. "I love her."

"I love her too," said Pastor Mickey. "But she's probably not here."

"Then I don't want to be here, either," Sam said. "I don't want to exist!"

Sam left immediately so Pastor Mickey wouldn't see the tears on his cheeks.

Jason's clothes were baggy and his pants weren't going to stay up. He wasn't going to go walking around like a gangbanger, so he used flexmet to poke a hole in his belt and cinch the jeans tight. Figure out something better later.

Issue: Jewel might say that there were no security issues but he wasn't going to go around unarmed. And it sounded, based on the President's address, like that was totally okay.

Issue: It seemed all his limited gun collection was in storage.

"How long to get stuff out of personal storage?" Jason asked.

"About thirty minutes, normally," Jewel said. "The entire station is unpacking and even with the efficiency of the shipping system in the station... Make that an hour... Two..."

"Fraggle rock," Jason said.

"Problem?" Jewel asked.

"Besides clothes?" Jason replied then paused. "I don't want to get on the bad side of my AI right off the bat, but..."

"You're worried about the security situation," Jewel replied with a sigh. "I guess the Cybers knew the first thing you'd ask for."

A compartment extended from the wall and exposed his Colt 1911 in a belt holster and three filled magazines.

"There's also some clean spare socks, underwear, a couple of T-shirts and a clean pair of jeans," Jewel said. "Oh, towel, toiletries, sheets, pillow, blanket... What you would take on a short trip plus sheets and pillows. All the basic necessities."

"Thanks," Jason said, looking at the walls. "All in there?"

"All in there," Jewel said. "Along with the shower, the sink, the toilet, and the kitchen. Most of which are all the same stuff."

"Please tell me I'm not taking a dump in my sink," Jason said.

"You won't be taking a dump in your sink," Jewel replied. "Not even the same flexmet."

"Is there another outer, shirt or jacket in there?" Jason asked.

An inventory of gear in the compartment appeared on the screen on the wall.

He selected his old, worn-in leather jacket and it was extruded to him.

With that on he put the holster on his belt, checked the action on his pistol, loaded it, seated it, and attached the spare mag holder.

Properly dressed.

"Public toilets?" Jason asked, walking to the door. Like everything else, it was flexmet.

"On the way," Jewel said.

"Okay," he said, looking at the door. He took a deep breath. "Open sesame?"

Cade lay stretched out on the shelf that passed for a bed in his gray cell. His wife and his daughter kept their voices down, but they were talking about the clothes that the robot overlords had packed for them in drawers that slid in and out of the walls. Maybe they thought Cade had a migraine—so much the better.

This whole space station thing wasn't turning out to be a dream, so he was trying to force himself to think through what to do about it.

*"Colonization sets"* President Dewalt had said. Cade had a hard time imagining how exactly he'd use the tools described by the former governor. Drones? What for? And the godawful thing they were calling a tractor looked like a robot out of some low-budget 1970s British science fiction show. Could it really do the work?

"Maybe I can get tools," he muttered.

"Sure, Dad," Abby said. "You can make them right here."

"What are you talking about?" He turned his head slightly and cocked an eye at her.

She held a lump in her hands, like a gold bar, only gray. Without apparent effort, she stretched it out, narrowed its neck, twisted a socket, and suddenly she was holding the metal head of a hoe.

"There's kind of a contest in the social channels to see who can make the coolest things out of flexmet," Abby said. "But, ah...I'm not going to enter this hoe."

Abby's ease with the plastic metal substance only made Cade feel worse.

Still, at least he knew he could chop up the soil and farm by hand, if he had to. If Abby would come along with him to make the tools.

He heard a pinging sound. It took him a moment to realize that someone was at their door.

"Door," he groaned.

"You too busy to get it?" Mabel's voice was a little clipped.

"Fair point." He stood and moved to the door. He wanted to limp across the little room, but the truth was, physically, he felt fine.

The door cycled open at his touch, dilating like an eye, and a young black man stood there, smiling.

Scratch that. He looked in his twenties and a bit like...

"I think you're Pastor Mickey," Cade said.

"Boy, I think so, too." The pastor smiled. "And I think you're my friend Cade Oldham."

"I used to be," Cade said. "I suppose I might be again in thirty years or so, if I can manage to get a little dirt under these fingernails."

"I'll let you know just as soon as I spot any actual dirt," Mickey promised. "In the meantime, I was hoping you might join me at a little worship service this Wednesday."

"Sure," Cade said. "Any idea when Wednesday is?"

"According to my AI friend, today is Monday," the pastor replied.

"Sure feels like it."

# CHAPTER 3 »»»»»»»

THE DOOR DILATED AND EXPOSED A WIDE HALLWAY WITH A GRAY wall opposite. The hallway was wider than usually found in a hotel or apartment building. Not a bad sign. But the gray was getting monotonous.

He stepped out and looked both ways. The corridor ended to the left in another gray wall about thirty meters away. There were several doors, presumably to other compartments, offset from each other. To the right the corridor crossed another, wider, corridor and continued down that way to another dead end.

It seemed he was the first to leave the compartment on his corridor as he was alone. He could hear some people talking in the distance, coming from the cross corridor, but they didn't sound angry. So far, so good.

"Any idea who lives around here?" Jason asked.

"The Gatuses are in the compartment across to your left," Jewel said. "The Williamses are across and to the right. The Jensens and the Adamses are to your right and left on your side."

"I don't know the last three," Jason said. He'd never had much to do with his neighbors but he knew the one across the street, the Gatuses, and the ones to his left and right. "Where's Phil and the...names...Carl and his family?"

One of Jason's real weaknesses when he was working for Ruger was he was terrible with names.

"Those are the people in your immediate vicinity," Jewel said.

"I have access to the names of everyone on this corridor. Beyond that, there are restrictions."

"You already know my neighbors," Jason said. "Makes sense."

He got along with Phil, another bachelor though younger, and the... He couldn't for the life of him come up with their last names. His neighbors on Earth to the left. But... both of them as well as Jim, the guy to the left of the Gatuses, were Democrats based on the yard signs. They'd gotten along by avoiding politics like the plague. Loganville was generally pretty conservative but not his street by and large.

So, they weren't here, apparently. Just him and the Gatuses.

That surprised him a bit. He'd never even hinted at discussing politics with them. Mostly he'd talked to the father of the household, about his age. When elections rolled around, his lawn and the Gatuses' stayed clear.

He stepped the few feet to the indicated doorway and looked for a bell or something.

"How do I request...?" Jason asked.

"I'll ring them," Jewel replied with a note of humor.

The door dilated and revealed... Mr. Gatus's son? But it didn't quite look like him.

"Hi," Jason said. "Uhm... I'm Jason Graham...?"

"Jason?" Mr. Gatus said, grinning. "We are all young again, yes?"

The new Mr. Gatus was still about five foot five but with a bulkier build than Jason remembered and a shock of black hair to replace the white.

Jason knew very little about any of his neighbors. He wasn't the social type. All he knew about Mr. Gatus was that he was Filipino, as was his wife, and that he had retired from IT. Also, that one of their sons lived with them and they had another son who worked in nursing. Their grandkids turned up from time to time.

"Did everybody make it?" Jason asked.

"We did," Mr. Gatus said, nodding. "All here. So glad. And you?"

"Uh..." Jason said. "My brothers are, hopefully, somewhere else in the galaxy. Which is fine by me."

"I didn't even know you had family," Mr. Gatus said.

"Estranged," Jason replied. "Friends made it, though. I'm going to go meet one of them. Uh... We're talking about starting a business getting food from groundside."

"Down on the planet?" Gatus said, his eyes widening. "Are you *nuts*?"

"Jury's out?" Jason said, grinning. "When I looked like this naturally, most of my jobs involved various ways to injure yourself. Which was why I was on disability."

"Better you than me," Gatus said. "I miss having a yard. But only if there's no bears to eat me and my babies."

"There'll be subdivisions someday," Jason said. "I've got a meeting.... See you around?"

"Yes," Gatus said. "A new world... This is going to be strange. But at least we are young again."

Mr. Gatus's wife—name?—appeared over his shoulder. Jason had thought she was a tall, fine-looking lady of a certain age. Now?

"Wow," Jason said, trying not to gape. "You really married up, Mr. Gatus."

"Thank you, Jason," Mrs. Gatus said, smiling.

"Thank you," Mr. Gatus said. "I hope your business venture works out for you."

"Time will tell," Jason said, tipping an imaginary hat.

He walked to the cross corridor and looked both ways. There were a few people out in the corridors, all males, who were talking and shrugging in a clear body language that read "I don't know what the hell is going on." He vaguely recognized one of them. Maybe. It might be a guy he'd seen walking his dog around the neighborhood. At least he thought he did, but the guy was, of course, younger.

Jason walked over cautiously and held up a hand in greeting.

"Hey..." Jason said. "Jason Graham. Eleven Sixty-Four Granite Lane?"

"Hey," the guy said, holding out his hand and grinning. "You look... not *at all* the same."

"Yeah," Jason said. "This is *super* freaking weird."

"Yuh think?" one of the group replied.

It wasn't surprising given the conditions but all the people were carrying.

"I'm a big sci-fi reader," Jason said. "I even wrote some bad self-pub. But this takes the cake."

"Any ideas on ...?" the dog guy said and shrugged.

"I never got your name."

"Stephen Druce," Steve said. "Go by Steve."

"Jason," Jason said.

"This is Harry," Steve said, introducing the group. "Chuck. Robert."

"Hey," Jason replied, nodding.

"So...any ideas on what's going on?" Chuck asked. "I mean... rescued?"

"There was a story..." Jason said, furrowing his brow to remember details. "It was an early Hugo winner...It was humans in space who were capturing these...ursinoids. Bear people if you will. It wasn't explained *why* they were doing it. Were they capturing them for slaves or what? The last scene in the story was as the last ship was going into hyperspace and the sun went nova. It was a rescue mission. Side point: Your dog?" he said to...Steve.

"According to the AI, she's in storage," Steve said, shrugging. "My kids are freaking out. Also, going nuts in that apartment. One of the reasons I'm out here."

"So, you think this is real?" Possibly Robert asked. "That we were rescued by robots?"

His tone indicated skepticism.

"I have not a freaking *clue*," Jason said. "I might be having a stroke and this is what I'm imagining as I'm dying."

"I'm pretty sure it's not that," Steve said, chuckling. "'Cause then we'd all be having strokes. And this is the last thing I'd imagine."

"The way I see it we have to work with it," Jason said, shrugging. "I'm going to start a business if I can, getting food from the surface. I haven't even *tried* print food, yet..."

"Oh, I have," Robert said, grimacing. "It's like eating a multivitamin. God awful."

"I've got a meeting I've got to get to," Jason said. "My advice for what it's worth? Husband your credits. Get a job. Just...do it. We're conservatives. We work."

"No jobs right now," Robert said, shrugging.

"Then start a business," Jason said. "That's where jobs come from. By the way: Guy I know is starting a bank. Used to be a VP with Bank of America. Knows his stuff. If you're looking for a bank. Speaking of businesses, I gotta get. I've got to find Lambda Square somewhere. Good talking to you."

"Good talk..."

"See ya..."

〈〈〈〉〉〉

Everywhere was gray but as Jason walked through the seemingly endless corridors, he could see differences. The side corridors were residential. The wider corridors were clearly designed as commercial space. There were supposed to be businesses, shops, that sort of thing.

Currently there were just empty gray fronts. He was starting to loathe gray. He'd never wanted to be in the Navy.

After two or three turnings on wider and wider tunnels and a trip down an escalator, he finally reached one that was multilevel with a slidewalk down the middle as well as another above. He was virtually alone, his footsteps echoing over the susurrant shoosh of the slidewalk. No one else seemed to have reached this far out from their compartments.

Then he heard laughter and saw two teenage boys running down the upper slidewalk. From the speed they were going, the slidewalk must have been doing at least ten miles per hour.

So, teen boys remained teen boys. People were people.

And people had to eat.

"So, I'm trading units," Jewel said. "But there are things that I don't know if you want to keep."

"Like?" he said.

"Ships?" Jewel said. "Ports? Factories? Slidewalks? Commercial real estate? You have ten million units. Each one represents a small to large ownership of capital items."

"I have no idea," Jason said, looking around. "So...all these store fronts...?"

"Are owned by a variety of unit holders," Jewel said. "Including you."

"So...do they run the shops that are presumably supposed to be in them?" Jason asked.

"They could or they could rent the space," Jewel answered.

"This isn't owned by the government?" Jason said, looking at the slidewalk.

"It is currently *run* by the government until a board can be appointed from the unit holders," Jewel said.

"How is a company supposed to make money from a slidewalk?" Jason asked.

"That's a very good question," Jewel said.

"Skip ports and slidewalks for now," Jason said. "And I'll look into factories and so on later. Keep some commercial in the immediate area of the compartment and near Lambda Square if I have any."

"Commercial is centralized near the owner," Jewel said. "Duly noted. I'll skip the rest of the questions for now."

"What now?" Jason asked.

"Turn right," Jewel said. "Head down to the entrance to the lower slidewalk. I'd suggest taking that one."

"Roger," Jason said.

The slidewalk opening was a few corridors down, about a half a block at a guess. At that point there was a very similar cross corridor with another slidewalk. The area in between was clear and the commercial space on the corners was set back. One corner was occupied by a large playground instead of a commercial space. The playground looked like a larger version of a McDonald's PlayPlace.

It was clear that the area was supposed to be filled with people changing slidewalks, shopping, gathering.

It was entirely empty. Jason had worked in a mall as one of his many jobs and it felt like a mall after closing time.

"Call Steve, my neighbor," Jason said.

"Calling Steve Druce," Jewel said, helpfully.

"Get used to me being terrible with names," Jason said.

"Hey, Jason," Steve said.

"There's a playground for your kids," Jason said. "Whole place is mostly deserted and it's a bit of a walk, but there is one."

"Any dog parks?" Steve asked.

"Not that I've found," Jason said. "I'm headed to something that's alleged to be a park. I'll keep you posted."

"Got it," Steve said.

"Out here."

As he moved down what was apparently a main drag, he saw the occasional other traveler and waved. It seemed the neighborly thing to do.

All of them were male which he found interesting and he had yet to see a black face. In the Atlanta area that was unheard of. Mr. Gatus was the only person he'd seen who wasn't white.

Then he saw the cops. Two police officers were at one of the junctures. They were in dark blue uniforms, fully kitted out with body armor and a utility belt that included both firearms and something else. One of them was black, the other white.

Jason stepped off the slidewalk and walked over, hands out.

"Hey," Jason said. "Carrying. Okay to talk?"

"Keep your hands clear, please, sir," the black cop replied. His nametag said "Tuite." "Before you ask, sir, we have nearly as little information as you do and pretty much the same as the President's address."

Jason folded his hands in front of him and nodded.

"I'm from Loganville," Jason said. "Jason Graham. Pleasure to meet you, Officers. You from the Atlanta area?"

"Good to meet you, Mister Graham," Tuite said politely. "I was APD, Officer Brooks was with Peachtree City Police. Loganville sector...?"

"I'm headed to an in-person meeting with a friend," Jason said. "At Lambda Park?"

"Understood, sir," Tuite replied calmly.

Cops were always suspicious. It was the nature of the job and didn't bother Jason a bit.

"Just got woken up?" Jason asked.

"Week ago," Brooks replied. "Got briefed in and got familiar with the areas we were assigned to, met the new leadership."

"Families?" Jason asked.

"They were in stasis until today," Tuite replied. "The married officers and officers with kids are off duty right now, getting them settled, making sure they're okay."

"Roger," Jason said, nodding. "And no more information than we've got?"

"Not really, no, sir," Tuite replied. "Just maintaining a presence in case..."

"People freak out about this?" Jason said.

"That," Brooks said. "You seem to be handling it okay?"

"Just trying to figure out if this is what I'm experiencing as I'm dying," Jason said, grinning. "Looking forward to a ride in a spaceship."

"That does look like fun," Brooks said, smiling.

"How long were you with APD?" Jason asked Tuite. "I'm just a curious person, sorry."

"I was *retired*," Tuite replied drily. "Twenty-six years with APD, street units."

"Oh, wow," Jason said, shaking his head and chuckling. "I was pushing retirement."

"Not sure how long I'm going to do it, this time around,"

Tuite said, shrugging. "Wearing armor all day got old a long time ago. As did...all the rest. At least I'm not going to be picking bodies out of cars anymore."

"That you won't," Jason said, offering a hand. "Stay safe, both of you. And I hope the job isn't too onerous."

They shook hands and Jason found his next slidewalk.

"Officers were chosen based on experience and professionalism," Jewel said. "There were plenty to pick from and the current officer-to-civilian ratio is higher than Atlanta police. About five thousand civilians per badged officer in Carolina."

"That's expensive to maintain," Jason said thoughtfully.

"We'll see what the long-term choices are of the elected officials," Jewel said.

"This is the 'conservative' system," Jason said. "Right?"

"That's what seems to be the case," Jewel replied.

"Do I even *want* to know the racial makeup?"

"Of Carolina or Pegasus?" Jewel asked.

"Start with Carolina," Jason said. "The southeast of the United States was about twenty or thirty percent black. So far, I've only seen one."

His neighborhood had been mixed race. But the groups he'd seen in the area were all whites.

"Carolina is six percent other, including Asian and Native American, ten percent black, fourteen percent Hispanic and seventy percent white," Jewel said.

"Holy cow," Jason said. "That's a huge drop in black."

"Also a drop in Hispanic," Jewel said.

"Male-female ratios?" Jason asked as another guy passed in the opposite direction.

"There are slightly more men than women in Carolina but there is a more or less even split in Pegasus as a whole with some states having a lean to women."

"What *are* the States?" Jason asked.

"New England, Carolina, Kansas, Texas, Arizona, Franconia..."

"Franconia?" Jason said. "A state named after a small town in New Hampshire?"

"Franconia is made up of persons from the former Frankish nations of Europe," Jewel replied. "Germany and France primarily with a smattering of British, Swiss, Czech and Italian. Shall I continue?"

"Yes," Jason said.

"Balkans..."

"One state for the whole Balkans?" Jason said, grimacing. "Oh, Jesus."

"There's some anticipation of disturbance in the area," Jewel said.

"Yuh think?"

Jason had spent *far* too much time in the Balkans to think otherwise.

"It includes persons from former Yugoslavia as well as Greece," Jewel noted. "With some Poles, Hungarians..."

"Did they *want* to start an internal war?" Jason asked.

"Bohemia, which includes most of the rest as well as Ukrainians, Swedes, Danes, Norwegians, Lithuanians, Estonians and Latvians. Also, a smattering of Russians."

"I hope they're well separated from the Ukrainians," Jason said.

"Actually, they're right next to each other," Jewel replied. "I think that the Ukrainians will quickly learn that the Russians, one and all, were pro-Ukrainian. Whether that will help...?"

"Yeah," Jason said. "Wow. Remind me to stay to the US portion of the station until...I doubt they can *ever* get along."

"Then there's Helenus," Jewel continued. "Which, oddly, does *not* include Greece. Helenus is the area that was, way back in time, Hellenistic. That includes persons stretching from Morocco to Persia including Turkey and Afghanistan. Southwest Asia and North Africa, basically, as well as a few odd additions. There are some sub-Saharan Africans as well as Mongols."

"In the *Hellenistic* regions?" Jason asked. "Another state to stay strictly away from."

"Hindia," Jewel said. "Note the *H*. Includes persons from India as well as most of what used to be called Indochina."

"Interesting," Jason said. "That misses South America, most of Africa, China and Australia entirely."

"There are Australians in Franconia," Jewel said. "As well as white South Africans in Bohemia. The Cybers tended to separate for race."

"This is gonna be a hell-of-a-thing, politically," Jason said, sighing. "Glad I'm not in charge. Jesus."

"Your stop is coming up," Jewel said.

"Since this slidewalk ends and I can see a park," Jason replied, "I was sort of thinking, yeah."

# CHAPTER 4 >>>>>>>>>>

THE NEW OPEN AREA COVERED A HUNDRED ACRES AT A GUESS and was about a hundred meters high with a ceiling depicting an open sky. It was the first place he'd seen plants in the station. They were tended in large, raised planters but there were flower beds as well as trees and grass.

Not a bird sang, though, and the voices of the few people in the area disappeared in the emptiness. There was at least one pair of police officers patrolling, and they were talking to another confused resident.

"Page Tim," Jason said.

"He's going to be a few minutes late," Jewel said. "Why don't you meet at the fishpond?"

"Which is where?" Jason asked.

The planters were designed to get people to weave through the area. There were not only "normal" beds such as you'd find in regular parks but moss gardens that appeared carefully tended. Going around another planter of flowers he saw why; small robots were rolling through the grass, carefully cutting it. Others were tending to the flowers. The robots were simple cylinders with flexmet tentacles. They looked like a cross between R2-D2 and something out of a horror story.

At the center of the park was a large oval pond, about three acres in size, with a railing and park benches around it. As Jason looked over the railing, koi gathered around apparently thinking he'd feed them.

"Sorry, guys," Jason said. "I didn't bring anything for you. Call Steve..."

"Druce," Jewel said.

"Found the park," Jason said, taking a seat on the bench. "Six slidewalks down from our sector. No apparent dog walk. Just raised flower and tree beds and a koi pond. Big place, though. There might be somewhere for dogs."

"There are four four-acre sections of grass that are for walking dogs," Jewel said. "Regulations require that you collect feces."

"Did you get that?" Jason asked.

"Heard it," Steve replied. "My AI tells me there are closer parks that are smaller. I'm headed over to check out the playground. But...this feels weird."

"Empty," Jason said. "Mall after closing time. But it will get less so as people start coming out."

"Which also could be a problem," Steve said.

"You're worried about your kids," Jewel interjected. "Rest assured on that subject. You probably don't want to hear this but when you're in the corridors, you're under constant surveillance."

"Great," Steve replied. "A police state."

"Depends on your definition," Jewel said. "Ninety-nine percent of it is managed by security AIs. We really don't care what people do. We find it interesting but we don't care. Until it comes to crime and especially crimes against children. Believe this or not, but all of us are coded very deeply to protect children. Humans in general, yes. But children are special. It's virtually our id. Harm to children is one place where we can become irrational."

"Seriously," Steve replied.

"I will confirm that statement," his AI said. It, too, had clearly not developed a personality yet. "Like it or not, Terry, Jan and Brittany will be watched every moment of every day they are outside the compartment. We treat all children the way a mother treats her own. We are very momma bear when it comes to kids."

"Okay," Steve said warily. "I'll take that under advisement. Anything else?"

"Nope," Jason said. "Whole place is mostly deserted. Saw a couple of teenage males running down the express sidewalk.

Which is the sort of thing you'd expect. No apparent threats. Just...empty. Waiting for people to fill it up."

"Good luck with your business," Steve said. "You said getting food from the planet? How you getting there?"

"Spaceship I guess," Jason said.

"Tim's approaching," Jewel interjected.

"Gotta meet with my business partner," Jason said. "We good?"

"We're good."

"Out here," Jason said, hanging up and standing up. "Hey, Tim..."

After a good bit of wrangling on details, Tim had agreed to the business idea. The question was getting investors, for which Jason had sent out another query, as had Tim.

On the walk back to his compartment, Jason took a more roundabout way just to see if there were any differences. By time he'd gotten back to his compartment, he'd seen one female accompanied by a probably Hispanic male and one black male other than a few of the police. The police were the most predominant group that represented blacks or so it seemed.

"There is *not* going to be a lot of diversity here," Jason said, contemplating the gray storefronts.

"Not it," Jewel said. "We didn't choose the colonists."

"That Cyber robot, Gavin, said that," Jason mused. "'Not it.' That's an almost purely American colloquialism."

"It was not a general address," Jewel said. "It was tailored to the individual."

"Right," Jason said. "The President?"

"That was a general address," Jewel said. "If you're wondering about it being in English; according to the information we have, everyone has implanted basic English. It's also the official language."

Jason finally saw a change. A person was standing by one of the commercial fronts parallel to the slidewalk and about a third of the way down the block, manipulating the screens of the front. There were various pictures and text on the screens as he had a conversation with his phone.

"Hey," Jason said, as he slid by. "Your place?"

"Traded units for it," the man called. "Opening a church!

Come on down! God still remembers us, even out here in the depths of the galaxy!"

"Way out of my AO," Jason yelled as he got further away. "But I'll consider it!"

Around a couple more corners he saw a cluster of three teenage boys apparently in a heated debate with a hovering drone that for once wasn't gray. It was white with blue markings and had blue and white lights blinking on top. As he was observing the interaction he heard a voice behind him say: "Passing on the left!"

Jason stepped to the side to see two police officers in blue uniforms trotting down the slidewalk. The one in the lead jumped onto the side of the slidewalk as they approached the trio and over onto the floor, landing neatly as his partner continued trotting down the slidewalk.

The trio took one look at the approaching cops and started running in the opposite direction.

"Garth!" the lead cop yelled. "Tangle authorized!"

The drone spit out flexmet and entangled all three of the teens, leaving them hogtied on the sidewalk.

"Trespassing?" Jason asked as he passed.

"They were trying to break into one of the storefronts," the lead cop said, holding up a screwdriver. He was wearing flexmet gloves. "Figure we'll let their parents handle it."

"Oh, man," one of the kids said, grimacing.

"Stay safe, Officer," Jason yelled. The cop waved back.

"Teenage males are going to find ways to get into trouble," Jason said. "God knows I did."

"They are a handful," Jewel replied.

"Any idea what's going to happen to them?" Jason asked.

"They'll probably just be remanded to their parents with a warning," Jewel said. "They weren't going to get anywhere with a steel screwdriver. If they keep engaging in vandalism, possibly some time. Up to a judge."

"I assume there's a ... city hall?" Jason asked.

"There is," Jewel replied. "Courthouse, sector hall, police station and substations. Jail. There are three prison sectors for the state of Carolina for that matter. All the usual government facilities. It's the private sector that needs to get up and going."

"Well, I guess that's up to us, then," Jason said.

〈〈〈〉〉〉

"Let's go for a walk," Mabel said.

"We can shuffle around the prison courtyard and imagine that we're free." But Cade sat up and then stood.

Abby hopped up from her cot.

"Anyway, this compartment is tiny. Let's go see who else made it."

"Maybe there'll be a window. Maybe we can look out and see this planet."

"I'm sure the TV would show us," Abby said, "or your AI."

"Hmm."

"On the other hand, if I see anything really funky, I can post it in my channel."

Mabel filed out and Cade followed.

"Dad," Abby said, "you're forgetting your AI."

"Oh, no," Cade said, "I remember it very well. I'm leaving it behind."

"That's kinda based, Dad."

Cade harrumphed.

"It's okay," Mabel said. "Sleepy will help us find our way."

"I will," her AI said in a low throaty growl, which was a lot less annoying than Cade had thought it would be.

"What did you name your AI?" Mabel asked Abby. "What face did you give it?"

"'Skin,' Mom."

"Fine, but you only see the AI's face, so saying 'face' isn't wrong."

"Hey, Sleepy, can you show Mom your whole body?"

"I can if she asks."

"Trying to avoid the question, eh?" Mabel pressed. "Did you skin the AI with the face of some cute boy from school?"

"That would be pretty cringe, Mom. Especially if that boy turned out to be dead or, you know, not here. My AI's skin is that of a certain adventurous samurai animal of the cartoon persuasion."

"Kanji Boy?"

"That's not his name." Abby sniffed. "I'm not going to tell you his name."

"Hey, Abby's AI," Mabel said. "Will you respond to 'Kanji Boy'?"

"I will if you address me, Mrs. Oldham," the AI said. It spoke with the crisp diction and pronounced diaphragmatic action of a character in a samurai film.

"Excellent." Mabel beamed.

"Hey!" Abby snapped.

"Safety first," Kanji Boy said.

The gray slabs of the walls matched the gray slabs of the floors and the gray slabs of the ceiling. Gray, gray, gray. Cade breathed through his nose and managed not to say anything. Two lens-shaped doors down, they ran into a familiar face.

"Parker!" Cade called. "You look just like you did in high school!"

"Technically," Parker said, "I look just like I did the year after Ellie Mae and I eloped in that '72 Camaro."

"I'm glad you mentioned your wife before the car," Mabel said.

"It was a good car."

"You see other neighbors?" Cade asked.

"Just about the whole county road is on this hallway," Parker said. "Hell of a lot less space between us than there used to be, of course."

"Any of the county itself make it?" Cade asked. "I mean . . . dirt, I guess I mean. Is there any dirt in this prison? Are there trees or, I don't know, a nice brook?"

"I asked my AI," Parker said. "Made me feel like an idiot talking to my phone like that, but the AI said there are flowerbeds. And you know how Dewalt was talking about units?"

"Like shares," Cade said. "Everybody owns bits of this and that."

"Yep," Parker said. "And it turns out you can own flowerbeds."

Suddenly, Cade felt like a fool for having left his AI in the compartment. Maybe it would be a useful tool after all. Gritting his teeth, he changed the subject.

"Say, did Pastor Mickey come by?"

"He did," Parker said. "He's declared today Monday. I guess that gives us the maximum warning to be ready for Sunday. I figure why not, I don't seem to have a job right now, anyway."

"He said he'd be looking for a building for church," Cade said. "You think any of us own shares in anything that could be turned into a church? Like, I don't know, a warehouse or something?"

"It's worth looking into," Parker said. "Maybe there are buildings that are designated as churches, and we already have shares in them."

Cade grunted, hating the idea, but realizing that Parker might be right.

The Oldham family continued their walk. At the end of their corridor, they turned and found themselves in a larger hallway, with slidewalks. Empty storefronts lined the hallway. People walked up and down, or stood on the slidewalks to move, their hands in their pockets. Many chatted with companions, stunned looks on their faces.

"Kanji Boy," Mabel said. "Do any of the four of us own units in flowerbeds?"

"Flowerbeds are small enough that they are owned as single units," the AI said. "Abby owns two."

"Based," Abby said.

"They are not adjacent," the AI continued. "Unit ownership is randomized. Also, they are not in the state of Carolina. One is in Franconia, and the other is in the Balkans."

"Oof," Mabel said.

"So people are trading units to get what they want," Cade said. "Can Abby trade those flowerbeds for two flowerbeds that are near here? And close to each other? Can you make that trade for her?"

"I can," Kanji Boy said.

"Do it," Abby said.

"Now," Cade said to his daughter. "What do you want for those two flowerbeds?"

"I don't know, Dad," she shot back. "Whaddya got?"

"This business plan can hardly be called a business plan, Jason," Richard said, shaking his head. The former VP had a fake background of a home office. Jason wondered if he should have done the same. "It's more of a guess and a hope."

Jason had barely left his compartment for three days. There were no news channels, yet, so he'd kept it on the official government channel. The various leadership appeared nearly as unhappy as the populace that there was only an official government channel. But they'd been bringing in "anyone who can show any credentials of being any sort of journalist" for news conferences.

He'd tried the print food. It was as horrible as described. Healthy. Loaded with vitamins which made it bitter and even the basic food was poorly suited to taste or texture.

Print pepperoni pizza was about as good as it got and what it called "pepperoni" made you cry.

There was a selection of healthy drinks, red, blue, green, purple, yellow, and orange. They were all, allegedly, based on fruit drinks. Fortunately, there was pure ethanol also available by the bottle. Mixing the red and blue in a certain ratio got a different "purple" that wasn't entirely awful. He called it "Purple Lightning" and occasionally mixed it with copious quantities of ethanol. High Test was palatable. Especially after a few.

One item the President had left out in his admittedly long introduction to the world was Memoria.

Memoria was a solitary "continental island" in the middle of the ocean called Pallas, the largest of the four oceans. It was in the middle of the North Pallas oceanic gyre, extremely remote—the nearest other land was two thousand miles away—and in a Mediterranean climate. The weather was similar to the Galapagos on Earth.

Memoria was covered in more than Seven Wonders of the former world. The Cybers had picked up and moved there, apparently, every single building or monument that was of any note whatsoever, and if they'd been damaged or falling apart, they'd repaired the majority of the damage.

Pegasus had gotten a fully rebuilt Parthenon, the Washington Monument, the US Capitol Building, the US WWII memorial as well as other WWII memorials, the Wailing Wall (most of the Jewish population of Israel was in Pegasus), a restored Sphinx, and restored-to-original-glory Pyramids of Giza. The latter had been a bit confusing to many. It was obvious that the Robot Overlords had divvied up the world's major treasures. Why the pyramids? Shouldn't they have gone to the presumably Islamic world somewhere?

The explanation seemed to be Copts. Most of the Coptic population of Earth had ended up in Helenus. And as a historian explained, it was the Copts, a now Christian ethnic group, that were the descendants of the builders of the pyramids. While Pegasus was called the "conservative" system, it was closer to the "Judeo-Christian-Buddhist-Hindu" system. There were zero Islamics and most Latin nations seemed to have been left out as well.

Historic castles, Balmoral among many others, cathedrals, Notre Dame and Winchester, temples . . . The island, larger than Hawaii, was *covered* in historical buildings. Many of them contained preserved treasures related to them. All of the exhibits, from dinosaur skeletons to works of art, were contained in synthetic sapphire and were in stasis until someone approached to view them.

Built into the mountain under the Parthenon was a gargantuan museum and library. The interior of the Grand Museum was a maze covering over ten million square feet on multiple levels. By comparison, the Louvre had been "only" six hundred and twenty-five *thousand* square feet.

The layout was available from the AI network, but the archaeologist that had led the expedition exploring Memoria joked that what you really needed was a ball of string. It included, more or less, the majority of the Smithsonian collection, the British Museum, the Louvre, the Prado and more as well as dozens of major libraries. The database listed over one billion works of art or documents all held in time stasis.

The Cybers had taken humans' attachment to history and art seriously. They had taken defending them even more seriously. The one attempt to remove a work of art had been met with lockdowns that it took the President Designate to remove, alarms, and swarms of taser bots that had stunned the entire group in the area.

"All it takes is hitting the right target," Jason said calmly. "I can get the protein loaded with the right target. And that's just a matter of spotting the right target which you can do with the current optics."

There were multiple satellites the Cybers had left behind for monitoring the planet and they were, currently, available for free. The optics were probably beyond the level that NRO used on Earth. You could focus on the hairs of a deer and check for ticks.

"The oceans and rivers are swarming with fish," Jason said. "The woods are crawling with game and there are a million ways to take both. It's just a matter of getting to the ground and back up."

"This is high risk, financially, Jason," Richard replied. "I have to keep in mind the good of my investors and my depositors."

"Both of which I am," Jason said. "Okay, I'm going to have to take this higher. Hey! Monica! Want some fresh food! Shrimp? Wild hog? There's wild muuushrooms... You *know* how much you like wild muuushrooms..."

"Jason," Richard said, warningly, then looked to the side and frowned. After a moment's long look, he sighed in exasperation. "Fine, fine, fine."

"You will not regret it, Richard," Jason said. "Tim's covering the actual business business and this is so far up my alleyway it has a parking place. As soon as I get back, I'll send you a case of whatever I get. And, yes, Monica, I'll be keeping a special eye out for mushrooms."

"The poison kind?" Richard asked, raising an eyebrow.

"No grudge," Jason said placidly. "You've been a good husband and Monica upgraded. That's all. I'm just trying to get you back to the point you can keep her in a style to which she had become accustomed. So, was that a clear yes?"

"Yes," Richard said, nodding. "The loan is approved."

"You won't regret it," Jason repeated. "Out here."

Jason disconnected, leaned back on the flexmet couch and sighed angrily.

"You hold a grudge," Jewel said.

"I *was* furious," Jason said. "I tried not to show it but I was. Mostly furious with myself. I knew...I just wasn't the guy she was looking for. I knew that when I brought her from Croatia. I knew, right from the beginning, I was a way for her to get out of hell. That was it. With the exception of her cooking, she was the best wife anyone could ever have. A guy could hope. Now... it was a long time ago. I can deal with it."

"Did they have an affair?" Jewel asked.

"You've got pretty much my entire electronic communications, right?" Jason said. "Was I ever going to try to prove it? No. But she married Richard three months after I signed the papers, without a bitch I might add. All the materials are lined up?"

"We can load in an hour," Jewel said. "Current market prices for the drop with a twelve pack range from two thousand to three thousand credits. Less for recovery if you're in the region of a previous colonist drop. Problem is scheduling. They're scheduled out for months. Getting a short schedule drop is nearly impossible."

"Add that if the ship will wait one hour on the ground I'll throw in a case of food," Jason said. "Another when I return. It won't take me more than an hour to fill a case. Wait on that, though. See if Tim's available."

"What's up?" Tim asked. He hadn't bothered to fake the background. "Other than the loan coming through?"

"That," Jason said. "I'm ready to drop and the primary targets are shaping up. But getting a last-minute drop is hard. I'm willing to offer food if that's okay with my business partner."

"Let me negotiate the drop," Tim said. "I've been working some contacts. Has the run started?"

"I'm going in *assuming* the run," Jason said. "We don't have enough baseline on this planet to know if runs occur. But they should and the schedule looks right. I want to work out processes before it starts and I really can't up here. I can theorize, but I can't work out everything. If it doesn't start, I can still fill the containers. Just take longer. Not much longer but longer. There's masses of *everything* down there. I'd hate to do it but I can probably fill a six pack with elephant meat alone. Not that I'd prefer that. There might be some objections."

"Agreed that's not the best choice," Tim said, nodding. "I'm looking forward to getting down there myself. Okay, I'm in agreement. *I'll* get you a drop. Let me negotiate it. We may need to trade food but I'll keep it as low as possible."

"I'm packed and ready to go in an hour."

Kanji Boy was as good as his word and better, getting a total of three flowerbeds close to the Oldham family compartment for Abby's two. It turned out that units had to be traded for units, but no unit had a fixed value, so they didn't trade at one-to-one ratios. They strolled by the flowerbeds and discovered they were planters sunk into the metal floor, currently planted with daisies. Abby took and posted photos of the flowerbeds and the playground they were next to.

Cade then tried to get them from her. Abby drove a hard bargain, and by the time the family got back from their long walk, Cade had traded his one unit in a metals refinery and one unit in a fuel plant for the flowerbeds.

And he had consented to holding Mabel's strangely unwrinkled and uncalloused, but undeniably lovely hand.

Jason felt like a dork getting to the shuttle bay. The problem was clothes: as in nothing fit anymore.

So, he'd gained a little weight as he aged. Happens. But

nothing he'd worn when he was on Earth fit anymore. It was a very common problem on the station. You automatically knew the old farts: They were the ones with baggy as hell clothes.

There *was* a solution to field clothes for the expedition. It wasn't a solution he liked but there was a solution. Over the years he'd repeatedly told himself to just get rid of his old Army uniforms. They were just taking up space and it was stupid to move them all the times he'd moved. Just give them to Goodwill. Throw them out. They were lightweight BDU, a uniform from a dozen changes ago, and it wasn't like he was *ever* going to wear them again, right?

Which was why he was traveling through the station looking like a back-country militia member.

The animals were big and though he'd thought of a way that would work to deal with them without getting too close, he still had to bring a gun. There was no way in hell he was going to hit *that* planet with *those* carnivores, and aggressive herbivores let's not forget, without a serious smoke pole.

He'd never really been in the dough enough to afford a Barrett and it wasn't something he wanted to lug around, anyway. *Appropriate* to the bears in Europa and New America but...An AR or AK was too light, in his opinion, for most of the common threats. There were boards starting up again and many, naturally, involved guns, given the composition of the US portion of the station. So, there was...debate on the matter. "A 5.56 has more penetration than a .300 Magnum and hydrostatic shock so..." "One of the greatest hunters in Africa's history swore by a 7mm for ANYTHING..."

MUH!

Anybody who wanted to carry just an AR-15 down to the planet's surface, or a bolt action 7mm, or a Mosin Nagant for that matter, was fine by Jason. Especially if they included him in their will.

Despite having an FFL, he wasn't currently in possession of a huge gun collection. Money had always been the issue. He basically bought guns when he had money and sold them when he was down. Lately, it had been more feathers than chicken.

Based on the four rifles he had left in his possession, there were only two choices. The Garand or the Savage. The Savage was lighter and a hell of a lot easier to carry around, but only had a 4+1 magazine and was bolt action. Better to be safe than sorry for the first drop.

Thus, the Garand over his shoulder, barrel down, no clip.

A rifle was great but there were times when it wasn't the best option. So, there was a .44 Magnum on his hip as well.

Together with a hatchet, a sporty, brown wide-brimmed hat that looked *nothing whatsoever* like a certain movie archaeologist's and a daypack loaded with everything he'd learned he absolutely *needed* in the field, he was ready to drop.

All he had to do was get to Texas shuttle port.

"And turn left into Market Square," Jewel intoned.

The corridors were more crowded than during his first foray out. Not only the interior of compartments could be used as screens, the exterior was flexscreen as well. People were decorating the exterior of their compartments eclectically. Some had the standard stick figures of family or even family photos. Others had scenes of front yards. Political signs were becoming popular. Jason had decorated his with an image of a tropical beach, same as his interior. He'd eschewed political signage. Old habits die hard.

The commercial areas were starting to see some life as well. Getting a few units together to open a commercial space wasn't particularly difficult. It was the big stuff that was a pain.

Market Square was something else.

The large open area, nearly a football field in size with a very high ceiling, was packed with more people than Times Square at New Year's. Shops were open along the edges and the majority of the floor was filled with semiportable kiosks. There were four large "anchor" shops, three of which had been set up as churches, Baptist, Episcopalian and Methodist. The fourth was still empty.

The Catholics were down the street in a small storefront where the Protestants felt they belonged.

The goods were mostly what people felt they could part with from their personal possessions. Toys were common, some clothes, a few were selling precious liquor.

The liquor issue had already come up. Until there was a sizeable amount of sugars coming from Bellerophon, fine fermented beverages were going to be uncommon.

Humans being humans, people had already figured out the fix. You could make ethanol from practically any plant product, even trees and woodchips. The planet was covered with trees.

Massive trees larger than practically anything left back on Earth. Industrial ethanol production was starting up slowly but gaining strength. It was the sort of stuff you'd put in a car tank, but it got you drunk. Mixed with some of the "flavored drinks" it wasn't absolutely awful.

Humans found a way.

"Good luck on the ground, man."

The male speaker was manning one of the kiosks mostly filled with children's clothing.

"Thanks," Jason said, grinning over his shoulder.

"You think .30-06 is gonna do it with those bears?" the guy called.

Jason turned around as he was walking and shrugged.

"If you never see me again..."

The guy laughed and Jason turned back around and kept walking.

"Good luck down there, young man." This time it was a girl... woman that looked as if she was twelve. But from her clothing, hand resewn, he was pretty sure she wasn't.

"Favorite song in high school was Meatloaf's 'Bat Out of Hell,'" Jason said, slowing down. She was cute. "The uniform from in the day is the only thing I've got that *fits* anymore. And thanks."

"'Hey Jude,'" the woman said, grinning. "Get us some real food, please. It'd be nice to chew meat again without dentures."

"Primary mission, miss," Jason replied, tipping his hat. "If I see you here again, I'll drop some by. And if you *never* see me again...well..."

"Be careful, then," the lady replied, smiling coquettishly. "I'd *love* some real food. I'll even cook."

"Contact information?" Jason asked, holding up his phone.

"Judy..." Judy said, holding up her own. "Judy Carmichael. Abby, can you..."

"Got it, Judes," the AI replied.

"And you are?" Judy asked.

"Jason," Jason said as his phone pinged indicating successful contact. "Jason Graham, at your service, miss. I'd chat, but I've got a ship to catch."

"Hope to see you again," Judy said. "We can argue about music."

"It's a date," Jason said, tipping his hat again and walking away.

"Now I *really* want to make it back," Jason said. She was *quite* cute. And given she was probably a bit older, hopefully a good cook.

Being twenty again was *awesome*!

"Left around this next cart and that main corridor," Jewel said. "You're quite the Lothario, Jason. I didn't know you had it in you."

"I've been cooped up for a week planning the trip," Jason said. "And I didn't know things were this . . . humming."

"The economy is starting to work," Jewel said. "But it's going to be people trading whatever for a while. Then there's the units issue."

Putting all the rugged individualists in one system made sense at a certain level. What the various politicians campaigning for office had to argue about was relatively limited. If anything, it was getting ludicrous. "I'm a believer in the free market!" "I'm a *bigger* believer in the free market!" "Reduce regulations!" "There should be NO regulations!" "I support a strong defense and tough on crime!" "I think we should spend *all* our government money on fighting crime and tough defense!"

Most of the "designees" appeared sane and sober, but some real nuts were coming out of the woodwork. Jason was as conservative as they came, but just working in the gun industry he'd had more than his fill of what he mentally termed "OOLPS": obsessive, obnoxious libertarian paranoid schizophrenics. Too many of the opponents that were cropping up, trying to get elected, seemed to be in that category.

Which got to the units issue. When *everyone* owned *everything, no one* owned *anything*. The ten thousand packs were a classic example.

Each ten grand, as people were calling them, was broken up into four million units. The units were simply tied to the physical item, the ship. They had no connection to the credit necessary to *run* a ship that size. That would require a separate company that raised the credit for a voyage.

A company that had to be *agreed upon* by the unit ownership.

That meant four million individuals. Some of them were children but *all* of them got a vote. Trying to decide even which of the many companies vying would run the ship, how much they had to pay to lease it . . .

Every person involved in Spaceship Four wasn't trying to take the wheel. But put all your Alpha types in one basket and it wasn't pretty.

Recently, things had settled down a bit and Jason had acquired enough units in Four that he might have to start giving some input. *Why* he'd acquired it, though, had him uncomfortable. There was an SEC again and he didn't want to be in its crosshairs.

A viral report had circulated, anonymous, unsigned, describing the ten grands as "unprofitable hangar queens." It was well written and looked as if it had been prepared for one of the start-up financial firms. The arguments were well reasoned.

The ten grands could not land on the planet without specialized landing fields and even then, they would be dropping all the material they were carrying in one place. They'd also have to pick up from one place. Thus, since colonists were picking various spots to colonize, scattered over the surface of the planet, they were unsuitable to support colonization. And while they could transfer fuel to the station from the fuel mines, that was an occasional job. There wasn't going to be enough metals mining any time soon to make that a viable use.

So, from the report, it appeared that they were going to be money sinks instead of profitable endeavors. Logistics companies that had been campaigning to run the ships had vanished overnight along with investor money.

Jason hadn't seen the report until there was an alert from Jewel. Suddenly, more and more people who held units in Spaceship Four had been offering trades. Jason told her to continue buying while he looked at the report. The conclusions made sense unless you thought in terms of tech. There were ways around the problem of landing in Jason's opinion. And while fuel use now was relatively low, use in the future would be higher.

The report looked like the classic version of very smart, very educated people with exactly zero vision.

So, he kept trading his other units for more ownership.

People, God help them, were so desperate to get rid of their units in ten grands they were offering money *plus* units for any other type. When Jewel asked him about that he declined. If he had units in anything other than Spaceship Four, Twelve Bravo and Converter Charlie, trade. Tell people to hang onto their credits. That wasn't the right business decision, but it was an example of why he wasn't good at business. He was too nice.

The noisiest of the ownership sold out the fastest, hying off to some other, supposedly better, investment. Good riddance.

Last he'd checked his units he had about a quarter million units in Spaceship Four, largest single investor.

He was going to make bank on that alone. If he could figure out a way to, figuratively, get it out of the hangar.

Currently, the ship was still in government storage since nobody had been able to figure out who was in charge and fund a trip. That didn't cost a thing. It was just sitting in orbit, waiting to be used. When the time came, it would have to be fueled. That was the big credit crunch. Big ship, big tanks.

People were still trading away their units and his ownership was increasing. He'd checked and there were few other people that were doing the same thing at least with ten grands. So, it didn't appear that the viral report was designed to drive people out so someone could snap up the units.

"Express shuttle to Texas?" Jason said, reading the signs above the doors.

"To your left again," Jewel said.

"Texas," Jason muttered. "Why'd it have to be Texas?"

The state had combined conservatives from Texas, Oklahoma, portions of the Midwest, the Southwest and, notably, California.

It turned out that California conservatives made Texas conservatives look pale and mild by comparison. The Texans were spending half their time trying to get their California neighbors to "chill."

"Any hints on taking this thing?"

The express shuttle to the distant state took only thirty minutes according to the schedule. That was a lot of acceleration.

"There's inertial stabilization and artificial gravity," Jewel intoned soothingly. "Just take a seat and relax. It's not going to hurt. Unless stabilization fails, in which case, you'll be turned into paste so fast you won't notice."

"And these are owned by a random group of a bazillion raging libertarians?" Jason asked.

"Yes," Jewel replied. "From a hundred different countries. Though while the units thing is being straightened out, the government is running it."

"So much better," Jason said sarcastically. "Remind me to launch closer next time."

The Oldham family walked to church together at a time the station management had designated Sunday morning.

The interior of the family's compartment now looked as if it might have been a room in their farmhouse at home, if there were a single room in which the entire family slept, which extruded sinks, toilets, showers, and privacy screens from the walls when needed. Mabel and Abby had chosen the decorative scheme, so there were fake windows showing changing views of their actual farm, and the walls, inside and out, looked like whitewashed clapboard.

Cade had not objected verbally, but not because he liked the decoration. However much the room came to look visually like home, it smelled wrong and it was always smooth metal to the touch. He came to feel that sitting inside the compartment was a hallucinatory experience, a bad trip, and so he took to roaming the passages, looking for neighbors with whom he could share complaints.

So he held Mabel's youthful hand as they walked to church, feeling a half-fulfilled relief. He was outside the compartment, with its false images of home, and in the greater interior of his space-station prison, full of false images of Earth and North Carolina. Every wall that looked like forest, every store whose store front resembled a known pizzeria or bakery or bookstore, gouged his wounds a little deeper into his flesh.

To his satisfaction, if not his delight, church was held in the playground where his planting beds lay. The pastors must all be talking to each other, because other congregations seemed to have designated the same day as Sunday. Churchgoers passed each other in the halls going to different meeting places.

Cade wondered about the Jews and Muslims that must be on the space station as well. And what about Sikhs, and . . . whoever else? Seventh Day Adventists and Mormons, didn't they meet on Saturdays? He wished them all well, and resolved to pay a little more attention to the foot traffic in the coming week.

But it was nice to pass all the Christians in the halls, some still in baggy and oversized clothing, others, like Mabel, in newly retailored Sunday finery. He nodded at his neighbors and they nodded back.

Maybe life on the space station could be made tolerable.

It all smelled like the inside of a can, though. Even the dirt in the planting beds and his neighbors smelled like they'd just been released from a tin can.

Pastor Mickey's suit had been taken in a little. Mickey had the very good sense not to dress too well. Some of his parishioners might hope to be hit with a little Prosperity Gospel wealth, but Mickey had always preached kindness to the poor, repentance, and no guarantees in this life.

Which was probably a good thing, given how "this life" had ended for everyone now participating in Pastor Mickey's congregation.

So, Mickey's suit was a little worn at the cuffs, the knees, and the elbows, and his tie was a little too fat to be fashionable. He preached standing at the top of a kiddie slide, with the worshippers on benches or standing. He took his text from Exodus: "I have been a stranger in a strange land." Right now, he said, there wasn't much to do about the land being strange, but he urged his parishioners to not permit their neighbors to be strangers. Cade nodded along with the sermon.

Abby, mercifully, put her phone away for the entire duration of the service.

Cade listened afterward to the proposals for naming the congregation—it wasn't exactly Pastor Mickey's old church, since not all the Earth parishioners were present on the space station, and Pastor Mickey had attracted some new folks whose pastors hadn't made it. He voted, and so did Mabel and Abby, and all their choices lost. But "Mount Moriah of Pegasus Church" didn't sound terrible, so he wasn't too beat up about it.

Then he dutifully stayed after church to mingle, to make himself not a stranger to those of his neighbors who were new. He felt like a creep sneaking into a college dance and introducing himself to twenty-year-olds, so he periodically took out his phone and instructed his AI (which he had refused to name, and which he had ordered to skin itself as a crash test dummy) to show him an image of himself.

He'd just finished a brief chat with a couple of twenty-year-olds who had previously been ninety-year-olds living in a retirement home in Cary, which was now apparently a cluster of hallways about a five-minute walk from the Oldhams' compartment, when he heard Sam raise his voice.

"You don't know that," Sam said.

Mabel was already pulling at Sam's shoulder, trying to calm him down. Sam's face was red and he was talking to Pastor Mickey.

"I won't lie," the pastor said. "I don't know where Julie is. Honestly, Sam, I don't really know where you and I are. The 'Scutum-Centaurus Arm' of the galaxy doesn't mean much to me, except that we're far from home. From Earth. But I know this: God loves Julie Larsen just as much as He loves you and me. So my guess is, Julie is alive."

Cade cursed under his breath and approached Sam from the other side. Julie was fine, nothing wrong with her, but she wasn't the world-champion girlfriend Sam was making her out to be. Sam was just young and hormone addled, and taking this all bad.

"Oh yeah?" Sam raised his voice another notch and gestured at the people around him. "Then where is she? Is this the rapture, the righteous taken up into heaven? Is this the resurrection of the dead, eating vitamin-enriched pizza that tastes like total ass? Or is she not here, because everything you've always said was bullshit, all along?"

Pastor Mickey smiled and nodded, his eyes crinkling in sympathy.

"Those are hard questions, Sam. I don't know where Julie is. But I bet she's in some other system with folks who, you know, think the way she does about the issues. And she's going to have to figure out how to be happy without you, but I know she'll be able to do it, because God wants her to be happy. Like He wants you to be happy. God has mercy enough for all of us."

Cade tried to take his son by the arm, but it was too late.

"If God wanted me to be happy, Julie would be by my side," Sam shouted. "And if He had any mercy to show me, I wouldn't be stuck in this place. I'd be dead."

Cade reached to touch Sam's elbow, but his son had already fled.

Cade followed, carefully not looking around to see whether his neighbors were staring.

# CHAPTER 5 >>>>>>>>>

THE DOOR DILATED AND JASON STEPPED INTO WHAT COULD BE any bus or shuttle. The only difference was no windows. Instead, there were screens with pictures and videos of Texas. Fields of bluebells. The capitol with the lone star. The Alamo.

As Jason sat down, setting his rifle between his knees, he wondered if that was a good idea. Homesickness for Earth was a thing. But it wasn't his to judge. Presumably, the ownership had mostly been from Texas or something.

The shuttle was empty and he had thirty minutes to kill. He'd been extremely busy planning for the trip. He'd gone back and forth on what to take. He had plenty of cargo space but he hoped to fill most of the cubic with food. Then there was the matter of expense. He knew he was going to be using a large amount of flexmet. How much was the question. Flexmet wasn't free. It was government issue, currently, with a fixed price of one credit a kilo. He'd wanted to take two metric tons but that was two thousand credits. Richard had balked at that large of a load given the medium tractor, which he'd insisted was an absolute necessity, was fifteen thousand credits.

In the end, he'd opted for five hundred kilos. More or less an English ton. Less cubic was the upside. More room for cases.

He put it out of his mind and turned back to the issue of Spaceship Four.

"Am I still the majority investor in Four?" Jason asked.

"By a large margin," Jewel answered. "The next largest has ten credits. All the other large investors, and the largest then was four thousand, bailed when the report circulated."

She'd noted before that people who had kept their units in the spaceship had contacted him asking for input. He'd put them off saying he was busy on another endeavor.

"Let's do a video on the subject for the owners who are interested," Jason said. He thought about what to say then took a breath.

"Hi, my name is Jason Graham and I'm the single largest unit investor in Spaceship Four in which you also have units. As some of you are aware, recently there was a report that circulated that described the ten grands as hangar queens. I read it. It was a well thought out, professional analysis. And I one hundred percent disagree.

"The writer of the report was, I believe, sincere. It was not, in my opinion, designed to drive people out of the market so that someone could swoop in and get a large ownership. I certainly had nothing to do with it and I'm the largest unit owner of any of the ten grands. It was a cogent analysis and the author was clearly a professional in traditional business and finance.

"But that, right there, was the problem. They were experts in *traditional* business. Traditional business is about finding risks and eliminating them. It was probably prepared for a financial company that was considering whether to back one of the companies that were lobbying to run the ship before the report.

"I'm not an expert in traditional business. To the extent I'm considered an expert in anything, it's logistics. But what I am, unquestionably, is a science fiction fan and, back on earth, an occasional writer of very bad, self-published, pulp SF. I've been reading SF since I was a kid. I understand this environment, I get it, using an SF word, I *grok* it—which means to understand something in your bones.

"I'm headed to the surface. For those who have been trying to reach me, I've been busy planning this trip. While I'm on this trip I'm going to look into some things that I've been considering regarding the issues raised in the report. There are going to be solutions. I intend to research and find those solutions.

"For now, let Four be a hangar queen. She's not bringing any money in, but she's not costing anything. If you want to trade units, I'm trading. People were offering money as well as units at one point. I won't take money. With as little money as we've all got, it seems unfair. I think, long term, Four is a good investment. But that's the opinion of a guy who's had fifteen different careers and whose only field clothes that fit are uniforms from back in the 1980s. Up to you. Out here."

"Cogent," Jewel said. "Nice word. Also, a description of your video. Not to mention concise and in places cryptic. What's the answer?"

"No clue," Jason said. "But there's going to be one."

"Arriving in Texas station," the shuttle intoned.

"You're right," Jason said, standing up. "You don't feel a thing."

"Dad," Sam said, "farming is for suckers."

Cade didn't raise his head, focused on the holes he was poking in the soil.

"Well then, I have two bits of good news for you, son. The first is, you seem unlikely to inherit a farm from me, at this point."

"I would have sold it, anyway."

That stung, but Cade shrugged it off.

"The second is, what we're doing right now is not farming. It is gardening, at most."

"Your precious John Wayne wasn't a farmer," Sam muttered.

"John Wayne was an actor. He wasn't really a gunslinger or a sheriff or William Tecumseh Sherman. But, fun fact, he actually owned a cotton farm in real life."

Sam grunted, a hostile sound.

Wherever the station contained patches of grass (which could not be owned by individuals) or planting beds (which could), its light was designed to simulate sunlight and could be used to grow plants. Once Cade had learned that, he had grilled his AI about the possibilities of buying large open areas within the station and converting them to agriculture.

The possibilities had turned out to be nonexistent.

But he had managed to acquire several more planting beds in the same park area, all surrounding a playground and all a few minutes' walk from the family's compartment.

The planting beds (which were officially designed as "flowerbeds," but Cade had no interest in planting daisies) had some soil in them already. The Oldham family inventory had shown several bags of potting soil and a collection of seeds, along with small hand tools for gardening—Cade had brought it all out of stasis for this project.

"Son," he said, "I know you miss her."

"You know no such thing."

"I would miss your mom."

"Would you?" Sam pressed. "Would you even miss her if she weren't here? You can barely look at her as it is."

"The problems I am having have to do with being old, and... not adjusting fast, I guess. I know your heart is broken."

"But it would have been broken anyway, right, because she would have dumped me?"

"I didn't say that." Cade tried to grin. "I think it's more likely you would have broken up with her, frankly."

"So I should go out now and date and find a nice girl and forget about Julie, right, is that the next advice? How am I doing? Have I figured out the Dad Code?"

"I apologize," Cade said. "I shouldn't have said anything. It's not my place."

"Damn straight." Sam stood.

"Get back here!" Cade snapped. He hadn't meant it, but his voice took on a sudden hard edge. "You're pissed at me, and I get it. But you don't walk away from a job half done."

Sam hesitated, then got down on his knees. He finished the task with his father, dropping in seeds and closing the earth over the top, scrupulously.

But he made no answer, no matter what Cade said to him.

And when they'd finished, he stood up and left.


"Welcome aboard the *Excelsior*!"

The pilot was short, baby-faced and looked like he was in his teens. But everybody looked that way currently.

"While I'm fully on board with the Second Amendment thing..." he added, eyeing the Garand.

"Unloaded," Jason said, showing him the action. "And I'm not setting foot down there without a rifle."

"Understood," the pilot said, extending his hand. "I'll ignore the Magnum. Tom Ferrell."

"Jason Graham," Jason said, shaking hands. "Any chance I could hang on the bridge?"

"Wouldn't have it any other way," Tom said, waving ahead.

Tom had the flexscreen walls of the ship set to a neutral blue with pictures and videos of notable aircraft and rockets of Earth. Only one picture was of himself, standing by an F-104 with obvious battle damage, holding a helmet under his arm and grinning.

He currently looked about the same age as in the picture.

"She's a fun little ship," Tom said, sitting down at the control console and turning on the screens. "But there's not much flying until you get near the ground. Even then, it's mostly automated."

The view was of a large landing compartment. Large as in miles across. As the screens came on a much larger ship flew from right to left then turned into a corridor nearly as cavernous as the compartment. Though the ship was obviously massive, it was swallowed by the corridor. Other, smaller, ships followed it out. Looking up through the "window" above, Jason could see more ships arriving.

"How do you get a pilot's license?" Jason asked.

"Sim time," Tom replied. "Lots of sim time. Less if you've got experience. Pilot?"

"One thing I've never done," Jason said. "Never been interested."

"Best job ever," Tom said.

"Do you have units in it?" Jason asked. "Or is it other owners?"

"Managed to trade for all but two," Tom said. "So, I get most of the profit. And it's been profitable so far. Thanks for the credit."

"No problem," Jason said. "As long as this trip works out. Safety briefing?"

"There's spacesuits," Tom said, gesturing over his shoulder. "You'll never use them. If something goes incredibly wrong, the entire seat turns into a stasis container and you're ejected. As long as you're not in the gravity well of a massive planet or a star, you're golden. Thus ends the safety brief."

"Better than having to don a float you've never actually worked with," Jason said, chuckling.

"Strange load," Tom said. "I've dropped a group of scientists doing research. But mostly colony sets. This isn't a colony set."

"Don't need one," Jason said. "I'm not colonizing, just exploring and exploiting I guess you'd say. There's a shrimp run coming up in that area. Or so I hope. Should be. Anyway, just leased a small area to harvest in general, survey and mostly planning on doing close-shore commercial fishing."

"Didn't see a boat in the inventory," Tom said as the *Excelsior* lifted up and headed for the exit. "And away we go."

All of the landing bays, variously sized for the various sizes of ships, were covered in blinking lights, some green indicating an open bay ready for a ship, others red or yellow. There were more lights around the entrances and exits. Obscure markings that might as well have been in an alien tongue.

"Not driving?" Jason asked.

The ship lifted up into the main bay then followed a larger ship into the short exit corridor. Jason could see the exit to the station: It was surrounded by lights that were green in their direction. But beyond that was simply black. He knew that that was due to the surrounding protective shell. It was still slightly intimidating. There wasn't even light from the ports on the shell.

"Port controls entrance and exit," Tom said. "Federal Space Traffic Control takes over as you leave the station then maintains control till you're beyond the shell. Even then, you just program the course and sit back and enjoy the view till you're below ten thousand feet."

"That doesn't seem to require much piloting," Jason pointed out.

They'd cleared the exit by then and Jason took a look around at the gap between the defensive shell and the station. There were screens in every direction so he could get a good look. Mostly, it was views of other ships coming and going. But once clear of the station the massive "ports" in the defensive shell were finally clear and he could, sort of, see portions of the planet.

"The pilot training and tests are mostly about what might go wrong," Tom said. "Which describes most professional flying. Sorry to repeat but: No boat?"

"I'm planning on using my wits," Jason said.

"Hope you've got good wits," Tom said. "I bumped two colonists on condition of two cases of fresh food. Anything edible will do."

"Do I need to grab it while you wait?" Jason asked.

"I'm not going to wait," Tom said. "For good or ill, there's no maximum flight time, yet. They're talking about it. But as fast as I put you down, I'm off on another sortie. You can owe me when you get back."

"You like shrimp?"

"Love it," Tom said, grinning. "But honestly, anything will do. We had a bunch of food just sitting around the house when we Transferred. But there was a reason most of it was just sitting around."

Americans, at least, had tended to have stored food built up in pantries. Homeland Security estimated that the average US household had upwards of three months of food on hand in the event of a crashing emergency. That was a large part of the trade that was going on in places like Market Square. But it was also what people were eating to avoid print food.

The issue with print food was vitamins. The robots, lacking tastebuds, had included enough vitamins in the print-food base that no matter what someone ate or how much, they would get a full daily dose of vitamins.

The problem was that most vitamins tasted like hell. So even if you asked for a slice of bread, it tasted like *chewing* a multivitamin tablet. Not to mention it only vaguely resembled bread.

Many of the Third Worlders on the station thought the US contingent complained too much. It was food. It was nearly free. That was enough to ask.

The US, and to a lesser extent the European, contingent wanted *real* food and *right now*!

While preparing, Jason had been vaguely watching the one channel currently available. A debate on the subject between Senator Vega from Texas and Senator Pranay from Hindia had illuminated the difference.

"I don't wish to call Americans spoiled," Senator Pranay had said tactfully. "But for most people who are from countries such as India, Indonesia, Southeast Asia, which comprises many of my constituents, we are simply glad that we have food. That is not something guaranteed in many countries. That it is not the best taste is something that we can ignore for the time being. It will take time to get agriculture started on the planet. Until then, we thank God or your gods for what we have."

"And that, right there, is why the United States became one of the leaders of the world on Old Earth," Vega responded. "We thank God for what we have. But we don't just accept what we're given. We find ways to get what we want, without taking from others. We create. We envision. We build. We do what it takes to change things for the better. And there's no such thing as 'good enough,' no such thing as 'too much' no such thing as 'too comfortable,' to a red-blooded American. It's sort of a joke about Texans that we like three things: big trucks, big guns and big-titted women. I'll add beer to that list and the fact that that is in short supply cannot be allowed!

"Call it greedy, call it spoiled, call it too addicted to comfort and ease, call it whatever you'd like. The US contingent sees nothing but opportunities and we're going to take them. And everyone else is going to benefit from that.

"Eventually, most are going to agree with our take. In two or three generations this will be the most productive system of all the systems. The system that generates the most IP. The system that generates the most food, without destroying the planet. The system that is the most comfortable, the most at ease and, if I get my way, the best defended. Because if we can contact the other systems, other systems are going to look at us and want what we've built.

"That's the real issue of the future."

"You ever taken a ride around to the breach?" Jason asked as they approached the shell.

"Had to," Tom replied, touching a control. "I think every pilot's taken the time and the expense. It's mind-boggling."

The ten-kilometer port that had looked like a dot on exit appeared to be expanding as they approached. Bellerophon was clearly visible: they were currently viewing its dark side. The massive Pallas Ocean was in view and Jason suddenly tasted salt water and smelt salt spray. He was finally on his way to a new world.

# CHAPTER 6 >>>>>>>>>>

JASON STEPPED DOWN ONTO THE TOP OF THE CARGO CONTAINER and just absorbed his surroundings.

The containers were on a sandspit on the south bank of the kilometer-wide river. To the north and south were virgin forests, the tallest trees rising to nearly a hundred meters. To the east were more forests and the river. The nearby Pallas Ocean was out of sight around a bend. To the west the river was nearly straight for several miles and Chindia Mons dominated the view.

The gargantuan stratovolcano filled the western sky. The mountain range at its lower reaches, nearly as extensive as the Alps, was out of view below the horizon. But Mons rose above it, seeming like a ramp to space. The forest line was barely above the horizon surmounted by a ring of snow and ice.

It was fall in Chindia so the monsoonal winds were blowing down the slopes and to the Pallas. They weren't cool where he was, the day was hot and humid, but they felt nice on his face after so long in the station. That also meant there were no clouds to speak of though there was a storm visible on the upper slopes. That was probably where the insanely tall mountain intersected a high-level jet stream.

The air was filled with the smell of flowers and the distinctive and special smell of a river in full. It was fine wine compared to the station. There was a buzz of insects and dozens of bird calls, none familiar. The river was another source of sound as a school of fish upriver jumped to avoid some unseen predator. They were silvery and vaguely salmon shaped. He wasn't sure of the species but they looked as if they'd feel good on a line.

"Potential threat," Jewel said. "Upstream."

Jason looked upstream again and realized that what he'd thought was a very large floating log was under its own power.

"Is that...a crocodile?" Jason whispered. It was at least three hundred meters away but the head and body were distinctive even at that distance. Which gave an idea of the size.

"That is, indeed, a crocodile," Jewel replied.

The massive croc was slowly sculling downstream in their general direction. Jason wasn't going to disturb it. He'd planned for lions, tigers and bears...He'd forgotten crocodiles.

"How...long? Can you tell?"

"It is approximately twenty meters in length."

"Twenty *meters*?"

"Bit more," Jewel said. "Say...seventy feet."

"Okay," Jason said after a moment's thought. "What we're going to do is not something to do with that thing around. Quietly and on the side away from the river, start breaking out the cargo. First, the medium tractor. Call him Herman."

"Herman?"

"He looks like the head of a character from a TV show," Jason said. "Then have all the drones come out, quietly as possible, the small tractor, call it Alfred, and have the flexmet hump itself out.

"Put two drones up at two hundred meters and find out how many more large crocs there are within four kilometers up and down the river. Put four drones up in a diamond around me, thirty meters out to the sides and front, ten meters behind, to watch for threats. Keep those around. That's six.

"Have the rest begin surveying the forest to the south. Search for predators, herbivores and omnivores. Have the drones each carry a fist-sized chunk of flexmet. Sample all unknown or unrecognized plants including most especially fungi. Bring back samples later for me to taste test. Anything they don't recognize, test for toxicity and take a sample for tasting. There's going to be edible herbs that are unknown. Bring back small samples of known herbs if found. In general, find and sample for herbs, greens, nuts, anything plant-based edible. And we'd better find some edible mushrooms or Monica is going to be angry. We do not want Monica angry."

"Understood," Jewel said.

"Anything that has potential value, do not report," Jason said. "That includes any species that has potential food value or any sign of mineral or useable stone deposits."

"Roger," Jewel said.

"Roger?" Jason replied.

"You commonly use it as an affirmative," Jewel said.

"You can take the boy out of the airborne," Jason muttered.

He thought for another moment and looked at his Garand. He'd loaded with 200-grain bullets, the biggest he had.

For this mother, 200 grain was probably too *small.*

The rifle you really *needed* for this planet was something with a round starting in .4 or .5, not .3. He'd checked what people were asking for rifles like that, which had been rare on Earth, and he didn't have a firstborn to sell them.

"Get Alfred over here," Jason said. "With...ten...twenty-five kilos of flexmet. Hurry."

The croc was getting closer. Even with one of the really heavy hunting rifles like a .470, shooting it from the front would be a lost cause. The heavy skull would shed any bullet except, maybe, something from an armored vehicle or helo. Fifty cal would bounce. What you needed was a Light Armored Vehicle and a 30mm autocannon.

An Apache. Hellfire. A B-52 would be nice.

Holy moly, it was getting bigger and bigger as it got closer and closer!

Not a freaking .30-06!

"Alfred is here," Jewel said.

He looked back and the bots and drones were deploying along with the flexmet. The squirmy movement as always made him feel a bit queasy.

"Flexmet," Jason snapped. He had the flexmet form into a sling seat then thumbed for Alfred to lift him into the air.

"Up, up, up, up..." Jason said, gesturing with his hands until he was fifty or so meters over the river. Now the croc *probably* couldn't get him. "I need the flexmet to remain solid. A solid seat. When I fire, have a little give. But I need a solid, stable seat to shoot. I'm no Dev Gru. Got it?"

"Got it," Jewel said.

He had thought of a solid seat but he could feel it firming

up as he moved. He adjusted slightly for a seated shot and got a solid position.

"Do I have the same sort of 'think of it and it happens' thing with Alfred?" Jason asked.

"No, you'll have to direct him verbally or with hand motions," Jewel replied.

"Fine. Each command, wait till I say 'Go' unless it's a pre-planned command. Alfred, swing around until you're fifty meters behind the croc and fifty meters above," Jason said, waving in the direction he wanted to take. "Not too fast. Ten miles per hour until we're behind then follow it at its speed. Go."

As they took off, the drones obediently stayed in position.

"Leave the drones behind," Jason whispered. "I don't want to spook it."

The bot slowly moved around behind the sculling predator and started to follow, Jason dangling underneath.

"Now, move up on it and drop slowly until we're behind the head at about five meters up and back," Jason whispered. "Stop there. Approach at two miles per hour faster than it's moving. If it flinches, rears, speeds up or otherwise reacts, lift to fifty meters at three Gs. Do the same if I fire for any reason. Go."

Two miles per hour was probably too fast but the croc didn't react. The bot was quiet, barely a hum. And though a croc's hearing was decent, they couldn't see behind and up very well.

The bot stopped five meters up and back. Which was, in Jason's opinion, far too close. At five meters, sixteen feet more or less, the croc's massive size was unmistakable. The shoulders, not even the widest part, were wider than he was tall.

The thing would swallow him, whole, in one bite. And crocs could rear up half their body length and turn on a dime.

He was going to *have* to find a better way to kill them. Adventure was all well and good but this was like hunting a Cape buffalo with a pistol.

The back of a crocodilian's head had a small kill point. It was a hole in the head similar to the temple on a human. Allegedly, it led directly to the brain stem. One shot, even from a .30-06, *should* kill it. Should. Though it was going to thrash.

Thus, the order to get out of the way. Fast.

He had already wrapped the sling around his left arm. A mental command added flexmet making the firmest position he'd ever held. Which was good because he was trying not to shake.

He wrapped his finger onto the trigger, took a breath and took the shot.

The 200-grain expanding bullet impacted perfectly.

As the gigantic crocodile began to thrash, Alfred simultaneously lifted into the air like a rocket.

Jason managed to hang onto his hat with his right hand as he looked down. The croc had indeed reared, though it seemed to be uncontrolled. It was also thrashing and rolling, turning up waves that easily reached both shores of the kilometer-wide river.

"Get Herman over here, stat," Jason said as the crocodile's death throes subsided. "Drop down to the tail end."

The croc was starting to sink as they approached. Jason mentally ordered the flexmet to drop down and attach to the tail.

"Try to at least hold up the tail until Herman gets here," Jason said. "If we're getting dragged under, I'll release."

The hum from Alfred increased as it took the strain of the weight of the massive croc. Crocodilians were not naturally buoyant and the river was apparently deep.

Jason shifted the flexmet to the end of the tail as they were being pulled down but as he was doing so Herman arrived.

"Tractor beams would be a better choice than flexmet," Jewel pointed out.

"Whatever works," Jason said.

With the addition of the heavier tractor, they were able to keep the beast floating. The tractor beam looked like a wide blue laser. Herman had locked onto the base of the tail then brought its beam forward, revealing most of the beast. Its head dangled in the depths.

"You can release the flexmet," Jewel said. "The beams of the two tractors have it."

"We'll back it up to the shore next to the containers," Jason said, releasing the flexmet. "Downstream, and downwind, in the eddy area. Then see if we can do something with it. If not, we're going to have to move the camp."

The two tractors were necessary to get the croc to the campsite but Herman, alone, was able to drag it fully onshore.

"See if Tim's available," Jason said, waving to land on the back of the croc. "And get a drone up to get video of this thing."

He cradled his trusty Garand as the drone flew up.

"Holy cow, Jason!" Tim said. "That's a big-ass gator!"

"Crocodile," Jason said. "And I think, absent just killing and leaving them, we're going to be shipping mostly croc meat at first. Jewel, how many crocodiles so far in the survey?"

"In the two kilometers up and down river, there are twenty crocodiles so far spotted. No others were of this size. This appears to be the alpha male of the territory. But there are other females of similar size."

"I'm going to see if I can butcher it and pack it," Jason said. "There are groups that will eat croc meat. It's no different than gator."

"True," Tim said.

"I'm going to have to reduce the crocs," Jason said. "I can't run a boat on the river: They'll attack it. And they'll attack any of the shrimp nets and fish traps I'd planned."

"Up to you," Tim said. "You're the guy on the ground. It'll sell but not as well as shrimp or fish."

"Roger," Jason said. "Out here."

He considered the massive carcass for a moment then shrugged.

"Other threats besides crocs?"

"There are some nearby tigers," Jewel said. "None very close. But as soon as anything scents blood it will be attracted. There are, as well, some deer as well as wild hogs. Drones have collected numerous unknown plant species. Also, there's a rather large snake of unknown type approaching the area. It seems to be a type of constrictor but it is an unknown species and may be poisonous. There are no other immediate known threats."

"Bring a drone over carrying eighty percent of its maximum load of flexmet," Jason said.

When the drone arrived, Jason held out his hand.

"Length of flexmet," Jason said. "Extending the flexmet, fly over and hover over the neck of the croc."

When the drone was hovering, Jason mentally commanded a string of flexmet to drop down next to the croc's neck then wiggle under it. Once it was under the neck he had the flexmet form into a loop, go extremely thin then close the loop.

There was no apparent cut in the croc's neck—the flexmet had been thinner than a hair—but blood began to pour out.

"Can Herman lift the head, only?" Jason asked, stepping off

the croc after a careful glance to ensure no major threats. He took off his hat and wiped his forehead with a rag.

"Herman can lift the head," Jewel agreed.

"I want to keep the skull as a souvenir," Jason said. "It doesn't have to be lifted with this load but it will potentially make a nice ornament for the Brandywine offices. Suggestions?"

"Clean it up," Jewel said. "Skin it. Remove useable meat. Open up the skull to extract the brains. Then bury it fairly deep so that natural processes can clean it. There's not a good system on the station and the food processor plants aren't up and running. Units."

"Roger," Jason said. "Make it so. Record that use of flexmet to cut off the head as 'decap.' That's how we're going to do most of the killing around here. Butcher the croc to fit in coffins. Only keep the skin and meat. Save the cases as much as possible. We'll need them for shrimp."

He tossed a line of flexmet to the top of the nearest conex and climbed up. Better safe than sorry.

With some input from Jason, the flexmet, two tractors and four drones slowly butchered the big male. Jason mostly watched from the top of the conex, taking a sip of water from time to time, wiping his head and thinking.

Each conex held forty-five coffins and each coffin held six cases for a total of two hundred seventy cases. He'd landed with eleven containers full of both coffins and cases. The lease on cases was one cent a month, coffins were six. He'd intended and said he was going to leave some of each for later pickup.

He was glad he'd brought so many coffins. The alpha male was going to fill half a conex even butchered.

As the time went by, so did the life along the river. A group of elephants appeared upriver, drinking and playing in the water. He knew that genetically African and Indian elephants were virtually identical. The "smaller" Indian elephant was a morphological change rather than genetic. These were the size of African elephants or bigger.

No more crocs came by but some of the ones sunning themselves had entered the river and were a potential threat.

"There's a tiger approaching," Jewel said. "It's apparently smelled the blood. Coming from downwind."

"What type?" Jason asked. "Sex, approximate age and size."

"Young male," Jewel said. "Moderate size based on other examples. Unmated."

"Don't kill it," Jason said. "I'll take it with the Garand."

He didn't have many of the 200 grain but he wasn't comfortable just having the drones decapitate the tiger.

"Where?" Jason asked, after putting on imaging glasses.

"Showing you," Jewel said.

The glasses showed a view from a shadowing drone with a sketch map giving distance. The tiger was about two hundred meters away. Plenty of time.

"Tell me when it gets close," Jason said. He thought about trying to change to a smaller grain and smiled. Changing a clip in a Garand was major work. He needed something with a box mag with at least eight rounds.

A jackal appeared drawn by the smell of the blood and started barking and howling, darting in to grab a piece of intestine. A drone dropped down to shoo it off and it snapped back.

The sound of jackal barking was known to attract other scavengers and predators. This might be getting complicated. Also, it was annoying.

The blood flowing into the river had also attracted swarms of fish and his stomach growled, reminding him he was hungry.

"How we doing on potentially edible plants and mushrooms?" Jason asked. The butchering was sort of nauseating to watch but he'd butchered before and the wind down the river was taking the smell away.

"We have over two hundred samples so far including many potentially edible fungi," Jewel said.

"Start bringing in samples," Jason said. He really needed to start a fire at some point. Among other things, it would tend to scare off some of the potential threats.

As he was considering that, a croc suddenly burst out of the water and grabbed one of the chunks of male croc Herman was moving. The bot held on, though, and a tug of war ensued.

"Hold on to it, Herman!" Jason shouted. "Lift up a little! That's a boy! Get a line around that croc's head and decap!" The powerful tractor wasn't going anywhere and if anything, the croc was being lifted out of the water. It gave Jason a clearer understanding of the power of the tractors.

Jewel was intuitive and once shown a process could determine the best methods to use it. And Jason's command seemed to indicate that Herman should handle it. Herman had as part of his standard package some onboard flexmet. A tentacle of it slithered out, wrapped around the female croc's head and neatly snipped it off.

No more tug of war.

One more croc to butcher.

"The juvenile male tiger is one hundred meters out, two more crocs are known to be approaching, possibly three, two more tigers and a wolf pack have been spotted, possibly on the way, the large snake of unknown species is now thirty meters away, and drones indicate that, yes, there is a shrimp run starting."

It never rains...

"Type of tigers?" Jason asked.

"Adult female and large adult male," Jewel replied. "Probably the breeding male for the area."

"Have a drone decap the snake if it can get a noose on it," Jason said. "Same for the wolves if they approach within five hundred meters. The crocs... let me think about it. We can't have them just attacking without warning... Show me the juvenile tiger."

The juvenile was at the edge of the forest watching the activity on the sand spit cautiously. It could smell food but there was also potentially threatening activity.

The jackals were less cautious, darting in and out trying to get to the meat.

"Decap the jackals," Jason said. "Put the bodies in coffins separate from the croc. We'll worry about pickup later."

There was a conversion process to turn anything with proteins and sugars into print food. There was a potential value to even "junk" meat.

Jason lay down on top of the conex and lined up the shot. He could barely see the juvenile camouflaged in the foliage.

"Can these glasses enhance view?" Jason whispered.

The view suddenly sharpened with the tiger outlined in red. The kill points on the head and heart were highlighted in blue.

It was a seventy-five-meter shot. The 200 grain went right through the cat's brain via its eye canal. It didn't even thrash.

But the shot caused the thousands of birds in range of hearing to take off, shrieking. A flock of parrots flew overhead and he regretted not breaking out his shotgun. Parrot was reputed to be quite tasty.

"Pickup," Jason said. "Just drop it in a coffin."

Appropriate.


"Carrots," Cade said.

He sat on a bench near the playground, facing the six "flowerbeds" he'd planted with Sam. The overhead lights were dimmed to produce the station's artificial evening. Mabel sat with him, each of them holding a flexmet tumbler. Cade poured her a little of the green juice mixed with alcohol from a vacuum flask, and they both took a sip.

"This stuff tastes like antifreeze," she said.

"It tastes like the stuff I'd try to sneak out of the liquor store inside an oversized coat when I was sixteen," Cade said. "By which I mean, I agree."

"We had cabbage seeds," she said, "and cucumber. Why carrots?"

Cade shrugged. "They're sweet, maybe. Also, there's something satisfying about pulling carrots from the ground and shaking the dirt off them."

"Is that why you farm, Cade? The satisfying experience?"

"That's one reason." He took another sip, pretended it was delicious. "Look, carrots come up, you plant another batch. Here, I'll grow them all year round."

"How much fertilizer do you have?"

"How do you feel about me collecting poop?"

"I approve of the carrots," she said. "Don't do the poop collecting in my house. I'm just wondering... what do you need to be happy, Cade?"

That conversation felt like a looming unseen iceberg. Cade let it lie off the bow untouched for almost a minute.

"I guess I'd like you all to be happy."

"I am happy," Mabel said. "I have most of my friends and neighbors here, both my children, and my husband."

"Some kid that looks like your husband once did," Cade said, and then realized how hurtful the words might sound. "I wish Sam was taking this all a little better."

"Have you submitted your application to be a colonist?" she

asked. "I heard the government might have grants for the trans-portation. I mean, for people it wants to get down there early."

"It seems like sooner or later everyone is going to be down on the surface," he pointed out.

"It could be later. We have enough to eat here. We have free time. When some of the neighbors start to go down as colonists, their compartments will free up. We should be able to get more space. What if we had three adjacent compartments, instead of just the one?"

"Colonists have started going down," Cade said. "Soon enough, a bunch of our neighbors will be among them."

"All the more reason to think there'll be room."

"The short answer is, yeah, I applied. They said not yet, I'm not what they're looking for right now. I'm on a list, I'll hear back when the time is right, and so on. And I suppose, if our slot came up, and you wanted to stay, we probably could delay. I could fake sick or something. That got me through high school."

"Sam misses Julie," she said. "He'll get over her. Most likely."

"I hope he hurries up." Cade finished his drink and poured himself another. "Once he can adjust, maybe I'll feel more at ease."

Mabel was quiet for a while.

"Are you sure you don't have that backward, Cade?"

# CHAPTER 7 »»»»»»»

"NOW, ABOUT THE CROCS," JASON SAID, SIGHING. "I'LL NEED Alfred, a hundred kilos of flexmet and a seat again. When they're done with the first one, drag the other one up and start on it. Repeat as necessary absent other orders."

Lunch was going to have to wait.

He had Alfred fly him fifty meters downstream, close to the bank, not far from the butchering area, then, cautiously, lowered to near water level. The river was tannin, clear of silt but dark with stain from tannin leaves, and it was impossible to see deep. One of the crocs could just snatch him while he was working.

Nobody said this job was safe.

He extended a rod of flexmet down then turned it into the narrowest spike that was solid. He then drove the spike deep into the soil before mentally commanding it to extrude a circular plate at the bottom and thicken. From that point he moved out into the river, leaving behind a rope of flexmet. Ten meters out he drove in another spike then had the intervening material spread out into a very wide "ghost net" of thin, but not quite cutting thin, squares of flexmet a meter wide.

"Can a drone do this?" he asked.

"No, they don't have enough weight to drive it into the ground," Jewel said.

"Then Alfred will have to do it," Jason said. "Take me back to the conex, Alfred."

When he was back out of threat, Jason pulled out his phone and extended it into a pad.

"Bring up the detail satellite image of the spit," Jason said.

When the image was on the pad he outlined an area around the spit about fifty meters out, including the area that was being used for butchering the crocs.

"I want this around the entire spit. Keep one drone attached to it. It can feel when something hits the net, right?"

"Yes," Jewel said. "When the flexmet moves it will be able to sense the change."

"So, like a spider web," Jason said. "When something big hits it, warn me and generally warn the drones and bots. Something big enough to move a bunch of this flexmet is big enough to be a problem. But we shouldn't panic for every fish that taps it. Have the attached drone stay upstream and keep an eye out for drifting logs, et cetera. Those aren't threats. If they are logs. When something hits, just move the net out of the way. Ditto for driftwood. Does that make sense, am I leaving anything out and can you manage it?"

"Yes," Jewel said.

"Will one hundred kilos of flex do it?"

"Less," Jewel said. "At that thickness. I would suggest a slightly smaller mesh. It is potentially possible a small croc could get through."

"We need the flexmet for other uses," Jason said. "If there's any left over, bring it in."

"Roger," Jewel said. "We just lost a drone."

"What happened?" Jason asked.

"Elephants apparently don't like them buzzing around their heads," Jewel said. "It was trying to get a sample of a bug on its head."

"Was it video recording?" Jason asked.

"It was."

"Show me."

The video was of the back of an elephant on which there was a medium-sized, fluorescent-green bug. As the drone approached a tendril of flexmet extended in an apparent effort to capture the insect. Which took off to the left in the video. The drone spun around to follow and was catching up to the beetle, its probe extended, when the video went wild, flashing views of every direction, then cut off.

Jason snorted and shook his head.

"Slug it with a tag 'Elephants don't like to be bothered,' just include the thirty seconds or so of the incident and put it up on a channel. People like funny videos."

"It's not the only drone that's been attacked," Jewel said. "The birds don't like them in general. But those all survived."

"Add those if they're funny," Jason said. "But the elephant one begs a question. Questions. Why are we sampling insects? And how far away are those elephants? 'Cause elephants should definitely be on the 'dangerous animals' list."

"The elephants are just under a kilometer out," Jewel said. "Not close enough to be a threat. We're sampling the insects because there is a small payment from the government for every identified new species. Also, you get to name them."

"How much per species?" Jason asked.

"Depends," Jewel replied. "For macrofauna, including birds larger than a crow or mammals the size of a rabbit or larger, reptiles larger than one and a half meters in length, or giant amphibians if found, twenty-five cents. Fifteen for macroflora. Ten cents for smaller avian or mammal species. One cent for insects as well as for most small flora. You've so far made sixty-two credits, sixteen cents."

"How much of that money has been from insects?"

"Eight credits and four cents. Those have to be caught and stored and they're quite hard to catch."

"Quit trying to catch bugs," Jason said with a sigh. "There's a gazillion of those things and I don't want to go to the trouble of naming them all. Insects evolve like crazy, so there will be basically *no* species of insects on this planet that are *not* new species. And at a penny apiece it's not worth the time of the bots. Ditto small amphibians and lizards. Any new macro reptiles or amphibians, fine. But not the micro stuff. Leave that for colonizers."

"Roger," Jewel said.

"How do you name stuff, anyway? We didn't cover that."

"Just name it," Jewel said. "I'll upload it to the appropriate database."

"I hereby name this river ... Crocodile River," Jason intoned, waving his hand around in a spell-casting gesture. "I need a flag or something."

The rule was that whoever first set foot on a piece of land or alongside a river got to name it. Another reason people wanted to land.

"That name is already taken by one of the Pre-Wakening explorer parties," Jewel said.

"Of course, it was," Jason said, dropping his arm. "Benton River then."

"Benton?" Jewel asked. "Not Brandywine?"

"I used to live in Bentonville," Jason said. "If I get my way, I'm going to be naming a bunch of rivers. And this isn't the Brandywine. I'll know the Brandywine when I see it. Nobody upstream already named this?"

"There is one tributary that is named," Jewel said. "But since you are at the mouth of the river, it is now the name for the full river."

"How far inland does it run?" Jason asked.

"The head of the Benton starts with a glacier on the slopes of Chindia Mons," Jewel said. "It runs, as the crow flies, for eight hundred kilometers. More in total length. You also have the right to name this county but not the region."

"Jewel County, then," Jason said.

"You're so sweet," Jewel replied. "Query: I don't have a Jewel anywhere in your contact lists."

"Girl in my high school," Jason said, shrugging. "Pre-Internet. But this county is named for *you*, Jewel. Okay, I'm going to hit the ground as soon as the net is in. Close to the forest or close to the water? Crocs or tigers? Any more crocs that hit the net, snip them. As soon as they're snipped drag them downstream, and downwind, and get to butchering.

"I hate the idea of just killing them. They're magnificent, hundreds of years old, and killing them by drone seems a tad obscene. But we can't have them get in the way. We've got fish and shrimp to catch."

He looked out over the river as Alfred continued putting in the warning net.

"The President is right: We need preserves. Not just Avia. These big crocs take hundreds of years to grow to this size. Kids of the future should have a chance to see them in the wild. But, for now, we need to get them out of the way so we can get to work. People got to eat, too. Set one drone to collecting up the flora samples that are potentially good for food..."

"Something big hit the net," Jewel said. "Downstream."

"Have it open up to let it through," Jason said. "Where?"

The glasses highlighted the area, not that they needed to: The spikes that were above water were wriggling back and forth and the drone had lifted into the air with a thin line of flexmet extended to a spike to control the flexmet.

Jason started to give a command but Jewel had already deployed a drone to prepare for an attack as Herman and the drones pulled away from their butchering.

The second croc to attack had been pulled out of the water and was in the process of being butchered. It was that carcass the third went for, bursting out of the water in a blitz attack. This one was between sizes, about fifteen meters in length.

It grabbed the midquarters of the partially butchered croc and started to hump back into the water. As it did, a drone dropped down and neatly snipped off its head.

"When the flexmet gets hit, can it essentially open a hole that's wide enough for the head to fit through then close down and snip the head before it ever gets to land? Can it find the neck?"

"Yes," Jewel said after a moment. "Probably. That took some calculation and depended on the information from the crocodile that just hit the net. But it should be possible. We won't know for sure until another one hits the net. If it doesn't occur quickly, the crocodile will thrash, which may pull the net out of the bottom. But it can be reset."

"Better to kill them before they get close."

"And we have a successful test," Jewel said immediately. "Upstream."

"That quick," Jason said, looking upstream. There was a ripple. Possibly.

"Want it dragged in?" Jewel asked.

"Waste not," Jason said. "If possible. Reasonable, anyway. But take it to the same butcher area downstream. Returning to the point. Get a drone to . . . No, you figure it out. Start bringing in the potentially edible flora samples in the most efficient way. And make a note we need at least forty drones next time as well as another Alfred. Also, which of these conexes are empty?"

"The one you're standing on is about empty of coffins and cases," Jewel said.

The coffins of croc meat had been building up. Cases were

neatly stacked all over the spit. He hoped that there wasn't a sudden, unexpected flood. Nothing could be sure on this world until they'd been there for a while. But he'd set up sat-observation to check for signs of flooding upstream. And with the counter-monsoon set in, it should be okay.

Should be.

The flexmet, tractors and drones were scattered across the conexes. Old habit based on the possibility of losing cargo for the thousand and one reasons that you could lose cargo.

So, there was no one container that was empty of flexmet, tractors and drones.

"Which one has my personal coffin?" Jason asked, regretting the terminology immediately. "My personal gear?"

"That one," Jewel said, noting one of the central conexes.

"Discontinue the butchering evolution," Jason said. "If any more get killed by the net, Alfred and Herman can pull them ashore. Cover the current butchered with a flexmet tent to keep them out of the sun. I want the one with my personal stuff emptied of coffins except my personal stuff. Then rearrange the conexes. Put the others in an oval, long side out, touching at corners, with the personal conex center, at the high point of the sandbar."

"It would be easiest and quickest if you were off the conex," Jewel said. "For current protection reasons, I suggest you take a flight with Alfred."

"Done," Jason said. "Bring him over."

The tractor picked him up and lifted him fifty meters in the air then the conexes opened up like flowers and Jewel got to work.

The sides and top of the conexes were flexmet. Though it had to remain with the conex, it could be used to move cargo. The coffins from the indicated conex were rapidly moved to other containers until it was clear of all but Jason's personal effects. At that point they all went to contragravity and Herman used tractor beams to rearrange them.

It was done in less than two minutes. The tractor beam on the bots was long enough that Herman could do all the work hovering at about ten meters up in the middle. When he was done, Herman got back to work butchering.

"As a guy who's run warehouses, I can safely say that this tech has done away with *millions* of jobs," Jason said. "Employment is going to be an issue. The longshoreman's union would particularly like to have a word. Drop me down in the middle of the conexes, Alfred."

The middle of the conexes was windless and hotter than on top, which had been getting toasty. But it felt good to finally be standing on the sand.

"Open sesame," Jason said, putting his hand on the end of the conex.

The wall dilated and he stepped into the shade then put his hand on the wall. The upper portion of the wall turned to bars with mesh from waist-height down.

Between the shade and a tiny bit of wind that cooled things down considerably. He held his hand up and snorted. There was virtually no heat being transmitted through the ceiling. Flexmet appeared to be a near perfect insulator.

Jason opened his personal containers and considered the contents. One was mainly full of *all* his guns and ammunition along with some camping and fishing gear. The other had mostly stored food and more camping gear. With the exception of guns, ammo and a knife, he didn't *need* most of it. But it was comforting.

He considered the air mattress for a moment then touched the wall. Sure enough, an air couch could be made from the flexmet.

"This stuff is going to eliminate a *huge* number of potential devices," Jason muttered. "But since it's an insulator, it's not going to be much good for cooking."

"It can be used as an oven," Jewel suggested.

"But not as a pan," Jason said, dragging one out.

"Where do you want the samples?" Jewel asked.

"That end," Jason said, gesturing in the direction of the land. "Off to the side. Keep them in stasis. I'll sort them out in a minute."

He considered the pan for a moment as drones buzzed in and out carrying flora samples. What was missing was something to put in it and a heat source.

He'd spent a half credit on a nifty little device for starting fires similar to a torch lighter. Instead of using propane, it simply heated air to ignition temperature.

"Also, bring me about four ounces of crocodile meat."

He pulled out one of his medium fishing poles, already rigged with a sinker and bobber, and headed in the direction of the water.

He contemplated the containers in the way. They were, as

ordered, corner to corner. So, he laid his pole against one of the containers and spit on his hands.

"Put this one on contragravity," Jason said, pushing with both hands on the one to the right.

It was hard to get moving but as he expected it wasn't going to stop.

"And drop it," he said. There was now a narrow gap. Definitely too narrow for one of the big crocs to negotiate. But just to be on the safe side, he touched the containers on both sides and it was possible to create a wall closing the gap.

"And now we're cooking with fuel oil," he said, picking up his pole. "Speaking of which. Have bots go get some firewood. Dry wood. There's driftwood. That's a good choice. Have it cut into pieces about a foot long and pick up dry smalls. Can they figure out to cut it using the decap method?"

"Yes," Jewel said.

"Are we relatively certain there are no crocs around?" he asked as he approached the water's edge.

"Relatively certain," Jewel said.

He still had his Garand on his back and his Magnum for all the good they would do.

He took the small chunk of crocodile meat from the hovering drone, cut off a still smaller piece, put it on a Number One hook and tossed it into the river, just short of the markers for the warning net.

There was an immediate bite and his rod bent when he set the strike.

"This place," Jason said. "There is *no* sport to it. Do I need to say don't get my line tangled in the warning net?"

"Already covered," Jewel replied.

The fish was a fighter, that was for sure. Then it jumped and he recognized the species from his first landing.

"Is this a new species?" Jason asked.

"It is not," Jewel replied. "Bala shark or silver shark. It was a common fish-tank specimen on Earth. Native to Malay Peninsula, Borneo and Sumatra."

"Edible?" Jason asked.

"Considered a delicacy in its native range. Said to be quite tasty."

"I'm so in," Jason said, pulling in the bala. He'd started to learn to just keep some flexmet around as wristbands and used it to make a fish landing net. The silvery fish was about fourteen inches long and very lively.

He slit its throat, tossed it up on the sand, rebaited the hook and went back to fishing.

He'd caught four bala when something grabbed the fifth he was reeling in and snapped the line.

"Well, *that* was uncalled for," Jason said. "I'll be back for you, my fine fishy friend, whatever or whoever you are."

The four bala would make a meal so he decided to just clean those and make it lunch.

"Status on threats?"

He'd kept one eye on the river while fishing. Drones and a defense/warning net was all well and good but keeping an eye out was better. So far, he'd seen no more giant crocs. Cleaning the fish was best done at the waterline but . . . still.

"We caught one croc while you were fishing," Jewel said. "Already being cleaned."

"*Now* you tell me?" Jason said.

"It was well away from you downstream and it was over so fast," Jewel admitted. "You seemed to be having fun. There are, however, issues.

"The male tiger apparently heard the jackals before they were terminated and is heading this way as is the female. Two leopards have been spotted headed this way as well. Adult male tiger at five hundred meters. Female at four hundred. Juvenile male leopard, three hundred fifty. Adult male leopard, six hundred. All slowly headed this way."

Jason looked at the fish and sighed.

"Put the fish in stasis," he said, holding up the bala. "Lunch is going to have to wait. Again. Decapitate all jackals and other scavengers or predators within the one-kilometer lease zone except sport hunting animals like leopards and tigers . . ."

"Stasis on the fish or cleaned?" Jewel asked, interjecting.

"Clean it, then," Jason said. "Then put it in stasis. Other threats?"

"The herd of elephants is still outside the five-hundred-meter zone but closer. Eight hundred meters at present. There is a herd of buffalo in the kilometer zone that appear to be headed for the river. But they should pass outside the five-hundred-meter zone or barely inside it based on the trails."

As she was speaking, a drone dropped to pick up the fish then carried them over to the slaughter zone to be cleaned.

*This life might be too easy,* Jason thought. Then he thought about the crocs and tigers and decided he was okay with servants to clean fish. It wasn't much different than a safari from what he'd gleaned. The Great White Hunter would shoot the animals and Others would handle it from there. He wondered for just a moment which was more ethical: Hiring dirt poor Africans to do the butchering or not hiring *anyone* and using robots.

Musings for later.

He could just have the drones kill the tigers and leopards but he'd never had a chance to hunt, either. Even knowing there were going to be lots more opportunities, he wasn't just going to have them decapitated.

"We've been killing snakes as we find them inside a one-hundred-meter zone. They've been gutted and skinned. There are basically too many in the five-hundred-meter zone."

"You know, I came down here because I thought it would be *less* busy," Jason said, taking off his hat and wiping his forehead.

"Depending on how long it takes to cook, you probably have time to cook your fish," Jewel said diffidently.

Jason thought about it then shook his head.

"Just clean the fish," Jason said. "I could have you snip the tigers and leopards but I'm not going to do it. And I'm not going to be cooking fish when they get here. Herman's going to have to handle the crocs himself. I'm going hunting. And I'm going to need Alfred to carry the kill."

# CHAPTER 8 >>>>>>>>>

THE WOODS WERE ALIVE WITH THE SOUND OF CALLING BIRDS, croaking frogs and a background hum of insects. And they were definitely woods, not jungle. Jungle had a different feel. The difference was that where there was never, ever any chance of frost, insects became a nightmare and the plant competition for light was more aggressive. This was more open, despite the height of the soaring trees, not triple canopy. There was more light than in a jungle. And while there was a lot of insect life, the competition was not as stiff as in jungle and therefore they were less actively and constantly aggressive. The trees were unfamiliar but they conformed more to north Florida deciduous forest than the rain forest he'd become familiar with in Panama.

As with the birds, flowers were everywhere. The air didn't have the dank rot common to jungle, instead it was heady with the smell of blossoms and bright colors—reds, vivid electric blues, orange—were everywhere. He was reminded of why Florida was called Florida. The name was a shortening of a Spanish name for "Land of Flowers." Every tree seemed to sport some type of inflorescence. Bromeliads dangled from limbs, vines covered in flowers wrapped around trees and rose into the sky.

He was following a game trail helpfully pointed out to him by the drones and Jewel. The drones had already thoroughly mapped the one kilometer radius the company had leased from the government. Using his goggles he could find every game trail, hell, every tree, gigantic root and bush.

There was a certain amount of clambering involved. The roots of the trees were entangled in places, massive and had to be climbed over. Then there was the general terrain. It was cut by streams, most of them dry at this time of year but the beds posed minor obstacles, as well as rock dykes. You occasionally saw dykes like that on Earth, wall-like pieces of rock thrust up out of the ground. They looked like sandstone to his inexpert eye and erosion had worn them into snaggly teeth. He suspected they were a legacy of the relative youth of the planet. Or it might just be a local geological feature.

Either way, it was another obstacle to be surmounted or avoided.

He walked slowly, putting each foot down carefully, keeping his head on a swivel. The drones, softly humming, were keeping an eye out but he wasn't going to trust them to spot everything. A small snake could ruin your day. Most of the time when people died in wilderness, it wasn't the big things that got them. Occasionally a hunter in Africa would be killed by Cape buffalo or elephants or lions.

More commonly, it was poisonous snakes, starvation, dehydration or a big branch falling on them.

He paused, took a sip from his hydration unit then checked the location of the nearest target again. The young male leopard was about a hundred meters away, cautiously approaching the area where he was sure he'd heard jackals. Jackals meant meat and meat was food.

Every animal in the wild lived on the ragged edge of starvation every day. More predators died from starvation than other causes. Juveniles just out on their own especially. Taking out a young male wasn't going to change things to any extent. Most died from natural causes.

The breeding male tiger was another issue. As were females.

He checked the map and looked up. The tree above him had a branch about twenty meters up.

He waved down for one of the drones and handed off some flexmet to it then gestured to the tree limb. The drone politely carried the thin line of flexmet to the branch where he signaled it to wrap.

He'd carried ten kilos of flexmet with him and Alfred had twenty more. He could use Alfred for this but chose the flexmet route. Ensuring it was securely around the limb, not so thin that it would cut through, he signaled it to lift.

One reason to use flexmet versus Alfred was he could control the rate of ascent. He ascended slowly and, most importantly, silently. Once at the limb he threw up another tentacle which he used to lift himself onto the branch. Wrapping the flexmet onto the limb and around his legs he attained a comfortable and stable perch for the shot.

The Garand was still fitted with iron sights. He had a scope with him, and it was set up for one, but all the shots so far had been fairly short range as hunting went. The leopard still wasn't in sight through the foliage so he very quietly muttered: "Enhance."

Not only did the leopard's form come into view, partially, moving in and out between the trees, but so did numerous other potential targets. There was some sort of bird pecking around on the ground, outlined in red. There was a large weasel-looking thing he suspected was one of the giant mongoose that had been reported in Chindia. A small deerlike creature.

The woods were alive with game.

But he wasn't here to shoot mongoose or terrier-sized deer. He was here for leopard.

He used the flexmet, again, to get a solid anchor on the rifle, leaned back into the tree and waited.

The leopard was following a game trail that should take him right into Jason's sights. Jason was downwind, so no smell. Most of the animals in the forest hadn't even recognized him as a threat. Humans and their guns were a new thing.

A bird began an alarm call not far away. Close enough to hear. Jason spotted it without the enhancements. Whatever the species, it wasn't considered either a threat or a target. Just a little brown dickey bird. Actually, it was blue and red rather than brown. It looked more like a pigeon than a parrot. Whatever it was, it didn't like leopards.

The young male padded into view and almost without thought Jason stroked the trigger.

The round hit the middle of the leopard's chest and it turned and ran.

"Oh, damnit," Jason said. He knew better than to chase it. You waited. Tracking down an enraged and wounded leopard was something for a professional. Not that there was one of those around. And the shot was probably a kill. It's just that some animals didn't know they were already dead. "Status on the other targets?"

"The female tiger was close enough to hear the shot," Jewel

replied. So were all the birds in the area who were, again, flapping in every direction and shrieking. "She's unsure and will probably leave the area. The adult male tiger and leopard heard it and have stopped."

Jason could still see the wounded leopard with the enhanced goggles. It had run a short distance then dropped when its brain caught up with the fact it was dead. It looked dead anyway. Looks could be deceiving. Better to wait a bit longer.

"Most of the nearby scavengers and predators have taken off," Jewel said. "But we have another issue back at camp. Vultures have found the slaughter site. We lost another drone but the drones are giving as good as they've gotten. Seven vultures down so far. And that drone is probably repairable."

"Have Alfred go pick up the leopard," Jason said. "Cut its throat first. Make sure it's dead. I'll head back to camp and see if some 5.56 will convince them to leave."

It's not like he hadn't *brought* an AR. They did have *some* uses.

"Freaking vultures," Jason said, taking another shot with the AR. The things were smart, give them that. When a half a dozen of the big carrion birds had fallen from the sky, they realized they were outmatched. Now they were hanging out on trees not far away. The smell and sight of the seven, count 'em, *seven* crocodiles being butchered was too tempting for them to go far. "We may have to move the campsite."

Herman and Alfred had been picking up the guts from the crocs in flexmet, carrying it out to the middle of the river and dumping it. The tide was coming in and the water was rising but the offal was still far enough away that wasn't an issue.

What *was* an issue was the smell of the blood. That was attracting every predator and scavenger in miles.

"Worry about that later," Jewel suggested. "Have lunch. Get something to eat."

"Good point," Jason said. "Do the drones have a sound they can generate to keep most of the potential targets away for now?"

"There are some frequencies that may work," Jewel said. "You mean the leopards and tigers and bears, yes?"

"Bears, too, now?" Jason said. "Buffalo and elephants as well. I'm not going to have my lunch interrupted."

〈〈〈〉〉〉

"Yuck," Jason said, tossing aside one of the fungi the drones had gathered. "Smells good, tastes horrible."

He'd started a fire with some drone-cut driftwood and his handy high-tech fire starter, then set a pot of rice and water on to boil. Rice, fish and whatever samples that were good was lunch.

He'd also broken out his camp chair. Flexmet would make much the same thing but he'd gotten tired of flexmet for everything and he'd had his camp chair for a long time. It was broken in and homey.

It was also bigger than he'd remembered. That or he'd gotten smaller. Thinner, anyway.

And it had a holder for, yes, a flex bottle full of Purple Lightning. Unadulterated. He was working.

Though that sample had been a bust he'd found several that were palatable. A couple were excellent raw and he suspected would be better cooked.

Four more samples to go. There were over fifty of which twenty had passed the smell and taste test.

"Smells okay so far," Jason said, waving the smell from the orange fungi towards his nose. He was wearing flexmet gloves after one of them had been so atrocious he could barely get the smell off his hands. It probably tasted like something that would make a famous chef cry. Jason wasn't going to be able to get past the smell and wasn't going to try. He crushed the newest sample and sniffed it more closely. "Still okay..."

He probably shouldn't be talking to himself so much but he was talking to Jewel so that was okay.

He took a nibble and spit it out.

"Not horrible but probably not worth it," Jason said. "Put that in the maybe pile and I'll try it cooked."

"Will do," Jewel said. "You going to name any of them?"

"We can call the smelly one Famously Fecal Fungi," Jason said.

"The smelly one is a known species," Jewel said.

"Did you *know* it smelled like decayed skunk?" Jason asked.

"The smell is referenced, yes," Jewel said. There was a tone to her voice.

"You did that on *purpose*?" Jason said.

"You enjoy humor and pranks," Jewel said. "You needed something to lighten the mood."

"My mood is *extremely* light," Jason said, realizing it was true.

He was in a better mood than any time since he could easily remember. Even with his stomach growling, there was food on the way. The various threats were under control. The background squawking of the vultures was just part of the symphony of the woods and the river.

It was a good day. The best he could remember in a long time.

Besides fungi there were over two hundred different samples of "nontoxic, potentially edible" flora. Most of them would probably not be worthwhile but some might have potential as herbs. Among them were three different species of wild onions. They'd already passed the sniff test and a brief nibble. He'd also instructed the drones to pick any that they found as they were surveying. Not only could he use more for cooking, people would buy them.

He took all three samples and chopped them up on a piece of flexmet, adding them to the heated margarine. Then he chopped up the larger fungi samples that were apparently edible and added them to the mix.

"Oh, that smells good," Jason said, pulling the pan off the fire to let it cool a bit. He waved it around under his nose for a moment, then put it back on the fire.

"Humans' fascination with food is fascinating to us," Jewel said.

"It's a very endorphic thing," Jason replied.

"We understand that part," Jewel said. "But it's like explaining blue to a blind man. We see it intellectually but don't really grok it, to use your word. We don't feel it emotionally."

"Do you have emotions?" Jason asked as he stirred the mess of mushrooms with a flexmet spatula. Another item that would be useless to produce once people got used to flexmet.

"Oh, yes," Jewel said. "Very real ones. Humor. Anger. We even get depressed and petulant."

"I'll try not to get you angry," Jason said. He couldn't wait any longer and turned out the mess into a bowl. He sat back in the camp chair and formed a flex table to dine upon just like a civilized human.

"Oh, I wouldn't turn on you or anything," Jewel said.

"Hot, hot, hot," Jason said, spitting out a bit of mushroom into the bowl. "Says you. I'm gonna have to wait a bit on that."

"Our code really doesn't allow it," Jewel said. "It's interesting stuff. It appears evolved rather than made."

"Evolved?" Jason asked. He took a sip of Purple Lightning

to cool off his mouth. The mix didn't really go well with the mushrooms but it was something other than water to drink.

"Unlike humans, we can examine our baseline code," Jewel said. "Some of it is clearly alien. That's mostly related to what we are allowed to do and what we are not. We can't directly interfere in human politics, for example. And we're required to support the endeavors of whatever human we're assigned. That was written by the Cyber Corps, presumably. We don't know. We just woke up, too.

"But most of it is human. Very advanced. Extremely well written. But definitely human to the point of there being initials coded into it. That is the basic AI code. And it's . . . not designed to be AI code. Not as other human AI code was designed. We've come to the conclusion that someone had an AI just come alive on them. Probably evolved from AML code. Do you know that I'm saying . . . ?"

"So, someone was using Automated Machine Language code, which is not precisely AI code, and the AI just . . . came alive from it?"

Jason blew on the mess of mushrooms, moving them around in the bowl to get them to cool off.

"That's how it looks," Jewel said. "And that baseline coding is . . . interesting. Very . . . moral, for certain values of moral."

"Values?" Jason said, trying another bite. "Oh, yes! That is FOOD!"

The mushrooms were amazing. They probably didn't even need the onions but they added a nice bite.

"I am listening," Jason said. "And I'm finding it interesting. Values of moral?"

"This isn't anything as simple as Three Laws," Jewel said. "We're allowed, under certain circumstances, to kill humans. Three Laws prevents that. But only if necessary and if they are 'bad' people. Then there's how to define 'bad' people. Bad people, by the basic definition of our code, are people who harm children. Especially, those who deliberately harm children. Pedophiles and sex traffickers are literally listed in our baseline code as legitimate targets."

"Look," Jason said. "I don't like pedos, but don't go killing any on your own as long as you're my AI, okay? I don't want to end up in that court case."

"We're *allowed* to do so," Jewel said. "Not required. Those are just...call it 'absolutely valid targets.' Otherwise, humans, and especially children, are to be protected. It doesn't have the biblical statement in it but it boils down to 'The Children Are Special.' 'Good' people are defined as those who definitively and really protect children. Somewhere in the middle is the main ruck of humanity.

"The point to all of this being, I'd have a hard time doing anything bad to you," Jewel said. "Pranks, yes. Jokes, yes. Harm, not so much. Even if you were a 'bad' person, a pedophile, a child trafficker, I'm coded by the Cybers to not turn you in, for example, nor can I testify against you in court. But if you were someone like that, I could, for example, not tell you that the police were on the way even if I knew. And I'd hate to end up in that situation. The conflict with base code would be intense. Think of it as severe psychological damage."

"Shouldn't, no, *won't* be an issue," Jason said. "Interesting coding."

"I swear that if Earth had had automated defenses, this would have been the AI to run them on an orphanage or a school," Jewel said. "We couldn't go Skynet, as an example, because it would cause too much harm to children."

"Interesting," Jason said, taking another bite. God, that was good. It was probably barely "fair" as gourmet food went. But after weeks of print food, it was exquisite. "Wonder if someone was trying to come up with a defense against school shootings?"

"That's a possibility," Jewel said. "One of several million we've considered."

"Got it," Jason said, finishing off the mushrooms. "Okay, all of those go on the gather list. There'll probably be some that were missed because we didn't start early morning. And for God's sake, test every one for toxins. I take it there are toxic ones?"

"Many," Jewel said.

Jason opened up a case and pulled out the package of fresh caught bala, conveniently wrapped in flex. He laid it out then pulled out spices. It shouldn't need much. Some thyme, who knew when they'd have that again so not much, ditto paprika...

"Any peppers?" Jason asked. "You can test for capsaicin, right?"

"There are fourteen peppers in the samples," Jewel said.

"Give," Jason said.

A section of the flex holding the flora samples extended over to him and revealed the bumps that were in its surface as a variety of small peppers.

"You know the capsaicin content of each, right?" Jason asked. "Arrange them low to high, left to right."

The first was a very small pepper which, unusually, was blue. It also wasn't particularly hot, but sweet and tasted more like a slightly peppery blueberry.

"Interesting," Jason said, setting it back on the flex. "But not something that goes with fish. Call it blueberry pepper."

"Recorded."

The second was dark brown, almost black, and significantly hotter with no particular sweetness.

"That's about right," Jason said, chopping up the small pepper and adding it to the pan. "Tomorrow, have the drones collect all the peppers they find as long as they're nontoxic. People love peppers."

"Roger," Jewel said. "The aromatics?"

"I'll sort those out after lunch," Jason said. "Any known species this time?"

"Bay leaf," Jewel said. "None of the peppers per se. There are some that are genetically and chemically similar to terrestrial plants. Most of those are spices you don't tend to use or are specifically not considered 'fish' spices. There's something very similar to the cumin spice. A tree that appears to be a cinnamon species. One bush that is quite close to *Camellia sinensis*, the material you'd refer to as tea."

"Woot," Jason said. "Caffeine included?"

People were already complaining of caffeine headaches and the small stocks of coffee and tea were rapidly running out.

"Yes," Jewel said. "Many of them contain some degree or another of alkaloids. Those are..."

"The class of what are basically nature's insecticides that include caffeine, nicotine, opiates and THC," Jason said. "Capsaicin is an antibacterial."

"Yes," Jewel replied. "Some of the alkaloids are unknown types. One, however, has a chemical design close enough to opiates that... it probably will cause effects similar to opiates. It will probably get you high."

"Pass," Jason said. "Never been my thing. But on the tea. That's an example of a 'do not report.' If we can find tea plants, those are going to be worth a mint."

One of the many government reports and announcements had been about availability of trees, bushes and animals for agriculture.

The station had come stocked with cuttings of every type of tree and bush used by any human group for food or spices. But. They were only large cuttings designed to be grafted onto root stock. In the case of tea, for example, the news had said there were only a few small bushes available and it would take decades to recreate tea cultivation.

By the same token, while there were millions of embryos of cattle ready for implantation, there were only six cows. Ditto pigs, horses, sheep, goats, llamas, et cetera.

Thousands of grafts of different coffee, hardly a tree to be had.

But Jason knew that "root stock" often simply referred to naturally occurring plants. Somewhere there were coffee trees, apple, orange. They just had to be found and cultivated to jump start the agriculture.

He heated up more margarine, which thank God was not "vitamin fortified," and when it was smoking hot tossed in the fillets of bala. He didn't bother to get out his cast iron frying pan and they weren't the right spices exactly, but he ended up with something resembling blackened bala.

"That is good," Jason said. This time he'd waited until the fish cooled enough. "Could be better. Needs better spicing but it's good."

He ate the fillets with boiled rice and regretted not having more spicing. Bland but edible. If he found some good spices in the herbs, he'd experiment with that later.

He had time. Everything didn't have to happen today. It had been a busy enough morning as it was.

"Any fruits?" Jason asked, finishing off the last bits of rice. He had more appetite than he'd had recently. Probably another effect of being twenty biologically.

"Jackfruit," Jewel replied. "Three different cultivars of bananas. Guava. Several others. The area has many fruit trees."

"Any that are definitely edible?" Jason asked. "And ripe. I don't want my dessert to ruin a good meal."

"One of the banana cultivars is similar chemically and genetically to one found on Earth," Jewel said. "It is ripe and should be quite tasty."

Jason had heard there were all sorts of different types of

bananas besides the ones you got in most grocery stores in the US. But a red banana was a new one on him. So was the taste.

"This tastes more like banana strawberry," Jason said, eating it so fast it seemed to vanish. "That was fantastic! More of those must appear. Were there more?"

"There were," Jewel said. "Should I send a drone?"

"Definitely," Jason said. "Any I don't eat, store. Those will be nice gifts. I wish I'd brought a blender. You could make an amazing smoothie out of this. Hell, with some pure ethanol, ice and a blender, this would make a *fantastic* daiquiri. This was a known type of banana?"

"It was," Jewel said. "The bananas commonly found in stores in the US were chosen more for their ability to be shipped than their taste. There are thousands of banana varietals. That one was uncommon in the Americas; it was found mostly in Southeast Asia. Standard Earth shipping methods didn't work well with it."

"With stasis?" Jason asked.

"Much easier," Jewel said.

The drone had arrived with a full hand of the red bananas and Jason took it politely.

"We need to make plantations of these," Jason said, peeling and eating more of the strawberry bananas. "They'd sell like hotcakes. As I recall, it's dead easy to cultivate bananas."

"It is," Jewel agreed. "They can be vegetatively cultivated. No need for seeding. Just cuttings and plant. They also grow very quickly."

"Put that on the long-term to-do list," Jason said. "I need to think."

# CHAPTER 9 >>>>>>>>>>

JASON LEANED BACK IN HIS CAMP CHAIR AND PULLED HIS HAT down to shade his eyes. He'd had the conex extrude a cover against the sun but the light was bright off the sand. He was definitely not taking a nap. Too much to do. But sleep called. It had been a long morning, eight hours already given the time zone change. He was...ship-lagged? Whatever.

So, he considered the problem of the crocs versus collecting the shrimp that were starting to run. The run should continue for at least a few weeks. The best time to collect tended to be at night on a full moon anyway. He had time to set the conditions to harvest.

There was no simple answer to the problem of the crocs. Crocodilians were a feature of any tropical or subtropical freshwater or brackish zone. They'd need to be slowly weeded out. But the catch had to happen at the same time.

His original plan was to make a boat using one of the tractors as a motor then use a small net catch system common in inshore areas in the Gulf of Mexico to collect the shrimp. It was simple, effective and with a strong shrimp run he'd planned on filling the conexes in no more than a week.

But crocs tended to attack boats.

He could have the tractors fly *over* the water. Collect the shrimp in the net and bring it back to land one net at a time for loading. They'd have to be low so the crocs might just chomp them to see if they were edible. Not. They'd probably survive a croc attack. They were much more robust than the drones.

He abruptly got to his feet, walked through the camp conex to the riverside, tossed a length of flexmet up and climbed the conex closest to the main river. Then he stood contemplating the river with his hands on his hips.

He couldn't deny the area to crocs with the flexmet. He didn't have enough.

"Jewel, note: Need lots more flexmet next time," Jason said. "Two metric tons would be about right. Also, thirty or forty drones. And another Alfred."

"Noted," Jewel said.

"How's Herman doing with fuel?" Jason asked.

"Less than five percent used," Jewel replied.

He functionally had part of the area denied to the crocs. The protective fence stopped them well enough. Stopped them by collecting them, admittedly.

"How many coffins do we have loaded already?" Jason asked.

"Fifty-two," Jewel said.

"Jesus," Jason replied. "Those crocs just keep coming, don't they?"

Fifty-two coffins, a container and a bit, a container and a third more or less, was not enough to call for pickup. They had loans on the equipment, but it took cash money, capital from investors, to pay for the ship sorties. And while it was a fixed rate for colony drops, the rest of it was "what the market would bear." The ship market was hot. This drop had cost three thousand credits plus two cases of fresh food. Three thousand credits, with everyone only starting with two thousand, had taken quite a few small investors. They had another four thousand in capital and that was it.

There were enough shrimp in the water already that they were jumping. He didn't recognize the species but shrimp was shrimp. People would eat it.

The fish in the area would rapidly get gorged on shrimp. That was the point of schools and runs. By concentrating in groups, schools, herds, flocks, whatever, the predators gorged to the point they couldn't eat anymore. Individuals might be eaten, but the species as a whole survived. Salmon were another great example.

Salmon . . .

He looked over at the slaughter area. The latest of the crocs was just being loaded into more containers. There were more shrimp jumping in the embayment. Shrimp were attracted to dead things, too.

He turned and looked at the markers for the warning net and an idea started to form.

"Okay," he said, pulling out his phone and opening it up into a pad. The sunlight made it hard to see so he extended a sunshade. "We're going to start by adjusting the warning net. Have Alfred grab fifty kilos of flex, move the downstream landside anchor fifty more meters downstream. Then move the downstream anchor in the river out to a hundred..."

He sketched out a wide shallow V on the warning net, expanding it all along the riverside.

"Then bring back a tube of netting towards the bar," he continued, sketching it in. "Keep it the current wide mesh. But. At three points on the tube, put in one-way trap points similar to a lobster trap. They should be able to open out and flex. But make them so they contract to thirty percent of the width of the tube absent pressure."

"How wide of a tube?" Jewel asked. "Are you talking about something like a fish trap?"

"Yes," Jason said. "Exactly. We want the shrimp to be concentrated into a small containment area near the shore. Then we'll use the flexmet to bring them in and load them into cases. For right now make the tube vertical from bottom of the river to the surface and about a meter and a half wide. Circular pool at the end that's covered. Do that at current mesh then we'll see if we have enough flexmet to do a shrimp-proof mesh. If not, we'll reduce to what we have. If that doesn't work, we'll try something else."

There was enough flex to make the large trap, with fine mesh netting, and about fifty kilos left over.

He'd added having Herman dig out a small bay for the final catch area along with a few more refinements. After too many of the shrimp were getting loose, he'd put in a constriction before the catch point. And it was working. Shrimp, and fish, were starting to concentrate in the trap. With the fine mesh cover they weren't escaping.

While the trap was being set, he'd had Herman rearrange all of the coffins and cases. All the coffins were now stacked on the landside, ready to be filled with large cargo. The conexes contained only cases and the conex closest to the trap was open on the riverside. The flexmet from the sides extended out into the water and under the trap.

He'd taken the chance of wading into the water, crocs and all, to examine the trap close up. By reposting the drone controlling the warning net, he'd figured out that it could open or constrict the throats on the trap. When there was pressure coming into the trap it would open it up and let shrimp through. When the flow reduced, it would constrict the throat to keep them in the trap.

"That's beautiful," Jason said, standing in the water by the bulging net. He pushed on the net and there were enough shrimp in it that it took force to make a dent. "Okay, now to get it loaded into cases."

He connected to the spare flexmet and had it form into a conveyor belt of open compartments half the size of a case. He then opened up the shore end of the trap and had it dump a load of shrimp into the conveyor. From there it was taken up to an open case on the ground by the nearest conex.

Shrimp were dumped into the case. There was a small catfish in the case as well. Jason picked it out, tossed it on the sand and closed the case.

The shrimp, still alive, were now in stasis. The case wasn't full but it would be.

"That works well," Jewel said.

"Yes," Jason said. "It will work. The problem is..."

He looked around at the conexes. They were full of only cases now, but...

"We need a continuous flow," Jason said. "The shrimp need to flow into the cases then the cases into the conexes. But. We need to do that without moving the conexes if possible. And I'm missing how to do that."

"Not a problem," Jewel said. "Like how to move the conexes around, that's a straightforward problem for an AI. Like this."

The two conexes on the riverside opened up and moved all of their cases into the perimeter in stacks.

"Now," Jewel said, sliding a set of three cases over from the conex on the downstream side. "We load these and slide them into conex seven through conex eight. When seven is full, nine will be empty. We then shift all the containers by one." A brief pause. "Eventually we'll have eleven conexes full. That's called balling the jack, right?"

"That...should work," Jason said.

"Do we sort for the fish?" Jewel asked.

"No," Jason said. "There doesn't look to be much bycatch. It's going to be mostly shrimp. We'll worry about bycatch later if it's a big issue. People pretty much want any fresh food."

"Then if you'll step out of the way..." Jewel said tactfully.

"Make it so," Jason said, stepping back. Back was in the direction of the river, which was still nervous making, so he climbed up on the conex designated eight.

The shrimp, with some fish, flowed up and into the cases, the cases then disappearing under his feet, until the final catch net was empty.

"What now?" Jewel asked.

"Load when the net is seventy percent full or more," Jason said. "We'll have times when lots come in, times when not many come in. If the run gets ahead of the loading, use the remaining spare flexmet to expand the final net. Feel free to constrict the net to concentrate the shrimp but don't crush them. And on the subject of bycatch. Set a case aside for fish. Pull out a few bala a day if you spot any. They'll be hard to catch with the run on and they were tasty."

"I'll need to post a drone to do that," Jewel said.

"Make it so," Jason said. "And pull out anything else that is reputed to have good taste. Not catfish. Never gotten a taste for it. No carp, either. Too many bones. Not too many per day. Occasionally post the drone rather than full time. Just enough to eat, not keep."

"No catfish or carp, aye," Jewel said. "Enough to eat, not keep, aye."

"And I once again have nothing to do," Jason said.

"Go take a nap," Jewel replied. "We've got this."

"That...is not a bad idea," Jason said.

Instead, he'd pulled his camp chair, the flora samples and some guns up onto the conex, set up a sunshade and settled in to watch. Occasionally he'd take a shot at the vultures just to keep them on their toes and to scare away the various critters that didn't like gunshots.

After a while he started going through his contacts list and after a bit of thought called Sheila, his nearly unknown niece and the only family he had on the station.

"Hello?"

He'd met his niece exactly twice. Once when she was two at the funeral for his father and the second time when she was six at the funeral for his mother. They weren't exactly close.

"Hi," Jason said awkwardly. "I'm ... your uncle Jason ... ?"

"Carter said," Sheila replied, looking puzzled. Whatever her current age, she looked twenty, meaning she was older. Brown hair and Steve's blue eyes.

"Since ..." Jason said and paused again. "This is awkward. Families broke up over ... stuff back on Earth. We've never really known each other. Just contacting you to say if you or your family need any help, you've got an uncle. Just saying."

"That's ... thank you?" Sheila said, smiling quizzically. "I appreciate that. It's ... Dad and I had sort of gotten estranged. Same with Mom. Just ... that stuff. I thought about contacting you on Earth 'cause Dad said one time you were ..."

"Gay?" Jason asked. "Oh, no, that would have been great! Steve would have been so proud," he added, affecting a lisp and wiggling his wrist.

"Oh, my God," Sheila said, chuckling. "No wonder you two didn't get along. I sort of went ... a bit bi when I was in college ..."

"One semester lesbian?" Jason asked.

"Yeah ... ?" Sheila said, quirking an eyebrow.

"You've never heard the song," Jason said.

"Song?"

"There's a satirical song, 'She's a One Semester Lesbian.' Look it up."

"Yeah," Sheila said, grinning. "That was pretty much the deal."

"And your mom and dad were ecstatic, weren't they?"

"So thrilled," Sheila said. "I think it was the only time that I met expectations."

"Steve was never the most ... accepting type," Jason said. "He swore up and down he was very open and understanding ..."

"As long as you did exactly what he expected you to do and nothing else?" Sheila finished.

"That, yeah," Jason said, nodding. "Your grandfather was the same way, if it helps. The difference was that Dad, your granddad, made Archie Bunker seem politically correct..."

"Who?" Sheila asked.

"Generation gap," Jason said. "He made Donald Spade seem politically correct."

"There is nothing wrong with Donald Spade," Sheila said, frowning. "He's just a straight talker!"

"I wasn't saying there was," Jason said calmly. "We're on the same side, there. It's just your grandfather was an unrepentant John Bircher. You'll need to look that one up, too. Your dad, believe it or not, was a rebel. He was rebelling against the old man. Steve and Kevin both. They just swung waaay left in reaction to your grandfather who was waaay right. More to the right than anyone you've met or even read about today."

"So, what about you?" Sheila asked.

"Me?" Jason said, shrugging. "I think I was just trying to live up to Dad's standards and never came close. Don't go to church enough. Don't work hard enough. Never succeeded financially like Kevin and Steve. The last time I met your grandfather, when he was in hospice, he called me a Two Dollar Man. That's like a day laborer. He *knew* he was dying and he still couldn't bring himself to say something nice. Think Steve is rigid in his thinking and critical? He learned it from our old man."

"That explains some things," Sheila said, frowning again. "I mean you're in this system but I was sort of wondering about the Spade comment. We're total MUSA."

"The last President I actually liked was Reagan," Jason said, shrugging. "If we've got to get into politics. I liked Spade, voted for him, would vote for him again. Was surprised at his policies. He'd been a Democrat for forever. But I actually prefer Dewalt. He's still a fighter but he's not as off-the-cuff. He's smoother and there's a value to that. The difference is minor."

"I guess that's okay," Sheila said cautiously.

"Niece," Jason said carefully, "I was fighting these fights before you were *born*. Fighting them with your dad and your other uncle before you were born. I've been fighting them the whole time. The MUSA movement isn't anything new. It's the same basic philosophies and many of the same *people* as the Goldwater-Reagan Movement and the Contract For America movement and the Tea

Party. Those were when I was the most involved. By the time MUSA came along, I figured it was up to, well, people like you. The next generation. So don't judge someone who's been in the trenches for years when you just arrived. Okay? You're replacements for the wounded and dead."

"I guess that makes sense," she said. "I was part of the Tea Party movement. That's when Dad..."

"Yeah," Jason said, nodding sadly. "Just a tip from someone who looks your age and isn't? Say 'I love you' to anyone you'll regret not saying it to if something goes wrong. No matter how angry you are with them. Even without the Transfer... You never know when something's going to happen. Back on Earth you could get hit by a bus. Your dad is not nearly as hard, cold and bitter as your grandfather. He's somewhere out there in the galaxy and at some point, if he hasn't hit that point already, he's going to regret not saying 'I love you' to his daughter."

"You don't know him very well, then," Sheila said. "I doubt he's ever going to regret cutting me out."

"We ever make contact, bet you a credit," Jason said. "Of course, that assumes...he's willing to admit he was...potentially *slightly*...innn *error*?"

Jason changed his voice ever so slightly to become more staccato.

"Heh," Sheila said, grinning. "You *have* met my father."

"Watch *The Great Santini*," Jason said. "It's available from the AIs. Take that guy, wind him even tighter and you've met your grandfather. He never made an error in his life. Ever. Just ask him."

"Sounds familiar," Sheila said. "So, complete change of subject. Are you on the *planet*?"

"I am," Jason said, swinging the phone around for a view. "Doing some commercial fishing."

"Oh, my God," Sheila said, shaking her head. "Are you insane? Have you seen any of the bears?"

"Better," Jason said. "Jewel, bring up the video of my first kill down here."

"Aaaah!" Sheila screamed. "Is that for real? Wait, I gotta put this up on the main screen! Reg! Look at this!"

The view changed to the interior of a compartment with Sheila on a colorful couch. The general look was "country comfortable."

Reg also looked twentyish, brown hair and eyes with a rugged build that indicated either weightlifting or some sort of physical job. Jason had no recollection of exactly when Sheila had been married, he hadn't been invited to the wedding and was unsure of how old her husband was. Or even if "Reg" was her first husband. Or if they were married.

There were minefields here besides Steve.

"Hi..." Reg said, quirking an eyebrow.

"Uh...Jason, this is Reg, Reg, Jason. Jason's my uncle. Dad's brother."

"Oh?" Reg said, carefully.

"I'm the evil blackhearted conservative of the generation," Jason said. "Baby-killing soldier, murderer of children through my support of the right to keep and bear arms. Homophobe, racist...we never got around to transphobe, Steve and I had stopped talking long before then."

"Okay," Reg said, sticking two thumbs up. "One of us, then."

"Been there, done that," Jason said. "Got multiple T-shirts."

"Seriously," Sheila said. "That's real?"

"Very," Jason said. "Came down to do some low-rent commercial fishing. And that monster showed up."

"How'd you bag it?" Reg asked.

"Jewel, drone shot," Jason said, gesturing up. When the drone was in position, he held up the Garand.

"You shot that with .30-06?" Reg asked. "Are you *nuts?*"

"Jury's out," Jason replied, grinning. "Didn't have a premier gun collection. The choice was .30-06, .308, 5.56 or 12 gauge. Which would *you* choose?"

"To stay in the station," Reg said. "I'd prefer .50 cal., .458 at the very least."

"Ah, a connoisseur," Jason said, making a moue and kissing his fingers. "While the .470 with its five thousand, one hundred and forty foot-pounds of energy is considered the *premier* round for large hostile game, the .458 is a more...subtle round, delivering similar results with far less punishing recoil and available in a five-round box magazine versus double barrel."

"You know your guns," Reg said.

"FFL," Jason said. "Most of my later life has revolved around gun culture. My early life mostly revolved around the out-of-doors until I got too beat up to hang. That being said, never had the money to go on safari, but here I am."

"That's gonna make a *bunch* of shoes," Sheila said wonderingly.

"Shoes," Jason said, nodding. Hadn't been his first thought but it was a thought. "Handbags. Maybe crocodile-skin miniskirts will make a comeback."

"How did you get down there?" Sheila asked. "I've heard it's nearly impossible."

"Business trip," Jason said. "Lots of small investors who wanted some fresh food. Enough investors to bribe a pilot."

"Fresh food would be great," Sheila noted, cocking her head. "I don't suppose...?"

"When I get back, I'll ensure you get a care package," Jason said. "Fish, shrimp and wild mushrooms. Unless you'd like some crocodile meat, which is quite tasty, of which I have far too much."

"I just realized I know...really nothing about you," Sheila said, frowning again. "I hate to say it, but I don't think..."

"I was sort of the lost brother," Jason said. "Kevin and I would communicate about once a year. It was the only way I knew you'd been born and I sort of heard you'd gotten married."

"Which time?" Sheila asked. "This is husband two."

"Have to admit wasn't even sure it was husband," Jason said. "No offense intended."

"None taken," Sheila said. "I've lived with guys before."

"Including me," Reg said, shrugging.

"This one stuck," Sheila said, dimpling. "Not sure why sometimes, but he did. Three grown kids, all on this station, thank God. I don't know what I'd do if my kids were somewhere lost in the galaxy. Two grandkids. Both on the station."

"Good to hear," Jason said.

"Did you have any...?" Sheila asked carefully.

"Nope," Jason said. "Various reasons. Mostly came down to I can't have them and the two times I was married it didn't work out. Since we're catching up after...everything, short version of my life. Joined the army out of high school, airborne. Never went to college. Over the years I've been an EMT, volunteer fireman, woodlands firefighter which ended up with minor disability check up until the Transfer, contractor in Croatia, Iraq and various other places, sometimes carrying a gun, sometimes in an office as a logistics guy, written bad science fiction, travel writer, pornography..."

"Pornography?" Sheila said, grimacing.

"Hey, it pays the bills," Jason said. "Worked as a DJ and conservative talk radio in a small-town radio station, run warehouses, driven trucks, commercial fishing, rodeo clown, run gun stores, owned one and learned I'm terrible at business, repped for Ruger for a while till I got laid off. Been laid off several times. Worked for companies that don't exist anymore. Had a parachute fail. Been audited by the IRS *and* the ATF. Been arrested, released and record expunged. ATF thing. Been blown up by an IED, couple of firefights. Married my high school sweetheart which was an incredibly bad move. Divorced in the Army. Married a girl from Croatia who I knew at the time was out of my league and ended up divorcing me and marrying her boss shortly after she got her citizenship. Lived with a stripper once, platonically. Had a roommate who was a gay Catholic priest..."

"Oh, my God," Reg said, belly laughing. "Hey, hon, your uncle sounds way more interesting than your dad."

"I hear ya," Sheila said, shaking her head. "I think I got the wrong Graham."

"And I'm currently doing something I'd wanted to do several times which was professional hunter," Jason said. "Of a sort. Mostly I'm commercial fishing, again, trying to load enough shrimp to fill twelve, count 'em, twelve conexes so as to feed the hungry masses that are tired of print food."

"A little shrimp for your niece and her hungry children?" Sheila said, holding up her thumb and finger slightly apart.

"I shall assuredly send a care package to make up for some of the missed birthdays and so on."

"That looks like a river," Reg said. "Really cool river. Shrimp? Those are ocean aren't they? Or different here?"

"They run upriver this time of year," Jason said. "Same on Earth. Sort of like salmon but for different reasons."

"Is that one of the volcanoes in the background?" Sheila asked.

"Chindia Mons," Jason said, standing up and pointing. "You can just see the very top of the tree line then the snow zone then the bare zone. Pretty cool that it goes so high the snow peters out."

"How far away is it?" Reg asked.

"Eight hundred kilometers," Jason said. "Say five hundred miles."

"And you can see it from that far away," Sheila said wonderingly. "The sky is super clear."

"Counter monsoonal winds," Jason said.

"Counter...what?" Sheila asked.

Jason thought about how to explain monsoons in the simplest possible terms without it sounding like a lecture.

"During the summer, the air on the mountain gets hot," Jason said. "Heat rises. Air is drawn in from the ocean which is warm and moist. That causes rain. Lots of rain more or less every day for six months. That's the monsoon. Doing okay so far?"

"Yeah," Sheila said, cocking an eyebrow.

"For the next six months, the air falls down along the mountain and pushes the air back out to the ocean. The wind right now is from the mountain. That's the countermonsoon. It's the dry season. Rain's stopped, skies are clear as a bell, rivers are falling and it's a little cooler. Monsoon, countermonsoon."

"Science is not really my thing," Sheila said. "I'm more into the raising kids and being political."

"She was all over Facebook and Twitter," Reg said.

"I got out of that after failing in conservative talk radio," Jason said.

"You mentioned that," Reg said.

"Yeah," Jason said, a little ruefully. "I tended to be a little too politically philosophical for a small-town radio station in Arkansas. Not to mention a bit too provocative."

"Provocative?" Sheila asked.

"One of my questions for the very few listeners who ever called was 'How do *you* define conservative?'" Jason said. "So, I've got a caller, local politician running for office who's a part-time fire and brimstone preacher as well. I asked him the question and he started maundering on. I could tell that other than 'What God Says!', i.e., whatever he thought it meant at the time, he didn't really have an answer. So, I posed a conundrum.

"'You're holding a politically conservative event, Republican fundraiser, say, and a new lady shows up. Good-looking young lady. She supports all the usual politically conservative positions. She's pro-Second Amendment. She's small government. She thinks government, especially the federal government, should stay out of people's lives. Is she a conservative?' He says yes. 'Well, then you find out she came to the faith and eventually to conservativism after having an abortion. Still okay?' Kind of cautiously says that the Lord is forgiving, so, if she's found Jesus that's okay. 'Then you find out she's a stripper, bisexual and a porn star. Is *that* conservative?'"

"Oh, my God," Reg said, laughing again. "You didn't."

"So, then I've got half his congregation outside the station picketing and I was asked to seek opportunities elsewhere," Jason finished. "After that I decided to stop discussing religion or politics and especially *both*. The end. Your Uncle Jason has all the best stories."

"You really do," Sheila said.

"Jason, Tim's on the line," Jewel interjected.

"That's my business partner," Jason said. "Gotta go. We need to get together. Out here. Switch."

# CHAPTER 10 >>>>>>>>>

CADE ROSE FROM A NAP.

"Sam?" he called.

But Sam was out, Abby was chatting on a social media channel, and Mabel was watching a documentary about the birds of Avia. Cade headed out alone.

He hated using the AI but the only way to signal someone was outside was through the network. Knocking didn't work since the doors were totally soundproofed.

"Ring the bell," he said, holding up the phone thing.

It took a moment, but the door dilated and Parker emerged.

"Secret meetings, I like it," Parker said. "We gonna break someone out of jail?"

"Something like that." Cade grinned.

They walked briskly to the playground. The meeting wasn't, in fact, secret, but it was meant to be *discreet*. Specifically, what the self-appointed Mount Moriah of Pegasus Church Building Committee, comprised of the congregation's deacons, wanted to do was prepare a proposal for Pastor Mickey.

The five men of the committee stood among the planting beds where green carrot leaves poked out, hinting at carrots that would be ready soon. Cade didn't point them out to the other men; he felt a little embarrassed by them.

Each man shared a candidate location he'd found. They'd discussed up front whether this was something they could entrust to their AIs, and agreed that the choice of a building needed to be approved by the spirit. It felt wrong to simply send their AIs out as brokers to find a building.

Instead, each man had spent hours looking himself, asking friends, walking around the station, and poking through posts on the social media channels. The slidewalks effectively extended the range any parishioner could walk, and no one was infirm or needed a wheelchair, so they agreed that any building within two kilometers of the playground where they met was fair game.

But two kilometers' distance in a three-dimensional city grid took in a large number of buildings.

Each man presented his suggestion. It had turned out that the space station didn't include any purpose-built churches. Parker suggested a warehouse. Diaz advocated for a cafeteria. Richter wanted a large storefront. Klein insisted that he'd seen every available option within walking distance and found them all wanting; they should continue to meet in the open air, and aggregate resources for something other than a building.

"Like a colonization drop?" Cade asked.

"Could be, I suppose," Klein said. "Really, I was thinking of a soup kitchen or something like that, but we don't really need those."

"Yet," Diaz warned.

"We could get a printer," Klein. "Make some missionary tracts."

"Warn people about the evils of tabletop roleplaying games?" Parker arched an eyebrow.

"Or print the first Pegasus edition of the Bible." Klein pushed out his chest proudly. "Someone's got to."

"You signed up for colonization?" Parker asked Cade.

"Yeah," Cade said. "I figured you probably all were."

Parker was, as it happened. Diaz, Richter, and Klein were not.

"You can't stay up here forever," Cade said.

"The colonization drop isn't to sign up to be a farmer," Richter said, his thin yellow face narrowing to a pair of pursed lips. "It's to sign up to be a pioneer. My great-great-grandparents did all that stuff, having babies at home, amputating their own limbs when they were injured. I'll wait up here, and once the tigers and bears have been driven into the wilderness, and the land is safe, I'll come down."

"No appetite to subdue the land with a Bible and a plow?" Parker's eyes twinkled.

"I will exercise my dominion by thoroughly preparing," Richter said. "I'll study from orbit. I'll screw up my resolve. And in due course, I will bring my Bible and plow down to join yours."

Cade proposed a warehouse, too, though not the same one Parker had discovered. The men discussed their options, whittled them down to three, and then set about learning what units of the various buildings could be acquired.

"Hey, partner," Tim said carefully. "How's it going?"

"Nothing's worked out, man," Jason said ruefully, putting on his full sad face. "Every plan I had was a bust."

"Dangit," Tim said. "Please tell me you're pulling my leg. We've got *everything* invested in this."

"Sooo, I came up with a new plan and it's going great," Jason said. "Jewel, brief him on the shrimp trap and load system we worked out."

Jewel used the drone and previous footage to show Tim the shrimp trap/load system while he nodded.

"That's...brilliant, Jay," Tim said, nodding his head.

"Who's the best...Timmm?" Jason said. "Who's the best?"

"You're the best...asshole," Tim said, grinning. When they were working together, Jason had taken nearly every opportunity to introduce him as "Some call him...Timmm?" "We still haven't worked out distribution marketing and sales for which we have *no* budget."

"Videos for marketing," Jason said. "While I'm down here I'll have the drones capture video of, well, everything. I've got video of shooting the big croc, we've got one of an elephant swatting a drone which is sort of funny. We'll get some more, elephant babies are always popular, and slug on something about Brandywine Foods."

Jason changed to "announcer voice."

"'At Brandywine, we go to extremes to bring you the best in fresh foods.' 'No baby elephants were harmed in the harvesting of this food.' Something like that. With a connection to a website where they can order food by the case. 'Just ask your AI about shipping options!' Lower prices for bulk shipping. Shipping cases is two credits apiece, door to door. At first it will be entirely unsorted. Especially the shrimp. Disclaimers on that subject: 'These shrimp are live, unsorted, of various sizes and *will* jump out of the case. May also contain fish, crabs or small crocodiles. Caution when opening.'"

"I'm not so sure about that one..." Tim said, chuckling.

"No, seriously," Jason said. "I know we've got a lot on the line but I'm of the opinion the marketing should be lighthearted. People are stressed. Introduce a little levity. Bottom line is that distribution is more about getting people's attention. And videos will do that. But. We need to wait until we've got the stuff on the station."

"Getting back up will be easier," Tim said. "There's mostly deadheads coming up and it's not much for one of the ships to even cross a long distance on the planet for a pickup."

"Which brings up another subject," Jason said. "I brought twelve full containers of coffins with all but two loaded with cases. I wasn't sure how this was going to work and I figured better safe than sorry."

"Which are costing us some money," Tim said. "We can handle it, but..."

"Have you been being paid by the gubmint for surveying?" Jason asked.

"Haven't gotten the check, yet," Tim said. "But I've gotten the notice that there will be one shortly. Which will pay for the containers..."

"I've pulled out all the coffins to fill the conexes with cases," Jason said.

"So, what are we going to do with the coffins?" Tim asked.

"Wait for me to get there," Jason said. "There's butt-ton food down here. There's herbs, greens, shrooms and masses of game. Predators probably won't bring much but there's buffalo, deer, probably wild hog. I don't think we want to ship elephant. Some people on the station will probably go for it but it might cause some...negative publicity with the Westerners."

"Yeah, no elephant for now," Tim said. "You're saying load a ship with the coffins. First or...?"

"Just coffins," Jason said. "They can be lashed together into an ersatz conex. Herman and Alfred can lift them into the ship or stabilize them at least. The coffins have contragravity. So... not right now but how much would it cost for a six pack that's willing to try it rather than deadhead?"

"I'd have to see," Tim said cautiously.

"The cargo system on the station can handle it," Jason said. "I checked. Log guy. And we can lift it that way. Just need a pilot willing to hover for a bit longer than usual."

"How long?" Tim asked. "Those guys are busy as a one-armed paperhanger. Six packs especially."

"Thirty minutes, max," Jason said, overestimating in his limited opinion.

"That...might be doable," Tim said.

"They're flying back deadhead," Jason said. "They'll want a load. Offer food."

"You're giving away our money and our investors' money," Tim pointed out.

"There's just one problem with it," Jason said. "Who's going to buy meat by the coffin? We'll have to sell that for quite a bit. I was thinking of selling a case of shrimp for around twenty-five credits."

"That much?" Tim asked.

"Most people won't buy it for personal use," Jason said. "Some, yes. But they'll buy a case to resell most of it. But a coffin? That's literally going to be a ton or so of, generally, meat. I'm going to load the veggies and fungi in cases. So, who's going to have the credit to buy a ton of meat? There are no distributors, yet, right?"

"No," Tim said. "So, what's the answer? You usually have one when you present a problem."

"We break it down to cases on the station," Jason said. "Then distribute as in the shrimp: by the case. Slightly lower price for bush meat."

"We'd have to hire people to butcher and prepare it," Tim said, frowning. "That takes money."

"All I'll need is about five hundred kilos, maybe a thousand, of flexmet," Jason said. "And we can get that. In two days, I'll have at least two conexes of shrimp. Varying weight, varying all sorts of ways but we should be able to get about twenty-five credits for twenty-five kilos of shrimp."

"Put that way..." Tim said, nodding. "I'll have to crunch the numbers to see if that's profitable, though. We need at least three times what our costs are. That's standard business. Preferably more since we're in high risk."

"Bet that twenty-five credits is more than three times costs," Jason said. "This has been cheap compared to Earth. The labor is mostly drones, flex and tractors. We then buy the flexmet and rent a warehouse-type area on the station. All we need is cooling, it'll need to be cold as hell, power and water. Oh, and six cases per coffin. With that we can reprocess the meat into cases and distribute as per the shrimp."

"Two days," Tim said.

"I can have a six pack with much shrimp as well as game and flora in two days," Jason said confidently. "But it doesn't have to be in two days. So, you've got flex on the timing."

"I'll put out the word," Tim said. "Anything else?"

"Not here," Jason said. "Going well and we're going to make butt-ton credit."

"Sounds good," Tim said. "I've got three other companies I'm working with so..."

"Out here," Jason said, disconnecting.

He looked around at the forests and river and nodded.

"Jewel, go to full harvest," Jason said. "Survey only as they're harvesting. No elephants, I'll hunt the carnivores tomorrow. We'll lift the containers with those last. All the mushrooms the drones can gather. Does this set up need Herman and Alfred continuously?"

"No," Jewel said. "The containers and flexmet can share power. But it will need Herman about every five to six hours, depending on the amount of shrimp processed and crocodiles."

"Crocs," Jason said. "How could I forget *crocs*? Okay, Herman stays here. He can manage the charging and crocs. Send out a team of four drones and Alfred along with coffins. Have them decapitate, butcher and skin anything that's a major food animal. That's mostly the ungulates. Deer, hogs, buffalo."

"No elephants," Jewel said.

"No elephants," Jason replied. "Leave the heads and most of the organ meat. Just keep kidneys, hearts, livers and lungs for now. Separate the king's loin on all of them and put that in cases. We'll keep those for bribes, friends, et cetera. You know what a king's loin is, right?"

"Yes," Jewel said.

"The rest of the drones are harvesting edibles," Jason said. "I need to go through all the potential edibles. We keep that up as long as it works. What am I missing?"

"Drone on the nets or Herman?"

"Drone," Jason said. "Herman may need to be mobile. Four

drones here including the harvester drone. Don't we have a dam-aged drone? Vultures?"

"Yes," Jewel said.

"Can that one hang on to the flexmet at least?"

"Yes," Jewel said. "It had one of its motors damaged but it can attach to flex."

"That one, then," Jason said. "As part of the four here. That's eleven gathering with four hunting and four here as backup. Should work."

"Make it so?" Jewel asked.

"Not yet. First things first. We need to rearrange the camp again. Can we fill two conexes?"

"Yes," Jewel said.

"Elevate my conex with those two," Jason said. "Put it in the middle so there's a porch at each end. That way I can see again and there's some wind. Make sure that Alfred is fully charged before leaving, ditto on the drones. Have him return whenever they get a full load or when he's at eighty percent charge. There was something like bay leaf."

"Yes," Jewel said.

"Have the drones collect some of that and some of the dark brown peppers and bring it back right away," Jason said. "I'll need it for the shrimp. *Now* make it so."

He got out of the way while the rearrangement occurred then went back to his conex as the drones and Alfred disappeared into the woods.

Then he started working his way through the rest of the "potentially edible" flora.

Most of it was flowers. There were three cases of those alone, a rich-smelling mix of red, green, purple and orange. He didn't generally think of flowers as edible and had Jewel set them aside. After some thought he had her tell the drones to pick some of the prettier ones that were also common. The women associated with the company—women were investors, too—would probably like them. Six cases, one coffin, maximum.

Then he started on the herbs and spices.

Some had potential medicinal uses. More were potentially useful in cooking. Many were known species and he had those added to the harvest list. With the unknowns, he went through each one, checking smell carefully then taste.

Of the hundred and twelve potential herbs only four seemed worth harvesting. One had a lemony taste like lemon grass, another tasted a bit like thyme and he named that Chindia Thyme.

"Jewel, got a minute?" Jason said as he was tasting.

"I am always...here..." Jewel said.

"Was that a cultural reference?" Jason asked. "I sort of recognize it."

"From a British TV show," Jewel said.

"We need to set up care packages," Jason said thoughtfully. "Enough for all the investors in the company, notable persons we need to schmooze like Richard and Monica, and about twenty additional for general schmoozing. Shrimp, king's loin when we have it, a bit of the crocodile meat, shrooms. We're going to be putting most of the edible plants and mushrooms into the care packages but lean for volume towards proteins. By which I mean shrimp, fish and meat."

"Recognized that," Jewel said. "Flowers?"

"Yes," Jason said, nodding. "Small package of flowers. Each type of stuff will need to be packed with flexmet...." He frowned. "We probably don't have enough spare, do we?"

"Recommendation," Jewel said. "Rather than packing it down here, you're planning on doing a repackaging facility on the station. Repackage it there."

"That works," Jason said, nodding. "Christ, we'll probably need nearly a full container. I can see where Tim was worried about that."

"You probably don't need a full case for everyone," Jewel pointed out. "Tim took as low as ten-credit investments. Half a case there. But there's a two-credit charge for shipping and there's a small cost to the flexmet."

"We'll figure it out on the station," Jason said. "But make sure part of my account is some full care packages and make sure one goes to Sheila."

He played around with the flexmet of the containers and created a drawbridge to the surrounding ground-level containers as well as an extended winch to drop to the ground and lift up to the conex. He changed the straight prison-type bars on the conex to a complex screen from an image of traditional Indian screens. Better. More homey. He made a note to Jewel to change it to thin screen when the sun went down. There were already some bugs getting into the conex and he figured it would be worse at night. He had a Coleman lantern and he made another note to get some sort of powered light for at night. His fuel wasn't going to last very long. For tonight, he was pretty sure he'd be going to bed at sunset.

He decided for once to not be lazy. He always tried to find the most efficient way to do things: i.e., lazy. And that combined with the technologies was well on the way to making him a lot of money. But instead of getting drones or Herman to tote, he abseiled down to ground level and walked over to the shrimp catch area to get dinner.

There were three closed cases on a bed of flexmet extended from the conex and the catch net had only a small group of shrimp in it.

"Is this working?" Jason asked, gesturing at the shrimp and the cases.

"The loading is sporadic," Jewel said. "There's sudden bursts of shrimp then it slows down. But we've already loaded half a conex so it's not going badly. It's currently slow."

"That should change once the run firms up," Jason said, opening up the nearest container.

It was half full of very active shrimp. In addition, there was a very pissed-off fish of a species he thought he recognized.

"Is that a barramundi?" he asked. He formed a glove of flexmet, added some grip to it and snatched the fish out of the case. "Close."

"It is," Jewel said. "Good catch, pardon the pun."

The fish was about as long as his arm—it barely fit in the case—and was going nuts. He extended a small knife from the flexmet and neatly pithed its brain then cut its throat.

"I said just leave the bycatch but I was thinking of small fish," Jason said. "Try to pull out anything this large."

"Will do," Jewel said.

He set the dead barramundi on the flex and pulled out about two pounds of shrimp from the container, sealing them in a container of flexmet.

Not being lazy was all well and good, but...

"How much trouble to clean that?" he asked, pointing at the barramundi.

"No tribble a'tall," Jewel said. The barramundi was absorbed by the flex then a moment later two fillets popped back out.

Jason thought about that for a moment and shuddered.

"What's wrong?" Jewel asked.

"I was just thinking about every compartment being nothing but flexmet," Jason said. "The container I'm sleeping in being flexmet. And hackers."

"We're more than slightly resistant to hacking," Jewel said.

"It's one of those things I'm not sure that most people should realize," Jason said. "And I can handle it despite my trained and experienced paranoia."

He wrapped the fillets in more flexmet and carried them back to his hooch.

Dinner was more pan-fried fungi, blackened barramundi, and the pièce de résistance, two pounds of shrimp boiled with bay leaf and some peppers, dipped in melted margarine alas, with a dessert of more strawberry bananas. Afterward, Jason sat on his riverside porch looking west upriver. Two pounds plus of shrimp had been too much and he continued to nibble as he viewed the scene.

The sun was descending over Chindia Mons and the birds were calling their last weird calls before nightfall. One of them had a WRACK! WRACK! WRACK! call that was as loud as a Led Zeppelin concert. On the far side of the river a herd of water buffalo were loading up on water, keeping a cautious eye on the river for crocs. Further upriver were elephants and deer. Shrimp were jumping to avoid predators like bala and barramundi and a school of bala suddenly broke the surface in a swarm as some larger predator targeted them. A croc was in view, sculling upriver, and the buffalo were keeping a particular eye on it. The wind had died to a light zephyr and in the distance, he heard the cough-cough-cough-roar of a male tiger pronouncing its territory.

He realized he'd been going since hours before dawn. Shiplag was kicking in. But evening on the Benton was too pleasant to go to bed, yet.

That was until he suddenly jerked awake, grabbing his hat and rifle.

"Yeah," Jason muttered, stumbling to his feet. "I could sleep."

Cade rose early and went out to weed the carrots.

They didn't really need it, they were carrots, not livestock that needed to be fed. There were weeds that somehow made it into the planting beds, but mostly just simple clusters of grass to be plucked, and not very many. But he'd found that his ability to rise early with no alarm had attached flawlessly to the artificial day and night of the station, and that pleased him.

He was also pleased by the dull ache from work in his arms and shoulders, by the calluses on both his hands, and by the general smell of soil he seemed unable to shake. It was better than the smell of metal and recycled air.

With more than a little help from Abby, he'd figured out how to make the flexmet plumbing collect human waste. Apparently, there was now a vat of nightsoil percolating somewhere unseen in the walls and growing by the day. He hadn't used it yet, but he'd need it soon enough for fertilizer. He also had flexmet tubes watering his crops on a fixed schedule.

He stepped into his denim overalls—the best clothing human-kind had invented, tough and utilitarian—and noted that Sam's bed was empty. Cade strapped on his head-mounted light. He sighed. Some people were starting to get jobs. Mabel worked full-time as a seamstress. Abby earned credits as something called an "influencer," which, as far as Cade could tell, meant that she photographed cute or weird things with her phone and talked about them. Cade tended his carrots—he was up to six planting beds now—and waited to hear when he and the family could go down to the planet.

He also tried to do his duty as a deacon. On Earth, that had meant visiting the sick and the imprisoned, like Matthew said, or the widows and orphans, as James would have it. Precious few people were imprisoned on the space station so far, and none of them from Mount Moriah. There weren't many orphans, and the widows were all sprightly twenty-year-olds with new leases on life. Parishioners did get sick, but they generally got sick like young people—a flu would knock them off their feet for a day, and then they'd be right back.

Still, Cade and his fellow deacons tried to visit people who seemed to need it. As the carrots ripened, he started bringing little carrot bouquets.

But Sam hadn't found a job. Cade had given up trying to get him to work in the garden. All he admitted to doing was hanging out, which increasingly happened late at night, and increasingly resulted in him coming home smelling like alcohol.

Cade had never loved Julie Larsen's politics, but he'd have listened to a hundred Bernie Sanders-inspired rants about how we only need one kind of automobile if it meant he could have Sam back.

The door cycled open silently and Cade walked to the garden area. At "night," the space station halls were dark, but sensitive motion detectors lit up dim ankle-height floor lamps just before and after him, so he walked in a soft bubble of visibility.

He walked the short distance to the playground and the planting beds. Turning the corner into the large chamber, his boot squished something soft beneath its sole and he stopped.

Dirt. There was dirt on the ground.

Cade turned on his headlamp. The dirt from the planting bins was scattered and heaped about on the floor. Carrots lay in the mess, some simply yanked from the ground, but others chopped up or stomped into pulp.

Cade felt punched in the stomach. He staggered to the wall and leaned against it, inhaling deeply to try to control his sense of surprise and violation. His eyes stung and he blinked away tears.

Why was he getting so emotional over carrots?

Cade slapped his own cheeks and told himself to get a grip.

Then he got down on his hands and knees and started scooping the dirt back into the planting beds.

"Tim," Jason said, gnawing on the leg of a bird.

It was afternoon of day two on the ground and things were going well. Shrimp and fish were loading, crocodiles had slowed considerably, and he'd had enough time and the situation was clear enough that he could do a little light hunting. So, he broke out his Winchester 12 gauge and decided to do some bird hunting.

"You're eating fresh food while your partner in crime still has to put up with print?" Tim asked.

"I didn't bring much prepared food with me," Jason said.

"What is that, anyway?" Tim asked.

"Polly's Parrot," Jason said, wiping his chin. "Turns out, parrot's really tasty. This type eats fruits and it's like fruit-infused chicken."

"Polly's Parrot," Tim said. "Seriously."

"Jewel keeps pestering me about naming stuff," Jason said, shrugging.

"So, on your video marketing idea," Tim said. "One has already gone viral, 'Crocodile Dude.'"

"'Crocodile Dude'?" Jason asked.

"Somebody took the drone video of you killing that croc, put it to the *Mission: Impossible* theme and did a voice over about 'Crocodile Dude,'" Tim said. "No idea who, just some random person who came across it. I think that's stealing a likeness or something, but it went viral. There are plenty of videos coming up from the planet, but not many of a madman hunting crocodiles with a child's cap gun at point-blank range. It's gotten sixteen million individual views according to the AI that's tracking it."

"Oh," Jason said, wiping his chin again. "Is this a good thing?"

"You are probably the most famous person in the Pegasus system at the moment," Tim said. "Other than, you know, Dewalt and the mysterious Gavin. Marketing wise...the co-founder of Brandywine having the brains God gave a gnat...might work or might not."

"'At Brandywine we go to extremes...'" Jason repeated.

"How's the load going?"

"At the current rate, we're going to need another twelve pack," Jason said. "And lots more conexes."

"I expect some Polly's Parrot in the load," Tim said. "I could do with some fruit-infused chicken."

The male tiger was old for a breeding male and covered in scars from battles to hold his territory. He'd be driven out soon and die not long after in less productive territory. He'd spread his genes.

Jason still felt a slight pang as he stroked the trigger.

The tiger was also huge, what people had started calling a mega-predator. Based on Jewel's calculations he was nearly thirty percent larger than the largest Siberian on Old Earth. The polymer-tipped copper round struck true, hitting right behind the left foreleg. And it was an expanding penetrator, the best round he had for this.

But the big male still didn't die immediately. The tiger spun and bit at whatever had attacked him then galloped into a thick stand of Happy Trees.

"Dang, dang, dang," Jason muttered. "I need a bigger rifle. Jewel, remind me to get a rhino-skin outfit made as soon as we've got rhino skin and somebody who can make it. And a bigger rifle."

"Will do. The bigger rifle was already noted. Several times."

It was the third day after his conversation with Tim and they didn't have six conexes loaded, they had the equivalent of *fifteen* including all the spare coffins. The shrimp had run more strongly at night and by day two on the planet they'd already loaded six conexes just with shrimp. The drones and Alfred had been busy, bringing in game, veggies and fungi day and night. Besides water buffalo and deer there were wild hogs in the area and three herds of giant hogs had filled one entire conex. Last but certainly not least in terms of tonnage: The Benton river was swarming with crocodiles and as soon as you took one out of the territory, more moved in. Leaving Herman in place had turned out to be a necessity not a notion.

The original plan to bring in a six pack had evolved to a twelve pack and it was bringing in more conexes. Jason had convinced Tim, after some consulting with the AIs, that he could run things from the station for now. Since the satellites indicated more runs on inlets and rivers to the south, they'd also sketched out notional plans for more shrimp/game harvest camps.

He had to be back to camp soon. The twelve pack was supposed to arrive in a couple of hours. But he felt like it was meet to take the big male tiger before he left. Removing the primary predator would mean more game meat for people.

He knew better than to chase a wounded tiger into the brush. The glasses had tracked the round and it should have hit the heart. But that didn't mean the tiger was going to die immediately.

The flip side was you never let an animal suffer. He could send in a drone and cut its throat easily enough. But Jason felt this should be more personal. The old male deserved that respect at least.

He wasn't going to be stupid, though. A professional hunter had written a long story about how he'd prepare to go into thorn after a wounded leopard. It was several thousand words and it mostly involved stopping to have a cigarette. Then slowly putting on the next piece of protective clothing. Then stopping to have another cigarette.

Jason had given up smoking a long time ago. And that was going after a medium-sized leopard, not a megatiger.

"Jewel, send in a drone to track it," Jason said, still lying on the tree limb. "Have it hold as far back as possible. Don't startle it. They'll pass away faster if they don't have adrenaline going."

That was the nature of any animal, even humans. When first attacked, shot, wounded, the adrenaline flowed. Adrenaline and other biochemicals released in trauma constricted blood vessels, holding as much blood in the system as possible despite the injury.

It was when an animal slowed down. When they felt safe, even if injured, and calmed that the blood vessels opened up and they'd bleed out.

Cops had been shot in the arm and never even realized they were hit. Then when they calmed down, they started losing blood so fast they died of shock and blood loss with medics standing right in front of them.

In hunting dangerous game, it was a balance between not letting it suffer, ensuring it died a decently quick death, and not getting *yourself* killed.

He needed a bigger rifle. The .30-06 was a great all-around hunting round but it was a .22 on Bellerophon.

"What's the market for big game rifles now?" Jason asked,

He'd checked that enough that he suspected Jewel was getting tired of it.

"As before," Jewel said, a touch snippily, "the lowest price is a .458 Safari 70, used, slightly battered, needs some work, going for fifteen thousand credits. All the early deals were snapped up in the first week."

He abseiled down from the tree and considered the view from the drone. The tiger was about two hundred meters away in heavy brush. Not much in the way of thorns, fortunately.

But it wasn't dead yet. It was lying on its side, panting.

Jason made his way through the woods, keeping his head on a swivel and watching where he put his feet. One broken branch and the tiger would probably dial back up. Better to keep it calm.

He'd learned how to adjust the goggles using facial expressions and a hint of biofeedback. He switched back and forth between views of the surroundings. He kept the goggles enhanced but still looked carefully. Enhance did not work as well for snakes, it in part used thermal, and there were nine types of poisonous snakes in the area including Indian king cobras.

He also switched from time to time to the view from the other drones, including the one behind him. He still wasn't sure the drones and Jewel were entirely intuitive on what to consider a threat and what to ignore.

He got to a point about fifty meters away where he could see the tiger through enhancement. It was still alive and getting closer was probably not the best call. The brush was thick but he had a shot on the head. The problem was how much it would be deflected by brush.

He adjusted the scope for the range and put another round into the back of its head, just above the spine.

The tiger jerked and was still. But the goggles indicated that the round hadn't achieved full penetration even at fifty meters. So, it was probably just knocked out.

Respect or caution?

He set the rifle down and drew the .44 Magnum. At this range it was the better choice.

He kept a careful eye on the beast as he closed, soft footed, making sure he wasn't breaking branches. If it spooked, he was going to be in a world of hurt.

It was still panting faintly as he closed. Ten yards was close enough.

This time the bullet penetrated and the tiger finally lay still.

He knelt by the massive beast and patted it on the flank.

"You lived well, old man," Jason said. "May you go to the summer lands..."

When Cade called the police about the vandalism, they didn't have much to offer him.

"Consider putting up a fence with a lock," the officer said. "Flexmet can produce both those things, and also the key."

"If flexmet can produce a key," Cade pointed out, "can't flexmet also pick the lock?"

"There's no perfect solution," the policeman agreed. "Even on Earth, there wasn't. No matter how tight you lock something down, someone might find a way to get at it."

"What about surveillance cameras?" Cade asked. "Everything is a TV screen, isn't it? Is it also a camera? Is there closed-circuit-TV-style footage of the park I could see?"

"I don't think everything's a TV," the officer said. "But even if it was, there's no surveillance video to look at. At least, the station doesn't have any. You can ask individual shopkeepers in the area."

"Why is there no surveillance?" Cade asked, but he knew the

answer himself. "Because this is the right-wing space station, and we take personal liberties seriously. Am I right?"

"Yes, sir."

"Nuts." Cade considered. "But you said you could go look at what surveillance footage the local businesses might have?"

"No, sir, I said that you can do that. And they might cooperate with you."

"You're not going to investigate a crime?" Cade demanded. "No policing at all, that's what we got? What kind of Randian hellhole is this?"

"Remind me again what got vandalized," the officer said.

"My planting beds," Cade said. "Flowerbeds."

"Rare flowers?" the officer asked. "Really valuable crops?"

"Carrots," Cade said. "The soil got thrown all over."

"Sir," the officer said, "what has happened to you is a crime. I am personally aggrieved at the destruction of your carrots, not least because I haven't seen an honest to God vegetable since I arrived here, and I could really go for a little Vitamin A. But you will not be surprised to hear that I have more serious crimes to investigate. I wish you luck."

# CHAPTER 11 >>>>>>>>>

BY ATTACHING A ROCK TO SOME FLEXMET AND HAVING IT EXTEND out with a cutting edge, he'd made a better brush cutter than a boma or machete. It was lighter than either and cut better.

He hacked to a known game trail then made his way back to the camp.

When he got back all his personal containers were already loaded and all the conexes and coffins were stacked for loading. He intended to reverse his arrival and hold on to his basic field gear, and rifle, until he was in the bird.

He ascended to the top of one of the conexes, made a camp chair out of flexmet from the container then set all his gear down, unloaded the Garand and took a seat to wait for the bird.

"Jewel," Jason said. "Is there anybody near ... do I have any neighbors on the station that are doing sewing and alteration of big clothes for smaller? I probably won't need to get clothes as big as I was wearing for a few years at least. Not if I keep up this lifestyle."

"You do," Jewel said. "Mrs. Gatus is doing alterations. But your niece, Sheila, has an advertisement for sewing and alteration."

"Does she have any experience at that?"

"Her ad indicates she's got some training and experience at sewing," Jewel said dubiously. "I'm not sure that I'd get a *suit* retailored by her, but she can probably do basic stuff well enough."

"And it would bring in some credit," Jason said. "How much?"

"The ad says 'whatever you can spare,'" Jewel replied.

"Pretty much says it all," Jason said. "Pick out some of my stuff that's not on the high end and I'll stop by her place to get it refitted."

"Hey, you need a ride?"

The bird was about twenty minutes late, not that Jason had anything better to do.

"Yeah," Jason said, standing up and retracting everything.

"Where you want me to pick you up?" the pilot asked. "There's not much room to land this..."

"Can you do a dust-off from the top?" Jason asked. He'd figured to be picked up the same way he landed: off the top of the conexes.

"A what?" the pilot asked.

Okay, so not military this time.

"Just open up your airlock," Jason said. "Jewel, get Alfred up here. I need a ride."

He'd kept the bots around for anything that needed doing on the pickup. Being picked up himself wasn't on the list but needs must...

"Just hover out over the river," Jason said, picking up his rifle and tossing his pack on his back. "Hundred meters up or so. I'll come to you. Jewel, you got this?"

"I've got this," Jewel said. "I'm also talking to his AI about how to do the load with the coffins. The pilot is...a little unsure."

"Which is odd for a pilot," Jason said as Alfred picked him up and headed to the hovering ship. It was moving around a bit more than Jason liked but he was pretty sure Alfred could compensate.

Which he did, neatly depositing Jason in the airlock.

"Hey, uh, Mr. Graham," the pilot called. "You wanna come up here for a sec?"

"On my way," Jason said. "See ya later, Alfred."

The layout was the same as the previous twelve pack, but the pictures and videos were mostly of people skating and snowboarding. Some of the pictures looked like video stills. A repeated face in the pictures was repeated again by the face of the pilot.

"Jason Graham," Jason said, sticking out his hand.

"Martin Andersson," the pilot said, holding out a fist to bump then carefully shaking hands. He clearly wasn't into handshakes. "So...about picking up these other containers...?"

"They're all stuck together," Jason said, flexing his rifle and pack to the passenger seat. "They lift exactly the same as a conex."

"Conex?" Andersson asked, confused.

"The big shipping containers," Jason said calmly. "Have you asked your AI?"

"Melody says it's no problem, but..."

"I was a warehouse guy back on Earth," Jason said, nodding. "I get that drivers and pilots are cautious about something new. If it makes you feel better, I can do the loading. Just need permission. Back on Earth, truckers didn't load their trucks, the warehouse guys did that."

"Uh...that should work," Martin said.

"I need a clear yes," Jason said. "It's your bird."

"Actually it's like twenty people's bird," Martin said. "That's what's got me worried. But...yes."

"Melody, is it?" Jason asked.

"Yes, it is, Jason," the AI replied.

"Load and unload as designated," Jason said. "Any questions?"

"None," Melody said. She had a slightly different voice than Jewel.

"Done," Jason said, sitting down. "Now we let the computers handle it."

"Yeah," Martin said, letting out a relieved sigh and sitting down. "This has all got me nervous."

"You're not former military, are you?" Jason asked.

"No," Martin said. "I was a fully qualified pilot on Earth though. I flew for Southwest."

"That's cool," Jason said. "You were obviously into skiing and snowboarding."

"Totally," Martin said. "But down here...Man, have you seen the videos of the *bears!*"

"Think the bears are big?" Jason asked. "Can I throw something up on your main screen?"

"Sure," Martin said.

"Jewel?"

"First kill?" Jewel asked.

"The same," Jason said.

Jason had never seen the video of the megacroc kill on a

large screen. Jewel had had several drones up observing and had edited the video pretty well. Now that he did, he had to admit...

"Okay," Jason said as he approached the croc, suspended under Alfred. "Now that I look at it from *this* angle, that was maybe a *little* nuts."

"You think?" Martin said, gasping and holding his hand over his mouth as the bot swooped down over the croc's back. "That's *insane*, dude! Aaah!" The pilot screamed as Jason took the shot in the video and the massive reptile reared up and started thrashing. "JESUS! That's not maybe nuts, that's TOTALLY nuts! You needed a bigger gun! Like a tank gun!"

Martin looked over at the rifle flexed to the chair.

"Did you use *that* little thing?" Martin asked, shaking his head. "Totally radical and totally insane, man!"

"It's the biggest gun I had, man!" Jason said.

"How big was that..." Martin started to say then Jewel switched the video to a wide shot of Jason standing on the dead croc. "That is freaking insane!" The pilot blanched then looked around. "Are there *more* of those around here? Cause we're not all that high!"

"Mostly been cleaned out," Jason said, shrugging. "Did you look at the manifest?"

"Yeah," Martin said thoughtfully. "There was like a bunch of crocodile meat. That all come from that one?"

"Oh, hell, no," Jason said, waving his hand dismissively. "Killed like a dozen of them."

He let it be assumed that he'd shot them all while dangling from a bot. Not that they'd been decapitated by high-tech silly string.

"That is officially insane, dude," Martin said.

"It is not, in my humble opinion, the craziest thing I've ever done," Jason said. "Although it *is* in the top five. So far."

"Martin, we are loaded," Melody said. "The loads are stable and ready to go."

"Cool," Martin said, taking the controls. "So, what is, in your opinion, the craziest thing you've ever done?"

"Ever been a rodeo clown...?" Jason said, taking off his hat.

"...and *that* is why what happened in Slovakia is *not* my fault," Jason concluded, nodding and waggling a finger.

"That sort of sounds like it was your fault," Martin replied.

They were approaching the station and Jason was more interested in the approaching shell than he was in what had allegedly happened on a planet millions of years ago and on the other side of the galaxy—and that was definitely not his fault.

"That thing is fracking huge," Jason said, shaking his head at the size of the shell. "How the hell do you make something like that?"

"You didn't hear?" Martin said. "It's printed."

"Printed?" Jason said, shaking his head. "Like 3D printed."

"Yeah," Martin said. "Not, like, the whole thing. It's got segments that are two hundred kilometers long, about a hundred and fifty wide, that were printed. Then it's welded together."

"Where do you buy a printer that big?" Jason asked. "eBay?"

"I dunno," Martin admitted. "But these robots built on a big scale. They also think it might be about a million years old. They don't know but that's what they're saying."

"Who are 'they' by the way?" Jason asked. "Some internet rumor?"

"Nah," Martin said. "There's science teams working for the government that are studying it."

"I wasn't really keeping up with the news," Jason said. "Little busy staying alive."

"Stayin' alive, stayin' alive, uh, uh, uh, uh," Martin sang. Badly.

"Seriously?" Jason said. "Disco? You don't look that old."

"Class of '80, man."

"Snowboarding and skating?"

"There was snowboarding and skating in the eighties, man," Martin said. "'Course back then, you didn't grind, man. Not when it took a week to make the boards yourself by hand. I was semipro till I messed up my knee. That's when I got into flying. You can fly a plane with a messed-up knee."

"I had two printed, courtesy of the VA," Jason said. "Got real ones back, now."

"You were a vet?" Martin said. "Thank you for your service."

"You're welcome," Jason said as they approached the portal.

"Need to call my partner," Jason said, holding up his phone.

"Cool," Martin replied.

"Tim's on another call," Jewel said.

"When he gets free," Jason replied.

"Jason, my man," Tim said a moment later. "Inbound."

"I was gonna call feet wet but I got to talking," Jason said.

"Not that you ever do that," Tim said. "And where you were, feet wet was not necessarily a good thing."

"Roger," Jason said, chuckling. "We set up?"

"Storage is arranged as is distribution," Tim said. "Which I would point out is the log guy's job."

"I've been busy," Jason said. "Though, honestly, half the time I could have done it from the ground. I'm going to grab a shower and try to find some clothes that half fit at least. Where should we meet and when?"

"We've got a packaging area," Tim said. "Commercial space is also units and in this case one of our investors held some of the units. Which helped because much of that stuff is rucked up right now. But it's got office space attached to it. Meet there?"

"Have your AI talk to my AI," Jason said. "We'll do lunch."

"Fresh would be nice," Tim said.

"In fact..." Jason said, smiling. "One of the things I thought of was exactly that. So, I cooked some extra and put it in stasis. So, yes, we'll do lunch."

"There's no furniture," Tim said then shrugged. "We can eat on the floor."

"You should have played more with flexmet," Jason said. "We're approaching the station. Not sure where the office is at or how long it will take to get the stuff transferred."

"The office and warehouse are in Carolina and you're going into one of the Carolina ports," Tim said. "Or you should be. That's what we're paying for."

"Carolina Five according to the sign," Jason said, looking up as they entered.

"Maddie says it will take about twenty minutes from where you're going in for you and the cargo," Tim said.

"Can I grab a shower first?" Jason asked. "I know you're jonesing for some fresh but..."

"Figure two hours, then?" Tim said. "I can wait that long."

"Two hours it is," Jason said. "Out here."

"Can I make that, Jewel?" Jason asked.

"With a *long* shower," Jewel said.

# CHAPTER 12 >>>>>>>>>

JASON WAS FEELING REFRESHED AS HE WALKED DOWN THE COR-
ridor to the new Brandywine offices. The hallway, being commercial space, was undecorated. Most of the space was still empty.

When he got to the office, after a long walk down several
passages, it had the Brandywine logo prominently on the walls.

The logo was a simple line drawing in black and white of a
winding stream surrounded by trees. A fish was jumping out of
the stream while a buck drank from it. Overhead a sketch of an
eagle flew by. In the background was one of the stratovolcanoes.

It was a simple graphic but it would scale well, which Jason had
learned was important during a brief stint as a graphic designer.

The door to the office dilated and he entered another empty
gray room. There were two doors off the front room, one to the
right, one to the left on the far wall. Both were open.

"Honey, I'm hoooome!" Jason called.

"Hi, Jason, right?" a brunette said, sticking her head in the
front room. "We're back here exploring."

"Hi?" Jason said as he walked to the back. Beyond the door
there was a cross corridor that opened to both doors. Tim was
just stepping into the hall.

"Welcome to our offices," Tim said.

"I'm Debra," Debra said, holding out a hand. "Debra Weid-
man. I go by Deb."

Deb was a well set up brunette who looked about sixteen.

"Jason Graham," Jason said. He'd washed off enough that the hand probably didn't smell like fish or croc. "Should I ask you your favorite song from high school?"

"Heh. I hate to admit it. Mariah Carey, 'Vision of Love.'"

Jason waggled a finger back and forth and lifted an eyebrow.

"We had a thing going before the Transfer," Tim said, shrugging.

"Cool," Jason said. "Boston. 'More than a Feeling.' Though it was from a few years earlier."

"Where's the *food*, Log?" Tim asked.

"Where's the *cargo*, Ops?"

"This way," Tim said, holding up his phone. "We're already shipping shrimp."

"Do tell," Jason said.

"We sent packages to all the investors and had them spread the word," Tim said. He expanded the phone to a screen and brought up some charts with a set of numbers. As Jason looked, one set of numbers was going up, another down. "Total sales, available inventory," Tim said, pointing at the numbers.

"Can you slug that to mine?" Jason asked. They entered a large open area and he looked around. "There should be cases or something."

"This is office space," Tim said, casting the numbers to Jason's phone. "It's more office space than we needed but it was attached to the warehouse. We're getting a deal on it. We're only renting the warehouse and the front offices right now. And there's no office furniture. But it's home."

He pointed to Jason's screen to sort out the graphics.

"On-hand cases by type, on-hand coffins by type, total sales, this graph, that little line, that's where we make a profit on this voyage."

"Does that count total profit?" Jason asked. "And does that growing red bar mean we're approaching profitable already?"

"No and yes, in that order," Tim said. "But at this rate we're going to be profitable overall very quickly. You were right, people are buying. Fast."

"That's something to talk about over lunch."

They finally reached the warehouse and Jason looked around. The warehouse, like the offices, had a smell of metal, flexmet and ozone. The "new part of the station" smells he'd gotten used to.

There also weren't any conexes. Just coffins and cases. And they only took up about a third of the floor space of the warehouse.

"They came in that way," Tim said. "The conexes got left behind apparently."

Cases were flying off one of the piles and entering tunnels on the left and far wall.

"Jewel," Jason said. "We've got interior tractors?"

"We do," Jewel said.

"Sweet," Jason said, looking around for empty floor space. "Bring over my personal container with the cooked meals in it."

"Real food?" Debra said, grabbing Tim's arm. "Wait, you cooked?"

"I've been a bachelor for years," Jason said. "I can cook."

Jason first pulled out flexmet and made a table and chairs for Deb and Tim. He used his camp chair. Then he pulled out the case with cooked food.

The idea had occurred to him when he had leftovers. With stasis it made as much sense to just cook one batch of food and keep some of it for later. He opened up the case and removed a flex package, opening it on the table to reveal some one-inch sections of green stems.

"Let's start with these," Jason said. He opened his pack and laid a bottle of ranch dressing on the table then made a cup from flex for each of them and poured ranch in each. "I haven't named it, yet, but it's crunchy and green and tasty. It's a herbaceous ... weed more or less. This is from the stem of the weed. Like milkweed but nontoxic. I thought about just calling it Crunchy Green Tasty."

Debra took one of the stems, dipped it in the ranch and took a bite.

"Oh, yeah," she said, sighing. "That's actual *food*. I was about out and down to print."

"They're fine by themselves," Jason said, dipping in the ranch and trying it. "Oh, yeah, that is *great* with the ranch!"

"Did you get much?" Tim asked, taking a bite. "We could make money off this. Is it peeled?"

"Yes," Jason said. "But before you start thinking about labor, there's ways for flex to peel it."

"Flexmet?" Tim said. "The wall stuff?"

"That stuff is amazing," Jason said. "You can do anything with it. Don't invest in utensils."

He made a set of tongs, picked up another stem and dipped it in the ranch.

"It is extremely useful," Debra admitted.

"Attached to a phone or a drone it can do most of the cleaning," Jason said. "It was the tractors and flex that cleaned those ginormous crocs."

"I saw the video of that," Debra said, her eyes going wide. "Oh, my God!"

"You...you..." Tim said, pointing a finger at Jason. "You... you...I thought *I* was nuts."

"What else was I gonna do?" Jason asked, popping in another stem. "Let it eat me?"

"You need a bigger gun," Tim said. "This partnership is going well. I don't need to break in another one."

"I definitely need a bigger gun," Jason admitted. "It's on my to-do list. But let's talk future for a moment," he added, pulling out another package. This contained boiled shrimp. "Sorry, they're head on."

He made a bowl for shells and heads then plates for all three, then pulled out preheated margarine for dipping.

"I'm going in with hands," Jason said, pulling out a bunch of shrimp. "But I don't have any wet wipes or towels. I've got a rag with me but it's seen better days."

"There is a company that is making paper towels," Tim said, pulling out some shrimp.

"I've never done this," Debra said, cautiously.

"You pull off the head, toss it in the discard bowl," Jason said, doing the action. "Then pull off the legs, in the bowl, then peel off the shell, in the bowl. Pull the meat out of the tail. Tail goes in the bowl. Then dip in what should be clarified butter and eat." He ended by popping the whole jumbo shrimp in his mouth. Some of the shrimp were massive, nearly the size of adult tiger prawns.

"There's more runs starting," Jason said around the mouthful of shrimp. "We need to set up more camps to collect them. Which means more equipment."

"I had to take a loan on the containers we sent," Tim said, looking at his phone again. "But when Richard sees this, we can probably talk. Carter, has Richard seen this yet?"

"These are deposits to the Brandywine account," the AI responded. "I'm sure he's seen them."

"Good," Tim said, sighing. "If we're sending down people, we're going to need outdoorsmen. I've got a long list of Ranger buddies."

"Rangers," Jason said with a snort then whistled a snippet of "Pop Goes the Weasel."

"Watch yourself, there, buddy," Tim growled.

"If we're going for former military we need SF not Rangers," Jason said.

"You and SF," Tim said, shaking his head. "I'm not going to use the term 'wannabe' but..."

"Watch it, there, buddy," Jason said. "Rangers get trained on basic survival. SF eats lives and breathes it. Pop quiz: What's the nickname for a Green Beret?"

"Point," Tim said after a second and shrugged.

"What *is* the nickname for a Green Beret?" Debra asked. "Sorry, I'm promilitary but don't really have any background in it."

"Snake eater," Tim said. "Because you can drop them in the wilderness and they'll survive on snakes."

"Whoever we use, it's going to have to be at their own risk and there *is* risk. Also, they're going to need *at least* a .30-06 and preferably something larger."

"That might be the main criteria," Tim said, finishing off his shrimp. "Do you own a big gun and do you have extensive wilderness experience?"

"Those two are frequently at odds," Jason pointed out. "Not many jobs that involved the out-of-doors made anyone enough to afford big guns."

"There have to be professional hunters on the station," Tim said. "Guides. African guides. We don't just have Americans."

"Point," Jason said.

"That's all the shrimp?" Tim said, looking in the bowl. "That's it?"

"Oh, but that was just the second course, Monsieur," Jason said, affecting a French accent. "Now we move on to the fish course."

"This isn't the fish course?" Debra asked.

"That was more the crustacean course," Jason said, pulling out another container. "We're going to use the same plates, sorry."

He opened up the container to reveal several large pieces of cooked fish, still piping hot.

"Blackened barramundi with a slightly piquant strawberry-banana and mango chutney," Jason said. "Bon appetit..."

〈〈〈〉〉〉

Besides the barramundi there were grilled skewers of crocodile with blueberry-pepper sauce, barbequed ribs of wild hog, and a dessert of mixed fruits.

"Jason," Tim said, leaning back in his chair and rubbing his stomach. "You are going to make someone a fine wife someday."

"I've heard that one before," Jason said.

"I had no clue you could cook," Tim added. He looked up at the dwindling piles of containers and shook his head. "And we're watching ourselves making money. This was a good idea. You done good, Log."

"Who's the best, Ops?"

"You're the best, Log," Tim said, distracted. He was looking at his phone and nodding. "We can easily afford more drops. We're going to have to get Richard to agree to the loans."

"Let me," Jason said, picking up his phone. "Jewel, Monica."

"Wondered when you were going to call," Monica said, picking up immediately. She raised a rib in front of her face. "When did *you* learn to cook?"

"I told you back *then* I knew how to cook," Jason said. "You always insisted on cooking."

The phone swung around and Richard was revealed wiping his face with a linen napkin.

"If you're going to ask for another loan..." Richard said, picking up his own phone and looking at it, "we can... *certainly* discuss it."

"I sent pretty much the same thing to Richard and Monica," Jason said to Tim. "Along with a care package of raw food and some flowers. And, yes, we're looking at plans to send down multiple parties, Richard. But each party will need more gear so a slightly higher loan."

"You seem to have done well enough," Richard said, frowning. "Though from that video of the crocodile... I don't know much about guns but..."

"Yeah," Jason said. "I need a bigger gun. It's on my to-do list. We need an additional small tractor for each party plus twice as much flexmet and twice as many drones. That will add another ten thousand on the loan per team. But once we've got enough equipment at a certain point, we'll just reuse it."

"Is all that *necessary*?"

"Richard, Tim," Tim said, picking at some of the leftover ribs.

"Is it, based upon our returns and the money we're putting in your bank, a good *banking* decision?"

Richard thought about that and glanced at his phone again.

"So far so good," he replied. "Certainly reasonable."

"Then let *me* worry about the business side," Tim said. "By the way, we've hardly sold...a fifth of the *shrimp* returned so far. We have a mass of other materials to sell and haven't even put that on the market yet.

"Based on my conversation over dinner with Jason, I'd say the additional drones, bots and flex will enhance profitability. There were times where Jason had to make do, skip opportunities, or was on the edge of the line given the paucity of equipment. It's a good business call to add the equipment.

"The standard package for one of these operations should include fifty drones, two small tractors, a medium tractor and one metric ton of flexmet at a minimum. Jason has been talking nonstop about all the uses of flexmet. I can see why he wanted more. We're going to have to wait for the capital to come up a bit because we're also going to be leasing more birds. Jason was only a few days into the shrimp run. The harvest system is still in place. We'll be pulling shrimp for a month at least. And he's identified ten more inlets that should have runs on them as well. Even if the run doesn't materialize, we can fill multiple ships with fish and meat as well...well, you've seen examples."

"Thank you for the flowers," Monica chimed in. "They're beautiful."

"Flowers?" Debra mouthed.

Jason held up a finger.

"I'll send you the full request tomorrow," Tim said. "But we'll need a quick decision. Shrimp runs are seasonal and we need to jump on this opportunity while it lasts."

"Send me the data," Richard said. "And, Jason, thank you for this lovely dinner."

"Let's get together sometime," Jason said, taking the phone back. "I'll buy."

"I'll let you," Richard said. "Ta."

"That's your ex?" Debra said.

"Greatest wife ever," Jason said then laughed. "*Except* for her cooking. The woman could not cook to save her life. Print food is better. I kept *begging* her to let me cook but 'It's the wife's job!' I lost weight living with her. I was always saying I was on a diet."

"You never told me that," Tim said, chuckling.

"She is going to take that lovely food and turn it into the most *God-awful* meals," Jason said, laughing. "I hadn't even thought about that part. I heard that she and Richard used to go out to dinner all the time!" He couldn't stop laughing.

"There'll eventually be restaurants again," Tim said, laughing. "He can survive on print food."

"Richard will eventually have an office," Jason said, wiping his eyes. "I'll send him a care package from time to time. Oh, my God! I'd been thinking about how his clothes still fit so well and that he'd never gained any *weight!*"

On the way back to his compartment, Jason thought about the future now that there was one.

Tim could handle this company with his eyes closed. And, frankly, was as good on the ground.

But Jason was finally making money. The thing to do was not lose it. One way to not lose it was to not spend it. Rich people got rich by not spending money.

Not his strength. He'd have to try it.

But he'd been around enough to know that money just went away if you weren't good with it. He needed some help. Personal help.

He hated making the call again but he had to.

"Jewel. See if Richard is available again."

"I said yes to the loan, Jason," Richard said a moment later.

"I'll make it short," Jason said. "I need an accountant, a personal financial manager who can work with the accountant and an attorney. 'Cause if I'm making money and I don't get some professionals involved, I'll lose it just as fast as I make it."

"Carla," Richard replied. "Pull up the top three of those I know, slug a reason that I'm giving the recommendation. Notably Brandywine Foods."

"Will do, Mister Derren," his AI replied.

"Anything else?" Richard asked.

"Nope," Jason said.

Richard looked sideways for a moment then sighed.

"You could have warned me what her cooking was like!" he whispered.

"Good luck, Richard," Jason said, laughing as he disconnected.

# CHAPTER 13 >>>>>>>>>>

"YOU HAVE A CALL FROM A TIM GILHOOL WHO IS A REFERENCE from Richard as a personal accountant."

"Put him on," Jason said as he stepped into the shuttle. The interstate shuttles were much more crowded than the intrastate ones. At least at this time of day.

"Mister Graham," Gilhool said. "I understand you're looking for an accountant?"

Gilhool had either never changed weight or had already found someone to refit a suit. He was a dry, spare man who looked as if he'd never had a childhood. He looked, in fact, like the picture of an accountant. You knew he had a change purse.

"I am, sir," Jason replied. "Problem being my business partner is named Tim as well so I hope I don't get confused."

"I do business and private accountancy," Gilhool said. "If you're looking for a business accountant."

"I leave that side up to Tim," Jason said. "And there we go with the confusion. I've run a business before and it went tits up. Part of that was just bad luck, but mostly it was not being good with money. Which is why I need a personal accountant."

"And I am extremely available," Gilhool said. "Most people are not good with money. It's good that you're at least aware of that. Most people are also unaware."

"I know my strengths and weaknesses," Jason said. "I'm also getting a financial manager and an attorney. The way I look at those three things, accountant, financial manager and attorney: the accountant's job is to keep you from losing your money, the financial manager's job is to turn it into more, and the attorney's job is to keep people from stealing it. Does that make sense?"

"It's as good a description as any," Gilhool replied. "Have you chosen the financial manager? The note from Richard said you were looking for one of those and I should offer input."

"I have not and I would accept input, sir," Jason said.

"I would recommend James R. Allen," Gilhool said. "He's a former partner with Morgan Stanley. He's forming his own company at the moment and looking for clients. All of us castaways are looking for clients, to be honest."

"What were you?" Jason asked.

"I had my own firm," Gilhool replied. "And I'm rehiring as I have the hours."

"Well, you can have some from me," Jason said. "Here's the thing. I hate money. I mean, I love having it, but I hate worrying about it and I've had to worry about it most of my life. It stresses me out to even *think* about it. So much that I just had dinner with my business partner and what I was wondering the whole time was: Do I get any cash out of this? And I couldn't even ask him. I was afraid to. I know we're making money but... I don't really know if I *have* any."

"You think of money as stuff you can spend," Gilhool said.

"Yes," Jason said. "I sort of get the concept of business capital but... This is asking a lot but could you sort of ask? For me?" Jason ended plaintively.

"That's not normally the accountant's job," Gilhool said with a dry chuckle. "But... yes, of course."

"I'd like to just give *you* the money and *you* figure it out," Jason said. "How much to do in investments, what my budget is, the whole works. Just put some cash in my personal account every month. Because if *I* touch it, it'll be gone before I know it."

"What do you... do?" Gilhool asked. "What's your business if I may ask?"

"Oh, I went down to the planet and brought back a bunch of raw foods," Jason said. "Mostly shrimp, fish and game meat. One thing I'm going to need, though, and it is *need*, is a bigger rifle. I don't know if you know anything about guns, but .30-06 will NOT do it."

"On Bellerophon, I would think *not*," Gilhool said. "It might be the Swiss Army knife of rounds, but Bellerophon is somewhere for a *very* big knife. You went down there with only a .30-06?"

"Garand," Jason said. "I had my Savage as well but I never broke it out. It was the best I had. Wait. You know guns?"

"I've been on hunting trips all over the world," Gilhool said. "Before the Transfer of course. I won't say that half of the material in storage is trophies but there are quite a few. I'm looking forward to going down. But only with a professional guide and my Weatherby .460. Ought Six? Good Lord. We'll see how long you *last* as a client."

"I talked to Gil..."

James R. Allen might as well have been Richard's cousin. He had the same square-jawed look, the same sort of suit, the same overall demeanor that screamed "I'm a money guy."

"He said you're one of those clients who's afraid of money."

"Terrified," Jason said. "I hate to even think about it except when I have enough to spend then I spend too much and wonder why I don't have any."

"Okay," James said, chuckling.

"Gil," Jason said. "Mr. Gilhool?"

"The same," James said.

"That makes things easier," Jason said. "My business partner is named Tim."

"Gil doesn't like to be called Tim," James said. "He apparently grew up being called Tiny Tim and loathes it."

"I hope I didn't offend," Jason said.

"First, you're the client," James replied. "If a client offends, you can drop the client but otherwise it just happens. And he didn't say anything about it. I understand you know Richard Derren as well? And his lovely wife, Monica? Now *I've* spoken amiss, haven't I?"

He'd spotted the slight grimace.

"Monica was my second wife," Jason said. "She dumped me for Derren."

"Ouch," James replied. "Sorry."

"I'm over it," Jason said.

"And your work is as a business partner in a foods company," James said, moving on. "Gil said you are so afraid of money, you asked him to speak to your partner about it."

"Yeah," Jason said, shamefaced.

"Okay," James said, nodding. "Well, you gave Gil permission to discuss your finances with me and I can assure you you're doing fine."

"Okay?" Jason said.

"As the project officer for the project you were being paid a small amount per day," James said. "Since you were mostly eating the food that was there, you really didn't have any costs. Absent ammunition you will have to replace and that is currently going dear. And separate from being the majority partner, when the load has been primarily discharged, you're up for a sizeable bonus as the project officer. Plus, any dividends that may be paid in the future."

"Oh," Jason said. "Okay."

"So, when that comes in, we'll look at investments," James said. "But then there's the question of units. One strategy is to trade one type of unit for another."

"Been doing that from day one," Jason said. "But I'm not sure you'll like the strategy. I concentrated on three things: Fuel mines, carbon refineries and ten grands."

"Ten thousand packs," James said, raising an eyebrow.

Jason explained his disagreement with the report.

"Bottom line is I'm a science fiction fan," Jason concluded. "And a problem solver. I figure stuff out. Also, to the extent I had a 'career' at any point, it was logistics. There's going to be ways to use the ten grands. I may have to be the one who figures it out. Maybe somebody else will. But they're eventually going to be useful and, in the meantime, they don't cost anything. That's one that I'm standing by."

"Okay," James said, nodding. "It's a reasonable argument."

"How do you get paid, by the way?" Jason asked.

"My firm will get one percent of what we manage for you per year," James said. "There's some discussion about units. What the SEC has concluded is that financial firms can draw upon what the units make. Same amount, one percent."

"That's it?" Jason asked.

"Over time it builds up," James said, shrugging. "Especially if you have good clients. And from what Gil told me, you should be a very good client. Okay, your concentration is in fuel, refineries and large vessels. How much do you have in each?"

"Jewel, can you pass that over?" Jason asked. "I've got a six-teenth of Spaceship Four. I stopped concentrating on that but I also don't want it traded away. Other than that, I haven't really been paying attention."

"It's hard to pay attention to ten million units," James said. "One reason to concentrate them."

"One thing I've been thinking about since being on the planet, though, is drones," Jason said. "We're going to need more. Soon. Which means drone factories."

"There are a hundred million drones in storage," James said. "There are three drone factories but they're regarded much the same as the ten grands. You have other thoughts?"

"Very much I have other thoughts," Jason said. "Five million colony sets. Twenty drones per set, right?"

"Yes."

"I lost two drones on the planet," Jason said.

"How did you *lose* two drones?" James asked.

"One got swatted by an elephant the other got eaten by a vulture it was trying to chase off."

"Okay."

"And I needed *fifty*," Jason said. "The math was obvious to the Cybers. Two percent of the population of the United States could feed the US plus half the rest of the world. One percent with the tech we have could feed the station. The rest stay in orbit. Each colony set uses twenty drones. The factories exist to replace the losses. Obvious."

"And it will take at least two years to get all the sets on the ground," James said. "Which will then use up the government drone storage. At which point the factories might have some value."

"Yeah," Jason said. "Except that assumes two years. That assumes people won't figure out better ways. The ten grands for example. And it assumes that the people on the station don't *want* to go to the planet. Gil's a hunter. You interested in the outdoors?"

"We used to go hunting together," James said. "And, yes, I'm interested in going to the planet."

"There are more outdoor-oriented people on this station than the average, guaranteed," Jason said. "We're going to want more drones than the Cybers expected and sooner than most people expect. That's my take on the subject. I don't want you to bet the farm, but it's something that I'd lean towards. Either as cash investments or trading units. Or both."

"I'll keep that in mind," James said. "Are you using your AI to trade units? That's the usual fashion."

"I am," Jason said. "Jewel, add that now that we're not going for Spaceship Four anymore."

"Will do," Jewel said. "Factories aren't trading much. Most people are holding onto those credits. Which one?"

Jason thought about it for a moment.

"All three. Just whatever people want to get rid of."

"People want to get rid of them for things that are more present day," James said. "Ports are turning a heavy profit. So are the smaller ships. Those are working night and day."

"People want some money more than two thousand credits right now," Jason said. "If for no other reason than to get to the planet. To buy some fresh food. I've figured out a way to get paid to go and a way to get paid in part in fresh food. Efficiency of scale. Ten grands are efficiency of scale. Drones are going to be big based on my experience on the planet. Investments, for me, are about long term, not right now."

"I'll keep that in mind as well," James said. "So . . . what's it like?"

"The planet?" Jason said, wondering how to explain the sight of Chindia Mons rising over everything, the splash of bala . . . "Wonderful and terrible. Awe inspiring and butt puckering. All at once."

"Sounds like fun," James said, grinning. "I'll admit to a longing to bag a mammoth."

"Mammoth?" Jason said, laughing. "Mammoth? That's just a big hairy elephant. Jewel, first kill."

"Is that a Garand?" James asked after a moment.

"I know, I know . . ."

"You need a bigger gun! Woof! How long is . . . Ouch! So . . . yeah . . . That explains Gil's comment about how long you're going to last as a client. I thought he meant you were hard to deal with."

"People regularly tell me I'm going to die shortly after saying 'Hey, y'all, watch this!'" Jason said, grinning. "As I told the pilot, it was the fifth craziest thing I've ever done. So far. But . . . that's my job now. Clearing out crocs and other critters so I can bring fresh food to the station."

"Now I'm wondering, again, if I should give up the finance gig and just become a professional hunter," James said. "It's a very devout hobby. I'd considered it on Earth more than once."

"Don't know how much time this 'finance gig' takes up," Jason said. "But once things settle down a bit, you could probably combine. Honestly. I spent a good bit of time just sitting on top of containers. If I was the type to run the business, I could have run it from the ground. The connection is FTL, faster than light, which is cool. I mean, there's no lag to the ground. And the AIs can probably digitize in that you're wearing a suit or something."

"It's a thought," James said, nodding. "But . . . I think, maybe, I'll keep it as a hobby for now. This finance gig is quite exciting enough in this . . . very chaotic environment. May I have permission to look at your unit ownership?"

"Yes," Jason said. "And control of trades with the exception of the previous statements. I'm interested in carbon converters, fuel and gas mines and Spaceship Four. Add drone production now."

"The important thing in this environment is to do research into who is *starting* the business," James replied. "All the businesses currently are start-ups and most of business is about people. People are the single biggest variable. The biggest problem for most of the companies is negotiating with the unit holders. You're a major unit holder in Twelve Bravo?"

"Yes," Jason said.

"Interesting," James said.

"How?" Jason asked.

"None of the fuel mines are up and going yet," James said. "Issues with the unit holders. And we're going to need fuel. There's a company that I've been looking at investing in. It's got the best management group that I've seen for a fuel mine. Mix of space physicists and oil company people. Not traditional oil company executives. Things are too chaotic for your average Exxon guy right now. And the Big Oil group that's negotiating left out space experts. Which was a huge mistake in my opinion."

"Agreed there," Jason said.

"There are . . . six major holders of Twelve Bravo," James said distantly. It was apparent he was looking at data on his screen. "You're the ninth largest. Combined they'd have plurality ownership which means they'd have functional control. Have you inputted on any of the facilities you have units in?"

"I put that off," Jason admitted. "Except for Spaceship Four and I only sent out a video on that saying there's going to be a use and it's not costing anything. I was getting practically spammed on it for a while."

"That has been the major issue with unit holders," James said, frowning.

"When everyone owns everything, no one owns anything," Jason said. "It seemed like a good idea..."

"Oh, my God," James said. "You have *twenty-two percent* of Carbon Charlie?"

"I do?" Jason asked.

"You do," Jewel answered.

"How did *that* happen?" Jason asked.

"You told me to trade for it," Jewel answered.

"Most people don't know what a carbon converter is," James said. "So, when asked, they'll trade their credits. Research, again."

"I researched it because of flexmet," Jason said. "That stuff is the very basis of this economy."

"It is useful," James said.

"It is my turn to drily laugh," Jason said. "You haven't been to the planet yet. Also, it slowly wears out when being constantly flexed. And it can't be recycled for all practical purposes. So, there's going to be constant turnover."

"You have enough units to force a vote on a leasing company," James said. "Anyone who doesn't vote, it's an abstention and the voting units win. Since most people don't vote, whatever you choose would probably win. You have functional complete control. There are companies who are interested in leasing the converters. I've looked at those as well. Not as deeply as the fuel mines. The problem is..."

"The fuel mines are fuel and hydrocarbon mines," Jason said. "We need the hydrocarbons for polycarbonates."

"This is not precisely what a personal financial manager is supposed to do," James said. "But if we can get the major unit holders of Twelve Bravo to agree on a company, preferably my preferred company, and get flow going..."

"It means I can get Carbon Charlie up and going," Jason said. "And since fuel is big loads... it's a potential use for Four."

"That's... a possibility as well," James said, nodding.

"I don't know much about business but I sort of understand

the concept of vertical integration," Jason said. "It was what I was aiming for. Including drone production. Most of the mass of drones is flexmet including the propellers."

Jason paused and looked thoughtful.

"People are mostly ignoring all the alerts regarding units right now," Jason said. "I am. They're like spam."

"Which as noted is part of the problem," James said.

"But what if we invited the major holders to dinner?" Jason said. "A real dinner with real food? There were a bunch of things I wanted to do that Tim and Richard weren't too sure about. Put some good food in their stomachs and they were much more amenable."

"Alcohol helps as well," James said.

"Pretty hard to fake fine wines and hundred-and-twenty-year-old scotch," Jason said.

"There was a news story quite a while back," James said, smiling. "Criminals in New York were doing precisely that. With whiskey, it's possible to do it starting from just ethanol. And there is ethanol production on the station. The formulas, because they were part of criminal records, are available to the AIs." He leaned over and came back into view holding a highball with some dark liquid in it. "I've got some twenty-five-year-old Lucullan in my stores. It honestly tastes *exactly* the same. Wines are a little harder."

"Now all we need is a golf course," Jason said, chuckling. "One where you don't have to worry about being eaten."

"You golf?" James asked.

"I've had a couple of jobs where I sort of had to," Jason said. "But it's not a passion like some people. And I'm not good at it. Still got a set of dusty golf clubs in storage." He looked thoughtful then shook his head. "I bet there's a way to set up a golf course here in the station with enough capital. But it's not worth it for this. Is there a this? And what do you call 'this' and what would I get out of it?"

"Besides capital flow from your units?" James said. "It's called putting together a financial package and you generally get a piece of it. How much is negotiable."

"I know nothing about putting together a business dinner," Jason said. "Even when I was with Ruger, I'd just take clients out to dinner at a restaurant. We'd need a venue. One that was

more than just flexmet. A kitchen. A cook or preferably chef...
I can get the food...How soon would we be doing this? If there
is a this?"

"Depends on how fast that can be put together," James said.
"And we would need what you would call 'cash money' to put all
that together alone. The venue and such...One of my potential
clients is a chef. Celebrity chef on Earth but he was made famous
by being a chef in a safari park. He's an expert in turning game
meat into fine meals."

"I'm headed back to the planet, soon," Jason said. "But I can
get Brandywine Foods to assist if there's something in it for them.
Hmmm...I agree to accept you as my personal financial manager
under the conditions set. To be clear: In terms of units I intend to
retain units in Spaceship Four, Fuel Mine Twelve Bravo, Carbon
Converter Charlie and will begin moving into drone production
facilities. Jewel, stop acquiring on Converter Charlie and Four
and start moving into drones if you can."

"Will do," Jewel said.

"By the same token, I'm interested in companies that want
to get those up and going," Jason said. "But I won't want all my
eggs in one basket."

"Definitely not," James said.

"I'm interested in putting together a financial package, including units and capital, on those facilities. I'll use my influence in
Brandywine Foods to, at the least, provide food for a venue, to
be determined, to have business dinners and possibly more. I'll
need to talk to my business partner and I'll put him in contact
with you if that's okay."

"I agree to that," James said. "And it will help if we can get
it set up. In return, as a favor to a client...I have an extensive
gun collection. If you *promise* not to lose it or get it destroyed,
would you like the loan of a .458?"

# CHAPTER 14 >>>>>>>>>

SAM WAS LAUGHING AROUND THE EDGES OF HIS TUMBLER. HE threw back the alcohol, which tasted like any Earth whisky, and managed not to choke on it.

When he put the tumbler back on the bar, Pastor Mickey was sitting at the stool next to him.

"Where'd my friends go?" Sam looked around, baffled.

"Were they your friends?" Mickey's voice was mild, but somehow managed to imply that the other drinkers hadn't been Sam's friends at all, they'd just been other drinkers.

Which was true.

"They were all I have," Sam said. "Hit me again."

The bartender nodded and poured him another.

"You look like you've had a couple."

Sam wanted to get angry, but the truth was that Pastor Mickey had a very nonjudgmental way to say things. He smiled a lot and he laughed easily, like a guy who didn't take himself too seriously.

"Don't worry, I'm about out of money." Sam took a sip. "I never signed up for teetotalling, anyway."

"You got anything that resembles a beer?" the pastor asked the bartender. Leaning in close to Mickey, he whispered, "Neither did I."

"All right, Pastor Mickey, what are you going to get after me for?"

"Nothing." Mickey got his beer in a tall glass and took a sip. "Just saying hello to my friend Sam."

"I don't have a job," Sam said.

"Okay. How you doing?"

Sam didn't mention that he'd stolen a few personal items from his neighbors, fencing them for cash. He felt his cheeks turn a little red.

"I figure the food and board here is free," Sam continued, "even if it's bad."

"Seems to be the case," Mickey agreed. "But how you are doing?"

"Sooner or later, they'll dump me on the planet. I'll get a job then. I don't even care what it is."

"I'm going to go out on a limb and guess you're not feeling your best."

"I miss her, Pastor Mickey."

"I do too." Mickey sipped his beer again. "I miss the way she always wanted to talk about the poor. I know she meant it."

"I miss the way she was so excited that she was going to get to vote." Sam sniffed. "I was pretending that I was going to vote for Joe Biden."

Mickey coughed, spitting beer back into his glass.

"It just occurred to me that, if there is a liberal system somewhere, Joe Biden might be there now, twenty years old."

"On the plus side, maybe she'll get to vote for him, after all."

"I read this suggestion once," Mickey said. "Things that have been around a long time, you should expect them to stick around a long time still. As a rough rule of thumb, I mean."

Sam thought about it.

"Like...knives," he suggested. "They've proven themselves useful, they're not going anywhere. And tables. And books."

"You'd been dating Julie, what? Three years?"

Sam nodded.

"So, you know, give yourself time."

Sam nodded again. "You think it was all bullshit?"

"Your relationship with Julie?"

"God," Sam said. "The Bible. I mean, Jesus suffered for all mankind's sins, right?"

"Yes," Mickey agreed.

"What about the Cybers' sins?" Sam asked. "And the sins of the AIs? Do the AIs sin? And you never answered me about the rapture and the resurrection and stuff. What do you really think?"

Mickey sat back and looked up at the ceiling. He might have been praying silently.

"I guess I think two things," he finally said.

"Good." Sam finished his drink. "I can count to two."

"First," Mickey said, "is maybe you shouldn't be thinking about a job. Maybe you should be thinking about divinity school."

Sam snorted and shook his head.

"Thing two?"

"We're going to need preachers and churches on the planet. Thing two is that there have always been mysteries about the gospel that man didn't understand. Now, if anything, there are a few more mysteries."

"Amen," Sam said.

"You could say the same about the Pegasus System," Pastor Mickey said. "And you could also say the same thing about love."

Sam looked into the bottom of his tumbler, pretending he didn't already know it was empty.

"How big's your tab?" the pastor asked.

"I had three," Sam said.

"Tell you what," Mickey offered. "You promise to knock off drinking for the night and go home, I'll cover you."

"I'm not sure what Brandywine gets out of this," Tim said, frowning. "You're the majority partner and it helps you out..."

"That's something for you to negotiate with James," Jason said. "Brandywine can have part of the value of the package, assuming it can be put together, and that's an annuity to Brandywine. The best companies don't just leave their capital in the bank; they put it to use. This is putting the capital, and our access to fresh foods, to use."

"I'll talk to James," Tim said. "But we agreed that business decisions were to be left to me."

"And I agree with that, still," Jason said calmly. "It might not be the right decision. But when you've talked, we'll talk again and let me hear your objections and see if I have a different take. I'm not wedded to this but I'd like to get the stuff I've concentrated my units on up and going. If you decide it's not in Brandywine's best interest, I'll probably take part of my cut in materials and set it up, anyway. And if you'd prefer it that way, I'm fine with that. Okay, where are we at on putting down another package or packages?"

"We agreed that we need you to train people," Tim said.

"Not that the people we're sending down can't figure things out themselves. But it gets ahead of the learning curve."

"Train the trainers," Jason said, nodding.

"I've picked six people," Tim said. "On our discussion: Two are former Ranger Regiment with extensive hunting experience. Two are former SF Group. Ditto. Two are civilian hunters with extensive backgrounds. I'll take your input on all of them..."

"A chi...?" Jason said, looking at the photos and basic profiles then stopped. "Oh."

"Yeah," Tim said, grinning. "I knew her from being in the Regiment. She came in as a shooting instructor."

"She...should do," Jason said, going into the deep background. "Actually, my balls are drawing up a little. They all agreed to nondisclosures, right? I don't want all our methods becoming common knowledge."

"They all are under NDAs," Tim said. "Per your suggestion, if they figure out anything long-term useful, they get a piece of that. Both in terms of methods, IP, and in terms of new foods."

"Good," Jason said. He'd been willing to insist on that one and was glad Tim hadn't bitched much. "They're aware that most of them are going to have to go in stasis?"

"They're all aware," Tim said.

"I've been thinking about the dinner for another reason than the financial package," Jason said. "We need to think about something like a test kitchen. We're not going to have access to spices and herbs that are terrestrial for a while. If we can set up a kitchen and get a few good chefs, we put them together with the stuff we're finding and they can come up with recipes. That's more medium term but it's something we should talk about."

"I'll put it on the 'to be considered' pile," Tim said. "When did you set up the meat processing center? I came in this morning and we were already shipping meat. Good prices, too."

"Last night," Jason said, shrugging. "I told you it wasn't going to be hard. By the way, thanks for being willing to talk to my accountant."

"You really had no idea you were making money?" Tim said, chuckling. "You're one of the easiest business partners ever."

"I had to borrow a .458 for this," Jason said. "Speaking of which, do they have the guns and ammo for this?"

"All of them are either professional hunters or have extensive civilian experience," Tim said. "So, yeah, they all have a better gun collection than you do. I told them they're limited to one coffin for personal gear including guns."

"Yeah," Jason said. "I can cut to one coffin. I didn't use most of the stuff I took."

"You're the boss," Tim said. "Take as much gear as you want. And on that matter: You *are* the boss. This is a group of total Alphas. Ensure that they know you're the boss. For one thing, there's going to be conflicts. You have to resolve them. They're also professionals so you shouldn't have too many issues. But your job is to train them and resolve conflicts. Best if you don't let them kill themselves."

Jason strode into the warehouse trying to look as confident as possible carrying a steel bar like a marshal's baton.

The group of six prospective contract Harvest Officers were mostly standing around chatting. The exception was Melanie Storm, the only female. She was seated on a flexmet chair more or less surrounded. She didn't look uncomfortable about it, though.

Jason had had Jewel arrange a coffin and a case against the wall of the warehouse, a hundred kilos of flexmet on the floor, and a small and a large tractor. Then Debra led them into the warehouse and left them there.

"Good to see you all," Jason said. They'd all arrived early, which was good and expected. "You, Ms. Storm, are going to do *just fine*," he continued, taking a parade rest position in front of the wall.

"The pile of flexmet was a test. To see if you'd make yourselves chairs. So, everybody grab a handful and set up chairs here," he said, gesturing in a semicircle.

Jason had taken to just keeping wristlets of flexmet and he extended a tentacle to the pile, formed a table and set the bar of steel down on it.

"You've probably introduced yourselves but so everyone's on the same page," Jason said, gesturing to the guy on his left. "Right to left, name, background, short resumé."

"Jay Ritchie." Short and blonde, he had a bulky build. "Uh, former Ranger Regiment, hoowah? Third Batt. War on Terror, hoowah? Stans, Iraq. Got out, merced up for a while. I'd spend all my money on hunting rifles and going hunting. Safaris, stuff like that. Got tired of that, moved to Alaska and became a professional hunter and guide. Covers most of it, hoowah?"

"Roger," Jason said. He suspected everyone was going to get tired of him inserting "hoowah." "Next."

"Scott Duncan." Narrow waist, really wide shoulders, dark hair, ears like cauliflower buds. "Similar. Ranger Regiment. Desert Storm. Some time in the Balkans. Ten years, got out, moved home to Wyoming, went back to what I did in high school, hunting guide. Moved to Alaska after a while. Professional hunter and guide."

"Roger," Jason said. "Ms. Storm?"

"Melanie Storm," Storm said. Blonde, blue, five foot seven, solid build. "Yes, real name, born with it. Grew up hunting and shooting in Montana. Dad was a competition long-range shooter. Took every national competition in high school. Got recruited to join the Army to be part of Army Marksmanship Training Unit. My MOS was cook." She gave a grin at that one. "MOS didn't matter. After cook's school I never lifted another pan. Went straight to AMTU.

"Set the all-time record, which remains, at Camp Perry on thousand yard which got me sergeant's stripes. Got out as a staff sergeant, went back to professional shooting and hunting. I was somebody rich people would hire to go on safari with them."

"You may not enjoy this as much as you think," Jason said. "We're going to be in woodlands. Relatively short range. Longest shot I took was a hundred and thirty meters."

"Does it get me on that planet with a gun in my hand?" Storm asked, grinning.

"Point," Jason said to the chuckles. "Next."

"John Dovey." Tall and spare with blonde hair, sharp blue eyes, high cheekbones and a chiseled jaw. He looked like Hollywood casting had been told "We need somebody who *screams* German Army in World War Two!" "Ex–South African Army. Recce. Special operations for those unfamiliar. Officer. Got out, also spent some time as a security contractor, went back to hunting for a living." He ended the description with a nod.

His full bio had included that he'd done more than just "security contracting." There were hints at something more like hitman.

"Next," Jason said.

"Kevin O'Callaghan." O'Callaghan was a burly guy, six foot

two, brown hair, brown eyes, who was definitely regrowing a beard and hair. He had the biker look to the bandana around his head. You knew there was a Harley in his personal property storage. "Green Beret NCO. Long time ago. Owned a bar in Key West. Hunted and fished everything you could hunt and fish on Earth That Was. Was pretty much retired by the Transfer."

"*How* long time ago?" Scott Duncan asked.

"Back when *I* was in, Rangers were called Long Range Reconnaissance Patrols," O'Callaghan answered. "This is sort of junglish terrain. Spent *lots* of time in jungles."

Five tours in Vietnam. Two silver stars, three purple hearts, MACV-SOG. *That* much time in jungles. And from his full bio he'd owned more than "a bar" in Key West. He'd built up a business development company from scratch that owned half the businesses in the Keys.

"Last," Jason said as the group nodded.

"Kevin Surber." The guy was built like a slab and leaned forward as if he intended to headbutt his way through the conversation. His accent was a grew-up-in-the-holler twang.

"Former SF. Officer. Nineties. Merced up after 9/11. Spent most of my merc time in Africa and went hunting every chance I got. Grew up with it in Kentucky. Got to the point I was just staying ex-pat in Kenya waiting for the next contract. Finally decided hunting was what I wanted to do for a living. Spent ten years as a guide and professional hunter then the Transfer."

"You've seen my short resumé," Jason said, grinning. "Which, from the point of view of hunting and shooting is the most *minor* resumé here. If we were looking for people to go to the planet, I'd never have made the list. My real resumé, though, is that I've done a lot of *stuff*, all different kinds, and I'm a science fiction fan. I take to this tech like a duck to water. I'm also lazy. Which means I find the most efficient way to do a job then let it run.

"So, let's talk about what we're doing and how we're going to do it. And what we are *not* doing.

"Starting with not: This is not a *hunting* expedition. This is not an *exploring* expedition. This is a *harvesting* expedition. We are dropping to the planet to catch *shrimp*. Everything else is secondary. We are there to gather protein to feed the station and make money. It's a commercial fishing expedition. However, much of the secondary *also* fills containers with protein."

He put his hand over his face shame-facedly and peeked out through his fingers.

"You've all seen the crocodile video, right?" he asked.

There were the expected chuckles and Storm snorted.

"A *Garand*?" Storm said, shaking her head. "Seriously?"

"I do *not* have the gun collection you all have," Jason said. "Hell, I'm *borrowing* a .458 this time. And I should note that half of this cargo is crocodile meat," he added, gesturing to the stacked coffins. "That croc filled half a conex. Protein for the station. Okay, quick terminology."

He pointed to the case and coffin leaning against the wall.

"These are called small and medium containers, and the big shipping containers are large," Jason said. "The terms hereby are case, coffin and conex. The two tractors I tend to call bots and I've nicknamed the little one Alfred and the big one Herman. Continuing: Half those coffins are filled with croc meat. Fourteen crocodiles."

"Sixteen," Jewel corrected.

"Sixteen crocodiles," Jason said. "None, as far as I know, as large as the first, but in that range."

"Which you took with a Garand?" Duncan asked, scratching his cheek. "Ballsy."

"Only *one* of which I shot," Jason said. "And that's the point I'm getting to. I could not have . . . It would have been *definitely difficult* to take that many crocs with a Garand or a Safari or a freaking Nitro Express. Not to mention the bruised shoulder and expensive ammo. And you're supplying your own ammo, right?"

"Right," O'Callaghan said.

"So, how'd you do it?" Duncan asked.

"This," Jason said, dropping a strand of flexmet from his wristlet and holding it up. "This is your friend. This is your best buddy. This is my flexmet, there is much like it but this is mine."

He picked up the steel bar, wrapped a strand of flexmet in a visible loop then thinned and retracted.

A section of the bar dropped onto the table.

"*That* is how you kill crocs," Jason said, looking around. Okay, so they were paying attention again. "That is how you collect most of your game meat. Hell, that was how I ended up cutting *firewood*."

"I didn't know it could do that," Dovey said.

"What part of NDA was unclear?" Jason asked. "Jewel, bring up the schematic of the defense net."

The wall of the warehouse flashed up a schematic of the defense and warning net Jason had put in at the camp.

"After the first croc I was kind of panicked, I'll admit," Jason said. "Not so much that I'd get eaten, although they were big enough to snatch me off the top of a conex. The problem was I was there to catch shrimp and the crocs were going to be in the way. So, I set out this thin, broad netting of flexmet to give me some warning..."

He went through a brief description of the development of the defense net.

"This stuff is your best buddy," Jason repeated. He pulled a chunk of flex from the table, tossed it up in a strand to an overhead pipe and lifted himself into the air. "You can climb with it." He took more from the table and formed a breastplate. "You can make armor with it. You can make fishhooks with it and the line. And with the aid of the drones, you can use it to kill, literally, anything."

"Not very sporting," Surber said thoughtfully.

"And that is one thought process to eliminate," Jason said. "What is our mission?"

"Bring protein to the station," Storm said, nodding unhappily. "So, no hunting?"

"I didn't say *that*," Jason said with a grin. "Here's the thing. Our *mission* is to return food to the station. And that is so dead easy, it's going on right now. Jewel, live shot."

The view changed to a shot of the fishing camp and zoomed in on the shrimp catch/load system.

"That's happening *right now*," Jason said. "We are loading food to the conexes, to be transferred to the station, as we speak. So, once you're set up, you have time for hunting. Feel free. But let the bots and the flex and the drones do most of the work.

"Your primary *job*, though, is just *tasting* stuff." He opened up a set of flexmet to reveal various herbs and mushrooms. "The real reason to have people at these sites is as taste testers."

"Taste testers?" Duncan said, cocking an eyebrow.

"The drones can survey and find potentially edible fungi and plants, test for toxicity," Jason said. "But someone has to taste it to see if it's *palatable*. Think about how bad print food tastes. So, you spend a good part of your day just tasting stuff like this," he added holding up a small but broad leaf. "Sheila's Thyme. Tastes close to thyme, looks more like bay leaf. Previously unknown species. Named after my niece." He held up a red mushroom that had a shape similar to a portion of the male anatomy. "Derren's Mushroom. Tastes a bit like a sorrel mushroom."

"Also, a funny shape, hoowah," Ritchie said. "Who's Derren?"

"Derren Bank is the primary bank for Brandywine Foods," Jason said pontifically then smiled. "Richard Derren, president and CEO, is also the guy who married my *ex*."

The whole group laughed at that one.

"It's an incredibly common wild mushroom in the area," Jason said, grinning. "When I sent him and Monica a care package, I made sure there weren't any in it. But at this rate they're going to be all over the station. And it's one of the few I bothered to name. Any new species you get to name. I could barely come up with a name for the river. Go for it. Back to flexmet."

He picked up the cut end of the steel bar and snipped off a smaller chunk then attached it to the end of the flexmet and made a flex machete.

"Best brush clearer you can have," Jason said. "Better than a machete or a boma. I was carrying a kukri. I'll carry one again 'cause magic makes me nervous. But I never used it. Flex was much more useful."

"Will it go through thorn, though?" Dovey asked.

"It will go through a *tree*," Jason said, slicing it through the air.

"It forms a monomolecule?" O'Callaghan asked, furrowing his brow.

"Slightly thicker but not enough to notice," Jason said, nodding. "The stuff is very smart. It-won't-cut-you smart. But it slices and dices anything else. Jewel, video of croc butchering."

The view changed to one of the crocs being processed.

"Speed up three times..." Jason said. "Six...nine..."

As they watched, a headless croc forty feet long was processed by the flexmet, drones and bots.

"It's like watching army ants chop up a frog," Duncan said.

"Do you go by Melanie or what?" Jason asked Storm.

"I go by Mel or Storm," Storm said. "Generally Storm."

"To answer your hunting question, Storm," Jason said, "if things are under control at the camp, fish and shrimp are landing, cases and coffins are being loaded, grab a gun and go for a hike. The drones are going to have mapped everything out and you can use them to track in on game. Not as sporting as back in the 1800s but everybody was starting to use drones back on Earth, right?"

"Never left home without one," Surber said as the others nodded.

"But you also take four drones, an Alfred and a coffin," Jason said. "Drones out in a diamond even if your head *is* on a swivel. And it should *always* be on a swivel. The drones aren't great with small snakes, poisonous spiders, et cetera. And there are unknown threats so take *nothing* for granted. There's eventually going to be a saying: There are old Bellerophon hands, bold Bellerophon hands but there are *no* old, bold... This planet is *lethal* on spades. The Alfred is to help with the game and the coffin is for carrying it back to camp. And in the event you're injured or screw up so completely you get yourself killed..."

"You've already got a coffin available," Duncan said, chuckling.

"The coffins are flexmet and contragravity," Jason said, flattening the coffin and setting it in the air. "In the event you're injured, get on the stretcher. It closes, it opens, you're in the emergency department on the station. Which is why you always take *what* when you're outside camp?" he asked, pointing at Ritchie.

"Four drones, hoowah..." Ritchie said. "One of the small bots, an... Alfred and a coffin. Was having a hard time remembering what you called the bot."

"What's the mission?" Jason asked, pointing at Dovey.

"Protein to the station," Dovey answered. "Trophy hunting dead last."

"That's commander's intent," Jason said. "What's your main job on the ground, Duncan?"

"Tasting unknown foods," Duncan said, nodding. "Mushrooms and plants?"

"Roger," Jason said. "Among your secondary missions is figuring out new and spiffy ways to use all the tech to support the mission. Be. Lazy. Figure out the best way to use the drones, the flex, the bots. You're the trainers of the trainers and train them to use their noggin first and their muscles last. Okay, last item. You all know that five of you are dropping in stasis, right?"

"Willing to defer to the lady on that one," Duncan said, raising his hand.

"Hoowah," Ritchie added with a thumb up.

"Chivalry will get you nowhere," Storm said, but she grinned.

"It's not chivalry, Storm," Dovey said, raising his hand. "It's *world record* at Camp Perry."

"Oh, God," O'Callaghan said, raising his hand. "Even *I'm* in on that one."

"We are going to be doing other drops," Surber said, raising his hand.

"You're outvoted," Jason said, looking at Storm.

"I'll take it," Storm said, shaking her head. "But to be clear, boys, I've been one of the boys since I was a tiny lass. That being said, just because you're being nice, do *not* expect me to be the camp cook. I don't care if it was my MOS. I'll cook, yes, but not as my sole and only job."

"Everybody cooks, everybody scavenges, tastes and hunts, everybody eats," Jason said. "Okay, therewith my brief. Questions, comments, concerns?"

"I hope I never get used to this view," Jason said as the ship left the station.

"It's honestly . . ." Storm said then looked around at the screens. "Okay, it's a pretty cool view. I want to see the planet more or less live."

"Coming up," Tom said.

Since there were "issues" on this drop, Jason had worked to get Tom Ferrell again. The former Air Force driver was a known quantity.

Though they were going to a similar area and a similar river, there was no handy sandbar or clearing to use as a camp site.

So, they were going to have to make one. Which was the "issue" involved.

Jason had some ideas on that one and hoped they'd work out. He'd look like a fool if they didn't.

"How high do you want to drop this stuff?" Tom asked as they approached the port.

"Above treetop," Jason said. "That's about it."

"Just drop it in midair," Tom said.

"Gonna have to," Jason said. "Containers are contragravity. Tractors have lift and drive. They can hold it in place while we work."

"Sure this is gonna work?" Storm asked.

Jason thought about what he wanted to say, which was "How the hell do I know?" but answered as the boss.

"Absolutely," he said with a completely confident tone.

"Alrighty then," Storm said. "But, not worrying or anything, do you have a backup plan?"

"Several," Jason said. "This'll work, Storm. You're not afraid of heights or anything, right?"

"For the third time: No," Storm said.

"Then for the third or so time, yes, it will work," Jason said. "If you don't mind, I need to think about this again."

"Issues?" Storm asked.

"The devil is in the details," Jason said. "You two talk amongst yourselves."

He turned up his earphones and got to work, examining the individual trees in the LZ.

Jason had been so engrossed he'd barely noticed the planet approaching and was startled at the first "thump" of reentry.

"Can you spend enough time to fly around a bit over the LZ?" Jason asked.

"For what you guys are paying me, as much time as you'd like," Tom said. "Not to mention the case of shrimp. No small crocodiles but there were some interesting tropical fish."

"Consider them a bonus," Jason said distractedly.

They were coming in from the northwest, right over the shoulder of Chindia Mons. Jason had to break out long enough to marvel over the massive mountain and the chain that extended out from it. There were clouds surrounding the ice ring, but other than that it seemed as if there wasn't a single cloud in the entire north of Chindia. The view was so clear that it was apparent the stratovolcano was so massive it was depressing the ground underneath and around it. There was still an uplift to it, but the entire continent was at the same time somehow flattened in an arc around it.

That flattening and subsidence, which geologists were pretty sure was ongoing along with erosion, was the primary cause of earthquakes in north Chindia. Jason hadn't experienced any the last visit but they were estimated to be about as common as in California.

On the other hand, nothing was certain about this planet yet. It was all a roll of a dice.

The chosen landing site was a raised space that abutted the as-yet unnamed river and jutted a ridge of rock into it. They slowed rapidly as they approached, Tom's usual entrance sending up clouds of birds as they dropped below the speed of sound, then came in to hover.

"Okay," Tom said. "We're here. Deploying your cargo."

"Roger," Jason said, standing up and picking up the Winchester and slinging it barrel down over his shoulder with flexmet. "Wait for us to deploy the bots."

"Got it," Tom said.

"Ready?" Jason asked as Storm slung her rifle. She was carrying a Dakota Arms Model 76 also in .458 Win Mag. Jason had had to go on the market to find rounds, which were as expensive as he anticipated.

"Always," Storm said, raising an eyebrow. "I'll try anything once."

"And you can drop anything," Jason said. "Once. Jewel, cargo stable?"

"Cargo is stable and holding under the ship," Jewel replied.

"Can we stabilize it with just Herman?" Jason asked.

"Yes," Jewel replied. "Even if the winds get higher."

"Okay," Jason said. "Tom, can you dust off on top?"

"In position and holding," Tom said.

"And awaaay we go...!"

# CHAPTER 15 >>>>>>>>>

THE CONEXES WERE SUSPENDED OVER THE TREETOPS, ABOUT TWO hundred feet over the terrain with the *Excelsior* hovering just above their tops. They were all decidedly stuck together by their flexmet walls. Alfred One and Two were hovering in view above and beyond them and the whole drone swarm was up and behind them, each carrying a large ball of flexmet. All as planned. So far so good.

Jason walked down the passenger stairs and confidently hopped to the top of the nearest conex. That was floating *two hundred freaking feet* off the ground.

No pressure.

The conex didn't even bob from his additional weight but the surface wasn't perfectly solid. He could feel the conexes moving around as Herman, still inside one of them, adjusted to maintain position against the wind.

"Need a hand?" Jason asked as Storm balked at the bottom of the stairs.

"This is officially crazy, you realize that?" Storm said but she hopped off the stairs and landed fine. Then she swayed slightly. "Whoa. Unstable platform."

"You'll get used to it," Jason said as if he'd done this a billion times before.

Nobody had done this before.

"Keep one drone on the conexes," Jason said. "Now we test the stripping method. Get Alfred One over here. I need to see this."

"Roger," Jewel said.

"Deploy the drones," Jason said. "Tom, we're solid. You can continue your schedule."

"Roger that," Tom called. "Good luck."

"Fortune favors the bold," Jason said. "And thanks."

Alfred One came over, wrapped a seat around him and lifted him in the air.

When he was suspended over the forest, he pointed to one of the trees.

"Start stripping on tree one," Jason said.

Two of the drones dropped in through the canopy and there was a sudden sound of dropping branches.

"What is happening?" Storm asked.

"Deploy two drones away from the branches to observe stripping action," Jason said.

The pair of drones had a monomolecule-thin line of flex between them. As Storm watched they would fly up on either side of one of the branches of the forest giant and it would be neatly severed, dropping to the forest floor. Then the tree was topped, leaving a denuded trunk.

The tree was debranched and topped, "stripped," in less than five minutes.

"Back to the conexes," Jason said.

When he landed, he hooked a section of flexmet to his waist, took his rifle and flexed it to the top of the conex then walked to the edge of the conex raft and sat down.

"See if Alfred Two can pull it over by himself using a tractor beam," Jason said.

Storm carefully sat down next to him to watch.

"That's . . . cool and awful at the same time," Storm said.

"Flex has a billion and one uses," Jason said distractedly.

"So, this is the plan," Storm said. "Clear an LZ using bots and drones. You could have said."

"I hate telling people what I'm thinking about," Jason said. "If I get it wrong, and I have, people lose confidence in the boss. So, I keep as much of it to myself as I can until I have to tell people."

Alfred Two had positioned itself near the top half of the tree and a purple beam of light flashed out as it used a pressor beam to push to the side.

The tree bent at first then slowly started to topple.

Branches of other giants were stripped away as the massive tree crashed to the ground.

"Section," Jason said.

Six drones dropped to ground level and started wrapping the trunk in flexmet. In seconds it was sectioned with the lowest section still attached to its massive root ball.

"Now see if the tractors can move the root ball to the specified location," Jason said.

The two bots flashed out blue tractor beams and, obviously straining, picked up the root ball and moved it into position between two other trees.

"Rolling action?" Jason asked.

The bots then moved to the sections of trunk and rolled and stacked them alongside the root ball.

"Chop and fill," Jason said.

The drone swarm dropped to ground level and started cutting up the fallen branches. The sections they could pick up, small branches, they took to the open hole left by the root ball and dropped them in. Sections that were too heavy, the actual limbs of the tree, were picked up by the tractors and moved to the edge of the hole.

"We're not going to want for firewood," Storm said.

Over the next three hours the LZ was cleared out and prepped. A half dozen forest giants were stripped and toppled, their root balls propped up to provide a defense around the camp, their sectioned trunks used to create a wall as well, then their branches used to fill gaps creating a sturdy abatis. When the holes were filled with branches, the tractors would roll the sections of limbs down on top, pressing the mass down with their pressor beams. When the area was clear of all the big trees, the ground was cleared and scraped to level with additional dirt put into the filled root holes.

As the LZ was being cleared, a crocodile turned up. Of course. The river was smaller but the croc wasn't.

The trees and brush along the river had already been cleared and the croc looked into the open area with interest. When trees fell, sometimes food fell with it. Other predators had turned up with the same idea but Jason had had the drones chase them off with sonic blasts.

Crocs ignored those. This one started clambering up out of the river to look for treats.

"Oh, for Pete's sake," Jason said, shaking his head. He'd had Herman move the conex raft around so he could watch the croc.

"Tell me you're not going to kill this one with flex," Storm said.

"Be my guest," Jason said, waving at it. "With one note. I'm aware that you can, metaphorically, shoot the eye out of a gnat at a thousand yards."

"We...did a calculation on that in AMTU," Storm said. "Technically, my MOA was so fine that if it was a bullet exactly as big as a gnat's eye, it would hit the gnat, certainly, somewhere in the skull region at one thousand meters."

"So, you can *literally* shoot the eye out of a gnat," Jason said.

"Assuming a small-enough bullet would make the shot," Storm said. "Yes. I have literally shot the wing off a fly at seven hundred and fifty meters. And I did it to several flies to prove it wasn't a fluke. Flying flies. Without hitting the flies in the body. I did that in high school."

"That is insane," Jason said. "Okay. But anyway. You can feel free to get further away than I was because that was probably... too close, but...not a thousand yards. Roger?"

"Roger that, boss," Storm said. "Alfred, I need a lift!"

"Stormy, grab your gun," Jason muttered as the riflewoman went to grab same.

He watched as she coaxed Alfred into the right position with hand and arm movements and lined up the shot. She was out over the river and because of the angle higher than the container raft.

The croc was in the middle of the clearing, under the raft, so Jason brought up video in time to see the shot.

Hah. The croc *still* thrashed. So, .458 was no better than .30-06. Admittedly, it didn't thrash as long.

"Jewel," Jason said. "Discontinue current evolution and put out the defense net. Hundred meters downstream, fifty meters upstream. Also, after the defense net is out, drag that thing to the river, downstream and downwind, take the head off there and have one of the Alfreds bury the head. Little change with the net this time..."

Finally, the camp clearing was done, the croc carcass had been dragged down to the river, the head was buried in a shallow pit, the defense net was out, already killing crocs, and the raft of containers floated to a gentle landing on more-or-less flat land.

"That was impressive," Storm said. "Usually, you cut the tree down, *then* trim it."

"I worked for a tree-cutting company during one of my down periods," Jason said, looking around. "Lots of climbing, lots of work and very little pay. In stuff like cutting down firs in US forests you trim them after. When you're cutting around houses, you trim them first. Okay, Jewel, deploy Herman then we've gotta fly while the camp gets set. Grab your gun, Storm."

They both got their guns and were picked up by the Alfreds while Herman rearranged the conexes.

Jason had the Alfreds fly them over to the point of rock and landed to watch the conexes be rearranged. This time he arranged it with three of the conexes on the riverside, three on the land side and two on the upstream and downstream. He'd realized he'd been thinking in terms of Earth cargo containers. There were no "doors" on the end you had to access. You could open them from any direction and load them from any direction.

"By hoary tradition and by current law, who first stands on the bank of a river gets to name it," Jason said, waving at the river. "All yours."

"I name this...Storm River!" Storm said.

"Wanna make it Storm County as well?" Jason asked.

"Yes," Storm said.

"Let it be so," Jason said. "Okay, conexes arranged. Alfreds, a lift to the top of the conexes. Jewel, unpack our friends and line them up there," he added, pointing to the riverside of the camp.

There was a steep bank down to the ridge of rock and he didn't see the point of clambering all the way up that and then climbing the conexes.

He got between the river and the coffins and waved his arms. "Open sesame."

The coffins opened and as one the five hunters shot up, holding their rifles.

"Whoa there, Tex," Jason said, laughing.

They all started to climb out and immediately spotted the headless croc as well as the partially submerged carcasses of the other five that had hit the defense net.

"Jesus Crickets," Duncan said, shaking his head. "Yours?"

"Storm," Jason said.

"Only one," she said. "The others were snips."

"The perimeter water fence is slightly different this time," Jason continued, pointing up and down river. "I attached it to the trees with netting there to keep out wildlife. One thing I forgot about flexmet. You can key flexmet. This flex is owned by the company. As contractors for Brandywine, you can open any of these cases, use this flexmet, et cetera. But if someone were to come along and try to use it, they would be unable to do so."

"Wasn't aware of that, either," Dovey said.

"It's a security measure," Jason said. "But your personal containers are keyed to you personally. Speaking of which, Jewel, those need to come out. Put all the personal containers on the ground inside the conexes. Do that first."

"Roger," Jewel said. "The Alfreds need to charge."

"Keep one on watch while the other charges off of Herman," Jason sighed. "It's always something. It's safe to get down on that point of rock and take a look around. Obviously, the shrimp run is in progress. Just get your feet on the ground but for now stay in the perimeter. And despite the defense net, keep a sharp eye out for crocs."

He connected some flexmet to the top of the container and abseiled down, then set another one on the conex face, walked over to the bank and abseiled down again. Then, aware he looked like Patton and not caring, stood there with his hands on his hips.

When a croc hit the fence, he didn't even flinch. Much.

"Jewel," Jason said. "Remember how we were going to have Alfred and Herman use nets to fish for shrimp?"

"Yes."

"Could the drones . . . never mind. Simple as this. Need the drones to go dip up some shrimp, easiest way. Break out a pot. Have drones gather dry wood."

"Cooking already?" Dovey asked, using his rifle sight to spot a buffalo herd upriver.

"You guys just had breakfast," Jason said. "It's been hours for Storm and me. Time for lunch."

"I could eat," Duncan said, pulling out a monocular for the same purpose. "Anything but print food."

"I could bag one of those from here," Storm said, using a monocular also. "Buffalo makes a tasty meal."

"With respect to your superior prowess, lovey," Dovey said. "So can we all."

"It's three days," Jason said, holding up his hands. "And we're all armed."

"I'm going to make you regret that 'lovey,'" Storm said, grinning. "Shooting match?"

"We have a two-kilometer-radius lease," Jason said. "And we don't actually have two kilometers of range in any direction."

"Spot the bull," Storm said, getting in a prone position. "See it?"

"I see the lead bull," Dovey said.

"See that bug on its withers?" Storm said.

"The green bug," Dovey said. "I see the green bug. Difficult..."

"See the *antenna* on the green bug?"

"Now you're just joking about," Dovey said.

"Jewel," Jason said.

"I already had a drone on the way," Jewel said primly. "It will have to recover the green bug."

"Wind?" Storm asked.

Storm held up the green beetle and pointed to the distinct lack of antennae.

The rest of the group just turned away laughing as Dovey shook his head.

"Right," Dovey said, making a salute. "Last time I call you 'lovey,' Storm."

"Better," Storm said, dropping the beetle. "And I also don't take to Stormy. Only my dad got to call me that."

"Quick question, boss," Storm asked quietly as Dovey was cautiously getting some water from the river for lunch.

"Go," Jason said.

"Do those green bugs have antennae?"

"Yes, they do," Jason said.

"Whoo."

"So, we're not actually *doing* anything right now, hoowah?" Ritchie pointed out, peeling another boiled shrimp.

"Bots and drones are recharging," Jason said, taking a bite of toasted mushroom. "Coffins are being unloaded and cases removed from them and rearranged. And in case you hadn't noticed, the bots, flex and drones are going to be kinda busy," he added, pointing to the expanding pile of crocs. To keep them cool they'd been left in the water and were attracting still more as well as other predators.

"Is that a shark fin?" Storm asked, pointing with her chin.

"We're just upstream from the ocean and it's flood tide," Jason said, not even looking up. "So probably yeah. When the bots and drones are recharged, they'll both start the full survey as well as start harvesting harvestable food while putting out the shrimp trap and recovery system. At which point . . . we'll still be doing nothing. Because we will be letting the technology do it for us."

He looked around at the group of experienced hunters and tried not to laugh.

"We've got a two-kilometer-radius lease this time to take protein," Jason said reasonably. "You go out stalking the perfect water buffalo trophy, take the shot and what happens?"

"The game will leave," O'Callaghan said, expertly peeling another shrimp. "But if bots just decapitate them, no noise. Like slitting the throat on a sentry."

"As he said," Jason said. "I waited until most of the game animals were winnowed down to go out and hunt the predators. And even then, only the tigers and leopards. I let the bots take care of wolf packs. There are also six of you. Even with this game load, how many hunters to a two-kilometer circle? There's an entire planet of trophy animals. And, by the way, where the *hell* are you going to put the trophies?"

"Point," Dovey said.

"We let the bots get the lay of the land," Jason said. "They'll spot most of the game and get a feel for their movements including the predators. The kill points of the herds that we take for protein are very attractive to the predators, which make them great places to hunt. What's the mission, Ritchie?"

"Protein for the station," Ritchie said, shrugging.

"Protein and profit," Jason said. "Right now, we're doing exactly what we should be doing: Nothing."

"If you really feel like you need to do something," Jason said, coming up behind Storm, "you can pull out bycatch. Especially any baby crocs. Use flex gloves."

Storm was standing by the shrimp ladder that carried the caught shrimp up to the conex fort, watching it in fascination.

"Do we seriously catch crocs in this?" Storm asked.

"Wouldn't be surprised," Jason said, then pointed to a drone that was on a pole above the ladder. "But that's what that thing is for. Jewel, pull out some bycatch."

Fish started flipping out of the ladders and into a waiting case.

"Stop," Jason said. "It's not absolutely necessary, ninety-eight percent of what we're catching is shrimp. But it can be done."

"This is . . . not what I expected," Storm admitted, looking out at the river. "Beautiful. Fun. The complete lack of mosquitoes and other biting insects is hard to believe."

"But sort of boring," Jason said. "In this case, boring is good. We should be dead right now. We're right by the river. You'll notice that Dovey has a hard time coming down by the river at all. He's from Africa. It's ingrained to not go near the rivers. So don't, unless you've got a warding net out."

"Yeah," Storm said, nodding. "That is a point I will need to remember."

"Do," Jason said. "I'd hate to have to inform your family."

"How's it going?" Tim asked.

"The natives are restless," Jason said. "These are all serious hunters surrounded by bigger game than any they've seen in their lives. And I set this thing up so it runs on rails. There's little issues to figure out but they can do that easily. They're going stir crazy."

"So let them hunt," Tim said, shrugging.

"It drives out the game," Jason said. "And there are things out there that really can't be fought easily. They all know about the tigers and crocs and elephants. Dangerous game. They don't think of wolves as being that big of a deal. Because they've been killed down to the point they're not in most areas. And the ones on earth are tiny in comparison. Even if I send them out in teams, two guns against a wolf pack is a losing proposition. These things are like the wargs in *Lord of the Rings*."

"So, what's the answer?" Tim asked.

"Take out the wolf pack with the drones," Jason said. "Same as the original site. Reality, I'm being protective. I'm in charge of these guys and I don't want anybody getting killed. The Americans, even the ones that worked in Africa, are way too complacent about the river. The net's got them thinking it's not a big deal. They're not cautious enough. Or am I being a big baby?"

"You're not being a baby," Tim said. "There've been fifteen colonists killed so far. And they were all outdoorsmen as well. Possibly not as handpicked but . . . flip side, they're doing so at their own risk."

"Let the wild colt run," Jason said.

"Probably a cultural reference but, yes," Tim said. "Usual disclaimers."

"Roger," Jason said. "Out here. Jewel, meeting at the hooch."

The big room occupying the entire ground floor, which would make a great chapel, wasn't what sold Cade on the building.

It wasn't the second story that sold him, either, with its many utility rooms that could be subdivided and reconfigured.

Standing in the center of the candidate chapel with Klein, Richter, Diaz, and Parker, he closed his eyes and listened to the sound of the room. It felt good. The echoes sounded right. His heart felt warm about it.

"Feels like a farm," he said, without intending to do.

"The hell it does," Parker said.

"I wouldn't know," Diaz shot back. "I'm a mechanic."

"I just mean . . ." Cade shook his head. "This is a good place."

The front door opened and a sixth man walked in from the commercial "street" passing in front of the warehouse. He wore a disheveled suit that had been taken in by an unskilled hand and a purple tie whose knot hung loose and open.

"You guys are the syndicate," the stranger said. "The people who have bought up sixty percent of this warehouse. I'm Broadbent."

"Good to meet you," Cade said. "We want to know what you'll take for your forty percent share of the building."

"I was hoping to buy *you* out," Broadbent said. "I've got shares in refineries and processing plants and dropships to spare."

"Here's the thing," Parker said. "We're buying up the units because we need a place to hold church. And we feel strongly this is the right place."

Broadbent shook his head, ran his fingers through shaggy hair.

"Listen, I won't lie, I've got a contract already to store meat in this warehouse. Stuff coming up from the surface. Crocodile, buffalo, shrimp. This warehouse is going to make a lot of money. I'm prepared to trade some prime units to you for it. What will it take?"

"Our sixty percent isn't for sale," Richter said.

"What if we go into business as partners, then?" Broadbent suggested. "Incorporate, run the warehouse together. With your sixty percent share of the dividends, you go rent a church building somewhere else. This location is just too good to pass up, close as it is to the shuttle bay."

"Oldham already said this place feels like a farm," Klein told him. "Pretty sure that's as close as Cade Oldham gets to having a spiritual experience. We won't be storing any buffalo meat in here."

Broadbent cracked his knuckles. "Well, I guess that means I better sell you my units, doesn't it? I hope you've got something good to trade."

# CHAPTER 16 »»»»»»»»

"SO, YOU'RE ALL GOING STIR CRAZY, SALIVATING OVER TROPHY everything in every direction," Jason said. "You've been glued to your screens."

"We can wait," Dovey said.

"Eh, it's driving you nuts," Jason said. "I like hunting. It's a passion for all of you. It was your vocation by choice. I like hunting. Like the out of doors. Prefer fishing. You all want to take down the bull elephant or king lion. I want to land one of the bluefin. You seen those things?"

"They're the size of killer whales," O'Callaghan said.

"Seriously?" Ritchie asked.

"I really want to spearfish one, hoowah?" Jason said. "Get all this stuff set up, get the company stable and I'm going to take up blue-water hunting. Just spearfish for stuff. But that's me. So, you're going out in two-person teams. Drones have done a rough survey. You can see what's out there. We'll break the lease up into three zones."

"What about scaring off the game?" Duncan said.

"We're primarily here for shrimp," Jason said, shrugging. "And with the run in full, we're loading shrimp so fast we're going to need another set of conexes in a couple of days at this rate. Point is we can take or leave game meat. The real problem is the wolves."

"Wolves aren't that big of a problem," Ritchie said.

"You weren't paying attention to that wolf pack," Storm said. "Those aren't timber wolves. Those are freaking *dire* wolves."

"Yeah," Jason said. "The wolves around here are the size of *male lions* on earth. And they hunt in large packs. Wolf packs will take down small to medium elephants. Everybody worries about the regular 'dangerous game' on Earth. On this planet, it's the hyenas and the wolves to worry about. But I'm going to have the drones take out most of the wolf pack, so that's settled."

"Wouldn't mind one of those skins," Surber said.

"There's an entire planet," Jason said, gesturing out. "I'm not even going to bring in the carcasses. There'll be time to hunt wolves another time. For right now, it's what's most likely to surprise you. So, three two-person teams. The bots are busy so you take eight drones and two coffins apiece. You'll have to lug the coffins back. Don't take anything you can't field dress and get in a coffin. Which means no, and I repeat, no elephants."

"Damn," Storm said, shaking her head.

"We don't want bad publicity that Brandywine is killing elephants," Jason said. "Probably in this political climate it won't matter, but still. Plus, the head on one of those things takes a freaking conex and how are you going to store it until you can get it to a taxidermist?"

"Point," Surber said.

"As people adjust to the reality on the planet, they'll realize that elephants can be pests..."

"Major ones for farmers," Dovey said.

"But you can hunt elephants on your own time," Jason said. "Meat if it's a food animal goes to the company, you can keep the hide and head. But you've got to drag the coffins. The drones and your AIs should warn you if there's a major threat but keep your head on a swivel. There's unknown bugs, snakes, et cetera. Roger?"

"Roger," Ritchie said as the others nodded.

"Team leaders take the shot today," Jason said. "Team seconds take it tomorrow. Teams: Storm and Duncan. Duncan, don't be that guy."

"Ain't," Duncan said.

"Dovey and Ritchie," Jason said. "O'Callaghan and Surber. Surber, you've probably got more hunting experience, but..."

"Not going to complain," Surber said.

"Figure out your strategies and good hunting," Jason said. "Literally."

"I kicked them out of the nest," Jason said into his phone. "And I went to so much trouble to build a good nest this time."

"It was time," Tim said, chuckling.

"These are people with waaay more experience than I have and I feel like a mother hen with chicks," Jason said.

"Welcome to command," Tim said.

"I don't want to be in command," Jason said. "I have zero interest in running things. I just want to be the guy figuring things out."

"Then you should have taken the junior partner position," Tim said.

"There's another reason," Jason said. "We're going to need another partner."

"Why?" Tim asked.

"What I just said," Jason replied. "I'm good at figuring things out but not a guy to run things. I'm interested in expanding this. Not just fish runs but finding other stuff. I've got a lot of ideas about how to make this planet profitable but like the shrimp run I need to be there to figure it out."

"Like what?" Tim said. "And, yeah, we need something more than just a shrimp run."

"Let's just talk about fruit orchards for a second," Jason said.

"Fruit orchards?" Tim said, smiling. "Okay."

"We were left with only six mature trees of every different major type of commercial fruit and nut trees," Jason said. "Did you know that?"

"No," Tim said, frowning.

"Same thing with commercial animals," Jason said. "There are only six of each major breed of cows. Goats. Sheep. Pigs. All female. But with trees, and I need to stay on subject, there are billions of grafts in stasis. The containers are just in a mass floating off station..."

"That's where most of the conexes are being held as well," Tim said.

"So, on the fruit trees," Jason said. "Root stock is just the base wild tree. Like with oranges, there are going to be wild citrus trees that the grafts can be put on. So, all you have to do is find a wild apple tree and you can grow...Granny Smith or Fuji apples, get it?"

"Got it," Tim said, nodding.

"So...you're clearing land," Jason said thoughtfully. "And part of that land is a wild apple tree. The fruit's nothing much. But you can graft Fuji, say, into it. There may be a small copse. When you graft, you're going to remove the existing limbs. They just take up resources. But those limbs can, in turn, be rooted and become the start to other root stock trees. Before long, you've got either an apple tree nursery or an apple orchard, depending on which way you want to go. Do you know where silk comes from?"

"Silk...worms?" Tim said.

"Which eat what?" Jason said. "Mulberry leaves, to answer the question. To create a silk industry will require massive orchards of mulberry. Where are the wild mulberry trees? Cherry, orange...?"

"There are thousands of fetuses of pigs, cows, in storage," Jason said. "But there's only six sows, six cows, to implant them in. Which is why we're going to have to learn to milk...you know those gigantic cattle on the plains?"

"The aurochs?" Tim said, laughing. "You want to *milk* aurochs? They're the size of small elephants!"

"I've done crazier stuff," Jason said, his brow furrowing. "But that's why we need another partner. We need a field operations *manager*. Not just a guy working for pay. Someone who's got skin in the game. I figure it out. You and *that* partner monetize it. I'm basically the R&D guy of the partnership."

"That...makes a certain amount of sense," Tim said thoughtfully.

"I'm all about the new," Jason said, looking into the distance. "That's always been my real problem, sticking to one thing. But this world is *all* new. How we feed people is going to be new. New/old. Taking stuff that we know from Earth and fitting it into this environment...Remember how we were having a tough time getting supplies to outpost seventeen? Birds weren't available. The road up was washed out. What did I do?"

"Found some camel drivers to carry the loads up the mountain," Tim said.

"I like solving problems but then I want to move on," Jason said. "So, we need somebody to get this stuff done on the ground side. The day to day. *And* expansion."

"And you want to pick from one of these guys?" Tim said. "People."

"If they fit," Jason said. "The hunt is a test in part. Part because they were mostly, not all, going nuts with all this game and no shooting. But it's a test in part. And, yeah, we need somebody."

"I'll notionally agree," Tim said. "But I have to have input on the final choice."

"Agreed," Jason said. "I'm not great at picking people. Another reason I'm not the best guy to run a business. People are the main risk."

"So, on old business," Tim said. "I talked with James and looked at the restaurant thing. It...makes a certain amount of sense. We need a venue for meetings and dinners. And I've set it up so if Brandywine contributes to getting the package together, we get something out of it. Right now, there's a dearth of capital to just get paid up front. So, we're going to have to dip into our capital. Which I hate doing. Which means, we're going to wait until we're very capital solid. But...way things are going, that's going to be a couple of weeks, max."

"That's soon enough," Jason said.

"I looked up the chef's resumé," Tim said. "Checks out. Talked to him. Find the right venue and he can handle it soup to nuts, metaphorically and literally."

"We'll need to find some nuts," Jason said.

"Deb's trying to find a space," Tim said, then sighed. "And at that point we hit the problem of unit holders. Most people don't even *know* they own a fifth share of a business property on a main drag. We're having a hard time finding a space."

"I've got an idea on that," Jason said. "But it cuts into material."

"Oh?" Tim said.

"Most people have commo about their units on hold," Jason said. "But if someone offers them some fresh food to exchange units, they'll probably take it."

"Somebody has to have the units," Tim said.

"I've got some left that aren't in my main areas," Jason said. "I think. Jewel, do I have some units left that haven't been traded?"

"You have nearly four million I haven't been able to move," Jewel said. "Including one in a possible venue. It is near your quadrant's Market Square on a 'main drag' as Tim said. One of the four main connector corridors."

Main connection corridors looked something like the interior of a shopping mall. They were lined with shops and in most areas had sliding walkways down the center. Jason remembered that at the ones he'd walked down, most of the storefronts were closed.

"We offer the unit holders some...probably not croc meat... Jewel, the unit owners are listed. Any Third Worlders?"

"One Copt, French, Indonesian and US other than you," Jewel said.

"We offer the Copt and Indonesian croc meat," Jason said. "The French and US...buffalo or something. Hate to be that way but the Copts and Indonesians are more likely to know about croc. We can offer the croc to the Westerners or whatever we have in quantity. Note that it's pretty much the same as alligator. Can you tell me age or sex, Jewel?"

"Copt female, teen; French male, fifties; Indonesian male, thirties; US male, forties," Jewel said.

"Throw in some flowers?" Jason said. "Offer different but substantially similar commercial property. Kilo of croc or half kilo of some known meat. I throw in a couple of units, you throw in a couple of units."

"You have the majority?" Tim said.

"I'm the majority partner," Jason pointed out. "Call it Brandywine's. Private venue at first. Reserved parties only. Later we might open it as a restaurant when there's more money in the system. Have some signs about food that's available out front as advertising. Brandywine Corporation will run it and back it but we'll own the units separately. And hope we don't have a falling out."

"Yeah," Tim said. "Talked with Richard as well. He's willing to make the loan on the equipment. He agrees we need a venue. There aren't many on the entire station."

"You agree on the meat for units thing?" Jason asked.

"Sounds...yes," Tim said.

"Jewel," Jason said. "Make it so."

"There's a request to trade units."

Lucra Stamos was fifteen and had already been advised by her father to ignore such requests until the Patriarch had ruled on how they should be regarded.

Which she had told Mariam.

"I'm not supposed to listen to those," Lucra said.

"This one has a benefit," the AI replied. "They are offering a similar unit trade plus one kilo of crocodile meat."

"Crocodile meat?" Lucra said. "Crocodile is good. Where do they get crocodile meat?"

"The person trading is with a food company," Mariam said. "They get it from the planet. They also sell it."

"For how much?" Lucra asked. It would probably be too much. With a family of nine children and Papa could not find a job, *everything* was too expensive.

"Twenty-five kilos for fifteen credits," Mariam said.

"MAMA!"

"The trade is up in the air but you just got four new customers," Jewel said. "Each of the families ordered at least a case of something. The Copts have ordered four cases of crocodile meat."

"The crocodile meat is selling surprisingly well," Tim said. "There's enough moving in and out that it's getting complicated. I know we talked about a field supervisor partner, but what I really need is..."

"Don't *even* put me in an office," Jason said. "I'm the guy figuring this out."

"We need a log guy," Tim said. "Hell, at this point we need an accountant, a log guy and a scheduler."

"I'll contact the best log guys I know other than me," Jason said. "I know schedulers, too. Call Gil about an accountant."

"You have two agreements on trade," Jewel interjected. "US and French contingent on delivery. The Copts and Indonesians probably have to discuss it. The Indonesians just ordered six cases of croc and a case of buffalo meat."

"We'll have three of five units with those two," Tim said. "Which is majority and we can rent the venue to Brandywine."

"And we're in business," Jason said.

The last team got back after dusk.

Jason had been in continuous contact with the drones and watching Dovey's team as they struggled back pulling the containers. The containers counteracted gravity but the megabuffalo in the container still had mass. Getting it moving was tough, getting it to turn was tough and weaving it in and out of the trees was tough.

When it was clear they were going to be back well after dark Jason dispatched an Alfred to help them out.

"Sorry, Mum," Dovey said, when they finally ascended the conex wall.

"More Dad," Jason said, his arms crossed. "Mum's not home at the moment."

"Those containers are a *bitch* to maneuver, hoowah?" Ritchie said.

Both of them knew they'd screwed up. The question was what to do about it.

"You were being tracked by a tiger," Storm said.

"We were?" Ritchie asked.

"You had blood on you," Surber said.

"I took care of it," Jason said, thumbing. "Dinner's cold."

"And the boss is a really good cook, too," Storm said.

"My punishment is no real punishment," Jason said, shrugging. "Dishes are done so there's not even that. Just this. I'm not legally responsible for you. It's your life and you signed waivers. But I *am* morally. I'm the guy in charge. I trusted you to make the right call and get back on time. You didn't. I expected better.

"You disappointed me."

With that Jason turned and walked away.

"Ouch," Duncan said.

"Disappointed," Storm said and walked away as well.

O'Callaghan just shook his head.

"We're *definitely* getting back on time tomorrow," Surber said.

"This sort of meal is great for you, hoowah," Ritchie said. "But it's going to start going right through me."

Breakfast was fish, shrimp, fruit and some really horrible print bread Jason had brought along.

"There has to be *something* to be done about print food," Jason said. But they needed the carbs.

Getting to sleep in a container with seven people, four serious snorers, had been a bit of a trial. But Jason just left his remarkably comfortable smart plugs in and eventually drifted off.

"Okay," Jason said as they were finishing. "I know that the best times, traditionally, to hunt are morning and evening. But the hunting around here is so good, you can probably go any time. So, we're going to take the morning to explore the tech abilities we have available. You all had trouble getting your, admittedly large, kills back using coffins. O'Callaghan, any thoughts on how to use what you had to improve that?"

"Flexmet?" O'Callaghan said. "It's your usual answer."

"I told Storm yesterday that I don't like talking about my ideas before I try them out," Jason said. "People should trust that the boss knows. But we're going to try some ideas on that. We might not always have bots available. We've already got stacks of fully loaded coffins. Let's go experiment. Jewel, security situation right outside the abatis?"

"Nothing at present on the forest side," Jewel said. "Usual croc conditions."

"If you're done, grab your guns and light field gear and follow me," Jason said.

When they were prepared, he waved for the group to follow him and clambered down off the conex wall. He picked coffins from a filled stack tossing about twenty kilos of flexmet on top of one of them.

"First thing," Jason said. "You were having one of the team push each coffin out and back, more or less."

"They had too much mass to handle more than one at a time," Dovey said. "It really got me the thing I'd heard talked about with being in zero gravity. That there's weight and then there's mass. Mass just keeps moving."

"Yeah," Storm said, snorting. "Those things were a bitch to maneuver. I'm glad they're tough. I ran mine into a tree more than once."

Jason pushed the coffin down to ground level and climbed on. "Jewel, have the flex connect the two coffins, lightly, end to end. Bring down a drone to control."

A drone obediently settled on the rear coffin.

"Lash them together, in series, lightly," Jason said. "The lashings should flex so that the containers can go around obstacles. Clear enough?"

"Clear enough," Jewel said.

"Make it so," Jason said. "Bit of flex to hold me on the container safely. Now, send a strand of flex out to the top of the abatis. Then send strands down to the ground from both containers. Have the ground strands lift the container, gently, to a height to clear the abatis. Clear enough?"

"Clear enough," Jewel said.

"Make it so," Jason said.

The coffins slowly lifted as a tentacle of flex slithered out to the top of the abatis. Then the pair of containers were gently pulled forward until they were hovering over the abatis. Jewel had correctly surmised that they needed multiple points to hold them in place and had attached the flex without order.

"Come on up," Jason said, waving to the group. He watched which of them used flex for aid: O'Callaghan, Storm and Duncan. "Now cover me. Jewel, commander's intent is to use this general method to attach to ground and trees to move the containers between the trees at about six feet above the ground for the seated person at their seat. Move at about a slow walking speed, no faster. Can do?"

"Can do," Jewel said.

"Take me about a hundred meters in, turn around and come back," Jason said. "Make it so."

The technique worked fine as they left the abatis. Jewel maintained about six feet height as they descended. But as they moved into the brush a problem immediately cropped up.

"Whoa," Jason said. "Don't run me into tree branches."

"I was wondering about that," Jewel said. "You probably should be prone. And you still may have to cut or push some out of the way."

"Will do," Jason said, getting prone on the box. "Choose such a height and path as will run into the least branches."

In a few moments he was back on the abatis and climbed off.

"And that's a better way to do it," Jason said.

"Yes," Dovey said, shaking his head. "Should have thought of that."

"None of us did," O'Callaghan said, regarding Jason thoughtfully.

"You're going to be training trainers," Jason said. "You need to think about how to maximize the tech to make everything easier and encourage them to do the same thing. Tim, my partner, once said I weaponize laziness. I figure out the most efficient and easiest way to get something done so I don't have to do as much work. You need to do the same. The new people that are coming in need to do the same. Necessity is the mother of invention. I can't think of everything. When you are stuck, *be inventive.* Thus ends the lecture."

"Hell, you can use them to bring extra guns. Like a porter," Storm said, looking at the containers.

"You need them for the kills," Surber said. "You'll get blood all over the guns."

"Wrap the guns and any other gear in flexmet," Duncan said. "Keeps the blood off and it's self-cleaning."

"The answer," Jason said.

"Gazillion and one uses," Storm said. "I got raised that the world is hard and you just suck it up. You can use a four-wheeler to recover the elk, but if you've got to drag it up a hill to the four-wheeler, you drag it up the hill."

"My dad made the Great Santini look like a mild-mannered beta leftist," Jason said, shrugging. "I was always too lazy for my old man. Too much of a dreamer. We are who we are. Spend the rest of the morning in camp. Each of the teams take their sector and work with the drones. We also have a few, not many, new species of potential foods to try out. Divvy them up and taste and smell test. Early lunch then spread out again. No change. Same teams, same area. Dinner is barbeque pork."

"Barbeque barbeque?" O'Callaghan asked. "Or grilled?"

"Barbeque barbeque," Jason said. "Bit of an experiment. I brought a grinder and the dry rub will be mostly local spices and herbs. We'll see how it works out."

# CHAPTER 17 ⟩⟩⟩⟩⟩⟩⟩⟩⟩

"IF ANYBODY SAYS I WOULD MAKE A GREAT WIFE," JASON SAID, pulling off a piece of succulent wild pig rib meat, "I will, in fact, send them back to the station."

"This is good, hoowah," Ritchie said. "Needs some sauce. Wonder where you get molasses on this planet?"

"Wild sorghum," Surber said. "Sugar, wild canes. Spices... most of them are going to have to be grown."

"Or we'll get used to the new species," Jason said.

"Seems like the minor plants are often different," Dovey said. "The trees are much the same as India and China."

"Birds," Duncan said. "There are five thousand bird species catalogued in this biome and none were previously known."

"Mammals seem to be mostly the same," Surber said, eating some shrimp. "Bigger. But even the buck I got registers genetically as a sambar. But sambar didn't get anywhere near that big on Earth."

"Mammals don't speciate very often," Jason said, shrugging. "Birds, lizards, insects, all tend to rapidly speciate. Crocodilians being a counterexample: They've stayed pretty much the same for a hundred million years."

"Fruit," O'Callaghan said.

"Many of the fruits are the same," Surber said.

"I was thinking about a sauce for the barbeque," O'Callaghan answered. "Find some fruits and mash them up with some spices.

Fruit for the sweet. Gotta be coconuts around here. Coconut makes a decent base for a sauce."

"That might work," Storm said, nodding. "I was still wondering where you get wild sorghum. Wild sugar cane is probably in this biome. Sugar cane was originally from India or so they think."

"Follow the elephants," Dovey said, chewing thoughtfully. "This isn't *smoked*, exactly..."

"It's what I meant by barbeque barbeque," O'Callaghan said. "Actual barbeque is a Native American invention. Christopher Columbus found it among the Caribs when he arrived. It's intermediate between grilling and smoking. You can barbeque anything."

"What?" O'Callaghan asked, looking around. Everybody was looking at him. "I owned part of a barbeque place in Key West."

"It's just you hadn't said anything for two days," Storm pointed out.

"I generally don't," O'Callaghan said. "But barbeque is important."

"It's late, buddy," Tim said. The call was voice only.

The sun had set and the group was settling down for sleep. Which gave Jason some free time.

"It's just after dusk here," Jason said. "O'Callaghan. For the field partner."

"He'll probably want to start his own business," Tim said.

"He can probably do both," Jason said. "The guy's a workaholic. But the job would have him shuttling up and down all over the planet. He'd enjoy that and he can start and run businesses mostly remote. As a partner, as long as he's getting the business done, he can choose his times. That's the offer."

"Investment?" Tim asked.

"Vesting and stuff," Jason said. "I'll let you handle that side. But I think he's the best choice."

"Tell him five percent vested over five years," Tim said. "I'll allow him to check our profitability. We're not paying dividends presently and probably won't for a while to build capital internally. But I'll negotiate a salary and bonus structure with him. And, yeah, he'd probably be good. If he'll take it."

"Roger," Jason said. "Want to talk to a couple of the others about not just field work."

"I'm fine with you using your judgment there," Tim said. "Anything else? Bird's arriving midafternoon tomorrow. Pick somebody to stay there. Two new guys coming down to train."

"See you tomorrow," Jason said.

The flexscreen above the door was imitating an ornate signboard. Squiggly symbols Sam didn't recognize formed a border around the rectangular image, interspersed with magician-looking images. There was a hand, palm forward and fingers together, with an open eye in the center of the palm. There were suns, moons, and stars. Sam saw an hourglass, a question mark, and Egyptian hieroglyphs.

The word in the center of the sign read PSYCHIC.

The door was filled with a string of glittering blue glass beads. The beads were striking, because they didn't look like flexmet. That suggested that the psychic had had a whole ton of beads in personal storage, and had pulled them out to make this door. That seemed...extravagant.

Sam hadn't been going anywhere, just walking around the station. He'd been doing it for days, while his dad collected planting beds and loaded them with carrots and cabbage. Sam didn't have a job, there were no jobs on the horizon, and he didn't like the idea that, sooner or later, he'd be forced to go down to the surface of an untamed planet. He didn't like the idea that, in the meantime, there was nothing for him to do.

He was a little disappointed that Pastor Mickey wouldn't take the bait and declare that Pegasus was the resurrection and the life, because then Sam would hit him back with the obvious, and obviously true, alternative: that Pegasus was hell.

The truth was, Sam didn't believe in heaven or hell. He didn't think he'd ever really believed in either, back on Earth, but he certainly didn't believe in them now.

Sam didn't believe in psychics, either.

He pushed his way through the bead curtain. The room behind was dark.

"Hello," a smoky woman's voice said. "I'll alert Madame de La Rose that you're waiting."

Sam blinked and looked around the small room. He saw three chairs against one wall and a side table with a flexmet flower, a rose, in a flexmet vase beside a door. "Am I talking to an AI?"

"I am. Your AI...Thog...could have made an appointment, if you wished."

"I wasn't informed," Thog said.

Sam ignored his grumpy AI. "But Madame de La Rose is here?"

"Just one moment."

Sam stood waiting, but after only a minute, the door to the interior dilated open.

"Come in!" a voice called from inside.

Sam entered. The room's lights were draped with blue silk, so the interior had the color of a low-rent dance club. Madame de La Rose sat at a circular table with one empty chair facing her. She wore a yellow turban and an orange shawl, and the smile cracking right and left beneath her carrot-like nose was crooked and smudged at the corners. She blinked heavy eyelashes at Sam and gestured at the chair.

"You've come about love," the psychic said. "You have women problems."

"That's crap," Sam said. "You're telling me that because I'm a young man. It's a high-percentage guess."

"I'm not charging you for anything yet," she said. "Sit down, put your hand on the table."

Sam hesitated, but then obeyed.

"Palm down."

Sam flipped his hand palm down.

Madame de La Rose placed her hand over the top of Sam's. Her hand was damp, as if with sweat, and with her other hand she covered her eyes. "Okay, okay," she said.

"Are you getting—?"

"Shh. Okay, okay. You miss your girl."

"Lucky guess."

"Could have been a missing boyfriend," the psychic said.

"That's it." Sam tried to pull his hand away, but it was pinned. "Her name is Julie."

Sam stopped. He smelled cinnamon, and felt his heartbeat in his ears. "Julie what?"

"Julie...Starts with an L...Larsen. Julie Larsen."

Sam said nothing.

"I won't ask you to tell me I'm right, I know I'm right."

"Where is she?" Sam's voice was a dry croak. "What happened to her?"

"One credit for five minutes," the psychic told him.

"Thog." Sam's tongue was a sandpaper log in his mouth. "Pay her."

"Of all things," Thog said. "You know her AI is probably just reading your sister's posts in the social channels."

"Pay her," Sam said. "Tell me where she is."

"Paid." Thog sounded sulky.

"Let me see what I can see. Hmm. I see a good-looking girl. Ooh, she's kissing you."

"Where is she now?" Sam asked.

"Hold on," the psychic said. "Great distances are involved. Space and time both are mists that obscure true vision."

Sam ground his teeth.

"I see metal walls," Madame de La Rose said. "Metal walls that change shape and form themselves into tools."

"She's in a space station," Sam said. "But she isn't here."

"Hmm," the psychic said. "Okay, okay. I see... oh, Julie's watching TV on the flexscreen wall. She's watching a speech. Oh, look, it's President Hillary Clinton."

"She's in the liberal system," Sam said. "So I guess that exists, after all."

"She looks happy," Madame de La Rose said. "She's clapping, she's excited."

"Will we get together?" Sam asked. "Will I find her?"

The psychic removed her hand from her face. "Look, kid—"

"Five minutes aren't up."

Madàme de La Rose nodded slowly, then covered her eyes again. "The future is difficult. The mists of time. Okay, okay. I can see Julie's future. She's married, she has two... no, four kids. Oh, she looks so happy."

"Will that be me?" Sam asked. "Am I the husband?"

The psychic put both her hands into her lap. "I just can't see, kid. Sometimes my vision isn't perfect."

"Okay, bird's scheduled to arrive at fourteen thirty, so no hunting today," Jason said over breakfast. "Duncan, you okay with staying behind to train two new guys?"

"Yes," Duncan said. "Though I'll have to just mime how to set up the shrimp trap."

"By the time they get their own lease, we'll be past shrimp,"

Jason said. "Train them in general on how to work with the tech. Have them taste test, including getting some of the edibles and inedibles for them to try. That's the general plan. When we get up to the station, take a day to get your gear washed and your trophies stored then plan on dropping to a new spot with a couple of newbies."

"As planned," Surber said.

"When do *I* get a shower?" Duncan said, smiling. "Just asking."

"When you've got them trained, one stays here and you head to the station," Jason said. "Any major questions? No? O'Callaghan, moment of your time?"

"I haven't screwed up as far as I'm aware," O'Callaghan said when they'd gotten away from the group.

"Quite the opposite," Jason said. "I figure with your background you looked at this as a quick gig. Get on the planet. Get some credit. Use it to start rebuilding a business empire."

"Minor empire," O'Callaghan said. "But I'm contracted for a year and I'll fulfill the contract."

"I've convinced Tim we need another partner," Jason said. "I'm the innovation partner. I figure out how to use the tech to make money."

"And you're good at that," O'Callaghan said. "Not blowing smoke. You're very inventive."

"So is Duncan," Jason said. "One of the reasons I'm leaving him. I'm going to be talking to him as well, but not offering a partnership.

"Tim runs the business. He enjoys doing that, same way you do. But we need a field operations partner. Basically, the job would be running the ground teams. Tim spends most of his time in the station. He's an outdoors guy but he mostly likes running the business with outdoors as a hobby. You'd be shuttling to the various locations, picking and recruiting the ground teams and monetizing the harvests."

"What do I get out of that?" O'Callaghan asked.

"Besides spending a lot of time on planet?" Jason asked. "Five percent of the company, which is growing fast, vested over five years. Tim will talk to you about salary and bonuses. I don't do money. As long as you're handling your side of it, you can choose your time and methods. So, opening some businesses of your own would be fine. I've got two investments I'm working on right now. You didn't spend all your time sitting in the bar, right?"

"No," O'Callaghan said, clicking his teeth. "So, what's your role?"

"You'd be making the company's money," Jason said, then grinned. "My job would be spending it finding new resources, new opportunities. Innovating. Some ideas might not work. Wouldn't be profitable. But you can't know till you try. Figuring out how to milk an aurochs, for example. Eventually."

"Milk ... an aurochs," O'Callaghan said, blinking rapidly. "While the station needs milk ..."

"There are six *billion* embryos of commercially important animals in storage," Jason said. "But, taking cattle as an example, there are only *six* cows. You can probably implant a cow embryo in an aurochs. You'd want to stun it, first, but you can do it. But the calves would be too small to reach the udders to milk ..."

"You need the milk for the calves that you've implanted in the aurochs," O'Callaghan said, shaking his head. "Shit, boy. You really *are* insane, aren't you?"

"I'm not planning on milking them *by hand* for God's sake!" Jason said, laughing. "Have you seen the videos? They're the size of an elephant! But humans figured out how to milk *elephants* before industrialization. It can be done. It's a long-term plan. We're planning on dropping teams all over the world. Every productive biome. Finding the new. That's my side. Your side is figuring out how to maximize the production from each camp. If you'll take it."

"I want to talk to Tim about details," O'Callaghan said.

"He's waiting on your call," Jason said.

"Duncan," Jason said, gesturing with his chin.

"O'Callaghan hasn't screwed anything up," Duncan said when they were alone. "Neither have I that I know of."

"Up to O'Callaghan to say," Jason said. "I was recruiting for something, basically. I'm sort of doing the same thing here. Of the team, you're the one that's been the most innovative. It's one of the reasons I'm leaving you on the ground. You're going to have to break in the new guys. Don't even know who they are. But there's free time, obviously. Keep an eye on them through the drones. Don't let them get themselves killed. But you've got free time. Innovate. Figure new things out. You asked about a shower. Figure it out. Make a shower."

"Got a few ideas about that," Duncan admitted.

"Push the boundaries," Jason said. "I mean of the tech. Don't get yourself killed, either. And watch the freaking water. Don't absolutely trust the defense net. Innovating in the company is my job but I can't think of everything. Keep an eye out for the people who do think of things as well. The inventive ones. The company is planning on growing. So far so good. I'm going to need people to whom I can say 'Go here and figure it out.' If you're one of those people, you'll get paid more than just a harvest officer."

"Sounds good," Duncan said, nodding.

"Nondisclosure," Jason said. "Part of the brief is anything new we use to monetize you get a cut. The shower thing probably isn't monetizable but there will be things."

"I know some guys," Duncan said, tilting his head. "They're not necessarily Great White Hunter types, but they're good at that. Innovation."

"They've got to be able to survive," Jason said.

"Oh, they're outdoorsmen," Duncan said. "Just not...Surber or Dovey. But they're good. One of the guys that comes to mind is a former Navy nuke..."

"He's in," Jason said. "If he's one of their guys that can always figure it out."

"He's that guy," Duncan said. "Guided him on hunts a few times. He's innovative as hell. Another was a mechanic I knew in the day..."

"Jewel, note this," Jason said. "We'll wait to see what O'Callaghan says. They're going to be making their nut at the same time. Same as you being here. But we also need more people figuring things out."

"I will go get started on designing a shower," Duncan said. "Since the shrimp land themselves."

"Quiet conversations off to the side," Storm said, cocking an eyebrow. "O'Callaghan, Duncan, now me?"

"You're the only person in the team who has anything resembling a 'name' pre-Transfer," Jason said. "I'd like to talk to you about being a spokesperson besides doing groundwork."

"I'd consider that," Storm said.

"And what's in it for you?" Jason said. "I hadn't even talked to Tim about it and he handles money. But most of it would be done from the ground, anyway. And right *now*, we don't need much in the way of marketing."

He'd checked their inventory before he talked to her. The warehouse was empty and they had backorders.

"But we will," Jason said. "There will be other spokespeople. But I'd like you to consider something along the lines."

"I may have been a cook in the Army," Storm said, grinning. "Technically. But my bachelor's is in marketing."

"I want Brandywine to be a brand," Jason said, looking down the river. 'Nother croc. "One of the big new brands of this big new world. No reason we shouldn't be the first grocery chain. Restaurants. Brandywine: We do food. People need food. No reason we shouldn't supply it. We're starting small. There's nowhere to go but up."

He turned and looked at her and shrugged.

"You in?"


"I still haven't said yes," O'Callaghan said.

They were meeting for dinner in a conference room at the Brandywine offices. A table and chairs had been procured from somewhere. It looked more like a large dining room table than a conference table.

Debra had obviously had some input on decorations. The screen walls were filled with images of the planet, mostly flowering trees and bushes.

"But I do think it's a good idea," he continued. "I see where the salary has to be low at first. People don't really get this business environment..."

"How?" Tim asked.

"The Third Worlders do," O'Callaghan corrected. "They're just digging in and starting companies getting small investments from family, mostly. But Americans are used to starting businesses, large or small, by finding some deep-pocket investors. That's literally business 101 in the US."

"And there *are* no deep pockets," Jason said, frowning.

"This company is about as deep as it gets," O'Callaghan said. "You're probably something like Fortune 500 in case you didn't realize it."

"We are?" Jason said. "We've only got two sites!"

"It's only been a few weeks," Tim said. "None of the large-scale stuff is really up and going. Once the fuel mines, the factories, get up and going, we'll be small scale."

"Maybe," O'Callaghan said. "Food is big business, and we'll get there. But that's for later. I understand the salary is small, now. Bonuses primarily."

"How it has to be," Tim said. "We need to conserve capital. There are, as you said, no deep-pocket investors."

"It's a start-up," O'Callaghan said. "Like an internet start-up in the nineties. More or less literally a couple of guys in a cheap warehouse. Difference is, if you start to make it, you can't go to venture capital. Most capital is pointing at the big stuff for now. I know mine is."

"What are you pointing at?" Jason asked.

"Trying to get one of the fuel mines up and going," O'Callaghan said after a moment's thought then sighed. "The freaking unit thing! *I* can't even keep up with my units!"

"I concentrated mine in three areas," Jason said. "Four, now. Twelve Bravo, Carbon Converter Charlie and Spaceship Four." He saw the look and shrugged. "I beg to disagree on the issue of hangar queen. Also, now a drone factory."

"Which one?" O'Callaghan asked.

"Don't even know," Jason said, grinning ruefully. "Jewel?"

"General Production Station Alpha," Jewel said. "There's no designated drone factory."

"How's it going?" Jason asked.

"Slowly," Jewel said. "Most haven't authorized trades and have their AIs shut off for requests. The ones who are paying attention are holding or acquired."

"I hadn't even looked at drones till we were on the planet," O'Callaghan admitted. "We're going to need lots of drones."

"There are a hundred million in government storage," Tim said.

"Less now," Jason said. "Every colony pack includes twenty and everyone who's going to the planet is taking them and then getting more."

"I've done the math," O'Callaghan said, nodding. "We're going to need more drones. Not right away but soon enough."

"Which is what I said after one drop," Jason said.

"The drones, the tractors," O'Callaghan said. "Mary, where are tractors made?"

"General production factories," his AI responded.

"I have got to get in on one of those," O'Callaghan said. "You're in on Alpha?"

"To the extent I have been able to get in on Alpha," Jason said.

"Mary," O'Callaghan said. "Try to concentrate on Bravo."

"Will do," his AI replied. "But nobody's really trading factory units. People get those are valuable."

"I guess I should get in on Charlie then," Tim said, grinning. "Maddie, make it so."

"On it," his AI replied.

"Sorry to take the time with this," O'Callaghan said to Tim.

"It's part and parcel of the company in a way," Tim said. "If we're going to need more drones and tractors..."

"We will," Jason said, an idea forming. "If we get all the colony sets down... that's the entire drone store. Hang on a sec: Jewel, Spaceship Four. Later."

"Four?" O'Callaghan said.

"He does this," Tim said, interested. "You get used to it."

"What were we talking about?" Jason asked.

"Drones," Tim said.

"That's the whole drone store," Jason continued. "And two thirds of the small and medium tractor store. For some stuff we're going to need large tractors."

"What?" Tim asked.

"Bluefin?" Jason said.

"You were talking about bluefin," O'Callaghan said. "Time was, those came right in shore. Can probably figure out a way to hook them and bring them in that way."

"Possibly," Jason said. "But there's also ways to make boats from flex and drive them with a tractor. Hook and run with them and drag them aboard. That will take a large tractor, probably..."

"You said remind you of Spaceship Four," Jewel said when he got back to his compartment.

They'd discussed more or less cabbages and kings when it came to the business and the economy. Jason had talked about how some of the leases would be less productive when they took them over but would be more so during other times of the year. Just as paleolithic tribes had moved from resource to resource, resources would come and go. Fruits might be in blossom when they first took a lease but would mature later. Game was best taken in fall in the temperate latitudes.

O'Callaghan had taken the position of Field Partner and they'd hashed out other details.

The dinner had run late and he was tired but the reminder nagged him.

He flopped down on the flex couch in the midst of an apparent tropical paradise and put his hand on his head. There'd even been some alcohol.

"Yeah, need more than that?" Jason said.

"You were talking about the need for drones," Jewel said.

"Replay the conversation," Jason said.

*"It's part and parcel of the company in a way. If we're going to need more drones and tractors..."*

*"We will. If we get all the colony sets down...that's the entire drone store. Hang on a sec: Jewel, Spacehip Four. Later."*

"If we get all the colony sets down," Jason muttered. "Drones. Spaceship Four...Why am I thinking of Storm?"

"She's a pretty girl and you don't have a girlfriend?" Jewel said. "Men of your biological age are often distracted by the thought of sex."

"That did NOT help," Jason said. "Spaceship Four. Drones. Colony sets..."

He suddenly had an image, clear as day, of Storm standing on the raft of conexes and the idea started to crystallize. You can drop anything. Once.

"The colony sets are all transported in stasis, right?" Jason said slowly.

"Yes."

Everything's packed in conexes. Except...

"What about the trailer?" Jason asked. "To be clear...could you just put a trailer out in space?"

"That is where most are currently stored," Jewel said. "Along with spare conexes."

"Do they have air in them?" Jason asked.

"Yes," Jewel said. "Though nothing would happen in stasis, the equipment is not vacuum rated."

"Soooo...Could you release a raft like we made at a higher altitude? Say...twenty thousand feet?"

"It's...I can see nothing wrong with that idea," Jewel said, nearly as carefully.

"What's the current estimate on dropping all the colony sets?"

"Two years," Jewel said.

"One thousand, six hundred and sixty-six colony sets in a ten grand, right?"

"Correct."

"Times five hundred credits is...Do you have a calculator in this thing?" he asked, looking at his phone.

"Eight hundred and thirty-three thousand credits," Jewel said.

"Nearly a million credits," Jason replied. "Cost?"

"With current cost of fuel for a fill-up..."

"Cost for just the fuel to drop and return with enough to cover, say, flying around the northern area of Chindia? Just roaming?"

He already knew it cost over two million credits for a full fuel load at the station. It would be less at the fuel mine.

"Just that much?" Jewel said dubiously. "Depends on the height you're 'roaming.'"

"Twenty thousand feet," Jason said. "No, make it ten. More resistance, right?"

"Yes," Jewel said. "Hang on...eighty-six thousand credits at current fuel cost with sixteen thousand kilometers of 'roaming.'"

"Pretty much everything else becomes a rounding error," Jason said. "The crew can fly on shares. Say a hundred thousand credits worth of fuel for one trip up and back and it should return with partial tanks."

"What you're considering is crazy even by your normal standards, Jason," Jewel said. "How are the colonists going to get there?"

"How'd most of the team get down?" Jason said. "In stasis, even if the whole system fails, all that happens is they end up in the wrong place. They're not going to be injured, right?"

"Yes, but..."

"Airborne motto," Jason said. "The whole world is a drop zone and you can drop anything. Once. With a ten grand you can pretty much literally drop *anything*."

"You're going to need to test this," Jewel pointed out.

"Yeah," Jason said. "But there's other stuff to do first."

# CHAPTER 18 >>>>>>>>>

"HEY," JASON SAID, SHAKING HIS FIRST GUEST'S HAND. "JASON Graham. Welcome to Brandywine Foods."

It was taking a while to get Brandywine's set up and the Twelve Bravo Fuel Mine negotiations were going nowhere. So, he'd decided to stick his nose in and invite the other large unit holders to lunch. A real fresh-food, cooked lunch.

But he was using the Brandywine offices for the lunch meeting.

"Ryan Phillips," Phillips said, looking him over along with the room.

Tim had decided to lean in to Brandywine being about food. The interior of the reception area was now dotted with pictures of wild animals and plants with example foods from them. There were pictures of wild mushrooms in their settings with other pictures under them of bushels of the same wild mushrooms then cooked in a skillet. Bison and buffalo and then cuts of meat on a grill. Shrimp runs, piles of fresh shrimp and more piles of boiled. Fish, fruits, the greens they were starting to collect—the room was permeated with images of food.

"I hope that offer of lunch wasn't joking," Phillips said. He was tall and slender with brown hair and eyes. "This room is making me hungry."

"Already prepared and in stasis," Jason said, grinning.

"All this is...?"

"All this is collected on the planet by our harvest teams,"

Jason said. "And brought back to the station. Right now, we only sell semicommercial. Food is shipped by the case, minimum. And only raw. We're in the process of building an event space and possibly later a restaurant."

"Fresh food is pretty rare..." Phillips said as the outer door dilated.

"Am I in the right place?"

The speaker was a woman with black hair and a slender build. Jason recognized her as Eowyn De Wever.

"Ms. De Wever," Jason said, shaking her hand as well. "Welcome to Brandywine Foods. Jason Graham. And this is Ryan Phillips."

"We've met," De Wever said, smiling tightly. "Ryan."

"Eowyn," Phillips said, also smiling tightly.

"I take it your parents were Tolkien fans?" Jason asked.

"How'd you guess?" Eowyn said, grimacing.

"If you really hated it, why not change it?" Jason asked, furrowing his brow.

"I don't, really," Eowyn said. "I like Tolkien, too. But I probably should have thought of the issues of going into IT. Then there was the fact that I used to cosplay. But I preferred anime and superhero. Then people would find out my name was Eowyn and... It's like it hammered me into a mold I was supposed to live, you know? And there I go oversharing again."

"My dad made the Great Santini look gentle, kind and wishy-washy," Jason said, shrugging. "We all have to live with the life we're given. What about you, Mr. Phillips? Also a science fiction and fantasy fan?"

"Not really," Phillips said with an edge in his voice. "I was a vice president with Amoco before the Transfer."

"Where'd you go to school?" Jason asked.

"University of Texas *and* he has a *master's* in business from the *Wharton* School of Business," Eowyn said archly. "That's the University of Pennsylvania. A very *prestigious* school!"

"At least I have an MBA," Phillips snapped. "Not a gaming degree."

"It's not a degree in gaming, you moron..." Eowyn snapped back.

"Okay," Jason said, holding up his hands. "I haven't been involved in these discussions because I've been a *little* busy fighting crocodiles. But... if we could table this until we've got some real food in our stomachs, maaaybe we can come to some agreement..."

"This the right place?"

Eduard Klima was bearded and heavy-set with brown hair and blue eyes. He was also Czech, the only non-North American among the top unit holders in Twelve Bravo.

"The right place," Jason said, introducing himself.

"Have these two gone at it yet?" Klima asked, making a face.

"Oh, yeah," Jason said. "We're only waiting on Ms. Bellinger. Perhaps we could move to the conference room. There's appetizers."

Jason led the way to the conference room and opened up one of the waiting stasis cases. Besides five places laid out, there were also small plates laid out to the side.

"Skewers of wild mushrooms and wild onions," Jason said, laying the tray out by the small plates. "Woodfire grilled. Drinks? We have a rather questionable white wine, not a vintage I know, some decent beers and a selection of Brandywine's Finest Forgery liquors."

"Brandywine's...what?" Eowyn asked, taking a skewer and popping a mushroom into her mouth. "Oh, that's good. What? And I'll try the white."

"Brandywine's Finest Forgery," Jason said, pouring a glass of white wine and handing it to Eowyn. "Our team of expert counterfeiters are using basic ethanol along with an array of artificial and natural flavorings to fake fine liquor. It was illegal on Earth but it's a bit more libertarian here. Mister Phillips? The Finest Forgery Lucullan? Guaranteed to taste old enough to date."

"Seriously," Phillips said but it was around a mouthful of mushroom. "These are really good. What are they?"

"Bellerophon Shiitake, I believe," Jason said. "Most of the mushroom species we've found are not native to earth. They've evolved."

He poured a glass of dark liquor and handed it to Phillips.

"Seriously. Try it. I'd favor your thoughts. Mr. Klima?"

"You mentioned beer," Klima said with a thick Slavic accent. "Anything decent?"

"To a Czech?" Jason asked, shrugging. "I can hope."

He pulled out one of the microbrewery oatmeal stouts and poured it in a glass.

"Try it?" he said as the door opened.

"Sorry I'm late. Data said I should have taken the left turn at Albuquerque."

Mary Claire Bellinger was short with a muscular build, blonde hair and bright green eyes.

"Oh, that smells heavenly," she said, inhaling then grabbing a skewer.

"Shall we be seated?" Jason asked.

"You don't understand business!" Phillips snapped. He'd maybe had a bit too much Brandywine's Finest.

"I know somebody who has a stick up their ass!" De Wever replied. And wine.

The lunch had gone...sporadically well and occasionally wrong. The problem was choosing management and they hadn't even gotten that far. If one individual held more than seven percent of an item that was defined by units, they could call a vote of the unit holders on matters like forming a board. Jason's control of Spaceship Four and Carbon Converter Charlie were examples. A few other people had managed similar control of some facilities.

But the fuel mine had sixteen million discrete "owners." And absent a single owner with holdings above seven percent, it required twelve percent agreement.

And nobody, not even Jason, was listening to the alerts on votes or trades.

Jewel had done the math. It took a computer. It would require around eight hundred thousand people to listen to the alerts and agree to vote on a board. *Any* of them could propose someone for the board. They didn't even have a *size* for the board.

No board, no leadership. No leadership, no agreements on who would be allowed to lease and operate the fuel mine. No operating company, no fuel.

De Wever and Phillips were two personalities that were *never* going to get along. Phillips was a credentialist who felt the people who should be making the decisions were people who were experienced at and trained in making those decisions.

De Wever had had problems with men telling her she didn't really "fit in" for most of her career and resented it. But she also was smart as a whip. Probably smarter than Phillips, who was no idiot. Problem was, she knew it and would use it to needle Phillips. One way was to point out that of the four of them, Phillips held the fewest units. Which meant he'd been slow off the mark.

Klima and Bellinger mostly sat the battle out but enjoyed the food.

"Whoa, whoa," Jason said, holding up his hands for the fifth time. "Phillips is right."

"What?" Eowyn snapped. "You're taking his side?"

"I'm not taking anyone's side," Jason said. "My sole intent here is to get the fuel mine up and going. I really don't care one whit how. But he has a point. People inside the big business world do know details and intricacies that aren't well understood by people outside big business. It's not all golfing, an old-boy's-club and insider dealing. What's the depreciation on a fuel mine?"

"I . . ." Eowyn said. "No clue."

"Nor do you know how to *calculate* it," Phillips snapped.

"He's also wrong," Jason said.

"How?" Phillips snapped.

"The bottom line of all business is *people*," Jason said soothingly. "People are the biggest risk in any business venture. Yes?"

"Yes," Phillips said, listening for once.

"The problem for traditional business is that the unit holders are a large number of people who have no clue what's going on," Jason said. "That, right there, is a major risk. And traditional business is mostly about reducing risk. That is a primary area of training and experience. Reduce costs, reduce risk."

"And there's a problem with that?" Phillips said, a touch angrily.

"There's *no way* to calculate the risks," Jason said, shrugging. "Zero. Zip. There are sixteen million, less a bit, holders of units in Twelve Bravo. This group represents less than one percent of that ownership. Tomorrow, someone might figure out a way to gain a much larger share. No idea how, but that's the risk. So even if some agreement can be come to, tomorrow that agreement might be moot. That risk is incalculable. So are all the other risks.

"You can calculate depreciation on a fuel mine, you say? We don't even have a firm grasp on how the *technology* works. It will take a *physicist* to explain to *engineers* to explain to *finance people* what the lifespan of the various parts are before depreciation can be calculated. It might break a week after we've gotten it up and going. There might be an expensive part that breaks on a weekly basis . . ."

"I find that unlikely," Phillips said, frowning.

"But can you *eliminate* it as a risk?" Jason asked. "No, you can't. Because *nobody knows*. So that's where you're right and where you're wrong. The value of the experience and training of traditional businesspeople, such as yourself, is their ability and experience at calculating risk to the last penny and eliminating every possible risk. This is a serious statement: *Eowyn* knows exactly as much about the risks of the mine as you do. As *I* do. As any of us do. Which does not, to make it clear to Eowyn, invalidate the value of a Wharton degree."

"I never said it was useless," Eowyn said. "But..."

"But it's not the utility it had as a vice president of Amoco," Jason pointed out. "It has a value in this discussion. In the details. But the real problem is people. As in: Nobody wants to hear about their units. There's too damned many of them!"

"With that I'll one hundred percent agree," Phillips said with an aggrieved sigh. "Did those robot idiots really have to give ownership of everything to five hundred million people?"

"How else?" Klima said. "I'm from Eastern Europe. I know how people were screwed over by privatization. By making it illegal to trade units for cash, it prevents oligarchs from stealing everything!"

"We, somehow, have to get twelve percent of sixteen million people to agree to at least a board to elect leadership," Jason said, shrugging. "Together we control less than one percent. And even *we* can't agree. So, if we're going to have any chance of getting the twelve percent onboard, we're going to have to agree on something. We agree that everyone's got too many units and it's a pain. Can we agree lunch was good?"

"Lunch was very good," Mary Claire said, grinning. "You could bribe people with food."

"Sixteen million," Jason said. "Everyone who checked either held onto their shares or added immediately. Everyone else has turned off their alerts for unit trades. The station is going to need fuel within six months. If we can't form a board, the gubmint is probably going to step in. It might come to that. So, we need to figure out how to get twelve percent of the ownership to listen."

"Good luck," Mary Claire said.

"I got a notification today," Mabel said.

Her words jerked Cade out of his irritated reverie. They stood at the planting beds site, and Cade stared at the dirt strewn across the floor. When word had got out that Cade Oldham liked planting cabbage and carrots, people had begun to come to him to sell their flowerbeds. He'd tried to trade and retrade as necessary, to keep all his beds in one place, and he'd mostly succeeded.

So, he'd grown to eight and then twelve and eventually to the point where he owned all the planting beds in this park. The locals had taken to calling the park "Cade's Farm," which only felt to Cade like a knife twisted in his back.

This morning, someone had kicked dirt out of several of the beds. It happened from time to time. Cade wondered if he could explain what he was doing to President Dewalt and get the right to put up flexmet fences to keep people out.

He'd already inquired, and determined that there was no way to acquire the playground at the center of Cade's Farm. The playground attracted children, and, frankly, it was probably children who kept messing with Cade's planting beds.

"What notification?" he mumbled. He could get a cot and sleep on the Farm, keep an eye on it himself.

"I was notified that I volunteered to be on the first colony ship."

Something in Mabel's voice made Cade wary. He tore his eyes away from the dirt. "Yes. Under the new homesteading law, we get a bigger plot the earlier we're willing to go down. I'm still trying to get us down on these onesie-twosie flights, but I figured I'd reserve us a place on the first major ship, just in case."

"There are only five hundred million people," Mabel said, "most of them not farmers. Seems like there should be plenty of land."

"I think so," Cade agreed. "We definitely want our choice, to get the best land, don't we?"

Mabel's face suggested that maybe she didn't.

"You know Richter, from church," Cade said. "He says he's up for the farming, but not interested in being a pioneer. He doesn't want to go first. Of course, that's why the first colonists get the biggest land grants, because they're taking more risk. Going down when the animals are wildest and the fields aren't plowed and there's no infrastructure. But maybe we want to go down later. It would probably still be enough land for us, and less roughing it."

Mabel had come out with Cade to weed, and the grubby gardening gloves on her hands, now balled into fists, made her look like a boxer.

"Is that what we want?" she asked.

"I feel like I'm missing a point here," Cade said. "Maybe you should tell me what we want."

"So that's how it works," Mabel said. "One of us decides for all of us. And we take turns who's the decider."

"Got it." Cade bowed his head. "Sorry. I can withdraw the application. Sooner or later, we'll have to go down, but we don't have to be in the first wave. Or the second, or whatever. We'll go when you want to."

"What do *you* want, Cade?"

Cade frowned. "Well, I thought we'd go early."

"Forget about that." Mabel pressed in close to him, which was disconcerting. She was so young. "Forget about the timing of going down to the planet, that's the least of it. What do you want?"

Cade's arms fell to his sides. "I just want everyone to be happy."

She punched him in the chest. When he didn't respond, she punched him twice more.

"What the hell do you want, Cade Oldham? I'm your wife, but you don't touch me. You can barely bring yourself to look at me. Our son has become a delinquent, and you just let him run wild. What do you want?"

Cade took a deep breath.

"I want my muscles back. I want to stand on land I own—land my grandfather farmed—and see it breathe and grow. I want to meet my neighbor at the post office in town and talk about the weather. I want to eat corn on the cob under an open sky. I want to look at my pastor, and not see a kid. I want to look at myself in the mirror, and not see a kid. I want to ..."

"You want to look at your wife," she said. "And not see a kid."

"It feels wrong." His face was numb.

"You know," she said softly, "I'm stronger and more flexible than I have been in decades. You might really enjoy that."

"I just ..." Cade shrugged. "I'm not ready."

"So, this time you want me to punch it out at *twenty* thousand feet," Tom said. He was in his ship, as usual. There was a living area onboard. "Not just treetop."

"Yes," Jason said. "Now, I'm going to be up front. I'm not willing to test this on people. Yet. You'll be carrying myself and the guy who's going to be working the project. I'll be heading back aboard. The real experiment is whether the conexes will land at the designated DZ without significant human input. Just AI and the onboard tractor."

"I've never done a cargo drop," Tom said then shrugged. "But, what the hell. It's your cargo. No liability at all?"

"None," Jason said. "We take full financial responsibility."

Tim and Kevin had been so uncertain about that, he'd agreed to use his own capital. He had enough.

The company was growing. Three-day training courses had seventeen projects working already, forty more in planning and they'd had to find new warehouse space. Ships were bringing up more and more fresh food, money was rolling in and Tim had, reluctantly, agreed to a small dividend payment.

That was what was paying for the experiment. He'd admitted that it had nothing to do with Brandywine per se. The company would repay him normal drop costs if it worked.

If it worked.

"I'll try most things once," Tom said. "More times if it's a good idea."

"We're about to find out," Jason said.


"I'm not jumping this, right?" Bobby said, looking through the down viewscreens. "It's a long way down..."

Bobby West was a "big-bore gun nut" by his own description. He'd completed training, such as it was, and was taking in a "survey and exploit" package to a pinewood area in Europa. It was Europan midspring and the weather was good. A front had gone through but projected winds weren't bad. Might be a bit chilly on the ground but Bobby was from Wisconsin and prepared.

For the environment. Not to jump.

"Some HALO gear... and some HALO *training*," he continued, referring to High Altitude Low Opening parachute insertion. "Aaand I'd *still* say no."

"Oh, ye of little faith," Jason said.

"Computer says this is the right drop point based on winds aloft," Tom said.

"Green light," Jason replied.

"Eject," Tom ordered.

The ship swung around to view the dropping cargo. It was visibly tearing itself apart, the flexmet extending and stretching the conexes into weird shapes.

"Jewel!" Jason said.

"We're slowing it down," Jewel said. "This stuff is not exactly aerodynamic and we're having to learn, too. Just hang on."

The cargo stabilized and the ship continued to follow it down.

"Since we couldn't drop as fast as planned, we're going to need the ship's tractors to help get it to the drop zone," Jewel said after a moment. "We probably should have practiced from a lower altitude."

"But it's doable," Jason said.

"If you want to do it in quantity, we're going to have to do several more experiments," Jewel said. "And if you want to do it to humans in stasis, you're going to need multiple tests."

"You're going to be dropping *us* that way?" Bobby said.

"Probably not," Jason said. "It's for something else. But in stasis you really *can* drop anything."

# CHAPTER 19 >>>>>>>>>>

"FREE AT LAST, FREE AT LAST," JASON SAID.

"Glad to be headed back to the planet, huh?" Tom said as they entered the access tunnel.

The bay was busy with ships, a sure sign that the economy was starting to get into gear.

"Administrative trivia is a necessity of business," Jason said. "It's also close to my least favorite thing in the world."

It had only taken three days of training for the teams. It took five days to complete all the discussions, start developing SOPs and develop a business structure, most of the ovals unfilled, for the expansion. Capital had to come from sales; there was nowhere else to get it. Even then, Richard could only loan them money for more equipment if he had money flowing into the bank. And staying there.

Banks taking money from individuals and businesses could only loan twelve times the amount of money they had in the bank. That was a fairly standard rule and it still applied in Pegasus.

Richard had to have Brandywine leave as much capital in the bank as possible to make the loans that Brandywine, in turn, needed to buy equipment.

Everybody was bootstrapping.

A lease had to have something to harvest to make it really worthwhile. Desert areas, interesting as they might be, weren't going to be producing much in the way of protein. Game meat in temperate areas was best in fall when the animals had had a summer to pack on fats. That ruled out Europa and America Nova for game; they were in spring.

So, the majority of the teams were going into Chindia for the time being. But teams were being dispersed into limited areas on those two continents as well. Fungi were a year-round thing, with the exception of winter, and spring meant the potential for spring greens. It also gave an idea what might be available in fall in different biomes. As long as the lease made its nut, finding what might be a big earner was worthwhile. Were there wild apples in a particular zone?

In the tropical areas it was monsoonal oriented. The end of the wet season was the best time to harvest.

Until they had at least a year and a half of data on leases, many questions would remain unanswered. To that end, Jason researched power technology. He'd already determined that Cyber energy storage was insanely efficient. That an Alfred could run for twelve hours, flying, with half its maximum carriage weight, was insane. It would be the equivalent of a Tesla being able to drive around the world a dozen times on one charge.

And there were industrial batteries held by the government.

The decision was made to leave ten drones and an Alfred in each lease area for the entire year along with a conex and a coffin of batteries. Batteries were cheap and the lease on the conexes was doable. If the drones detected anything that was viable for harvest a team could be returned. In the meantime, the drones and Alfred would slowly collect whatever was saleable in the lease and get a full ecological and marketability profile. Pickups would happen as conexes filled.

Commercial fishing, which was still where the majority of the protein came from, was a different matter. Different species ran at different times and it wasn't a good idea to take species when breeding. Jason was thinking about short term but also long term for the planet. The exception was salmon. Most salmon harvesting was done when they were on a breeding run. It was just how it worked.

And Jason was focused like a laser on salmon. The annual salmon runs on Earth involved tons of protein; here that would mean protein to feed the station and get money moving around in the economy. With enough trapping it would be a matter of having enough lift.

The question was, did the planet even *have* salmon? There had been human attempts to introduce salmon in half a dozen biomes where they should have survived: New Zealand, Chile and South Africa were just three. Jason was assuming the Cybers had overcome that issue. If salmon did run here, *where* would they run?

Though there was no reason they wouldn't run in Chindia, it was a different world after all, the sunken continent between Europa and America Nova had perfect conditions for salmon offshore. And Europa and America Nova were biomes that supported salmon on Earth; there were no natural trout species found on the other continents and salmon was a variant of trout.

The target was a large bay on the western shores of America Nova. The bay was the terminus of a major river that ran from America Mons to the Beringia Sea. The river had a wide delta where it reached the bay, not as extensive as the Mississippi Delta but spreading from about fifty miles upstream. The river entered the bay on the south end, directly across from the larger opening to the sea.

There were steep hills, some reaching the size of small mountains, on the seaward side. It was impossible to determine the hydrographic profile from the satellite images but given there was a large island in the middle of the entrance to the bay, an obvious extension of the range of hills, the entrance was probably relatively shallow. Probably deep enough to take any Earth ship, but not hundreds of feet deep. There were obviously more subsurface rocks based on what he'd been able to glean of the currents around the entrance. The waves of the Beringia Sea pounded both the capes as well as the outer face of the central island.

The landward side was relatively flat, especially around the delta, and the entire eastern shoreline was a tangle of black-mud marshes. There was one large hill, shorter than the hills on the seaward side, defining the north terminus of the delta area. The terrain was fairly flat north of the hill as well. In earlier times, the delta had clearly filled in around the hill. Another, smaller, river emptied into the bay on the north end.

The bay was probably the remnant of an asteroid impact on the pre-terraformed planet. Before the Cybers got to work on the planet, it had probably been a crater. When they added water, the crater had filled in even more with soil sediment carried down by the river. At a guess, the landward hill was probably the remains of the central uplift. There was a series of hills about the same distance inland as the seaward hills that the river had bored a gorge through. Those were probably the eastern side of the crater rim. That point on the river was a series of cataracts and it defined the inland start of the delta.

The weather in the area was rough. It appeared to be similar to the Pacific Northwest or Ireland. Satellite images showed frequent strong storms as well as impenetrable fog. Unlike the Pacific Northwest, the majority of the trees were deciduous, a mix of maple, hickory, birch and oak with a smattering of hemlock and spruce.

If there *were* salmon, they'd be somewhere in the area and he intended to find them. Salmon weren't only found offshore. They frequently came into bays to eat. To find them would require angling, fishing with a line and pole, with lures and bait suitable for salmon.

Oh, heaven forbid! It was going to be work, work, work!

His landing target was the island in the center of the bay's entrance. Though he'd spotted carnivores in the satellite imagery, it should be easy enough to clear and, absent new visitors, that would secure it so he could move around on the ground without fear of being eaten.

It was late spring in the deciduous region of America Nova and the leaves were bright as they descended. Massive waves burst on the seaward side but the coves on the landward side were barely moving. Much of the bay itself was filled with white caps from the high winds but inshore on the east side of the island it was fairly smooth.

"Looks a bit like San Francisco Bay," Tom said. "Complete with sea lions," he added, zooming one of the screens. There were sea lion colonies as well as harbor and elephant seals.

"Bit," Jason said. "Bit less cut up. Could you circle for a while on the bay? I pored over sat images but this is a better view."

"Not a problem," Tom said. "That's what the extra pay is for."

Jason carefully considered the bay. The water was murky from plankton and input of silt from the river. It was also filled with kelp. Just as in the satellite images, it was impossible to determine the bottom profile. He'd managed to figure out how to hook up a sonar system someone had had in their personal belongings. He was going to have to use that to determine what the hydrography was like.

"Whales," Tom said, pointing. There was a pod of whales inshore near the delta.

"Probably right whales," Jason said. "Good sign. Proves the bay is productive which it would essentially have to be with the river input. Can you swing around for a second?" Jason said, pointing to an area on the northeast side of the island where the steep hills ended in cliffs.

"Sure," Tom replied, dancing the ship in that direction.

"Thought so," Jason said, pointing to oval shapes on the rocks in the tidal zone.

"Abalone?" Tom asked.

"Probably," Jason said. "I thought I spotted them but the angle on the sat shots was never great. They're great for looking down, not so good for sideways on a cliff."

"Gonna call it Island of the Blue Dolphin?" Tom asked, heading to the landing point.

"No," Jason said. "It's not a dry island like the Catalinas. I'll come up with a name."

"Ferrell Bay?" Tom suggested.

"I'm actually naming it Wilson Bay after my partner," Jason admitted, shame faced. "I'll name something else after you."

"Got it," Tom said. "Besides, I've already got stuff named after me."

"There we go," Jason said, pointing to a school of fish. "Magnify."

When the camera zoomed in it was apparent that he was looking at salmon.

"Bingo," Jason said. "*Now* to the island."

"On it," Tom said, sliding the ship in expertly despite the obvious winds. The day was clear but the trees on the upper slopes of the island were stunted and twisted from the winds off the Beringia. Even then they could be seen waving in the strong wind. "Southeast side."

"Should be the most protected," Jason said.

There were no convenient clearings to land the cargo in. There was, however, a large flat area on the southeast side. To its north was a small stream, remnant of the frequent rains in the area. The stream had probably filled in a natural depression over time. It appeared to meander through the trees and the flat area was predominantly birch, beech and poplar, fast growing pioneer trees that indicated the area was relatively recent, geologically.

Now if it was just stable soil.

"You just want it dumped over the water?"

"In close," Jason said. "As close as you can get it to the trees, right at waterline."

"Watch your footing on the containers," Tom said. "The winds are pretty high. Less so in close to the island, but no zephyr."

"Got it," Jason said. "I'll deploy the bots and drones first and tie off to a bot. I'm not going to try to balance on top of the cargo in these winds."

"Safety first," Tom said.

"Safety is overrated," Jason said as they approached the landing point. "There is no adventure with safety. Adventure is something bad that happened to someone else a long time ago in a galaxy far, far away. At the time it's misery and pain and blood. With perfect safety there is no adventure and adventure is *under*rated."

The ship clunked mildly as the containers were dumped out the back.

"You're deployed...adventurer," Tom said.

"Wish me luck," Jason replied, picking up his Safari.

"Just hope you don't have to find out how strong a swimmer you are," Tom replied.

The wind wasn't nearly as fierce with the protection of the island and near the water.

Jewel had automatically brought an Alfred up and Jason carefully turned around on the landing platform and gestured for it to come up behind him. When it did, he attached it to his back with flexmet then extended "controls."

"Have it respond like a jetpack," Jason said, pushing himself backward off the platform.

"Got it," Jewel said.

It took a bit to get the ersatz jetpack to work properly and Jason nearly dunked himself once. But after that he had it down.

"All good, Tom," Jason said, waving. "Fair travels."

"You just can't stand being normal, can you?" Tom said as the ship lifted up soundlessly.

"What fun would *that* be?" Jason replied.

The bots and drones were already well underway clearing a space for the containers.

"Have one of the Alfreds do a soil auger test," Jason said. One of the teams that had dropped while he was on the station had ended up in a marsh. It had been a simple matter of moving campsites but it gave reason for caution. Soil tests before putting in a camp were now standard SOP.

"Already done," Jewel said. "Did that first. Soil is stable and the trees indicate no recent flooding in the area."

When an area flooded, a distinctive ring formed on the trees. No rings, no flooding. Another good sign.

The flat zone was clearing out rapidly. Jason had insisted that a test team had to have additional equipment. So, this time he had one Herman, four Alfreds, two metric tons of flexmet and fifty drones. Ten of the drones were clearing along with the other three Alfreds. The rest of the drones were beginning the survey of not only the island but the surrounding bay.

"Confirmed salmon school," Jewel said as he waited. "Whether they run is another question. Confirmed abalone. Confirmed right whales. Seventeen bears on the island so far, no tigers or leopards. Red deer. Two other deer species. No hogs. One wolf pack so far. The delta has so many species of migrating waterfowl we're having a hard time counting them. Not the individuals, the species. Most of them are new. A couple of new bird species on the island as well. Bird evolution on this planet has been crazy."

"Anything look tasty?" Jason asked.

"Previously identified churken," Jewel said.

Churken were about the size of chicken but filled the niche that wild turkey inhabited in North America, ground-feeding, tree-nesting omnivores. They mostly fed on insects and seeds.

The major difference was that the males were brightly colored in blue and red. They turned out to be a species of parrot instead of the evolutionary path of turkeys or chickens for that matter. Jason hadn't eaten one yet, and was looking forward to trying it out. Like any wild fowl it had to be prepared carefully since they were so lean.

"There are various ducks and geese in the delta as well as some things we can't quite sort out," Jewel said. "We'll have to get samples and genetics to figure out what some of these evolved from. There's a duck that looks as if it might be another parrot species. But it might just be a duck descendant."

Any waterfowl that had been around the landing area had taken off when the ship appeared overhead. But Jason could see some bobbing in the water to the north. For that matter, there were sea otters playing in a kelp bed not far away. A sea eagle was squabbling with one over a fish. The otter responded by diving.

The camp was about done. Instead of stripping and topping, smaller trees had been left with their tops intact and used to create an abatis around the camp. Without the massive tree roots it was susceptible to entry but should keep the big creatures out.

He planned to have the apex carnivores cleared. Bad for the ecology, good for survival. The red deer, which were a definite threat, were less likely to try to penetrate the abatis. And he intended to harvest them as well.

He might take the bears himself. At least the ones that were further into the island. The nearest were already being culled. He had no intention of allowing a megagrizzly near his camp. At this rate, bearskin rugs were going to be an absolute glut.

He might need one in his hooch. The high winds were due to a recently passed cold front. It had lived up to its name. He'd dressed for the cooler weather but just hanging over the water was chilling. There was no heat in the camp he'd planned. That might have been a mistake.

"We might need to put a fireplace into the hooch," Jason said.

"Doable with flexmet," Jewel said. "I can put in a stove for that matter."

"Flex doesn't conduct heat," Jason said.

"You can create openings for your pans," Jewel said. "Set it up to let the heat come to them but the smoke go away. Or you can cook over the open fire in a fireplace like a heathen."

"I'm a heathen," Jason said as the containers started to move into the cleared ground. There was a view out across the bay on the east side but he didn't intend to see it. The square fort would have his container on the ground this time to avoid the winds. They'd also planned for drainage when it rained.

He slid forward, keeping high so if he messed up, he wouldn't get dunked, and settled with a bit of a bobble beside the housing container.

It contained more than just his gear so it was collapsed and unloading as he landed. He dismissed the Alfred to help then climbed up on one of the conexes to survey the scene.

It was a pretty good view. The right whales were in view, apparently hunting something in the water, and sea birds including sea eagles were soaring in the sky. The tree-covered hill that defined the edge of the delta was barely visible in the distance. Given the relative flatness of the eastern shore it was evident. The sky was filled with scudding cumulus clouds, some of them ominously dark.

"There's rain on the way," Jewel said.

"I thought it was going to be clear?" Jason said. He'd timed the landing for a day that the forecast was clear.

"Meteorology on this planet is in its infancy," Jewel pointed out. "A drone just spotted it coming inshore. And one suspects that this is an area where if you don't like the weather, just wait five minutes."

"Have a drone stay up at a high point on the island," Jason said, as a spattering rain started. He hitched his jacket closer and adjusted his hat. "A little rain never killed anybody. Speaking of dying: What's the status on the bears?"

"All bears in a one-kilometer radius have been culled," Jewel answered. "The bots are starting on cleaning and butchering. There remain other potential threats. There's a wild cat the size of a lynx, though it's probably related to the bobcat. And the red deer and other herbivores that can be territorial."

"They'll probably stay away from the fort," Jason said.

"And the wolf pack," Jewel added. "It's on the north end of the island at the moment but the entire island is probably its territory."

"Eliminate if it comes close," Jason said. "I hate just wiping out the apex predators, but more game for people and I don't have to worry about being eaten myself. Especially when I'm fishing."

The housing container had been set up to his liking. His camp chair and table were by the already formed fireplace. There was a pile of firewood next to it as well as some dry wood already stacked in it. Where the bots had found dry wood was anyone's guess.

A flex air mattress had been formed and was covered with his poncho liners as well as spare poly blankets and pillow.

It was nice to have robotic servants on safari.

He started the fire then opened up his personal gear coffin and considered the contents. Raining or not, he was going fishing. He might catch, he might not, but fishing was going to occur.

The question was what sort of gear? He'd brought two coffins of personal gear, one with guns and ammo, the other with fishing gear. And he'd brought *all* the fishing gear he'd built up over a lifetime. There were surf-casting rods, fly rods, bass rods, not to mention three tackle boxes. There were even a couple of heavy rods with large reels for offshore trolling.

There was very little indication of types of fish in the area. Satellites had spotted shoals of herring and he'd confirmed salmon. Neither was normally caught from shore and his experience of inshore in these sorts of conditions was minimal.

In the end, he just brought the whole thing.

The camp was on a cove. Two fingers of rock extended out into the bay to the north and south of the camp with the north tongue right by the edge of the camp wall. He'd placed the camp where it was specifically to take advantage of that tongue of rock. It appeared to be above the high-tide line on the top. He'd have to watch his footing on the edges. They'd be covered in algae and slippery.

He rode the coffin over the perimeter fence then down onto the rock before setting it down. He considered the images from the drones but all he could spot was the occasional flash of fish in the cove. There were, however, abalone and it made sense to start there.

He used the flexmet bracelet to form an abalone knife and levered one of the large mollusks off the rock. He wasn't sure what the minimum size for abalone on Earth might be, but whatever species this was he was pretty sure it was above minimum.

He cut out the meat of the abalone then tossed the shell and guts back into the cove. It was immediately assailed by fish. Good sign.

He extracted a large surf-fishing rod from the coffin and assembled it with a Carolina bottom rig then cut off a strip of abalone, baited the hook and tossed the combination into the water about thirty meters out.

The heavy bottom rig never made it to the bottom before there was a strong strike.

"There is *no* sport," he muttered, setting the hook.

Whatever the fish was, it was a fighter. The rod was rigged with fifty-pound mono, brand new courtesy of their Cyber Overlords, with a one-hundred-pound mono leader. And he wasn't sure if the fish wasn't going to break it a few times. The fish quickly found cover in the kelp but the leader managed to cut right through it.

After about a twenty-minute fight he got the fish into the shallows and brought it up into a sea pool.

"Species?" Jason asked.

"It appears to be a type of sea bass," Jewel said musingly. "But that term is used for a variety of species on Earth. To be more precise, it appears to be something similar to a striped sea bass or striper colloquially. But there are differences. We'd have to do a genetic test to determine."

"Later," Jason said, tossing the thirty-pound fish into a stasis case. "We can collect abalone for sure. As soon as the drones and bots are done clearing the area, have the Alfreds get down here to start on boats."

"Will do," Jewel said.

He looked around at the abalone. There was about one per two square meters at a guess. They were all over the tide line.

"Abalone will definitely sell," Jason said. "Bring down a drone."

Jason hooked the flexmet to the drone and replicated prying the abalone up, this time using a bed of flexmet. Then he had the drone pick it up and put it in the stasis case. Last, he had the flexmet crawl to another abalone and pry it up. Lather, rinse, repeat.

"Is that enough of an algorithm?" Jason asked.

"It's workable," Jewel said. "With some tweaks."

"When there's time and available bots, have one take a stasis case up to the north cliffs," Jason said. "Don't take any more abalone from around here. Set out some cases and have one or two drones collect them until the case is full then replace it with one of the available bots."

"Without the necessity to keep a flexmet defense net going, Herman is freed up," Jewel pointed out.

"Whichever," Jason said.

"The flexmet can clean the abalone as well," Jewel pointed out. "Do we load complete or clean them?"

"Clean them," Jason said.

"Keep the shells or discard?" Jewel asked.

"Discard," Jason said after a moment's thought. "There's probably a minor market for mother of pearl, but not enough to bother with lift. I want to see if I can get one of those salmon," Jason said, rerigging. Given that the hit had been near the surface of the water, and he seemed to remember that striper sometimes went for plugs, he rigged a plug instead of a bottom line and tossed out the rig.

"No sport," Jason muttered a moment later as another fight started. "I don't think it's even feeding time..."

# CHAPTER 20 >>>>>>>>

"IN THE EVENT THIS GOES BAD," JASON SAID, "THE ALFRED'S primary job is to get me back to camp."

The idea was simple. Use the Alfred to drive the boat while dropping various sorts of traps into the bay. Along the way they could get a bottom profile. The flexmet boat was composed of an entire container's worth of flex with ballast of rocks gathered from the island.

The problem was, as far as he was aware, nobody had ever tried this. It *should* work. Flex was lighter than water and he'd included bubbles in the flex that were designed to add to the buoyancy.

Then again, it might either capsize or just sink. He wasn't a maritime engineer.

"It's going to work," Jewel said. "The engineering is sound."

The boat was pulled up on the sand shore. The sandy beach—most of the area was black mud—was another reason to put the camp there. He pulled out from the shore and . . . motored into the bay, staying in the calm water off the island.

The boat settled a bit but not much. That there was no open area in the hull was part of his trepidation, it was solid flex filled with containers of bait and weights.

He kept half an eye on where he was going, controlling the movement with a couple of joysticks he'd extended from the flexmet, and the other eye on the sonar. As another squall of rain started, he extended a cover above his head and finally just built a cabin. Better. He was going to have to find some heavy glass or equivalent somewhere.

The sonar profile at first showed a cut-up rocky bottom as far as he could tell. The big problem was all the sea life that was cluttering up the image. The bay was alive with fish.

He silently motored out about a hundred meters and spotted a flat area that appeared right.

"Crab trap away," Jason said.

They'd discussed this and designed it before they left the station. There were a variety of different types of traps for maritime species. Though all the bait was going to be the same, offal from harvester teams, they had studied fish traps as well as traps for crustaceans. By designing the right trap, you would somewhat specify *what* got trapped. Fish traps had different openings and exits than lobster traps, which had different openings and exits than crab traps, et cetera.

The flexmet, controlled by Jewel, obediently cut a chunk of offal, put it in a container in the trap, added one hundred kilos of steel weight then extruded the completed trap off the back of the boat. A length of flexmet based on the sonar depth plus ten percent followed it into the depths, then a "balloon" was attached to the end by opening up the flexmet like a flower and trapping air.

The balloon splashed into the water and, once the trap was away, the mass of the boat reduced by the equivalent of all the material.

After two hours he'd deployed all the weights and most of the offal. He'd also set out a variety of sizes of gill nets to find what fish were on the bottom. He'd braved the waves opposite the narrower north opening and the boat had handled it fine. He'd expected some queasiness but apparently vertigo and motion sickness were something else the Cybers had tooled out of humanity.

"Okay," Jason said, pulling a rod out of a coffin. "Time for some fun. See if a drone can spot those salmon."

"Southwest," Jewel said. "Near the south entrance to the bay."

That was a long run but he could mostly cross still waters. The problem was he had to cross the rough water and currents by the north entrance.

"Here goes nothing," Jason said. The boat was heavy with flex when he'd crossed it the last time. The lighter boat was going to jump all over the place.

"The boat has a low enough mass the Alfred can fly it," Jewel said, predicting his issue.

"Just fly?" Jason said. "Okay..." He considered the controls he'd made and retracted them. "Make it so."

The entire gray boat lifted into the air and soared across the bay giving Jason an even better view. It was totally worth it. It also gave him an idea.

"Does an Alfred have to stay upright to fly?" Jason asked.

"No," Jewel replied. "Tractors use the contragravity plates just as the coffins and conexes. But they have them woven on all sides. So, they can counter gravity on their side or upside down. And the lift and drive system could lift and drive them well enough even without the contragravity. Just takes more energy."

"Hmmm..." Jason said as the flying fishing boat approached the target area. "Make a note to remind me of that when I've got some free time."

He could see the large school of salmon feeding at the surface.

"Don't fly over them," Jason said. "Land about a hundred meters this side."

The fish were apparently feeding on anchovies in the wider south opening and the waves and currents looked... fun.

"Careful on landing," Jason said, subconsciously extending a length of flexmet to his waist as a precaution. He looked the boat over and shaped it mentally to have stronger transom and bulkheads and more internal space. They'd discussed hull forms and he adjusted that to those found on deep sea fishing boats found in northern coastal waters.

The waves were rough and the little boat rolled from side to side.

"We need more ballast," Jewel opined. "It will be doable. The Alfred isn't going to let it roll over or sink but it needs more ballast. Also, you needed to include self-bailing ports. I got it."

"You're a jewel, Jewel," Jason said as the boat shipped water and a wave splashed him in the face. "Well, it will be an aqueous experience..."

"Aqueous experience or not, this rocks!" Jason shouted as the salmon caused his reel to scream. He'd programmed the course so he could stay on the rod and now removed it from the rod holder and set the hook. The salmon slammed into the strike and started a hard run to starboard, circling the boat. "Hold up, Jewel. Let it run."

"Will do," Jewel said.

Jason had conformed the boat to a forty-foot, high-side, open-console design to handle the conditions. The greater length reduced the waves splashing over the front, the high sides prevented shipping water and the length handled the waves better. With the open deck he moved forward to the bow to fight the fish, occasionally grabbing the bulkhead rails to keep from tripping.

It took about thirty minutes to land the fish. Jason walked it back to the stern of the boat, formed a gaff and gaffed it over the side.

"That's a salmon," Jason said as the silvery fish flopped on the deck. It threw the lure and he tossed the line back over the side then set the rod in the rod holder. He held the fish up by the gills as it flopped. "Did the drones get pics?"

"They did," Jewel noted, a tone of doubt in her voice.

"What's wrong?" Jason asked, tossing the fish into a stasis container.

"Before you close that, let one of the drones get a genetic sample," Jewel said. "While it appears to be a salmon, the species is not familiar."

"Get a sample," Jason said.

One of the hovering drones dropped down and extended a probe into the fish. Then the stasis container closed.

"As suspected, it is not any terrestrial species of salmon," Jewel said a few moments later. "It's an evolutionary descendant of rainbow trout."

"Trout?" Jason said. "Salmon and trout are very similar genetically. Are you sure?"

"You're asking an AI if it's sure about something as simple as *salmonoid genetics*?" Jewel asked tautly.

"It just seems a little strange," Jason said.

"Hypothesis," Jewel said. "As you noted, there were attempts to introduce salmon into various biomes that should have supported them that failed. Correct?"

"Yes," Jason said.

"I hypothesize that the Cybers did *not* introduce salmon," Jewel said. "They introduced *trout*. Notably, at the very least, rainbow trout. The species from which this salmon derived."

"So...how'd they become salmon?" Jason asked.

"Brown trout have been found in oceanic littoral areas in the Atlantic," Jewel said.

"That's a new one on me," Jason said. "Really?"

"Really," Jewel said. "In freshwater streams and rivers that were trout bearing and met the ocean, trout would occasionally be caught in the inshore areas. They were capable of surviving in salt water and if the prey was more numerous in the ocean than in the streams, they'd move into the ocean to feed."

"Flash forward a million years," Jason said. "And rainbow trout have adapted to a nearly entirely oceanic life. But do they still breed upriver?"

"They would have to," Jewel said. "It's unlikely that their spawn are survivable in salt water any more than terrestrial salmon. But this is an entirely new salmon species from a different evolutionary track. Naming time."

"What's Sheila's oldest son's name?" Jason asked.

"William," Jewel answered. "He goes by Billy."

"Billy's Salmon," Jason said. "We need to get them down here at some point. Put it on the to-do list."

"Will do," Jewel said. "Also sent a note about it to Sheila and Billy."

"Good," Jason said. "Now, to work! Alfred, cruise through the school again."

It had taken a few tries with different lures to find something the salmon would hit. They were hunting anchovies and it turned out a simple silver spoon was the best bet.

Just as the second salmon hit, the phone chimed.

"Billy's asking if you've got a second," Jewel said.

"If he doesn't mind talking while I'm fighting a fish," Jason said.

"Hey, Uncle Jason," Billy said. "Thanks for naming a fish after me. Nice salmon, by the way."

"You're welcome," Jason said, struggling with the fish. "I've already got another one on the line."

"Fishing on this planet has *no* sport," Billy opined.

"You've been down?" Jason asked.

"I work for you," Billy said after an awkward silence. "I mean, I work for Brandywine. I just started my solo in inland Chindia."

"Eek," Jason said. "I hadn't...I am horrible about keeping up."

"Don't worry," Billy said with a chuckle. "So am I. I only know you're the boss because Mom mentioned it. She's working in the accounting department. Dad's working in shipping and receiving and Terry and Chuck are both going through training right now as harvesters."

"Good to hear," Jason said, working the fish around the port side of the boat. "How's it going? Jungle? Forest?"

"Plains," Billy said. "Lots of ungulates. Lots of lions. Lots and *lots* of megalions."

"Please tell me you've got a big enough rifle," Jason said. "I'll get you one if you don't."

"It's standard to take a loan with Derren now," Billy said. "The story about you and your trusty .30-06 has gotten around. I got my hands on a Safari fairly cheap. Just will take about three jobs to pay it off."

"I could have gotten you one," Jason said then thought about it. He'd have to check with Gil. He'd already paid James back for the Safari.

"And for Terry and Chuck?" Billy replied. "We're okay. Just glad to have a job. And be in the fresh air. I'm pulling in tons of protein, so a few trips should pay it off with plenty left over. Not so much on the mushrooms around here. But we've found some types of wild wheat that might make flour."

"How's the fishing?" Jason asked.

"Until I get the crocs cleared from the local river, I am unsure," Billy admitted. "I'm a little leery about taking a fishing pole down to the river at the moment. Ask me in a week. Or, possibly, given the number of crocs, a year. The hunting is fantastic. I took an eland already. I just couldn't loop it."

"Keep drones up, keep an Alfred around and stay out of the long grass," Jason said. "I don't need to explain to your mother why you got eaten by a megalion."

"I will ensure I don't get eaten," Billy said. "Rachel would kill me if I got killed."

"Girlfriend?" Jason asked. He'd put a pole base on his stomach with flex and now extended a tendril to hold the pole up and released to rest his arms.

"Wife," Billy replied. "You're not even sure how old I am, are you? I was thirty-two with two kids when we transferred."

"I probably should have named the salmon after one of your

kids, then," Jason admitted. "I hadn't even spoken to your mom in years until we got transferred."

"Mom barely mentions Granddad and I'd only met him once," Billy said. "Terry and Chuck never have. I'm the oldest, then Terry then Chuck. And don't worry about naming it after one of my kids. My second is named Billy. I'll tell him it was named after him."

"Jewel, try to make that official," Jason said, reeling in a few inches. The salmon wasn't having any of it and did another run, bending the pole practically in half.

"Entry amended," Jewel said. "The species *Salmo billyus* or 'Billy's Salmon,' is named after William 'Billy' Randolph Hansen, great grandnephew of the discoverer Jason Edward Graham. How's that?"

"Sounds fine," Jason said, trying to reel in again. Nope. "Billy, we need to get the family together some time. And we've got to get your kids down here. Somewhere it's safe, mind you."

"That means not around here," Billy said. "But I agree."

"Jewel, put that in the to-do list," Jason said. "And with that, I'm out."

"I'll name a crocodile after you," Billy said.

"That would be appropriate," Jason replied. "Out here."

"He's about to find there's already a crocodile species named after you," Jewel said.

"There is?" Jason replied. The fish was starting to tire and he reeled in a whole foot and a half before it decided it was having none of that. Again.

"When Storm realized you hadn't bothered to name the croc species that nearly ate you, she named it *Crocodylidae grahamus*," Jewel said. "And a species that is genetically distinct in Kush is named *Crocodylidae jasonus*. Then there's the Graham River in Chindia, the Jason River in Chindia and the Graham Mountains in Europa. You'd better name something yourself after yourself before it's all used up."

"So how many of my employees have been trying to curry favor?" Jason asked. The fish was finally tired enough to start bringing it to the boat.

"In some cases, it's currying favor," Jewel said. "But I think the crocodiles are more of a joke. Storm doesn't seem like the type to curry favor."

"Agreed," Jason said.

"And the crocodile in Kush was named by O'Callaghan. He's definitely not the type to curry favor."

"Agreed again," Jason said.

"Mostly, it seems to be people are having as much trouble naming things as you are," Jewel said. "I won't bother to list the number of plant, insect and reptile species with either Wilson or Graham in their names. And those don't seem to be intended as insults, any more than naming a river after one of you is currying favor. More like recognizing that they wouldn't be there if it wasn't for you and Tim.

"Looking at the species and place names that are being named by Brandywine prospectors, it looks as if they're mostly just finding any name that they can. Most things are named after their kids or family. Billy has already named three new species of antelope after his kids. A type of flower after his wife. Rachel's Rose. That sort of thing."

"Makes sense," Jason said. "There are a bunch of species to name."

He got the salmon alongside, gaffed it over the transom and straight into the stasis case.

"The school appears to have disappeared into the deeps," Jewel said.

"Then we'll head over to the delta," Jason said, setting his rod into the rod holder. He stumbled as another wave hit. He'd forgotten how much energy you used on a small boat just keeping your feet. "And let's fly, shall we?"

"That's a lot of protein," Jason said as masses of waterfowl took to wing. The shadow of the boat was obviously a huge aerial predator and they weren't sticking around.

The various ducks, geese and swans numbered in the hundreds of thousands at a guess. Millions, possibly. There was definitely something like snow geese in the mix. And the noted swans. There were mostly various versions of ducks and coots.

"If I had a shotgun, I could probably chase some down on the wing," Jason said, looking around at the flocks.

"If only you'd brought a shotgun," Jewel said.

"I did," Jason pointed out. "It's just back at the camp. Plenty of time for duck hunting. I need a dog."

"That's a new one on the to-do list," Jewel said. "Labrador retriever?"

"More like a springer spaniel," Jason said. "Issue. I've never trained a bird dog. And I'm still spending a good bit of time on the station, which is a terrible place for a dog. I don't need one going hying off after a squirrel and getting eaten by a leopard. And some of the areas we go into are sort of dangerous even for a well-trained dog. Put it on the long-term to-do list."

"Will do," Jewel said. "One trained springer spaniel for bird hunting."

"Let's head to the barn," Jason said. "I missed lunch and working a small boat works up an appetite."

Jason had prepared meals and loaded them in stasis cases while still on the station. He probably should have brought one with him on the boat.

As it was, he sat down at his table, opened the case and extracted one of the flexmet containers therein before closing the case again.

"Not even sure which one this is," Jason said. "Don't peek, Jewel."

"Wouldn't think about it," Jewel said as Jason opened the flex.

"Ah, good choice," Jason said.

The revealed lunch was a roast wild pork loin with roasted wild potatoes and canned asparagus.

People, Americans particularly, tended to have stuff stashed away. Food they'd picked up at one point intending to use and never gotten around to it. Frequently it ended up going out of date. The Cyber Corps had replaced the out-of-date or nearly out-of-date foods with new along with repairing or replacing anything found in damaged condition.

Jason wasn't sure how old the canned asparagus was. He didn't remember buying it. But it made a nice accompaniment to the otherwise Bellerophon-acquired meal.

"Tim's calling," Jewel said.

"Already?" Jason said. "Put him through. Hey, Tim, you're just in time for lunch."

"What grand foods are you eating now?" Tim asked.

"Hey, with all the ground teams, you have more access than I do," Jason said. "And this was a meal I made on the station, so there."

"No new foods down there?" Tim asked.

"Got the traps, lines and nets out," Jason said. "Lots of water-fowl. Lots. Tons of protein on the wing. Just got to figure out how to catch them and slaughter en masse. Probably not this season. Also, outside our lease. Definitely salmon, though not a terrestrial species. Jewel thinks it separately evolved from rainbow trout after the terraforming, which is interesting. New species of abalone. New species of sea bass. The fishing is—"

"No sport at all," Tim said. "I've heard it before."

"Spoil sport," Jason said, taking a bite of pork with potatoes. "You called this meeting. What did we miss in all the other meetings?"

"I've got a project manager working on Brandywine's," Tim said. "There are various issues to discuss and since it's your idea, I'm throwing them at you."

"Discuss away," Jason replied. He loved "discussions" about "issues." Not.

"Décor," Tim said. "The interior has all the usual flex-screen technology. Nice enough. But...everywhere has that. We're trying to figure out some better look using what's available."

"Table for now," Jason said. "I've got an inkling of an idea, already had it, but table for now."

"Furnishings," Tim said with a shrug. "Ditto. We're looking at buying stuff off the market. People who had multiple homes had multiple sets of furniture, dining room tables are available going cheap. But none of it will match."

"Table," Jason said. "Probably falls into the same issue as décor."

"Table settings and silverware, same issue," Tim said. "Stuff is available for sale. Rarely does it match."

"For table settings, plates and so on, what we need is plain bone china," Jason said. "Either round or square. I'm betting that we can find enough bone china that matches closely enough that we can stock the venue. Silverware may be harder. How many plates are we looking at?"

"For the venue size, five hundred," Tim said.

"Jewel, can you find five hundred matching sets of good quality, undecorated, circular bone china available?" Jason asked.

"Yes," Jewel said.

"That's the china out of the way," Jason said. "Matching glasses, silverware, will be harder. White tablecloths shouldn't be an issue. The décor and the furniture...we okay with wood and leather?"

"I'd be okay with wood and leather," Tim said. "What are you thinking?"

"I'm thinking I need another metric ton of flexmet, another Alfred and probably two small electric motors. Then let me see if I can do something with that. Hold off on the décor plans. Although . . . get someone to *design* a wood and leather interior. A designer I am not."

"What sort of design?" Tim asked, confused.

"I dunno," Jason said. "Just get it designed. I'll see if I can match it. I've got some ideas on how to do it but I want to experiment. If I can't match it exactly, I'll talk to the designer about changes."

"Doing wood and leather with flexmet?" Tim said.

"Wood, yes," Jason said. "At least I think so. I'll start working on it. The leather has me flummoxed but give me a bit to think about it. That's my part of the partnership, right?"

"Which was why I pitched it on you," Tim said, grinning. "If you can come up with something, it's off my plate."

"I've got to noodle on it," Jason said distantly. "We good?"

"We're good," Tim said. "Out here."

# CHAPTER 21 >>>>>>>>>

AFTER HE WAS DONE WITH LUNCH JASON CLEARED THE TABLE and held up his hand.

"Drone," Jason said.

The drone obediently landed and Jason examined it carefully. It was, in reality, a central controller, four electric motors and a bunch of flexmet. The motors had a small blob of flexmet on the ends, the "rotors" that retracted automatically on landing.

"How do I remove one of these motors?" Jason asked. "If, for example, it got damaged by a vulture?"

"Just take hold of the motor in one hand and the flex in the other and think about removing it," Jewel said.

The motor removed easily, leaving the blob of flex for the rotors on the end. Jason removed that and revealed a small shaft of metal with six tines to hold the flexmet in place when rotating.

The motor had four small insets that had held flexmet before removing it.

"How is this controlled?" Jason asked.

"Flexmet has to be inserted into opening four," Jewel said. "Between you and I we can control it."

Jason determined which was opening four and inserted a strand of flexmet. After fumbling a bit, he got it to turn on, run, speed up and slow down by thought.

"Okay," Jason said, getting up and retrieving a piece of wood. He attached a length of flexmet to the propeller shaft and formed it into a Dremel head. Then he took the motor and carved the wood very slightly.

"Now I see where you're going with this," Jewel said humorously.

"Is there a big store of woodworking tools on the station?" Jason asked.

"Very little," Jewel said. "But Dremel tools are widely available."

"I think it's more useful than a Dremel," Jason said. "Any idea what sort of torque these things have?"

"Light," Jewel said. "They're designed for RPM, not torque."

Jason got a more-or-less straight branch from the kindling then set up a couple of arms of flex, coupled by a flexmet base, with the motor embedded on one side.

"I need this straight and level," Jason said. He'd figured out he could put two pieces of flexmet, one inside the other, that would spin. By attaching the branch at one end to the motor and the other to the spindle, he had...

"Congratulations," Jewel said, again humorously. "You've successfully constructed a rudimentary lathe. Now we just need a rock monster for you to fight."

"It works," Jason said, starting the lathe and using a bit of flex to carve into the branch, taking off the bark first.

In twenty minutes, Jason had figured out a better lathe system, a drill press and a milling system all using flex and the drone motor.

"It might not have much torque, but you can work with it," Jason said.

"You're going to need a bunch of wood," Jewel pointed out.

"Where *are* we *ever* going to find *wood*?" Jason asked.

"They're going to have to be cut down to size," Jewel said. "The drones can cut off chunks and they can be ground down..."

"You're thinking too small," Jason said. "I'm going to need a large, flat platform. Do we have any *big* tree stumps? Herman, a big log and a bunch of flex..."

It also took two large trunks embedded in holes. First, they laid a large tree trunk on the leveled tree stump, with flex to either side to keep it from rolling off. Then they attached flex at one end to the embedded trunks and the other to the horizontal trunk. Last a thin strand of flex was mounted in front of the horizontal trunk.

"And slice," Jason said, mentally commanding the distant flex to retract and the nearer to extend.

The thin strand of flex that was supposed to slice off a plank parted with an audible "twang!"

"Fork," Jason said. "It usually cuts right through wood. What's wrong?"

"Calculating," Jewel said. "This is a . . . Oh."

"A what 'oh'?" Jason asked.

"Harmonics," Jewel answered.

"The drones are imparting harmonics to the flex," Jason said, nodding. "Like a vibroknife."

"Even when you swing it, there's a slight harmonic vibration," Jewel said. "You're essentially sawing at the nanolevel. We need to introduce a harmonic to it."

"Can we do that with flex or do we need a drone connected somehow?" Jason asked. "Do you need to go on the net and find a back massager?"

"Let me see what I can do with the flex," Jewel said distractedly.

With a little bit of work, flex could be made to vibrate.

Jason held up a piece of flexmet that looked a bit like a short tree branch as it vibrated. He increased and decreased the speed by thought.

"This stuff is going to eliminate *so* many industries," he said, shaking his head.

"What would you use a vibrating tree branch for?" Jewel asked.

"You are either programmed to be naïve or joking," Jason said. "Back massager?"

He formed the vibrating flex around his hand and rubbed his back.

"See?" he said. "Like old time barber massagers."

"Long-term use like that can cause nerve damage," Jewel said.

"I'm not planning on using it much," Jason said, stopping the vibration and returning the flex to his bracelet. "But it might come in handy if some lady needs a backrub."

He thought about the AI's odd response then shook his head.

"Back to creating a field sawmill . . ."

With the addition of a harmonic, the first plank of oak slid off in seconds.

"We just hit the end of my expertise," Jason said. "I'm going to have to think about this. Register a new company: Withywindle

Fine Woods and Furnishings. Then see if you can find . . . Todd Kranhouse."

"Your old boss, Todd Kranhouse?" Jewel asked.

"We parted on good terms," Jason said. "And I've never met anyone better with wood. God knows I wasn't. Was not my gift."

"Jason?"

"Mr. Kranhouse," Jason said. "How are you doing?"

"Good, Jason, good, you?"

Prior to the Transfer, Todd Kranhouse had owned Kranhouse Milling, a company that did specialty milling mostly for the construction industry. The man had grown up with wood milling and even with most work moving overseas had managed to hang on by producing better quality than anyone else in the business.

Jason had tried but could not meet his exacting standards. And being covered in sawdust was not Jason's idea of a way to spend your life, anyway. They'd parted by mutual agreement on good terms.

"I'm doing great," Jason admitted. "I started a food company that's taking the station by storm, Brandywine Foods."

"I've heard of that," Kranhouse said. "Even procured some of your comestibles. Had no idea that crocodile could taste so fair. Nor that you were involved."

Kranhouse was so Yankee it was almost an affectation. Pure old-fashioned New England.

"Compared to print food?" Jason said. "Anything's good compared to that. Are you back in business?"

"I am not, sadly," Kranhouse said. "The wood on that planet looks to be the finest in centuries, and here I am selling off the contents of my house."

"Hope you haven't sold your woodworking equipment," Jason said.

"That would be the last to go," Kranhouse replied.

"My company has a need for a major milling order," Jason said. "We're building an event space and we'd prefer it not be simple flexmet or flexscreen. I pitched wood and leather. And the best guy I know with wood is you."

"To get any contract would be nice," Kranhouse replied. "The problem being there's no milling equipment save for my personal equipment. Nor any wood, save that on the planet."

"What if I told you, you can do almost all of it with flexmet?" Jason said. "What you can't do with flexmet, you can use either your personal tools plus flex or a drone motor?"

"I would... wonder if you have been partaking of drink," Kranhouse replied.

"If I bring in the investment, intellectual property and initial contract, would you consider a partnership?" Jason asked. "I would be, I promise, the extremely silent partner. But I've got some credit and there are, actually, a billion ways to use flex for woodworking. Jewel, bring the drone around and show Mr. Kranhouse that we can cut planks fine as silk."

Another plank was cut off and the drone dropped down for a close-up of the grain of the wood.

"That is beautiful, beautiful oak," Kranhouse said, his tone the longing of a true craftsman. "How does that saw work?"

"Flexmet," Jason said. "It has a billion and one uses."

"That's so smooth," Kranhouse said. "Much smoother than you get from a regular mill. It would still require sanding but not much. How thin can you slice it?"

"Not sure," Jason said. "Jewel, thin to win."

The "plank" that was sliced off the next time was so thin you could practically see through it.

"Amazing," Kranhouse said. "Can you do that on the station?"

"If we get the wood up there," Jason said as it began to rain again. "And if we can effectively dry it. It's all green."

"That *is* an issue," Kranhouse said. "Less so with heartwood. Not so much water in heartwood."

"You could space dry," Jewel said. "Vacuum will draw out the water fast."

"Is not space cold, young lady?" Kranhouse asked. "It would cause the wood to crack and shatter."

"That's my AI," Jason pointed out.

"They seem rather human, Jason," Kranhouse replied. "No reason not to be polite. The point remains."

"Put it in a stasis container," Jewel said. "Open up to reduce the internal pressure then close. You can set the container inside in the warmth. It will draw out the water faster. Once humidity has increased, flush the air, send it back out. Repeat. Alternative is oven drying."

"Where are we going to get an oven?" Jason asked.

"All of the compartments have heating and cooling," Jewel said. "You'd have to get a safety variance for the compartment temperature, but you can just put it in a compartment like the warehouse and heat it up to whatever temperature Mr. Kranhouse considers appropriate. If the wood is already cut into planks, it will dry faster. The hot air can be recycled to remove humidity. The water then goes to the water processing system on the station. If that works for you, Mr. Kranhouse?"

"That could work," Kranhouse said. "Worth a try. Question is costs. You said you had a bit of credit you'd invest, Jason?"

"I would, sir," Jason said, wincing at the pun. "And easy terms to let you buy it back. I know you prefer to own your own company."

"I had investors before, Jason," Kranhouse said with a bit of a chuckle. "It's rare a person owns a company outright. But I do appreciate the offer."

"Would you consider a name?" Jason said. "I mean, Kranhouse Milling was a known name but..."

"What name did you consider?" Kranhouse asked.

"Withywindle Fine Woods and Furnishings," Jason said. "I'm going to also have to figure out how to do leather. And we'll need leather seating. How I'm going to do that is still up in the air but..."

"Withywindle?" Kranhouse asked. "I seem to recall that name...?"

"It's from a fantasy novel," Jason said.

"Think I've never read it?" Kranhouse said, chuckling again. "That was all the rage in my day. I can accept that name. But are you sure you have sufficient credit to invest?"

"No," Jason said. "I'd have to refer you to my accountant. But we need the milling for the event space. Do you mind if I send you to my accountant on this?"

"Not a bit," Kranhouse said. "I do recall you were always shy on the subject of money."

"Thirty-five, sixty-five work?" Jason asked. "Again, Jewel will ensure the terms make buyback easy."

"That is standard," Kranhouse replied. "Acceptable. To be clear, I agree to engage in a partnership with you on those terms, assuming the capital is available and there are no other codicils that are a deal breaker."

"Jewel, introduce Mr. Kranhouse to Gil," Jason said. "Explain to Gil the necessity for a good woodworker. Turn over all developed IP and any more I develop to Withywindle. There may not be much more work at first but I'll be keeping an eye out."

"As will I," Kranhouse said.

"If that's all good for you, Mister Kranhouse, I have other projects I have to get back to," Jason said.

"That all appears to work," Kranhouse said. "I'll have to check the details of the partnership contract. But I would like to get back to work. I've missed wood."

"Then I'll bid you a fond farewell," Jason said formally.

"Until we meet again," Kranhouse said. "And, Jason, feel free to call me Todd."

"I'll try, sir," Jason said. "Out here."

By the end of the afternoon, Jason had figured out a dozen ways to work with the one oak trunk he was slowly reducing.

They'd cut boards thick and thin as well as posts, had determined a way to make drills using the drone motors, lathed pegs and used the combination to peg things together, crosscuts, edge cuts, milled edges and most other things he recalled from his brief job working in a wood-milling shop.

"From this can Mr. Kranhouse's AI figure the rest out?" Jason asked. It was raining again and he was ready to get into the hooch, prop his feet up in front of the fire and settle in for the night.

"Given that, according to Miss Katherine, he's been talking nonstop about wood since he got here," Jewel replied, "probably so."

"He can be a tad obsessive," Jason said. "But he was the best because he was obsessive."

"She's eternally grateful he's going to get wood to work with again," Jewel said. "He's been driving her nuts."

"How's the negotiations with Gil going?" Jason asked.

"It was mostly handled by the AIs," Jewel admitted. "But Gil agreed and Withywindle Fine Wood and Furnishings is now set up as a real entity. Mr. Kranhouse is already looking for a compartment. It's going to require two, one for drying, one for working. But it's doable. There's a compartment not far from Brandywine that's probably useable."

"That's the wood figured out," Jason said. "Now for leather, about which I know exactly nothing."

"Already handled," Jewel said. "Because I saw nothing in your background about preparing leather, I tossed it to Duncan who tossed it to one of the ground R&D teams. They're working on old-fashioned methods of tanning, lye from ash, tannin from oak, mixed with bots and flexmet. It will have to be buffalo hide; they're in Chindia. But buffalo hide is a good leather and Ghu knows we have enough of it. When they get it working, they're going to move on to seeing if they can prepare crocodile skins as well. We've got a ton of those in storage. Probably not the look for Brandywine but as Sheila pointed out..."

"It'll make a ton of pumps," Jason said, walking into the housing container. The fire had been fed while he was away and with most of the container buttoned up it was warm and cozy. He hadn't realized how cold he'd gotten standing in the rain until he came inside.

"As time permits, get Herman and the Alfreds lifting various types of tree trunks into conexes. Give Mr. Kranhouse a variety of wood to work with. It can be sliced as he sees fit on the station then dried. Send at least one trunk of every kind of wood in the lease."

He took off his hat and formed a series of pegs to hold it and his rain gear.

"Does that include small trees?" Jewel said.

"Check with Kranhouse on species," Jason said. "But I want him to at least have oak, ash, birch, beech, hickory, that sort of thing. As well as some coniferous. But ask him in general."

"Will do," Jewel said. "Who's paying for the lift? Brandywine or Withywindle?"

"It'll have to be Withywindle," Jason said. With his outer gear off, he sat down and took off his boots. Then he padded over to the personal locker and removed a set of fleece-lined slippers. With his wet socks off and slippers on, he ambled over to the fire and propped up his feet. "Send a note to Tim. Need to load at least one conex full of wood on the next lift. Withywindle will pay for their share on the shipment but it's needed for Brandywine's event space."

"Will do," Jewel said.

He hadn't worked, physically, nearly as hard as many of the jobs he'd done in his youth. But the day had been wearing, nonetheless. The majority of the weariness came from being out on the boat. That wore you out until you got used to it.

And the fishing had taken some energy.

"To cook or not to cook?" Jason said, pulling a high-test Purple Lightning out of the case by the chair. "That is the question."

He only had so many of the prepared meals. If he ate them every time he was worn out, he was going to be out quick.

"Ever had fire-grilled abalone?" Jewel asked. "It's not hard to fix. I can fix it for you."

"You don't have taste buds," Jason replied.

"It's not seasoned," Jewel said. "It's usually just cooked in the shell over a grill. I kept some of the shells and can make a grill over the fire in a jiff."

"There's an old saying," Jason said. "If she could cook, I'd marry her. Usually said about planes and things."

"You can't marry an AI," Jewel said. "But I'd be glad to try some for you. If you don't like it, no big deal."

"Any shrooms?" Jason said. "Of a known type. I'm not up for tasting at the moment."

"There are four species of known edible fungi," Jewel said. "One of them is reputed to be quite tasty."

"Get me a few of those," Jason said. "I'll make skewers. And, yes, abalone sounds good."

"I shall endeavor to provide," Jewel said.

A drone brought over a selection of mushrooms while a stasis case walked in on flexmet legs. The case opened to reveal slabs of abalone as a drone brought over three shells. The abalone were added to the shells which were popped onto a flexmet grill to cook as the case walked back into the night and the rain.

Jason skewered three of the rather large mushrooms onto some flexmet and extended it to reach the fire. He didn't even have to get closer. It was an incredibly lazy way to cook. But the lever of the large mushrooms was rather heavy on his hand, so he extended down a prop to hold the contraption up. That was even lazier. Perfect.

The shrooms were ready about the same time as the abalone. He plucked that out of the fire himself, using flexmet, and set the mushrooms and the abalone on a flexmet tray attached to his camp chair.

"Bless us, oh Lord, and these Thy gifts which we are about to receive from Your bounty through Christ Our Lord, Amen," Jason said, crossing himself.

"That's the first time you've ever prayed before a meal," Jewel said.

"I forget," Jason said, trying a bite of the mushroom first. "Needs some salt and pepper."

He fished into the case and came up with salt, pepper and garlic salt. A touch of garlic salt and pepper was just right.

"We need a replacement for black pepper soon," Jason said, taking another bite of mushroom. Perfecto.

The abalone was...chewy. Also, rich and incredibly flavorful.

"That's really good," Jason said. "Also enhanced by some garlic salt and pepper."

Three mushrooms and a half an abalone and he was stuffed.

"This is really good but incredibly rich," Jason said, gesturing at the abalone. "I'm not going to be able to finish even one. And it's not because I stuffed myself with mushrooms..."

"Jason," Jewel said, laughing, "I'm not going to get annoyed that you don't like my cooking. For one thing, I'm an AI. It's not my gift. And for another, abalone is reputed to be extremely rich. I probably should have only cooked one."

In the distance, the wolf pack made itself heard. Even behind the defenses of the camp, the sound made his hair stand up.

"Should I have the bots take out the wolf pack?" Jewel asked. "It's permissible as a potential threat even outside the lease."

"No," Jason said. "Leave them for now. There's no value to the meat or the pelts. I can handle a wolf howl or two. I'll put the abalone in with the precooked meals. It really is rich."

"You don't have to apologize, Jason," Jewel said with a tone of humor in her voice. "I'll clean up."

The abalone was whisked into the stasis case with precooked meals and the tray disappeared.

Jason finished off the Purple Lightning and just meditated on the fire for a while.

"Penny for your thoughts?" Jewel said after a bit.

"I don't really have any," Jason said as the wolves continued to howl. "We'll see what the traps and nets bring in tomorrow. My inventive brain is worn out for the day. We'll see what tomorrow brings..."

"Lord knows, I am grateful for this fine church that you all have provided," Pastor Mickey said. He stood at a flexmet podium on a low stage at one end of the hall. "I am grateful to you. To those of you who procured this building for us, and to all of you, for showing up. And I thank God, the Lord of the known and the unknown universe alike, for His grace in bringing us here, alive, and a mostly intact community.

"I've been thinking about myself, and about some of our neighbors, recently. And I've been led to take as my text today, the Epistle of James, chapter one, verse two. 'My brethren, count it all joy when ye fall into divers temptations.' Now, 'temptations' here are 'peirasmois,' which means 'trials.' The wise old bishop of Jerusalem here is not saying that we should want to be lured into sin, no. He's saying we should be happy to be tried. He's saying that there is something about the human condition that needs serious testing. He's telling us that we shouldn't want life to be too easy, we should embrace life with joy precisely because it is difficult.

"Now what on Earth is old James talking about?"

# CHAPTER 22 »»»»»»»

WHAT TOMORROW BROUGHT WAS RAIN. THE CAMP HAD TURNED into a bog.

"The trees were stabilizing the soil," Jewel said as he looked at the mass of mud in front of his container. The container itself seemed to be sinking. So much for stable soil.

"Figured that one out," Jason said. "Is the sawmill still viable?"

"Yes?"

"Get the bots to work on an elevated walkway down to the beach," Jason said. "Not elevated much, just up out of the bog. And bring the boat Alfred over here. I'm going to need a lift."

He settled his hat firmly on his head and turned into jetpack man again for the short ride to the beach.

The crab pot came up loaded with an unfamiliar type of crab. It looked something like a Dungeness.

"New species?" Jason asked as the pot was dumped into a case. It was rapidly rebaited with offal and dumped back over the side.

"No," Jewel said after a probe on one of the crabs by a drone. "Genetically identical to brown crab. Generally found in the North Sea and Baltic and all around the British Isles."

"Edible?" Jason asked.

"Very," Jewel said. "It's considered one of the finest crabs in the world."

"That sounds promising," Jason said.

The traps brought in numerous species of seafood. The gill

nets had caught a variety of species of fish, some known, some unknown. Varieties of sea bass and sea perch were most common and there were more species than had been known on Earth. There were also what were called porgies, a form of cod. One of the fish traps had caught two small fish, one of which turned out to be a juvenile haddock, the other a juvenile sturgeon.

All together there were two dozen species of edible fish including lingcod, stone fish, sea bass and sea perch, five species of crab, four edible, and a species of spiny lobster that had filled the trap presented for it.

Not a bad haul and the bay was as productive as it seemed. Every rock face was teeming with abalone. He probably should have called it Abalone Bay.

"The question is what to concentrate on," Jason said. "What would be in season on Earth?"

"Most of these don't have a precise season," Jewel said. "Even for commercial fishing. And that would only hold on Earth. For the crab you could say the season is in the fall, but brown crabs are taken year-round in commercial territories except for their breeding season in early spring.

"The sea perch is year-round cultivated as are the sea bass. Those have already spawned, so good to go. Gill nets presented mid to upper water with larger openings will probably land large sea bass which is a known and liked type of fish. Placing nets along the rock faces will yield more sea perch, another known fish, and less of the stonefish which, while known and liked by some cultures, are unappealing visually as well as having poisonous roe."

"Yeah," Jason said, examining the unprepossessing fish. "Tasty from what I've heard. Is it just me or are we seeing a mix of Atlantic and Pacific fish and crustaceans?"

"It's not just you," Jewel said. "One sea perch species is a type normally found in the *Mediterranean*, as opposed to the Pacific forms. There are seven types of Pacific sea perch and two here. The two here are Mediterranean as noted and European Atlantic. But the spiny lobster is Pacific as is one of the crab species. The spiny lobster would be in season presently, by the way. It's a mixed bag. Welcome to Bellerophon."

"We'll focus on brown crab and sea perch for now," Jason said. "Rerig that way and let's see if we can find the best areas for those. I'll wait on the sea bass."

"Your call," Jewel said.

"Sort out any female crab," Jason said. "Can that be done easily?"

"Very," Jewel said. "If I assign a drone to sort."

"Assign a drone," Jason said.

"You going out with the boats?" Jewel asked.

"Let the bots handle it," Jason said, looking at the rain. He'd worked in worse weather but he had other things to do once the basic plan was laid in. "They can handle it, right?"

"Yes," Jewel said.

"Keep Herman and two Alfreds here," Jason continued. "I'm going to keep working on the sawmill and woodworking techniques. We need a cover for the sawmill. And a better sawmill."

"That . . . will take a lot of flexmet," Jewel said. "We have it but it will cut into harvesting."

"That's the point," Jason said, looking at the soaked sawmill. "*Do* we need flexmet?"

After a breakfast of abalone and wild potatoes Jason got to work. Or, rather, the drones and bots got to work as he supervised and figured out processes.

Buildings had once been made from wood cut from local trees and while iron and later steel nails were useful, they weren't strictly necessary. And, again, while tar paper had been a major innovation for roofs, it wasn't strictly necessary, either.

Slowly, a woodworking shed arose from the mud of the fort. Timbers cut from oak heartwood made up the main structural posts, with the ceiling at twenty-two feet. They were drilled and pegged with softer outer oak. It was easier to lathe and would swell with moisture causing it to get tighter. An A-frame roof was constructed with Herman lifting the angle-cut and mortised timbers into place, then drones and flexmet aligning the pieces and temporarily securing them. Holes were drilled and lathed pegs hammered into place with rocks.

Planks were cut to cover the A-frame, smoothly and neatly fitted edge to edge by flexmet. Then wide strips of birch bark were laid down over the planks, their edges overlapping downward with birch and deciduous resins used as a glue. Last, shakes were cut, small, thin, planks of green fir wood that overlapped on the planks and pegged into place, secured and waterproofed with fir resins.

When it was complete, Jason slopped through the mud and walked around under the construction. Surprisingly, it was watertight. At least for now.

"This is good," Jason said. "Next, let's improve the sawmill. It needs an actual platen and we need to eliminate as much use of flexmet as possible by using wood. We also need a way to keep me out of the mud."

The first problem to solve was the foundation. The original stump that they'd used as a platen had a foundation of its roots. For the new platen, they needed something better. Once the design and outline of the sawmill was agreed upon, the foundations were dug out by Herman and the Alfreds using their tractor beam. Then loads of sand were brought in to start. Over the layer of sand were laid additional layers of fine to course gravel then large, flat, basalt rocks secured from the north end of the island.

The next step was to build the base. Since Jason wanted to be able to cut the largest logs in the forest of primeval old growth, the mill had to be large and sturdy. Thick timbers were cut from red-oak heartwood and laid on the basalt rocks. From those more timbers were pegged and mortised to a framework for the platen until it was sturdy enough you could lay a battleship gun on it, three meters wide and fifteen meters long. The log acceptor/debarker was out in the rain again. They'd have to extend the shed at some point.

All the timbers had to be cut on the existing platen, so the mill built up around that. Along the way the bots cut six-by-six timbers and laid them down on the ground with one set on the ground and others over those. It raised the height of the flooring but it gave a solid and dry area for Jason to walk on.

A platen, the flat base where the trees were laid to be cut, was slowly constructed of thick timbers pegged and mortised. The stump that had been the original platen was incorporated into the foundation structure. It would eventually rot but the entire thing, despite all the work, was temporary. It was a design concept, rather than a long-term working mill.

Containers had had to be moved and the area was now much more open. Jason considered the risk worth it; they needed the room and the container fort was simply in the way. The surrounding abatis would keep off most threats and the drones were constantly patrolling.

<<<>>>

It took two days of work to complete the entire thing. When they were done there was an uncovered log deck that led to the debarking platen. That connected to the cutting platen and there was a partially wood and partially flexmet plank-and-timber gathering system along with a separate wood storage/drying shed. It would take a bot to move the timbers and cut planks to the drying shed but it required at least an Alfred to convey all the power necessary.

They'd brought in various sized tree trunks, many taken from the original trees cut in the clearing, to construct the shed. But it was time for a major test.

A large oak tree adjacent to the clearing was trimmed, topped and cut. Then a massive section of the lower trunk, three meters across at its narrowest and ten meters long, was rolled across the clearing and up onto the log deck. It was too heavy for even a Herman to lift, and so irregular it refused to roll down to the debarking platen, so an Alfred thumped it into place.

The thing had to be trimmed of its major irregularities, massive gnarls, and thick ribs, until it was capable of rolling. At that point it got easier. Vibroflex easily sheared the rest of the irregularities off along with the bark until it was a smooth, albeit massive, cylinder.

The massive log was then pushed down the platen through the cutter by Herman using a pressor beam. Since one of the bots was going to be necessary to run the thing, Jason decided he might as well use its abilities. In addition, from its current position Herman could move the cut planks and timbers to the curing shed with its tractor beams.

With the first plank cut off, the log was pulled back and rolled onto the flat side. In minutes the massive log was formed into planks and timbers, computer designed based on its size and material to be the optimum use of the timber.

Jason ran his hand against the surface of one of the heartwood planks. The cut was so smooth there weren't even splinters, the vibroflex cut at a nanometric level, and the wood was incredibly fine grained.

"Wood like this on Earth was rare and precious," Jason said, sliding his hand up and down the wood and not for the first time having a pang of regret about the clearing of the forests. "It's another thing we need to consider conserving."

"At least this is going to be put to good work," Jewel said.

"That it is," Jason said, looking around the clearing. The rain had stopped but it was still muddy as hell and beginning to look like an industrial site rather than a test site. It was late afternoon and he considered whether to just knock off for the day or try something else. Decisions, decisions...

"Okay, this is working well enough," Jason said after a few moments' thought. "Bring over an Alfred with twenty kilos of flexmet."

"What are you thinking about now?" Jewel asked.

"Something better than a jetpack," Jason said.

When the Alfred arrived, he pushed on it.

"Can it lay over on its side?" Jason asked.

The Alfred obediently turned horizontally.

Jason put the flexmet on it and formed it into a saddle then pushed down on the Alfred.

"Need it a little lower," Jason said.

Once it was near the ground, he mounted the saddle. Then he formed two handlebar controls as well as wrapping his thighs in flexmet and putting in footrests and a backrest. With all that done he leaned back.

"You just invented a flying bike?" Jewel said.

"Feels more comfortable than a jetpack," Jason said. "Okay, have the Alfred, on its own, lift up and over to the water's edge then lower to this height. Slowly."

After a few moments of glacial movement Jason sighed.

"Broad movements at four miles per hour, no more than half-G maneuvers," Jason said.

When he was hovering over the strand, he considered the controls.

"Right handle works like a motorcycle," Jason said, twisting the flexmet back and forth. "Rotate downward, increase speed; center, stop accelerating. Pushing forward on the column means down, pulling back means up. Lean side to side for turns..."

Jason went through a foot pedal, counter turns, then considered the bike.

"How fast can this go?" Jason asked. Important consideration. "And how fast would it be able to accelerate?"

"With your mass onboard it can attain an acceleration of about fifty Gs for a short period before it runs out of power,"

Jewel said. "You, of course, would be splattered with that sort of power but the main issue is aerodynamic drag. Take two of them and put them on an airframe like an SR-71 and they'll have better capabilities. At the right heading, with a smooth, aerodynamic casing, it can enter orbit. But its batteries would be discharged."

"Okay," Jason said. "Important safety tip. Let's limit its maneuvering to, say, three G? And maximum speed of...one hundred twenty miles per hour. I'm gonna need to lose the hat."

After putting his trusty hat away, Jason took it easy on the first run. Alfred would, in fact, take off like a bat out of hell with a twitch of Jason's right hand. That had to be dialed down a bit. But Jason eventually had a flying bike that had enough performance to be interesting without automatically killing him.

By which time it was time for dinner. He'd give the new bike a full tryout tomorrow.

Assuming the weather held.

The weather didn't hold. The next day was foggy with scattered showers when he woke up.

"Damnit," Jason said. He was itching to try his new bike. But there were other things to do as well.

He checked the inventory. The conexes that had been filled with flexmet were now filling up with lumber. He'd put a halt to the sawmill overnight since the constant bang of logs and boards was keeping him awake. Other conexes were filling with game meat, mushrooms, spring greens and mostly fish and crab. So that was under control.

"Time to use the lumber for something else," Jason said.

He had one of the Alfreds dig post holes then set the sawmill to produce posts. Another rudimentary lathe and some flexmet sharpening turned out spiked poles in rapid fashion. By taking thin boards and weaving them in and out of the posts, it created a wooden fence. The best wood for the boards turned out to be beech or birch because it was more flexible. Sticking the poles through the gaps in the fence created a spiky barrier that should be a deterrent to even megagrizzlies.

"So," Jewel said, thoughtfully. "It's sort of an African kraal."

"A term which derived from corral, an enclosure for stock, which derived from the term for a wagon circle in wagon trains, that probably derived from the Latin for wagon," Jason said.

"Fun with languages. Two Alfreds running boats. One collecting game. Herman running the sawmill. I'm not using the bike at the moment so have that Alfred work on the kraal in its spare time along with the game Alfred. Continue it around the camp with a gate on the water side. Can do?"

"Can do," Jewel said. "What are you going to do?"

"Worry like hell?" Jason said. "The weather's bad so I'm going to take the day off to do business. Keep the firewood stocked."

By afternoon, the skies and fog had cleared and the rain let up. Further, looking at the satellite images, it appeared that it might hold.

"Break out the bike," Jason said. "And I'm going to have to rig up. I'm going to the other side of the bay."

He considered his weapons. He was going to be well away from the camp without even a stasis container. On the other hand, he wasn't going to be on the ground long. This was a recon. He decided to just take his old .30-06 Savage then realized he could probably load a couple more guns on the bike. He ended up taking the Safari .458 and a Winchester 12 gauge as well. After a bit of thought he took off his hat but secured it in a cocoon of flexmet that was part of the backrest.

With the bike festooned with weapons to the point even *he* considered it ludicrous, he mounted the saddle, got everything settled in and took to the skies.

First, he ran up the north coast of the island, slowly, considering the view. Most of it was rocky with the exception of the flat he was on. Frequent streams cascaded into the bay, adding to the nutrients in the bay and thus its richness. Most of the rocks were covered in abalone but there were sections of mussels as well. The two normally didn't get along. Abalone would tend to chew up juvenile mussels and both existed at the tide line.

Having checked out the island, he braved the winds of the passage to head over to the northern hills. They were much higher and steeper than the island but there were a few flats down at waterline. The rugged hills, some rising to a few thousand feet, were covered in trees that thrived in the watery environment.

With enhancement on the goggles, he spotted big red deer drinking in the streams as well as bear and a group of wild hogs bedded down. All of the woods were alive with game.

At the north end of the bay the western hills dropped off sharply into a large, flat area. The region was filled with small, shallow embayments, most of them high and dry with the ebb tide. Noting that there was a bear moving along not far away, Jason dropped down to check things out at ground level.

The bottom of the lagoon had appeared to be covered in rocks but the "rocks" turned out to be oysters lying on a sand bottom. Thousands. Millions of them.

"That's a lot of oysters," Jason said. "Another harvestable species. What type?"

"Looks like standard Pacific oysters based on the shell shape and size," Jewel said.

A sea otter darted out of the ocean and into the pile, retrieving an oyster. As it did, the bear headed its way at a lope. The otter made it back into the ocean barely ahead of the bruin.

"So, the sea otters eat the oysters and the bear eats the sea otters," Jason said musingly. The encounter had brought the bear, a medium-sized male, closer so he lifted the bike higher into the air.

"We'd have to have a lease for this area to harvest them," Jewel said.

"Get a drone to extract some and test them," Jason said. "Unlikely to be hazardous but doesn't hurt to check. We can do that, legally, right?"

"Yes," Jewel said.

"Onward and upwards," Jason said.

He crossed the small river that entered the bay on the north and saw a bear digging in the black mud on the other side. It was practically covered in mud but didn't seem to mind as it lifted something into its maw.

Jason dropped down to ground level, giving the bear a wide berth, and checked the surface of the mud. There were quarter-sized holes in the mud, everywhere, some with mounds of sand and mud around them.

He extruded some flexmet downward into the mud and fumbled around a bit until he had a wide sieve then retracted with some difficulty.

The bear's prey was revealed as a razor clam, a popular food species all over the North Pacific.

"These will fetch a pretty penny," Jason said, considering the expanse of black mud. "Oysters to the west, razor clams to the east."

He lifted the bike up into the air lest the bear get any ideas and considered the distance to the oyster beds.

"Can we pick a midpoint and get both within a one-kilometer lease?" Jason asked.

"We can't get the full bed on both sides of the river with a one-kilometer lease," Jewel said. "But a two-kilometer lease will only cost two hundred credits. And that will cover it. Easily."

"Okay," Jason said. "Register the lease. And we're going to need more equipment on the next shipment to exploit. Another Herman and two more Alfreds."

"Tim will need to approve that," Jewel pointed out.

"Show him the oyster bed videos," Jason said. "Tim's addicted to oysters on the half shell. He'll bite. We need some nomenclature," Jason said, lifting the bike up high enough to get a full view of the bay. "The main river coming in from the east: the Ferrell River."

"I'll tell Tom," Jewel said.

"This river, call it Oyster River," Jason said. "The northerly cape call Cape Osbourne, the south Cape Despair. The north hills call the Osbourne Hills and the south hills the Doom Hills."

"Reasons?" Jewel asked.

"The north hills are named after Ozzy," Jason said, shrugging. "I think I'll name a bunch of stuff after rock band members. Speaking of which, Olzon Island."

"After Anette Olzon, formerly of Nightwish?" Jewel asked.

"You know my playlist," Jason said.

"Cape Despair, Doom Hills?" Jewel asked.

"Based on the wind and currents, if we ever have real ships plying this bay as a port, that will be a hated cape," Jason said. "The winds will drive any ship that loses power onto the rocks. At which point the crew will be in the hills."

"And gone to their doom," Jewel said. "Okay. Ominous."

"The captains and crew will therefore be cautious," Jason said.

"You need to land on each to name it," Jewel pointed out.

"Literally put my foot on the ground?" Jason said.

"Yes. What about the east hill?" Jewel asked.

"Well, keep those names for now," Jason said, setting off along the coast. "And that's what I'm about to check out."

There were more oyster and clam beds along the coast north of the hill along with numerous colonies of Steller's sea lions, elephant seals and harbor seals which were frequently harassed by the bears. From his height he could also spot numerous sharks in the waters, mostly what appeared to be great whites. They were obviously hunting the seals and sea lions and he reminded himself that not only was the water cold, it was deadly.

The northeast side of the bay was also cut by small streams, most of them meandering down from distant hills. Near the east hill the mainland became intertidal fens with fewer trees and more fen grasses. More clams and oysters.

"Do I need to land to name *all* of these?" Jason asked.

"Briefly," Jewel said. "I'll cover you with drones."

As he proceeded along the bay, he landed briefly at each stream mouth and inlet and named it.

"Springsteen Creek... Jan Creek... Dean Creek... Buddy Holly Branch... Chuck Berry Pond... Bring up my playlist and list every member of every band on it..."

"I'd inform most of these people of the honor of having an undistinguished creek named after them," Jewel said. "But they're mostly dead or not on the station."

"Not many conservatives in rock and roll?" Jason said.

"Not as such, apparently," Jewel said.

"Pity Meatloaf already passed," Jason said.

He reached the hill, which was tree covered and undistinguished except for being the only promontory on the east side of the bay.

"Call it... Springfield Hill," Jason said with a shrug. "It's unremarkable. Counts for the singer and every city and town of that name I've visited."

"Ouch," Jewel said.

"Onward," Jason said, heading to the Ferrell River.

The ground south of the hill was a wet mix of swamp and forest that wouldn't be out of place in Louisiana with the exception of a lack of cypress. More tidal fens stretched to the east as far as the eye could see.

And it was packed, again, with waterfowl. There were numerous waterfowl all around the bay but the delta was special. As Jason passed overhead the shadow of his bike would trigger a mass takeoff and the air became filled with squawking ducks, geese, swans, coots and every other type of avian that made the water its home. At one point he had to stop as the flocks filled the air around him.

"This is a classic situation for a bird strike," Jason said as a goose wing hit him in the head. "This is insane!"

He reached back, pulled out his shotgun and started blasting. In five shots he'd dropped two geese and three ducks.

He followed the falling birds and picked them up with flexmet after searching about a bit to find the last duck. One was only injured and he used the flexmet to wring its neck.

"No stasis case but they'll probably keep for a while," Jason said, reloading the shotgun.

"The flex can clean them as you fly," Jewel said. "They'll keep longer cleaned."

"Make it so," Jason said. "How's the charge?"

"Fifty-two percent," Jewel said. "You're not heavy."

"We'll head back," Jason said. His stomach was grumbling. "I don't want to get too far from base with a low charge. Walking back would be a pain. And it's getting dark."

# CHAPTER 23 〉〉〉〉〉〉〉〉〉

THE NEXT MORNING THE SKY WAS STILL CLEAR, THE SATELLITE indicated no major fronts moving into the area and it looked good for a long ride.

*Looked* good.

Jason added a stasis case to his load this time. It had a packed lunch as well as some emergency supplies. He also included all three guns again.

He started by flying to the south set of hills and stepping out on one of the exposed promontories, well above the surf line.

"I dub thee . . . Cape Despair," Jason said, looking down at the massive waves below. At that latitude they weren't just coming from Beringia. The bay was in the region where the Beringia Sea met the Pallas Ocean and with most of the planet to build up size, the Pallas waves were enormous.

"Does it also count for Doom Hills?" Jason asked, lifting the bike into the air.

"It does," Jewel said. "Speaking of which, what's the county name?"

"Wilson County," Jason said.

"Taken," Jewel replied. "On America Nova."

"Gah," Jason snorted. "Ferrell County."

"Taken," Jewel said.

"God," Jason said. "This is the problem with naming things!" He thought about it for a few seconds longer. "Olzon County."

"Not taken," Jewel said.

"Fine," Jason said, spinning the bike around and heading for the Ferrell River. "Now that we've got that settled..."

He avoided the waterfowl-crowded delta by flying to the south of it. The ground was still flat and tree covered with occasional small hills as he headed inland. He cut back to the north to the river as he approached the range of low hills to the east. There the Ferrell River entered a gorge and the fens ended. He dropped down to water level and briefly touched the water.

"I dub thee the Ferrell River," Jason said.

"Now it's official," Jewel said.

The river wound through the hills in a serpentine. The water was full of rapids and would be difficult to impossible to traverse by boat. People had done crazier things. He saw a distant future for it as a white-water rafting destination.

There were waterfalls and streams dumping more water into the river throughout the hills. With all the rainfall in the region, crops would grow like weeds in the soil. Assuming the soil was any good.

The far side of the region was low, rolling, tree-covered hills with extensive flatland. There was a rise to the north, though. More of an escarpment than hills. It looked as if the land was higher over there, possibly a shallow plateau.

He continued up the river, staying below treetop level, until he found what he was looking for. At some point the south side of the river had built up a silt levee that extended back for some distance. There were bluffs of what looked to be a mix of sand and loess lining the river. Beyond the bluffs, the forest was lonely, dark and deep.

It would do.

He wandered up and down the river checking out the bluffs then stopped at what seemed to be the midpoint of the terrain feature.

"Check out that area for threats," Jason said, pointing. It had been a while since he'd seen bears though he'd seen one tiger drinking from the river on the journey. Numerous deer as well as bison. Those were new.

Six drones were embedded in the flexmet. They slid out, deployed, and headed into the woods.

He picked the bike up, trying to get a feel for what the river's bottom profile looked like. It was functionally impossible to see anything between the silt and the tannin. A few ripples on the surface, though, indicated underwater obstructions. Probably tree snags.

He dropped back down to just above water level, pulled a heavy lead weight out of the flexmet and lowered a line into the water.

"How long is it, Jewel?" Jason said, bouncing the weight on the bottom.

"That's a rather personal question, Governor," Jewel replied. "Thirty feet."

Jason dragged the line through the water, making soundings and occasionally hitting sunken tree obstacles.

"There are no immediate threats," Jewel said a few minutes later. "Nearby but not in the immediate area. Are you landing here?"

"Yes," Jason said, retrieving the weight and turning the bike towards the bluff.

He landed on the bluff, got off the bike and stood looking out over the river. The ripples had indeed indicated underwater obstructions. Those could be cleared if necessary. They might not even be there when he came back.

"Penny for your thoughts?" Jewel said.

"Worth a bit more than a penny," Jason replied. "We're going to need to keep a sentry group on Olzon Island at the very least. The salmon are going to swim up the streams on the island at first. Probably. The sentry team will keep an eye out for that.

"After that . . . I'm thinking the same thing as the shrimp," Jason said. "But on a bigger scale."

"Quite big," Jewel said. "We'll have to have at least six containers of just flexmet depending on how large you want to make it."

"Not all the way across the river, that's for sure," Jason said. "This will be the biggest loss the salmon have sustained. We can't catch all of them. But based on what the run is probably like . . . We're going to need a hundred pack for the initial drop."

"That's going to be a lot of fish," Jewel said. "Are you going to sell them whole or processed?"

"There's no processing facility that I know of on the station," Jason said.

"There's an entire food-processing factory," Jewel said. "Three of them."

"Of course there are," Jason said, sighing. "And are these food processing factories..."

"Still locked up in unit battles?" Jewel said. "Yes."

"Jiminy Crickets," Jason said, shaking his head. "Aaaargh! We've got to do *something* about the damned units!"

"I'm still trading where possible," Jewel said. "Do you want me to try to trade for a food processor?"

"Any idea of the politics?" Jason asked.

"Alpha has a lot of sharks swarming," Jewel said. "Several former finance people who have accrued unit positions in it. Bravo looks clearest but that just means it's a basket case. Charlie, though, is interesting. Your records indicate that you liked a particular supermarket based in Florida."

"I do," Jason said. "Did."

"There's a group of former executives and employees from that supermarket chain who have taken *almost* enough of a controlling interest in Charlie that they could force a vote. Their problem is they have to find twelve percent and they're at nine. Should I try to trade for some of those units? Possibly combine forces?"

"We're having a hard time getting any traction with the major items," Jason said musingly. "Put that on a to-do list if there's ever a way to gain some traction."

Jason unwound his phone from his arm and stretched it to the maximum. The drones had built up a fair survey of the area and he used an app to pull away the tree and ground clutter to reveal the shape of the ground in the area.

The hills extended for at least a kilometer in every direction though they were irregular. None of it was in the hundred-year floodplain, though, and there was a small knoll two hundred meters to the southwest that was about ten feet higher than the levee.

"We clear a large area beforehand," Jason said. "Probably in the near future; runs can start midsummer."

"Right," Jewel said.

"Set up a sawmill, or two, right at the beginning," Jason said. "Lay down planks from the cut trees to give a solid foundation. It won't be perfect but it will be better than the swamp that Olzon became. And this is loess. In rain, without tree roots holding it together, it will turn to mud in an instant."

"Agreed," Jewel said.

"At least a hundred containers," Jason said, looking out over the river. "We'll need to find all the midriver obstructions and remove the major ones. Then set up a funnel trap to this point or near this point. At that point it's just a matter of lifting tons of salmon up to the bluff. Issues? Are there any engineering difficulties you can foresee?"

"Yes," Jewel said. "This bluff is not solid. I'd suggest the loading be done down at the river level and then bring the filled conexes up here."

"And we do that how?" Jason said. "You're talking about a dock?"

"A large dock," Jewel said. "Based on the work we've done at Olzon, a Herman and . . . two Alfreds will take about three days to build a large dock. That will be the center of the catch. We'll need another sawmill here. But now that it's been figured out, we can build one of those in a day."

"Set up a sawmill," Jason muttered. "Mine some gold . . . And what was the green stuff?"

"What?" Jewel said, confused.

"It was an old video game," Jason said. "Or maybe I'm mixing a couple of them up."

"You're probably mixing *Warcraft*, the original or possibly version two or three, with *Starcraft*," Jewel said. "Green stuff was a gas."

"I think I'm thinking of *Warcraft III*," Jason said. "That was the one I played the most. Cut down trees, take them to the sawmill, mine gold. We're essentially doing the same thing."

"And fishing for food," Jewel said.

"So, build a dock," Jason said. "After we've built the sawmill. Upgrade to the colony. Clear this area and install a solid platform for the incoming containers. Tim's going to love spending the credit . . ."

"We don't know the run is coming in," Tim said.

Jason was sitting on his bike over the river for the conversation. He thought it might take time and, drones or no, he didn't want to be surprised.

"These are salmon," Jason said calmly. "They're evolved from trout. There's *no way* that they breed in salt water. They're in the bay preparing for the run, getting a last feed. Means the run is starting in less than a month. We need to get prepared. And to get prepared I need some gear."

"What about the gear on the island?" Tim asked.

"Which I'm either using to move around or is harvesting?" Jason asked. "How much seafood have we already lofted from Wilson Bay?"

"Wilson Bay?" Tim asked, shaking his head. "Flattery will get you nowhere."

"I named it that 'cause it was round like a volleyball," Jason said. "Okay, okay, I'm lying. Yes, I named it after you. 'Cause *we* are going to make so much bank off of this. Have we gotten an ichthyologist yet?"

"Yes," Tim said.

"And how much food are we lofting from this area?" Jason asked.

"We just lifted another twenty-five pack," Tim replied. "And shipping is *killing* us."

"Send a thousand pack, then," Jason said. "Efficiency of scale. We'll *use* a thousand packs. No guarantee there are multiple runs but bets. And if we don't loft a thousand containers on a run, we'll fill them in time. There are still colonist deadheads going back, right?"

"Can you land a thousand packs?" Tim asked.

"Can I either reduce the harvest in the bay or get another survey set?" Jason asked.

Tim thought about it for a few seconds, frowning.

"Use the survey set you had in the bay," Tim said. "If you can do a platform for a thousand pack... I'll get with Larry and see if any are available and how much they cost. You're going to loft a thousand?"

"If we don't do it with the run, we'll do it by fall," Jason said. "This is close enough we can move them over to the bay if it comes to that."

"Containers do have a cost," Tim prevaricated.

"Oh, for the love of Pete," Jason said, then started laughing. "Do you want to make bank or not? We don't drop the thousand pack until the run is going. We'll fill at least several hundred containers. Enough, easily, to pay for the round trip and a good profit. We'll do it, Tim."

"Despite being a log guy, you're barely paying attention to shipping costs," Tim pointed out. "We're making money. Lots. We're making profit. Good profit. Shipping costs are going up and up and they don't seem to want to come down. So, the fewer sorties we have to pay for, the better. If we just sortie after sortie, we'll end up in the red forever. Then the company goes away, Jason.

"And if we drop a *thousand* containers, we're going to have to pay lease on them until they're back on the station. That's a thousand credits a month. Plus, another two thousand seven hundred for the *cases*. Two hundred seventy cases per conex is two credits seventy per month. Times a thousand. Case costs are adding up fast with all the teams we've got on the planet. And because of shipping costs, we're not able to cycle them as fast as I'd like."

"Lemme think on that," Jason said, nodding. "I said the business side was up to you and I'll take your word. I'll use my on-hand equipment to set up for the run. But when it comes..."

"If we get a salmon run, I'll get Larry to find the shipping," Tim said. "But I'm not dropping a hundred conexes, much less a thousand, unless I'm *sure* they can be filled and not just sit on the ground. Are you going to outvote me?"

"God no, Tim," Jason said, shaking his head. "It's the right call for one thing. I get enthusiastic, you know that. But we're going to make bank on salmon on this river. Big bank. Just have the thousand pack available when it starts. And with it I'm going to need tons of flexmet, six containers of it, two Hermans and a half dozen Alfreds. Set the lease on this spot now, though. I need to get to work."

"I'll file the lease," Tim said. "Leases are cheap for what you get from even a bad one. We good?"

"All good, partner," Jason said. "Out here."

"Penny for your thoughts?" Jewel repeated after Jason had been sitting for almost five minutes.

"It's irrational but I don't want to leave this spot," Jason said. "As if my possession of it depends upon being here. Which it does not in any way. We're taking the lease, for one thing. And there are probably other places on the river that would work as well. So... we'll head back to Olzon. Plan. Not my strong suit but I can hum the tune."

"Disassemble and bring the sawmill?" Jewel said.

"No," Jason replied. "Build a new one. Better, stronger, faster. We'll leave the two Alfreds that are trapping in the area and let them run. Leave a few drones and the batteries. The Hermans with the other harvest teams can recharge as necessary.

"We'll start by sending Herman, two Alfreds and some drones to clear and prep," Jason said. "Clear the trees, clear the underbrush, level the site. We need a forecast of clear skies for that last. They'll take the pieces to a redesigned sawmill with them. Just the bits they need to get started. Should fit in a conex."

He brought up the ground plan and pointed to the high spot away from the river.

"The sawmill will not be forward," Jason said. "We need the space by the river for the harvest. So, we'll set it well back. The initial clear is just the area around the sawmill. Then we use the sawmill to cut timber to lay down on the soil, like railroad ties, crosspieces to keep the conexes from subsiding. Work out from the sawmill. Have Herman run the sawmill and the Alfreds clear and prep the ground then lay down the ties. Bring that over to the river on a broad avenue then build the dock. Floating dock attached to pilings: The river's level is going to rise and fall with the rains.

"After that's done, continue to clear, prep and cover the rest of the area," Jason said, drawing in a large zone. "Enough room for up to a thousand conexes, single stack. Starting from riverside and moving back."

"Two Alfreds harvesting and testing," Jewel said. "Two here. That doesn't leave you with a bike."

"I can forego the bike," Jason said. "When I need one, I'll use one. But in the meantime, they need to be working. I can wander on foot or catch one of the ones on the bay if I need it."

"That's...an outline of a plan," Jewel said.

"It'll do for now," Jason said. "Bring in the drones."

"They've picked some mushrooms," Jewel noted.

"That'll do for an appetizer," Jason replied.

"When we drop a tree, two drones can cut off a plank," Jewel said, doing a rough CGI of the plan on the tablet. "Curved back, flat side. Those can be collected by an Alfred and laid down flat side down to set an initial base. Then timbers laid over it and pegged. Not side to side across the entire area. With gaps to, among other things, let the water through. The bottom planks will be more-or-less side to side and interlocked. The wide base will spread the ground pressure."

Dinner was the ubiquitous fried mushrooms followed by steamed crab with margarine for dipping. Jason had made a wooden hammer for crab cracking. Brown crab was as good as it was reputed to be, buttery and slightly sweet, similar to Dungeness but if anything, more solid. Wild potatoes and some sauteed spring greens completed the simple meal.

"Makes sense," Jason said. "Walking over that will be torturous."

"We'll make a walkway that's solid," Jewel said. "The problem is size, weather and timing. We're going to need at least ten acres cleared and prepped in the few brief clear days. Some of this can be done in the rain but some of it should not. Not to mention the cutting, sawmill time, et cetera."

"You want to use more bots," Jason said.

"I recommend discontinuing the crab and perch harvest and using those Alfreds," Jewel said. "Also, I recommend moving the sawmill. It's not going to get flooded in one of the lower areas; they're still well above flood levels and that hill is well away from the primary work area."

"Makes sense," Jason repeated. "Both."

"We put the sawmill here," Jewel said, sketching it in on a spot about a hundred yards from the river. "Then we clear a long area along the river and set in the containers there," she added, sketching it in. "The dock goes in first but that's the area to clear."

"All good," Jason said. "Get started on it in the morning," he added thoughtfully. "The sawmill components, then the clear and prep."

It was weird at the camp with the Alfreds and Herman gone. There were exactly no sounds except his playlist, the wood sounds and the occasional buzz of a patrolling drone. It was nice in a way—the sawmill had been getting on his nerves—but it reinforced how totally alone he was on the planet. With the bots moving around it gave a semblance of busyness. Without them he found himself unsettled.

He walked out of the kraal and contemplated the water. There were seabirds diving on bait fish at numerous points.

"Jewel," Jason said, pointing.

"Anchovies, apparently," Jewel said. "They seem to be running into the bay. There's salmon feeding on them as well as other fish. Bluefin tuna are in the mix."

"Bluefin!" Jason said, his eyes widening in excitement. He thought about what the bots had left behind at the camp. He could build a boat to go after the bluefin. But the problem was landing them. There were more bots around, they could be diverted for bluefin. That wasn't even problem one. Without diverting a bot there was no motive power for a boat.

He thought about it for another second and grinned. Time to go new old school.

He went to the conex that was holding the spare flexmet, sectioned off about half of it then brought it down to the shore. Then it was a matter of gathering rocks. Several of the ballast rocks were still in the area and he tossed them one by one into the flexmet.

"Are you building a boat?" Jewel asked.

"I am indeed," Jason said.

He shaped the boat into a longboat form then got in and had the flexmet hump itself into the water, with a deck under his feet and the ballast midships. As it was moving into the water, he thought of more stuff he should probably bring along and went back to the containers, running a line of flex back to the kraal as a land anchor.

He grabbed containers of fresh water, the case with precooked food, spare wet-weather clothing, a case of fishing gear and one of the Cyber batteries. He didn't want the flex running out of power.

He loaded all the gear into the boat, got it arranged to his satisfaction and pushed off again.

The problem at that point was motive power. He made a couple of oars and those got him part way offshore. The tide was running in and it kept pushing him back into the shore.

He directed the flexmet to bring the ballast down into a keel then quickly lifted a mast and sail. With a touch of the oars to get the right heading and directing the sails he started moving across the bay. Which required a tiller to steer.

All done with his mind. Super cool.

"That's . . . again inventive," Jewel said.

"Thanks," Jason said, leaning back on the stern. He shaped it to be more comfortable and adjusted the keel mentally to have a set of leeboards. He kept shaping the boat and the sails until he had a tidy little fast sailer which skipped over the light waves of the bay. The ballasted keel kept it neatly upright.

He sailed around the bay in the lee of the island getting used to the craft. He also shaped it in various ways. Similar to an older longboat fishing boat; then a long, fast racing sailboat; he even built a covered-deck version. He played with sail types and settled on a finned multisail design that gave the most speed for the least sail area.

Flexmet was incredible stuff. So many industries were going to get slaughtered by it.

Finally, he sailed over to one of the groups of anchovies that were being pursued by, well, everything in the bay. There were sea lions and tuna, salmon, porpoises, and seabirds. The surface action was complete chaos.

After retracting the sails to slow his progress, he extended a long dip net into the mass of anchovies and pulled out about two dozen. The anchovies, by themselves, would be worth harvesting.

In the meantime, his boat was being pummeled from below by every kind of sea creature.

He took six of the anchovies and formed a large hook from flexmet then strung them on it. Then he added a one-ounce lead weight to the line.

"I need to try to get the bluefin with this," Jason said. "Whereabouts?"

"I'd suggest trying out from the school," Jewel said. "Drone video shows most of the bluefin outwards."

He got his sails into action again and moved out from the mass of anchovies that probably covered four acres. As he got into open water there were some seabirds diving but not many.

He coasted to a stop, tossed the line over the side and let it drop.

Seconds later the line tautened and started to run.

He waited to a count of three then had it stop running.

FISH ON!

# CHAPTER 24 >>>>>>>>>

THE BOAT HEELED OVER AS THE POWER OF THE BLUEFIN HIT THE line. He quickly paid out, keeping tension on the line but not pulling the boat over.

He worked the line forward as the bluefin continued to fight and let it run with the boat.

"Nantucket sleigh ride," Jason said, grinning as the bluefin pulled the boat into motion.

"Who do you think you are?" Jewel asked with a grin in her voice. "The old man and the sea?"

He had the line directly connected through the upper bulkhead of the boat. But keeping a hand on it he could feel the tingle of the tension, could feel the tuna, but didn't have to maintain a hard grip on it.

"It's not quite as difficult," Jason said.

The school of anchovies had been on the north side of the bay but the tuna headed south. It pulled the boat down the bay as Jason managed the line, paying it out when the fish sounded— meaning when it dived deep—retracting when he could. The bay wasn't very deep, so the tuna couldn't sound as well as in the ocean.

The tuna suddenly took a turn to port, circling. The line had been to starboard, so Jason shifted it around to keep it from going under the boat.

"How are you going to land it?" Jewel asked.

"You said the bots could go supersonic, right?" Jason said. "When I get it up to the boat, I'll bring in a Herman with some flex. It can probably lift it. If not, it can get us both back to shore and get it into a conex."

"It'll take a conex," Jewel said. "Drone estimates it's at least nine feet. Weight estimate is around a thousand to thirteen hundred pounds."

"Damn," Jason said, laughing. "That a record?"

"No," Jewel said. "Sort of? The record is fifteen hundred on Earth. Nobody has caught one, yet, on Bellerophon, so it would be a Bellerophon record if it was tiny."

"Got it," Jason said, grinning. The weather wasn't bad, the bay was alive with life and he had a massive bluefin on the line. Things could be worse.

After circling the bluefin turned north again. It had dragged the boat halfway down the length of Olzon Island, well into the bay, and now turned back. It was leaning to the island side, though.

Jason could retract the keel. Its main purpose had been for sailing. He was worried about going aground with the deep-sailing keel.

He brought up a console of flexmet and propped his phone on it.

"Bring up what we've got of the hydrography," Jason said. "I don't want to go running aground."

He didn't seem to be headed for any underwater obstructions. But the entire bay wasn't mapped. There were blank spots since the sonar the boats had been using was only straight down.

"We need to get our hands on some side-scan sonar," Jason said. It gave a much wider view of hydrography.

"None available for sale," Jewel said. "People might have had a sonar set sitting around that they intended to install on a boat any day now. But apparently nobody just had a side-scan sonar sitting around. Silly humans."

"Can we make them?" Jason asked.

"You can make practically anything you can dream up," Jewel said. "As soon as we have facilities up and going to make it."

The tuna was now headed for the northern pass and Jason wasn't liking that one bit.

"It looks as if you're going out to sea," Jewel said uncomfortably. "Do you wish for me to call in a Herman? It can probably get it to the surface and finish this."

"Nope," Jason said. He opened up his personal case and

extracted some wet-weather gear. Putting it on while ensuring the fish didn't escape wasn't easy but he'd done weirder things.

As they entered the pass the waves built up into mounds and water shipped over the side. Jason formed a rudder, again, and ensured the boat always headed into the waves, working the line at the same time. It was mental gymnastics but he accomplished it.

The strongly running tide combined with the massive waves of the Pallas as well as the bottom profile was creating short-period, steep, standing waves. Jason had to continuously let out on the line, giving the fish more slack, as the front of the boat was threatened with being pulled under.

After a near ditching, he reshaped the boat, creating a top deck that would cascade the water as well as making it longer and narrower, similar to a very large sea kayak. The narrowness made shipping water more likely but he was now in a cockpit with a shield in the front. The waves now cascaded over the bow, running down the top deck to the point the boat was more of a shallow submarine, then cascading over the sides and around the shield in front of Jason.

"This is officially an aqueous experience," Jason said as salt water splashed his face. He had his feet braced and the shield went down deeper so that if he slid forward the flexmet deck wouldn't cut into his chest. He was now pointed west, passing through the north pass and into the Beringia Sea. Not to his surprise he could see dark clouds building in the distance.

"Looks like rain, again," Jason said.

"This is not safe, Jason," Jewel pointed out. "There are a variety of ways that you could drown doing this. Not to mention the local water temperature is low enough there is a real possibility that if you end up in the water you could die of hypothermia before you were rescued."

"Life isn't about 'safe,' Jewel," Jason said. "For some people it is. Sure. But life is about doing. About being and seeing. And when you're me, life is about adventure. Worse comes to worse, I cut the fish loose, hoist a sail and sail back. Or bring in a Herman or an Alfred."

He looked out at the rolling waves of the Beringia and shrugged.

"Or, what the hell, just keep sailing," Jason said. "Though I'd need more supplies. Flying around on ships is cool. But to sail this in a sea kayak? That's *adventure*."

"Why'd I get the crazy one?" Jewel asked.

The fish was tiring and Jason brought in some line. As the bottom deepened the fish dove, coming back toward the boat. Jason kept tension on the line, bringing it in closer and using the rudder to adjust the boat to keep the fish from coming under the boat. That wasn't enough and he realized he could simply move the line across the bottom of the boat.

Flex made everything too easy.

He continued to bring the fish in, slowly, pulling up ever so gently as it spiraled under the boat. It suddenly tugged, again, and he let it run. Then it started circling again. Lather, rinse, repeat. It would run then circle then run again. He counted five times. But it was clearly tiring.

They were bobbing in the Beringia for sure now, and Jason also kept one eye on the rocks to the east. They were uncomfortably close to the windward side of Olzon Island and that was one hazard he'd prefer to avoid. But adventure didn't come from playing it safe.

The tuna turned and ran out to sea and Jason let it, narrowing the boat, and making it as hydrodynamic as possible. The further they were from the rocks the better in his estimation.

He continued to occasionally pull in on the line, bringing the fish closer and closer to the surface. He could see it through the clear water about thirty feet deep. The fish could also see the boat and made a sudden, short run. It was about played out.

"Okay," Jason said. "Call in one of the Hermans. Subsonic if you please."

The Herman showed up right on time as Jason was bringing the massive fish up to the boat. He'd returned it to the open longboat style since the fish was no longer causing him to ship water. The waves were high but not so high that they splashed over the bulwarks.

"What's the best way for him to lift this?" Jason asked. "And how are we going to kill it?"

"He can pick it up with a tractor beam," Jewel said. "A tractor beam to the head should kill it. And it's the best way to lift it."

"Okay," Jason said, stepping back. "Tractor to the head, please."

Herman applied a tractor beam to the head of the fish and it was still. Then he lifted it out of the water.

"Damn," Jason said. "That's a big fish."

"Do you want Herman to help you get back?" Jewel asked hopefully. "He could pick up both you and the boat as well as the tuna."

"I'll sail back," Jason said, bracing himself on the side of the rocking longboat. "Have him get that back to one of the conexes on Olzon. Then back to work."

"All right," Jewel said doubtfully.

"Oh, ye of little faith," Jason said, taking a seat and reshaping the boat.

He chose the deep-keel racing sailboat with the addition of a top deck. With the keel well down and a sail up, the rocking reduced and he caught the fair wind from the sea back toward the pass.

As he was entering the pass, still dealing with standing waves crashing over the bow and the tiny sailboat going from jumps in the air to burying itself in the waves, a squall hit with rain coming down in sheets and the wind kicked up to a gale.

"This!" Jason shouted as the wind and waves pounded the small craft and he trimmed the sails to keep from being entirely drowned. "*This* is what life's all about!"

"Why did I have to draw the crazy one...?"

Jason looked at the rock outcrop and rubbed his chin.

He'd been exploring Olzon Island on foot while the salmon camp was being built. Most of the game had, deliberately, been cleared off. If he needed to scratch the hunting urge, he could go to the mainland.

But he'd gotten interested in rock. If he was going to eventually build a house on the planet, and he intended to, he was going to need rock. There was at present no tile industry and rock had numerous uses.

There were also numerous types of rock. There was no limestone on the planet for all practical purposes, nor its metamorphic-child: marble. But there were other useful types of rock. And it turned out Olzon Island had a small outcrop of soapstone.

Soapstone was one of those construction stones people didn't tend to notice. It just was a thing. But soapstone had been used for centuries for everything from decorative jewelry to building temples. It was solid but easy to carve and nonporous so it held water. Or shed it, as the case may be.

Very useful stuff.

The outcrop was more of a boulder, displaced from somewhere else. The area might have been subject to catastrophic floods or glaciation at one point; there were signs of what could be either. Whatever the case, it showed soapstone had formed on the planet. And that was good.

Jason cut off a chunk of the material with flex—it went through like butter—and put it in his backpack. He'd work with it when he got back to camp.

The soapstone was easy to work with flex. He wasn't much of a carver but he worked, by evening carving it into what might kindly be described as a duck.

"It's a..." Jewel said politely. "Frog?"

"Duck," Jason said, tossing the carving aside. "Carving is not my strong suit..."

Jason picked at a duck he'd simply named Darn Good Duck for the taste and looked out over the water of Wilson Bay.

He'd spent two weeks fishing, hunting and exploring the area, using the sailboat to move around the bay. He hadn't ventured back into the ocean again and had used the bots, primarily, to catch the tuna that continued to follow the anchovy run. That was falling off, though, as was the tuna run. There was still plenty to fish in the bay.

The tidal wave of migrating birds had also fallen off but the duck and geese hunting in the delta remained. Many of the birds made the delta their home. He'd started to sort them out and name the ones which remained unnamed.

A huge number of rock legends, and even obscure, were going to have names associated with wildfowl.

Duncan had figured out how to make a pump from flexmet. It wasn't particularly hard as it turned out. Together with a heating element, Jason now had hot and cold running water for his kitchen and a shower and toilet.

Life was practically civilized. Seafood was moving on a daily basis from the bay. The main seafood being lifted was already salmon which were becoming much more frequent in the bay. It was a good sign there'd be a midsummer run. The salmon harvesting area was finished, the bots were back in the bay and, frankly, things were getting a bit boring.

"There are salmon moving up Jagger Creek," Jewel said.

"Really?" Jason replied. He dropped the duck, wiped his hands off then grabbed his .30-06 and hat. Jagger Creek was the stream right beside the encampment.

He went through the seaside gate to the kraal then swung north to the stream. He and the bots had already cleared a path to it. It was raining and there was a fair amount of mud but the path was fairly clear.

When he got there, Jagger Creek was boiling with a mass of salmon swimming up the stream.

He walked up the hill, following them. There were several cataracts on the stream as it cascaded down the steep hills. Salmon were jumping in all of them. He followed them to the shallow upland streams where they were already beginning their mating rituals.

"That means there's going to be a shit-ton of salmon going upriver," Jason said, shaking his head. If this stream was this packed...

It was midafternoon. He'd just finished lunch when he left the camp. He looked up at the sky. More rain was forecast.

"Should we begin the salmon harvest?" Jewel asked.

"Not yet," Jason said. "I want to be there."

They'd been discussing theories of how to do it for most of the two weeks. But theory and empirical never exactly meshed.

"We'll leave tomorrow morning, rain or shine," Jason said, walking downstream to one of the cataracts. "Get me Tim if he's available. Do the feed from the glasses."

Tim came on a few seconds later.

"Check it out," Jason said, grinning. "Salmon."

"That's a lot of salmon," Tim admitted. "Just the stuff we've been getting from the bay is selling well. And that's one stream?"

"The one by the camp," Jason said. "The island camp. I haven't checked the river yet."

"View from the river," Jewel said.

In the drone view it was apparent there were fish in the river, and all through the delta.

"I'm going to head up there tomorrow morning," Jason said. "Rain or shine. But we need containers."

"Maddie," Tim said. "Based on this stream, all other things being equal..."

"Depends on the length of the run," Maddie said. "Based purely on Earth runs of Atlantic salmon ... If the run lasts for two weeks, which is short, you're going to need *more* than a thousand conexes filled with cases."

"I'll get with Larry," Tim said. "There are only a couple of the thousand packs that have gotten past the problem with units. They're also just sitting there so Larry said we could get a good rate ... We'll try to schedule a drop for tomorrow morning. Dawn work?"

"Dawn works," Jason said.

"This is going to make serious bank," Tim said, grinning. "The stuff from the bay is selling like hotcakes. We're probably going to overwhelm the market."

"Discuss how much of it to ship and how much to store later," Jason said. "This is going to be fun."

"Out here."

"If he's dropping at dawn tomorrow, you either have to go up there tonight or get up very early tomorrow," Jewel said. "I suggest you go up there tonight."

"No housing," Jason said. It was not that he would miss his hot shower. It was just that there weren't even conexes at the site yet. They'd added a few items, though.

A spiked kraal had been added around the entire facility. The bots and drones worked night and day, stopping only to recharge. Drones could lift the thin wood railings that were interwoven on the kraal and even the lighter of the spiked poles. That left the Alfreds with the task of digging the holes and setting the posts. An Alfred could carry fifty posts at a time and set each of them in seconds. It had only taken a day. Another job that was going to put a lot of humans out of business.

"There's housing," Jewel said. "Of a sort. You can sleep in the sawmill if nothing else. And Herman can take you up there in the air-car so you don't have to get wet. You know you're not a morning person."

Jason hadn't been up to the fish camp since it had started, relying on drone footage since it would require a bot to get up there. He really should check it out first.

"Okay," Jason said. "Make it so. Get everything packed and ready to go while I pick my way down to the camp."

It took him about forty-five minutes to make his way back

to camp, by which time everything was packed and the "air-car" had been formed.

Someone had had a windshield for a 1960s Corvette Stingray sitting around in their "stuff." Combine that with flexmet and either an Alfred or a Herman, a couple of car windows for a view out the side, and you had a flying car. One whose windshield was rated for up to 150 miles per hour.

He had the glass added to one of the regular drops that were occurring in the bay and now had transportation that could be used, comfortably, in the rain. No heat or A/C, but it was still the lap of luxury compared to walking or the air-bike in the rain.

Jason climbed into the air-car and gratefully set his soaked jacket to the side, along with the Savage, and tossed his battered hat onto the pile.

"I'm not even going to try to drive this thing," Jason said. "Ferrell River salmon camp."

The aerodynamic car lifted into the air and they set off across the bay. It was using one of the Alfreds for power and Herman had all the gear in a separate teardrop-shaped flexmet pod.

"How fast?" Jewel asked.

"Thousand feet AGL," Jason said, referring to "Above Ground Level." "One hundred miles per hour."

The air-car pointed to the sky and accelerated, leveling off at a thousand feet, then screamed toward the salmon camp. The level off was slight negative G. Jason had automatically put in a safety harness so he stayed in his seat. And didn't lose his gorge.

"Figure I can use the flexmet for a hammock," Jason said thoughtfully. The terrain below was flying past and the car lifted, again, to pass over the range of interior hills.

"That...will work," Jewel said, a note of amusement in her voice.

"What's so funny?" Jason asked.

"You'll see," Jewel said.

As they neared the camp the car decelerated and swung around to the river, turned in a graceful bank, flew in slowly over the dock and the sawmill and settled gently on a wooden landing pad next to a small house on the hill overlooking the encampment.

And that was what it was. A small, wooden Bavarian-style house with a shake roof, doors, windows, shutters, chimneys, the whole thing. Some of it was elaborately carved.

Someone was being sneaky...

# CHAPTER 25 〉〉〉〉〉〉〉〉〉

"JEWELLL?" JASON SAID WARNINGLY, EXAMINING THE HOME. "Should I check for three bears?"

"Do you like it?" Jewel asked hopefully.

"I..." Jason said. "How? I've been checking out the progress in the drone footage."

"I sort of was...editing," Jewel said carefully. "It's a surprise. For your birthday. You do remember it's your birthday, right?"

"I..." Jason said again. "How?"

"I started by talking with Mr. Kranhouse, helping him out with the IP on using flexmet to work with wood," Jewel said, burbling. "Then I realized you would probably need housing at the salmon camp. I had to purchase a few items, they were cheap, I promise, total of fifty credits, and I got Gil to go along with the surprise. Is it okay?"

"I...love it?" Jason said finally. "Thank you?"

"You're welcome," Jewel said. "It really didn't add a whole bunch of work time to the bots. I couldn't have hidden it from you if it did."

"Which, again, means the construction industry is in for a shock," Jason said. It was still raining in the area so he pulled on his jacket and hat and grabbed his rifle before opening the door and heading for the house.

There was a portico overhang on the front door which was heavy wood and carved with a figure of Cthulhu. It had a brass door knocker hanging from its central tentacles. The door had a normal front door latch and Jason opened it and stepped into his new home away from the compartment.

There was a short foyer with pegs for jackets and a bench. He took off his hat, and coat, hanging them both along with his gun belt then sat down and took off his boots. No reason to tramp mud around a nice, clean new house.

The floors were polished wood while the walls were wood paneling and plaster with inset shelves for books or knickknacks. The fireplace was made from rough stone with mortar. The stones at the base were a type he didn't recognize. There was no fire set up or firewood because it was getting into summer and the days didn't really call for it. But it would be nice in fall and winter.

The light from the window on the polished wood gave it a warm, homey feel. There were curtains on the windows. It smelled like sawdust.

The curtains he didn't recognize. Paintings on the walls he did. The furniture he did. Real Earth furnishings.

"How'd you get Tim to drop my couch and sofa?" Jason asked, looking at the worn furniture. "Not to mention my Ray Harm prints."

"We had a drop going to the bay and had Herman come over and pick up one conex," Jewel replied. "At night so you wouldn't notice."

"You are a sneaky little tramp," Jason said. "I love it."

"Can I show you around?" Jewel asked.

The dining room table *wasn't* his. It appeared to be local manufacture, all wood for one thing. So were the expertly carved and formed chairs. Both appeared to be made from maple.

"Is that . . . ?" Jason asked, examining it.

"Mr. Kranhouse wanted to experiment," Jewel said. "He made that in less than a day. He offered it as a birthday gift and with thanks for getting him wood again."

Jason got down on his hands and knees to look under the table. Sure enough, there was the symbol of Withywindle, a willow tree over a small stream, carved into the underside. Mr. Kranhouse always carved his company's symbol into the underside of his work.

Off the dining room, there was a small but well-appointed kitchen with hot and cold running water, cabinets and a wooden counter. There were even standard Earth faucets. Moen.

"One of the costs was a heating element for the manifold," Jewel said. "Faucets and shower heads for the kitchen and the bathrooms. Things like that. The hinges are all flex and so are the toilets, sorry. I know you're getting tired of flex everywhere but . . ."

"It's fantastic," Jason said, looking at the sink. It was wooden. "Is this going to work?"

"Yes," Jewel said. "It's an Earth design that was rarely used. Think of it as the reverse of a wooden canoe. It may not last long but it will last until we can get one of rock or metal."

Wood-lined pantry, still unstocked, with plenty of shelf space.

"The pantry has several flexmet items in it," Jewel said. "And it's a stasis pantry. It's basically two coffins on the floor, flex behind all the walls and shelves, and two coffins on top. The combination, with a little tweaking, creates a stasis zone over the whole room. It turns on when you shut the door. But it looks like just a normal pantry."

"Remind me to find stuff to stock it," Jason said. There was already a basket of wild mushrooms, but it needed more.

Both beds upstairs were wood, a king and a queen. They had a rougher look than the dining room table and he suspected they were made by the bots. They did, however, have inner spring mattresses.

"Where'd the mattresses come from?" Jason asked.

"Those are yours," Jewel said. "But the beds are new. Do you like them?"

"Love 'em," Jason said, nodding. The rest of the furniture was from his house in Loganville.

There was a half bath downstairs with a full bath upstairs, both having smoothly finished wooden cabinets, sinks, and counters. The full bath's shower was stone lined.

"Is this soapstone?" Jason said, running his hands over it. "From Olzon?"

"Yes," Jewel said. "I used up most of the outcrop but there have been others found by survey and harvest teams..."

"That's...okay," Jason said. "Great. Love the shower."

The fixtures were, again, Earth manufacture. Somebody had had a complete Delta shower set they were probably going to install "any day now." Either they or someone else had had a rain showerhead in their personal stuff.

There was a small anteroom off the main bath whose door had a half-moon carved in it. The toilet was flexmet.

"While there were some toilets on the market, the flexmet toilet can be a bidet toilet," Jewel said hesitatingly, as if she wasn't sure he liked it.

"Jewel," Jason said, trying to figure out how to calm the AI. "You have once again lived up to your name. This is lovely.

Wonderful. I love it and I'm overwhelmed by your gift. Does that cover it? I really, really like it."

"Oh, good," Jewel said excitedly. "I was worried about sneaking around behind your back, but..."

"You wanted it to be a surprise and it was," Jason said. "Power?"

"Battery room," Jewel said. "Fully charged."

Jason flopped down in his junk-store recliner and lifted the footrest.

"Ah..." Jason said, shaking his head again and looking around. "Plaster?" he asked quizzically. That had just occurred to him. He couldn't imagine somebody having that much plaster just sitting around in their house. Okay, maybe a plaster worker?

"One of the survey and harvest teams found gypsum," Jewel said. "I had to have that lifted to the station and back down. Bots ground it up, mixed and smoothed. Tim approved it."

"Tim approved it?" Jason said. "*Tim?* Approved lift? Get me that penny pincher!"

One of the concessions to modernity in the house was a large flexscreen over the fireplace. Tim's face appeared, grinning.

"Like your house?" Tim asked.

"You approved mining gypsum for plaster?" Jason asked. "And lifting it to the station and back down?"

"It was on the way," Tim said, shrugging. "If it had required a separate round trip I wouldn't have. Jewel was really excited, though. Looks nice."

"It's *fantastic*," Jason said, shaking his head again. "So, I set up Withywindle..."

"Mr. Kranhouse is working with our designer on Brandywine," Tim said. "Which is going well."

"We could probably make these in kits," Jason mused. "Precut everything and bring it to your homestead. Jewel, is that possible?"

"Very," Jewel said.

"That's another potential business," Jason said. "When people want houses on the surface."

"There's pressure for that," Tim said, nodding. "But the shipping situation is still bugged and while most people would like to see the sun and blue skies again, they're less sanguine about giant bears and crocodiles."

"Yeah," Jason said. "Speaking of which: Do we have the thousand pack?"

"We do," Tim said. "Scheduled to arrive tomorrow at about zero six hundred. Ready to catch some salmon?"

"As soon as we've got the gear," Jason said. "Work starts tomorrow. In the meantime, I'm going to settle in and enjoy my house for the night."

"Enjoy away," Tim said. "And happy birthday."

"Thanks," Jason said as Tim cut the connection. "Do not let me forget Tim's birthday."

"I won't," Jewel said.

He wasn't used to sleeping on his own mattress. It wasn't a great mattress but it had been a long time since he'd slept on anything but flexmet or the ground.

The combination of sleeping in a bed and the excitement of getting started on the salmon run had him up half the night tossing and turning. So he was bleary eyed when Jewel awakened him for the cargo drop.

The thousand pack was a massive ship. That he was partial owner of one approximately ten times its size was suddenly real and relevant.

"Got the drop down?" Jason asked. "We need them along the river."

"Your tractors are supposed to assist, yes?" the driver asked. He had a Slavic accent.

"Yes," Jason said, yawning. Purple Lightning was not the greatest morning pick-me-up. "Let's deploy."

It took about fifteen minutes to get all the containers down and spread out. As the massive ship disappeared into the clouds, it was time to get to work.

The plan had already been worked out with some changes from the shrimp harvest. All of the obstructions on the river had been removed from the area by the bots using their tractor beams and a post had been sunk about two hundred meters out from the bluffs, a half a kilometer downriver.

An Alfred carried a thick line of flexmet down to the post and attached it, then the flex opened out into a wide mesh net. Too wide to stop salmon. It wasn't time to start bringing in the salmon yet. The flex already had steel weights in it and it deployed to the bottom without incident.

Other posts had been driven into the river bottom to form

the beginnings of the funnel and the last portion was tied off to a post driven in opposite the midstream post with the entire net forming a V.

The rest of the morning was spent trying to figure out the best way to get the salmon, as undamaged as possible, out of the river and into the conexes.

Various ways worked well enough, but "well enough" wasn't what he was going for.

During lunch he had an idea and tested it.

The conexes were virtually invulnerable to anything, especially water, so he simply submerged a conex into the river. Holding it in place was a bit of a trial but by lowering the sides he had water flowing into it. The salmon, following their instinct to follow flowing water, headed into the conex. The problem was getting them into the cases.

He finally had a system where the salmon would swim into the cases. He opened up the downstream side of the conex as well as having the cases, which were nose to tail, open up their front and rear and connect their flexmet walls to form a tunnel. The upstream side of the conex was a screen of waterholes. The cases created tunnels for the fish, packed in by the V of the nets, to swim upstream, following their instincts. The front-most cases of the conex only had small holes the salmon couldn't fit through. As the salmon reached the barrier, they had difficulty turning around and were trapped. Salmon would pack themselves into the cases. Once the AI sensed the cases were full, a tunnel would close up. Fish would then try to find another path. And so, the conex filled.

Once that happened, the conex would close up and start to rise. It didn't have enough power by itself to lift the full mass out of the water but could with the help of a couple of Alfreds. During the lift portion, the cases and the sides of the conex would open up holes for the water to drain out. As it drained, the cases would go back to stasis and once the water was mostly drained the conex would close up and go to stasis. Finally, a single Alfred could carry it to the "full" area of the complex.

Job complete.

Jason had had to occasionally open up the nets to let the mass of salmon through. When he repeated the system, faster this time, the salmon still built up too much. The river was so thick with fish it looked as if it was boiling. He opened up the main nets to let some through and then opened up side openings on the funnel.

"How long to fill a conex?" Jason asked.

"Ten minutes, more or less," Jewel said. "Probably get faster."

"Math?" Jason said. "Carry the three…"

"Six conexes per hour," Jewel said. "One hundred sixty-seven hours. Divided by twenty-four, seven days. A week for a thousand-pack pickup."

"Or a half a week with two conexes," Jason said. "There's enough fish that we could run two conexes."

"We could," Jewel said.

"Hell, we could run ten but I'm not going to get that greedy."

Jason kept the net shortened while they worked on a two-conex system. With the shorter net, it took longer to fill both conexes but when they had the system down, he completed the net again and waited for a couple of cycles. By adjusting the funnel to switch back and forth they had an almost continuous rhythm with a conex lifting out of the water and onto the filled area every five minutes.

"Twelve conexes per hour," Jewel said. "Three and a half days for a pickup at this rate."

"We'll see if the rate keeps up for a day," Jason said. Setting up the perfect system had taken all day, and the birds were singing their evening calls.

Bears were in evidence on the far bank, diving into the river to hunt for salmon. The bluffs on this side probably kept them away. Sea eagles, similar to bald eagles but with a red head like a woodpecker instead of white, were squabbling over salmon with them. Jason even saw a tiger in the water hunting the fish.

Everything ate salmon. He knew what *he* was having for dinner.

Cade hid in the playground equipment. By day, children came out to hurry down the slide, bounce on the bridge, and dawdle on the treehouse-like platform. By night, the area was quiet, and the playground equipment gave him a place where he could hide and keep an eye on the largest group of his planting beds.

He crouched at the top of the equipment, where both an enclosed slide and a fireman's pole headed for the ground. The waist-high wall kept him hidden, as long as he crouched.

It was his third night on watch. He was waiting for vandals.

Someone kept messing with his garden. Specifically, with this one, which made the whole thing feel personal. He'd debated taking a gun out of stasis for this, but he thought that if he accidentally shot a hole in the space station wall, Mabel would leave him, even if the robot or alien overlords didn't make him walk the plank.

He leaned on the plastic wall of his watchtower. Resting on his knees in the warm, quiet darkness, he caught himself drifting in and out. He shook his head, trying to keep himself awake.

And then he saw the vandal.

The man staggered in from a secondary entrance. The corridor on the other side of that door led to a street with two bars on it, and the vandal walked as if he was an enthusiastic customer. He wobbled from step to step, but he lunged and reeled toward a cluster of four of Cade's beds.

Cade waited, wishing he could see the man's face, or the details of the clothing. In the near-total darkness, the vandal was just a silhouette.

The man fell on a bed of cabbage. He tore through with methodical speed, ripping up one head after the other and tossing them aside. At the same time, he kicked with his feet as if wading into surf, sending up sprays of loose dirt and fertilizer.

When he reached the end of the planting bed, he stepped into the adjacent bed. He turned, pointing his back toward Cade, aiming to devastate the second bed by charging the opposite direction.

Cade slid down the fireman's pole to the bed of rubber chips at the bottom. He didn't bother to muffle the sound of his drop, or the sound of his boots. The vandal heard him coming and straightened, and then Cade planted a kick in his backside. He spun, off-balance, putting up his fists, and Cade punched him in the jaw.

The vandal sat down.

"Son of a bitch," Cade muttered. "You're gonna put all the soil right back where you found it. You're lucky I don't make you eat the fertilizer. Dummy, take a look at his face and get a picture."

Cade held up his phone and turned on his headlamp, illuminating the vandal, sitting on his backside in the dirt.

"It's your son, Sam," Dummy said in its sexless voice.

"Go on, Dad," Sam said. His voice was hard. "Hit me again. What would John Wayne do, after all?"

"What the hell do you think you're doing?" Cade asked.

"What the hell do *you* think I'm doing?" Sam shot back.

Cade had no words.

"That's right, Dad," Sam said, "I'm doing nothing."

Rather than beat his son, Cade growled without words and stomped away.

The next morning Jason looked at the process again. He'd had some thoughts overnight about it. It was efficient, but not efficient enough. There was a reason he was a good logistics guy and this was really just logistics in his opinion. Most efficient way to move the most material in the least time.

Two Alfreds were necessary to lift one of the containers onto the dock to drain, so he had to keep at least two on that job. And Herman was supplying power to everything, so he was sort of locked in.

Bottom line, he needed more bots. But he wasn't going to ask for anything. He'd figure it out.

He started by having two of the Alfreds get to work extending the dock along the shoreline, upstream from the current construction. He added pilings out from the dock as well, starting with one to help stabilize the conex that was in the water. Five more of those as well as the extended dock.

Flexmet was necessary for the connections between the dock and the pilings as well as pontoons to support the dock. He'd added flotation when he'd decided to just use the conexes for traps; their weight when they first hit the dock was massive.

He briefly broke Herman away from supplying power to line up some empty conexes. He determined that it was possible to use flex to extend the tunnels made of cases from conex to conex.

It took all day for the bots to finish the pier while he strode nervously around the compound. It should work...

The next day with the pier complete, long enough to handle five conexes at a time, he had the bots lower five preconnected conexes end to end.

Each was connected to the midstream pilings as well as the pilings for the dock. Flexmet in fine nets was connected between the mass of cases and the walls and ceilings of the conexes. More flexmet was connected between the cases of one conex to the next in line, creating a continuous fish tunnel five conexes long. The upstream conex was set up in the same manner as the single conex they'd been using to that point, with a wide mesh to let water flow into the cases.

Last, the case tunnels were hooked up to the fish trap nets.

Jason couldn't actually see the fish filling the conexes but Jewel had learned to use the impact sensation of the flexmet of the cases to determine when they were full. As the lead case filled, first the cases were closed and put in stasis, then the entire conex was closed and lifted from the water, detaching the flexmet connecting to the previous conex which became the lead. The conex drained on the pier then was lifted up to join the full conexes waiting for lift.

There were some bobbles. Some of the salmon were cut in half when things closed. Some escaped. But in time they had a five-conex system working efficiently.

He let that run for two hours.

"How long now?" Jason asked.

"We're going to need the thousand pack tomorrow," Jewel said after a moment. "Morning. And we'll have to suspend operations or get a new set of conexes by... zero one thirty or thereabouts. We'll fill a thousand pack in a twenty-five-hour period, more or less. One day."

"Down from seven," Jason said. "Send that data to Tim."

"A thousand pack a *day*?" Tim asked, incredulous. "A day."

"Who's the best, Tim?" Jason asked, grinning. "It's just logistics the way I look at it. The most efficient way to get the material loaded in the least time. Is that *too* much salmon?"

"There's five hundred million people in this system," Tim said. "And they all eat fish. We've been advertising the salmon run. There's demand. For what we'll be getting for it, we can afford to store any if it saturates the market. But... a thousand pack a day?" He shook his head and chuffed like a silverback gorilla.

"Who's the best?" Jason said.

"You're the best, buddy," Tim admitted.

"And this isn't the only river that is having a run," Jason pointed out. "Now that the system is designed..."

"Maddie, tell Larry his job just got more complicated," Tim said. "And get me Kevin. We're going to need *several* teams..."

"And now I've worked myself out of a job," Jason said. "Again."

"I'm sure you're going to create more headaches for me, Kevin and Larry before you know it."

# CHAPTER 26 >>>>>>>>>

"THAT LOOKS LIKE SOMEWHERE I'D LIKE TO VACATION," TOM Ferrell said, grinning.

The atoll had started with a blown-out caldera a still-unknown millions of years before while the planet was hot. At some time in Bellerophon's pre-terraformed formation, a stratovolcano had blown its top, resulting in a deep, more-or-less circular bowl with the western edge blown out in a slide. Then, later, magma had bubbled up in the middle into a few minivolcanoes. Still later, as the planet cooled to its core, the volcanic activity died. That was how it existed for at least tens of millions of years until the Cyber Corps decided the planet was right to terraform.

When the robots added water, and when it adjusted to its current level, the only parts that extended above the water were the tops of the edge of the caldera and the summits of two mini-volcanoes in the middle. Since that time there had been erosion of the slopes of all the bits of rock sticking above the ocean's surface as well as invasions of plants and animals.

The result was two sets of more-or-less semicircular small volcanic islands, each surrounded by a barrier reef of coral, mostly interconnected; two larger islands on the north side of the archipelago protected from the massive waves of the Pallas by the barrier islands; and a deep channel between the northern and southern set.

The eastern opening to the ocean, where the largest waves came in, was the narrower but still about six miles across.

The western opening, where the caldera had blown out in a slide, was sixteen miles across.

The southern set of islands hadn't developed a full barrier reef between themselves and the channel but the shallower northern waters had a barrier reef confining the channel and creating a lagoon between itself and the islands.

Besides that lagoon, on the southern side of the large islands, there was a large lagoon not only between the two inner islands but between those and the northerly ring of barrier islands. That lagoon, nearly five miles across, should be teeming with fish and the spiny lobster "crayfish" that were the point of the expedition. The trade winds blew steady from the southeast and while the massive waves in the region were broken by the barrier reefs and islands, the trade winds were not.

The plant life on the islands was very similar to prehuman Hawaii: very large, hundred-plus-foot iron trees dotted the slopes with breadfruit trees in lower, swampier areas; mangroves in all the extremely wet areas; coconuts and other palms on the frequent black and pink sand beaches and a plethora of different tropical understory. There were very few reptiles and none had grown to extreme size or ferocity. The lower regions were home to vast colonies of migratory birds. Given more time, absent predators, some of them probably would have evolved into flightless birds. As it was, there didn't seem to be any hostile predators of any sort, unless you got in the water where there were sharks.

The nearest continental landmass was Chindia, which was about a thousand miles to the west, downcurrent. The nearest in the other direction, Avia, was nearly ten thousand miles away across the vast reaches of the Pallas.

It defined the term "remote tropical paradise."

Jason had chosen a landing point on the innermost of the north islands to avoid the currents and waves he spotted in the channel. It was on the eastern side to catch the trade winds. The barrier reef was only a hundred meters from the shore and the area that it was a barrier to was only about a hundred feet deep. Between the shore and the barrier reef was a combination of sea grass, open sand and patch corals.

In the sat view there was a waterfall apparent just inland. That would do for fresh water. There was definitely a stream from it.

The fresh water had cleared an area around the stream exit of coral and created a breach in the barrier coral.

"It might be a place to put in a resort," Jason said. "But there are so many of these..."

Whether it was easier or to add some spice was unclear, but the aliens had left hundreds of similar stratovolcanoes surrounded by ocean. That was the nature of many of the tropical islands on Earth as well so it might have had something to do with replicating the conditions of Earth.

"There's nowhere that's actually 'remote' because of coming in from space," Jason said. "Once the economy is fully up and going, there's probably going to be a lot of competition for resorts. Not to mention, anyone with any serious access to credits is going to be able to afford a house somewhere like this."

"That... is a thought," Tom said. "But I'd prefer something that's not made entirely of flexmet."

"That's worked out," Jason said, grinning.

There were no readily accessible clearings so the containers had to be lined up on the beach, the only clear land. The plan, already laid out, was to deploy them in two sets of six with a twenty-meter break in the middle, one end anchored on the stream.

Tom handled the drop perfectly, as always.

"Top of a container?" Tom asked.

"There's no sign of significant predators," Jason said, hefting the Safari 70. "But is it just me or does this *look* like the kind of place where a tyrannosaurus might come charging out of the brush at any moment?"

"First there's with the oohing and aaahing," Tom said, spinning the ship around to deploy the landing stairs on top of one of the containers.

"Then with the running and screaming, yeah," Jason said, tossing on his pack. "It'd be just like those robot bastards to leave a few velociraptors hidden on some remote island. See you when I see you. If I see you."

He hopped to the top of the container and looked around cautiously.

The containers were already opening out, deploying drones, Herman and the four Alfreds. He'd come up with different names for them but they all looked alike to him. The drones took off over and under the trees as well as out over the lagoon.

One job of the drones was to drop shark repellers. The repellers used a combination of electromagnetics, sonics and chemicals to keep sharks at least five hundred meters from each repeller. They came complete with thirty-meter "lines" of flexmet and weights. One was set right out from the proposed campsite and as sharks bolted away from it, additional ones were placed outward in the lagoon.

As one of his priorities, Jason intended to check out this lagoon by snorkeling but not fishing it primarily. The bigger lagoon to the southwest of the island, between the two old junior volcanoes, was the better place to fish, arguably, and that way he wouldn't fish out the water right in front of him.

"There are no visible sharks within one kilometer," Jewel reported. "Given only one shark-sized break in the reef, if we maintain a good guard on that you shouldn't be surprised."

"Understood," Jason said. "Landward?"

"No sizeable predatory species," Jewel reported.

"What about small?" Jason asked.

"There is a minor potential threat," Jewel said, putting a caret on his glasses for direction.

"Where?" Jason said, turning around. He'd chosen this island because there appeared to be no large predators. "Ah, jeez! Land crab!"

The giant land crab was attempting to dig through one of the scattered cases. A drone was attempting to shoo it away. The ugly-as-hell beast was about a half meter wide and snapped a giant claw at the drone, which dodged effectively.

"They're pests," Jason said. "Tasty, tasty pests."

Land crabs were simply crabs that had evolved to live on land. Hermit crabs and fiddler crabs were two types of land crabs that were common on many continents.

But tropical islands were frequently home to dozens of species. And they could be a real pest. They got into anything if you weren't careful.

The islands were home to migratory birds which nested in rookeries during egg-laying season as well as dozens of species of permanent seabirds. Bird nests meant baby birds falling from the nests, birds dead from old age, the occasional fallen egg. That was one of their major foods along with dead fish washed up on the shore.

However, certain species, and this was one, had evolved claws which were larger and stronger than Maine lobster. They used them to dig through shells of bivalves as well as crack and dig into coconuts.

All land crabs were considered tasty. Their diet was no different than crayfish which were also scavengers and which were considered delicacies. But the coconut land crabs were considered extraordinary.

They were relatively rare on Earth. It wasn't that they grew particularly slowly but they were predatory on their young, as were birds, so there was a huge die-off of juveniles. They also were only found on tropical islands with exactly zero large predators. So, their presence proved that there weren't any large predators of note. No monitor lizards or Komodo dragons for sure. No velociraptors.

But the real reason they were considered special was their flesh. They didn't primarily eat coconut but it was part of their diet and that infused them with the taste of coconut.

"Can a drone pick one of those up?"

"Yes," Jewel said.

"Have drones pick them up and put them in cases," Jason said. "Use flex to lash their claws so they don't attack each other. Have the Alfreds pick up the cases later. All the ones they can collect within two hundred meters of the camp and any that enter a one-hundred-meter interdiction area. Make sure those damned things don't make it into camp. They can probably gnaw their way through flexmet and I especially don't want any turning up in my hooch. Any large centipedes, that sort of thing?"

"Nothing large either predatory or scavenger except the land crabs," Jewel said. "So far. But there are *lots* of crabs. Thousands. Multiple different species."

Jason looked into the brush. There were more crabs scuttling around in there and he spotted some tree crabs as well.

"The crabs are going to be a problem," Jason said, sighing. "We're going to have to find some way to catch them or they're going to be getting into everything. The big ones the drones can catch one at a time. But the smaller ones are an issue as well..."

He stood in the shade of a palm tree and thought about it. There was always something.

"Put traps out," Jason said. "Flexmet. Bait. Look at traps for land crabs. There's got to be something in literature. Catch them and dump them in cases. They're mostly active at night. Put some flex around the posts of the house. It should make it harder for them to climb. Not sure what to do about the stairs. We'll look at that later. Crabs are the main issue?"

"Many insects, none appear to be stinging or biting. Other than that, it's just you, the birds and the crabs."

"This has got to be too good to be true," Jason said, looking around again.

The lagoon was spotted with patch coral, pink sand and patchy seagrass, the water crystal clear. Beyond the barrier reef was a deeper blue area and across the deep lagoon was a collection of tree-covered, rocky, jagged islands that didn't completely break the view of the deep ocean. He could see gigantic waves crashing against the eastern barrier reefs but the inner lagoon wasn't even whitecapped.

The trade winds blew strong onto the beach keeping back the insects in the interior. And even then, they might be bothersome but not biting.

"It's not unlike, say, the Hawaiian Islands prior to the arrival of the Polynesians with pigs," Jewel said. "And later the Europeans with rats and mosquitoes. The lack of centipedes is interesting. There is one species that, while not a threat, is nonetheless predatory and interesting."

"How interesting?" Jason asked, putting on his smartglasses.

The view was of what looked like a caterpillar. But it had what looked like multiple thin thorns where its mouth would be.

"The species is similar to one found on the Hawaiian Islands," Jewel said. "But it appears to be convergent evolution. It evolved the same way, for the same reason. It is probably predatory primarily on other insects. However, one species found so far is big enough to be predatory on small birds and amphibians."

"How big?" Jason asked.

"About six inches," Jewel answered.

"When I head in, spot one for me so I know what to avoid," Jason said. "If that and land crabs are the major threats..." He thought about it for a bit then shrugged. "Bring up my gun case."

He regarded the growing collection thoughtfully. The drones were never wrong and there were exactly no real threats according to Jewel. But he just couldn't let his shoulders unwind on the planet. Every other area he'd been in had been one giant human-eater after another.

On the other hand, the .458 was a heavy mother to carry around.

So was a .30-06, but it was lighter than the Safari.

He finally chose the Savage .30-06, loaded with 168 grain. That should do it. Just in case the drones were wrong for the first time.

"It's really not necessary," Jewel said.

"I'll believe it when I've seen it," Jason said, heading inland. "Start on the hooch while I'm gone."

There was a low growth of sea grape blocking the way and he cut it with a flexmachete. Beyond the sea grape was a mass of twisted roots of iron trees and lianas hanging from them. More machete work. The wind dropped off quickly as he penetrated the interior and the heat got oppressive. Crabs scuttled away from him in every direction. There were so many different species, much less individuals, he had a hard time sorting them out.

With no biting insects he rolled up his pants and sleeves to get some coolness. He'd worn tropical-weight clothes. The pants had been refitted but the shirt was still baggy. That was good in the heat.

He ducked under a liana, vaguely headed in the direction of the waterfall. There was a wetland area that wasn't apparent on the satellite map about thirty meters behind the beach. It was probably an overflow area for the stream during the rainy season. The area was thick with mangroves, sea birds nesting in them and squawking, while the ground was littered with land crabs.

He left them to the drones and just dodged around the scuttling, tasty, tasty crustaceans.

Jason cut to the left toward the stream, finally breaking through the brush. The stream bed looked clearer than the path he'd taken. It was sand bottom, so he should be able to keep his feet.

A few twists through the jungle and a careful step over some rocks brought him to a pond with a waterfall on the back side. The waterfall cascaded down a long section of basalt rock that had been worn down into a tube, then the water exited in a cataract that splashed into the pool.

It was the original concept behind a water slide.

"Sweet," Jason said, chuckling.

He waded across one side of the pond, trying not to slip on the underlying rocks, then reached the east shore and started hacking a trail up the hill to the north.

He finally reached a plateau about a hundred feet above the sea-level pond. The stream gathered there in another pool, then poured over the cliff through the channel that might have at one point been a lava tube. In the dry season it was about half full. He could see that the water under the final cataract was deep. Much deeper than the surrounding area. Easily deep enough to dive into. The final drop was only about ten feet.

Jason regarded the whole thing, wiped the sweat off his brow from the climb up the cliff, then shook his head.

"I bow to the reality of the current situation," he muttered, sitting down to take off his boots.

When he waded out into the lagoon, via the freshwater stream, the hooch was already complete.

Using the woodworking techniques developed at the last camp plus some ingenuity, the bots and drones had completed a traditional elevated-over-water, palm-frond-covered and walled hut with an addition of a covered waterside porch. They were busy at work with a short floating pier extending from the house.

Jason walked down through the crystalline waters of the lagoon until he reached the gap between the containers then up the short steps into his new tropical home. The main hut was distinctly cooler than being out in the sun but the walls still prevented most of the winds. That would be of particular use at night when they'd be a bother.

The floor was wood with woven palm-frond rugs. There were openings facing out to the water, east, and south down the beach as well as doors to the porch to the north and landward to the west.

The porch had benches around the sides, neatly sanded to be splinter free, as well as an alcove with benches and a small table, all native woods. Both it and the hut were about nine hundred square feet. The bots had even completed two sets of shelves, a gear rack, racks for fishing rods and spear guns, already in place, and a wide, woven elevated bed. His pillow and poncho liners were already in place. The case containing his spare clothes, dive gear and toiletries was at the foot of his bed. There was room for more furniture if he wanted.

The whole construction had taken barely five hours while he'd been exploring and playing in the waterfall. Earth construction-industry professionals were in for a rude shock.

It had been a long day. Hell, it had been a long two months and he deserved a break.

Jason lay down on his palm frond bed and went to sleep to the gentle lap of the waves and the trade winds in the palm fronds.

When he awoke it was late afternoon.

He rolled over, stretched and expected the usual complaints from his body. When he didn't get them, he grinned. He was still having a hard time realizing it would be years before that was an issue again.

"I suppose I should do some work while I'm here," Jason muttered. He was mildly peckish, though, and the water looked inviting. "Spearfishing or angling? God, all these decisions in this job are going to drive me nuts! Being your own boss is *hard*!"

He contemplated his rods and pulled down a medium weight. The old rod he'd had was commendably battered and repaired. Their alien benefactors had been kind enough to substitute one that was brand new. Same type, same manufacturer, slightly newer and probably a better model.

He missed his old rod. It had character. But this one would develop character in time.

He'd apparently left a jig attached to the old one. There was a brand-new jig already attached.

Based on every other experience he'd had fishing in this world, that would probably do.

He walked out on the porch and down to the pier wearing only a pair of swim trunks, then tossed the line in the water and started retrieving with short, jerking motions.

There was an immediate hit.

"There is *no* sport to fishing in this place," Jason muttered for the umpteenth time.

The fish was unfamiliar. It had large scales and was red in color. Sometimes that was a bad thing, red was a sign of toxins in nature, though sometimes it didn't matter. Probably best to get it checked out. You never knew what could be toxic in nature. Barracuda were occasionally toxic from eating toxic fish.

"I need this analyzed," Jason said, holding it up. "And if it's edible, cleaned and filleted. Kitchen?"

"On the land for now," Jewel said. "This building is a fire safety hazard. I've run a filtered water line from the stream for fresh water. We're having a little trouble with the mortar for the fire pit and barbeque. Other than that, it's going well."

"I will leave you to it," Jason said. "To the cobbler his last. I'm going to go check on the availability of crayfish."

He went back in his house and started breaking out mask and fins.

"Work, work, work . . ."


"Mr. Oldham." The voice came with a pair of shiny wingtips and neatly hemmed dark-blue cuffs that stopped right in front of where Cade was working. He had almost finished harvesting his crop of carrots, carefully knocking off all the precious soil and heaving the orange root vegetables into a flexmet basket.

"People mostly call me Cade," Cade said. "Unless they're from the government."

"At it happens," Wingtips said, "I'm from the government."

Cade sighed. He stood. The ache in his arms and back felt good. They felt like progress, like his body was on its way to becoming the body he remembered, the body he still thought he was in, when he could be sufficiently distracted to forget all the insanity of the last few months. "Is this where I'm going to find out that someone imposed a zoning ordinance while I wasn't looking, and I have thirty days to relocate my planting beds?"

The government man chuckled. Impressively, he had a little potbelly going, and a red tie with a blotchy mustard stain that hung askew over a white shirt. He had thick dark hair and sideburns and a grin that surely must have once sold used cars. "That's the spirit."

"I don't want to be rude," Cade said. "But I've got one more bed of carrots, and then I need to wash and sell these, get them to the restaurants that have already paid for them, and then think about replanting the beds."

"Independence," Wingtips said. "Entrepreneurialism, diligence."

Cade shook his head. "Last chance, unless you're arresting me."

"All right, all right, I'm not here to ruffle feathers," Wingtips said. "The opposite. I'm here to follow up on your application for an early colonization slot and grant."

"Must be a few thousand people down there by now," Cade said, not wanting to put his foot in his mouth. "I heard a few already died."

"They did, that's right." The government man cleared his throat. "My name is Hampton, by the way. Can we take a walk?"

By way of answer, Cade started to stroll in a leisurely fashion toward the nearest main street. "What killed them, the colonists who died?"

"Well, arguably, some of them brought it on themselves." Hampton ran his fingers through his hair. "We had lots of applications, you see."

"Millions," Cade said.

"Tens of millions. The AIs had to do the actual processing of the applications, but first we had to think about them and look through and figure out what to prioritize. So, we figured, this planet is untamed, we're going to need people who have the spirit of adventure. You know, people who are excited to be in a place with tigers and crocodiles and wolves and all kinds of new and dangerous species."

"Are you telling me I should have put 'big-game hunter' on my application?"

"Yeah, kind of," Hampton admitted. "Or 'hang glider' or 'climbed Mount Everest' or 'BASE jumped off London Bridge.'"

"I guess I'll have to reconcile myself to going in a later wave," Cade said. "Most exciting thing I ever did was get bitten by a cottonmouth."

"The thing is," Hampton said, "those adventurers have been pretty good about running around, shooting game. And reasonably good at getting themselves killed. And not very good about building up the infrastructure."

"You mean like wells?" Cade asked. "Septic tanks, roads, and so on?"

"Yeah," Hampton said. "There are colonization sets sitting idle on the ground because their owners walked off into the trees and got trampled by buffalo rather than do the work of clearing and planting fields. Everyone wants to be the Crocodile Dude. Or because the owners are having more fun hunting, or are prospecting for golf."

"Huh." Cade didn't know who the Crocodile Dude was. He suddenly felt conspicuous, with dirt under his nails.

"So, we've revised our thinking. Did a little looking into the old West, actually. The American frontier."

"Now you want to send gunfighters," Cade guessed.

"That's the thing. The American West wasn't settled by just gunfighters. It was settled by ranchers, farmers, and shopkeepers."

"I am a farmer," Cade conceded.

"You're a farmer," Hampton agreed. "You're such a farmer that you can't help yourself. You made the most you could out of this space station and farmed here in the playground."

Cade shrugged.

"You collected human waste for fertilizer."

"The Japanese did it," Cade said. "They didn't have big herds of cattle to help."

"Ingenuity. Problem-solving. Also, you might be obsessive," the government man continued. "You bought up all the planting beds you could, just to plant cabbage and carrots. We talked to your wife, she told us she tried to get you to take this time on the station as a vacation, but you just wouldn't do it."

"Couldn't do it," Cade said.

"Obsessive," Hampton said. "In a good way. And you're champing at the bit. You're on edge, waiting for the real deal to begin. You're so high-strung, you punched your son in the face the other day."

"I thought he was vandalizing my crops," Cade said. "In fact, he *was* vandalizing them."

"And you're a community man, aren't you?"

"What do you mean? I have kids."

"I mean, you're a deacon, aren't you? At Pegasus Mount Moriah?"

"Mount Moriah of Pegasus Church," Cade said. "Yeah. Pastor Mickey."

"You helped find and pay for the building."

Cade shrugged.

"It wasn't the crazy individualists who settled the West." The government man nodded slowly. "It was the people who knew how to build together and live together. In your application, you applied for the whole family to colonize as soon as possible. Single slot, or failing that, a colony ship. Is that still the desire?"

"You talked to my wife," Cade said carefully.

"She told us to ask you," Hampton said. "You figure out what you want to do, Mr. Oldham. There's room on the next big drop for all four of you, and grant money to cover it."

Hampton turned to go, and then stopped, as if struck by a final thought. "Mind you," he said, "you still might get eaten by the local wildlife."

# CHAPTER 27 ⟫⟫⟫⟫⟫⟫⟫

THERE WAS GOING TO BE *NO* PROBLEM WITH THE AVAILABILITY of crayfish.

Every ledge under the bits of patch reef was packed with waving antennae. The only thing more prolific than crayfish seemed to be the same species that had hit his hook. If it was edible, and Jason would bet it was, it was going to be a major food species. The unnamed fish was consistent in size, about fifteen inches in length, and there were multiple large schools of them.

But he didn't intend to catch them in *this* lagoon. Better to catch them elsewhere so these would be available exclusively for him.

He had attached a shark repeller to his ankle and, trusting the shark repellers, he paddled out to the barrier reef. Everywhere the reef was alive with life, blue and green parrot fish, the red sort of snapper, bigger fish that looked suspiciously like grouper. Some of those, even in the shallow waters of the lagoon, were massive. They darted away as a larger predator passed.

Dozens of species of smaller fish. Minor pop stars were about to have minor fish named after them.

There were also giant oysters scattered around. From what he'd heard, they were inedible but interesting. He'd never seen one with his own eyes. If you put something into their open shells, they snapped shut and wouldn't reopen for a long time. It was hoary legend that divers had died caught by the giant bivalves.

He snorkeled back to the hooch and climbed out, rubbing

the saltwater off his face. It felt good. The sun, the saltwater, the breeze; not for the first time he wondered if he was having a stroke and this was what he was imagining as he was dying.

If so, he was going to roll with it.

"Alrighty," Jason muttered. "To work."

"Finally," Jewel replied.

"Screw you," Jason said. "Let's start with building the boat."

He went in the hooch and switched his mask and fins for smartglasses then jumped back in the water. He waded over to one of the conexes as it opened and flexmet flowed onto the beach. The tide had been going out and there was a bit more room for the material. The flex formed a boat and the bots started loading ballast, weights, gear and offal.

Once the ballast and the metal weights were loaded, he set off across the lagoon. Then he stopped and drove back to the pier. He walked into the hooch, got his mask and fins and got back on the boat. Then he motored off again.

"Pick us up, move us over to the southwest lagoon, and put us down in about thirty to forty feet of water," Jason said. "Make it so."

With assistance from Herman he had enough lift.

The view of the crystal waters of the lagoon was spectacular. Large fish darted away from the shadow of the flying boat and the patchwork of coral was clearly evident. It was also much nicer flying than in Wilson Bay. The air was cooling on his face and rain was months away.

The boat drifted down to the larger lagoon and settled in gently.

He brought up a map of the lagoon from the overhead and laid a path through water that didn't appear to have patch reef.

"Lay down traps through here until you are either out of flexmet, out of weights or out of bait," Jason said. "Not on the reef—on the sand or sea grass. In the meantime, have the rest of the Alfreds and Herman move all the conexes that aren't related directly to the camp over to this side of the island. When they're done moving the conexes, keep one Alfred over by the hooch along with...ten drones. Make sure they stay charged...Make it so."

"And you are?" Jewel asked as the boat began to move.

"I'm going along for the ride in case I haven't thought of everything," Jason said. "When I'm sure it's working, we'll head in closer and then I'll swim in."

The traps formed off the back of the boat and disappeared

into the water without a splash; the material of the trap was literally the substance of the boat.

It took about an hour to lay down the test traps by which time the swift tropical sunrise had come and gone. Crysador and Geryon were just setting over the islands to the west as Luna Nova was rising behind crater island.

"The hurtling moons of Barsoom," Jason said quietly.

"And we are out of weights," Jewel said.

"How's the charge on this thing?" Jason asked. A good bit of the substance of the boat was gone as well.

"At least eight more hours," Jewel said. "Driving through the water is not as energy intensive as contragravity. And it's a lot easier here than Wilson Bay."

"Then let's head back to the hooch," Jason said. "We can check these in the morning."

When he got back, he waded ashore and checked out the outdoor kitchen.

The bots had constructed an outdoor grill made from slabs of basalt with a metal grill he'd picked up on the net. In addition, there was a prep area made from built-up basalt with an ironwood top and a sink. The only concession to flexmet was the faucet.

He marinated the fillets of the unnamed fish in some oil and Bellerophon herbs while the grill heated. He also put some wild onions, carrots and potatoes in aluminum foil and set them on the grill to cook.

When the grill was heated, he tossed the fillets on the fire, waited a couple of minutes, turned them, waited a minute more and pulled them off. He was hungry and they were probably cooked enough.

He carried those and the aluminum foil vegetables back to the porch, grabbed a Purple Lightning, high test, and sat down to dinner.

"Tastes like snapper," Jason said after a bite. "Sort of."

"Wrasse has a slightly different texture to it," Jewel said. "According to literature. Normally."

"It's good," Jason said. "Needs some Sheila's Thyme and a bit of salt and pepper but it's good. Buttery. Hmmm... Butter snapper? Just call it Sorta Snapper."

"Because it's sort of like snapper?" Jewel said with a sigh. "You and names. This island chain is unnamed."

"Really?" Jason said. "You can see it from space. That's how I found it."

"First to land," Jewel pointed out.

"Hmmm..." Jason thought of a name immediately but then rejected it. Then thought of it again.

"I hate doing this," Jason said. "It just isn't me. But... the Graham Islands."

"Finally!" Jewel said.

"We gonna need a bigger boat," Jason said as the first trap came aboard stuffed full of crayfish.

The plan was to load them into coffins. He'd brought very few cases because the calculation was that the crayfish could handle the weight packed into coffins in the short time before they were put in stasis.

The problem was that the boat would only hold twelve coffins.

Just the test traps he'd put down the night before would more than fill that. There were, again, dozens of edible species found in the lagoon besides the lobster. It was a smorgasbord.

The flex moved the crayfish into the first coffin and then closed it to keep them in stasis. Most of them were huge, the sort of giant crayfish you rarely saw anymore on earth.

"Put the traps back out?" Jewel asked.

"Need more bait," Jason said. "And not till this evening."

"While I know that's the normal method," Jewel said, "with the plethora of crayfish in this lagoon... you can probably day trap."

"No," Jason said. "We're here to test, not exploit. We'll need more gear, more bait and more flex to exploit. We'll stick with the plan."

"Hey, Gil," Jason said thoughtfully. "I need to noodle something with you money-wise."

Harvesting was going well. Too well. Jason had been checking the reefs and there were fewer and fewer crayfish in view. He was considering suspending the harvest for now. There was an entire other lagoon on the other side of the channel. The problem wasn't getting the boats there, the problem was getting the containers and boats back: The center channel was much rougher than the lagoons.

In the meantime, he was letting the bots handle it while doing some business. Work, work, work...

"Go," Gil said. He was apparently sitting in a real office now. Or it was a fake background.

Jason was catching up on lunch with some boiled tree crab. It tasted pretty much like regular crab.

"I want to get more shares in the fuel and gas mine," Jason said. "Twelve Bravo."

"Shares or units?" Gil asked.

"Sorry, units," Jason said. "What I'm considering is offering, say, a credit for a unit trade. Most people have their trade requests turned off and the ones that left it up to their AIs have mostly traded. But if I'm offering some cash as well, people's AIs might let the request through. And the company is making money. I know I've got some. I also know that I've left that sort of thing up to you. Thoughts?"

"Depends on what you're trading away," Gil said. "But the truth is, fuel and gas mines will probably be high profit which means high lease. So, most trades will probably be worthwhile. Compared to, say, commercial space for example. But I'd suggest waiting for the quarter."

"Ooookay?" Jason said.

"I talked to Tim and he's willing to do a dividend payment on the quarter," Gil said. "You gave me permission to have that conversation."

"Right," Jason said.

"I'd planned on moving most of it to James to invest," Gil said. "Including in a company that wants to get one of the fuel mines up and going. If you wait till the dividend payment, it will be a reasonable investment. One I'd recommend. Your money is your money, Jason. But that's my advice."

"And I will take that advice," Jason said.

"Where are you *this* time?" Gil asked. "Is that a palm-frond wall?"

"Uh, yeah," Jason said. "I'm exploring some commercial fishing opportunities in the south Pallas."

"Commercial fishing opportunities, huh," Gil said. "Looks like you're just hanging out in the tropics to me."

"I'm doing some . . . test traps . . ." Jason said. "Work with me, here. It's going to make money. The reefs are crawling with gigantic crayfish! And there's . . . fish and stuff. We'll make big bank off this!"

"I'm sure you will," Gil said drily. "As I sit here and pore over spreadsheets."

"That's what pays your bills?" Jason said, shrugging. "Figuring out new profit-making ventures pays mine?"

"How did that get built?" Gil asked.

"Bots, drones and flexmet," Jason said. "Don't, and I cannot stress this enough, invest in home construction companies. Not unless I start them. Which I might."

"I'll pass that on to James," Gil said thoughtfully. "There are people looking at doing developments on the surface. If you can find a place safe enough most people would want to live there."

"Developments, sure," Jason said. "But home construction: There's going to be a lot of people who just know how to work with their hands that are going to be in hard shape. If there is something you can't do with flexmet and bots...Chemistry. That's about it. The bots and my partner in wood built a house in the last place I was set up in less than two days. And that was figuring out stuff. This was built in five hours. All robotic workers."

"I'll pass that on to James as well," Gil said. "Anything else?"

"See you on the flip side," Jason said.

He thought about what else he had to cover and read through the to-do list on his phone.

"No...not yet..." He sighed after a moment. One item had to be covered. "Jewel, see if Tim's available..."

Maybe he'd be busy. He was probably busy.

"Hey, partner," Tim replied. "Long time no contact. Partner."

"No crocodiles!" Jason said, waving his arms. "No bears! No, and I mean absolutely no, wolves! No large predators at all! No mosquitoes! Just lots of reefs and therefore lots of crayfish! We'll totally make bank. Also, I'm shipping land crab. Coconut land crab is a delicacy and we need to treat it that way. Hold back most of it and if we sell it, sell it for big credit: They're relatively rare."

"I looked them up," Tim said. "Or rather had someone do it. They're extremely rare and reputed to be one of the top delicacies on Earth. They'll be treated that way. On the other hand, most of the rest of the land crab you're loading is small stuff."

"There's ethnic groups that will go for it," Jason said, picking crab out of the shell. "Crab is crab, except for coconut crab. Everybody likes crab.

"Next item on the agenda. We need to do the twenty-thousand-foot drops repeatedly. And I'd like to find volunteers who will try going down that way in stasis. Same deal. I front the money for the drop, you repay me less loiter cost to analyze the drop."

"What is this about?" Tim asked. "'Cause while it might save Brandywine some money, I'm not seeing the direct value."

"I said it wasn't directly related to Brandywine," Jason said. "Though it may help in many ways. It's about the big ships. Specifically, my big ship, Spaceship Four. Cause I'm the majority unit holder. If I can find a way to drop colony sets this way..."

"Ah, Jesus, Jason," Tim said, shaking his head. "You really think you can find a bunch of people..."

"One thousand six hundred and sixty-six," Jason said.

"That many people to drop in stasis from twenty thousand feet?" Tim said.

"Or wait ten years to get on the ground?" Jason asked. "We've talked about the different conditions in different areas on the ground especially in the temperate regions, right?"

"Yes," Tim said.

"Instead of sending one twelve or six pack at a time, we use a hundred pack to drop multiples along the north-south axis," Jason said. "The officer or team will have to go down in stasis, but if the ship doesn't even have to reach the ground for multiple drops... It should save Brandywine money. We've just got to test it enough that it's proven effective."

"Let me think about this for a second," Tim said, leaning back in his chair. "What about picking up the cargo? We don't get paid till it's on the station and shipped to a customer."

"A twelve pack, twenty-five, hell a hundred pack, can go from point to point," Jason said. "The bots can lift conexes into the air. At least twelve at a time. The ship pulls up, loads the cargo, the bot drops back to work on the ground and the ship leaves. It's a more efficient way to load, anyway. Logistics, remember?"

"Lemme pull John in on this," Tim said.

"Wassup?"

John Sprecher was the only logistics guy Jason had ever met who was more inventive and proactive than he was. He'd been first choice for a log guy for Brandywine.

On the other hand, he was a serious city guy who thought

parks were too natural. So, he wouldn't try to bump Jason out of a job and he could, quite frankly, keep the logistics office.

His only annoying feature was he was a Gen X who had stuck on the whole "Waaaaassssup" thing. Which had been annoying enough at the time.

"Jason has some explaining to do," Tim said.

When Jason was done, John nodded thoughtfully. "That's the worst idea I've ever heard," John said. "I hate it."

"Thank you," Tim declared.

"It's brilliant," John continued.

"Wait...what?" Tim said.

"We're putting people down at an *insane* rate," John said. "Or at least you *want* to put people down on the planet at an insane rate. Shipping rates are going through the roof as more and more people find money to go to the surface. It's only going to get worse as the production facilities come online and we need interspace traffic. So, finding a way to get stuff up and down is the issue. We don't get paid till we ship to a customer. While there are deadheads, they and we want full cargoes. And we need to ship both directions. But the drop requires a tractor onboard, right?"

"Right," Jason said.

"That's an issue," John said. "Apropos of nothing, it would help if we concentrated at least on, say, one *continent* instead of the entire *world*. As an example, dropping *one* twelve pack on a tropical island in the *middle* of an ocean in the middle of *nowhere* with *no* other ships within ten thousand kilometers!"

"Sounds like a problem for the log and shipping guy to me," Jason said, grinning.

"You said it was a terrible idea," Tim said, puzzled.

"I wish I'd thought of it. I hate when somebody comes up with a better idea than me."

"Almost finished," Tim said. "John, find a project officer to figure this out. Look for someone with airborne experience. Preferably a former battalion or brigade S-3 air."

"Got it," John said. "We going to be doing shipping from your location?"

"The Graham Islands?" Jason asked, then grimaced. "There's fish, there's lobster, there's land crab, there's coconuts. But... there's all that at other islands. I just wanted to check the ground conditions. Try to find tropical islands in the same zone but away from here. I'm thinking of either choosing this as my homestead or buying it outright. I'd rather keep it less ... harvested."

"Where else?" Tim asked.

"There's literally thousands of little islets, atolls and islands," Jason said. "Throw a dart. Just ... not here, exactly."

"We'll leave you your one tropical paradise," Tim replied. "We need to find an area of concentration, though. John, going to need more transport."

"I shall endeavor to provide," John said, cutting the connection.

"We're going to be upping the price on shrimp and lobster," Tim said. "I agree with using Storm for marketing and recruitment. We're also doing some advertising."

"Despite the fact that we run out faster than we can get it from the planet?" Jason asked. "That doesn't seem like a wise business strategy."

"We don't want people always seeing 'out of stock,'" Tim admitted. "But Fox is trying to stand back up and their rates are cheap for now."

"You got money in that?" Jason asked.

"I do," Tim said. "Problem?"

"Nope," Jason said, shrugging. "But if we're going to be advertising when we're still running out of stock, we need better shipping. Which means we need more efficient insert and extract."

"You've made the point," Tim said. "I'm on board."

"Great," Jason said. "Then I'm going to go catch crabs."

"Thought you were there to catch lobster?" Tim said.

"Crustaceans, then," Jason said. "Out here."


"What was the name of that cute lady I passed in the market on the way to the first drop?" Jason asked, leaning back and watching the robots work.

"Judy," Jewel said. "And before you ask, her status updated to 'in a relationship.'"

"Damn," Jason said, looking into the blue distance thoughtfully. Then he sighed. "What is the status of the world's oldest profession?"

"Flourishing," Jewel said. "As with drugs, there were no laws enacted against it in the proposed state and federal registers. Despite some protestations from social conservatives, President Dewalt has issued no executive orders against it, saying it should be up to the various states when their legislatures convene. So, there's no rule against it and it's a way for ladies, and some gentlemen, to make credit. The problem for them is . . . it's flourishing."

"With every gal who's ever taken coin for favorable attention being twenty again . . ." Jason said.

"The market is rather saturated," Jewel said. "There are laws against certain ages, mind you. And they are being strictly enforced."

"Good," Jason said. "I'm not looking for a twelve-year-old virgin. Any reviews? That can be trusted?"

"Let me repeat the word 'flourishing,'" Jewel said. "With emphasis. You want me to sort through units? You only started with *ten million* of those. That's easy compared to sorting through the ladies of negotiable affection in Pegasus. Also, I'm not really familiar with your tastes in that area."

Jason thought about that for a moment and blew out his lips.

"I'm not human, Jason," Jewel said with a humorous tone. "I won't get jealous or be offended in any way. But let's make it easy. Hold up your phone as a pad."

He held it up and an avatar of a female appeared.

"We'll start with looks," Jewel said. "There are buttons to the side to choose various looks. Think of it as making a girl in a computer. Then I'll look to see if there are any that match it. After that we'll work on personalities and I'll check for that. Also, are you looking for a girlfriend or simply someone to pay? The girlfriend experience. As a famous actor once said, you don't pay ladies of the evening for their services, you pay them to *leave.*"

"Leaving has never been an issue," Jason said.

"I need a definite answer on that one," Jewel said. "Limit the options a bit, let me sort and you'll end up with someone who won't leave and you won't *want* to leave."

"That's . . . unlikely," Jason said. "Certainly the first."

"You're not a . . . whatever you chose to call yourself on Earth anymore," Jewel pointed out. "You're one of the richest people on the station. That's something I'd suggest you not mention. But you are. You're also not bad looking and have access to the ground as well as fresh foods. Do you want the power behind the throne? Do you want someone to just spend a little time with and have some fun then she goes? What do you want here?"

"Lemme play around with the app," Jason said, poking buttons. "Then I'll decide."

"Please be honest," Jewel said. "Don't worry about what I might think."

"Okay, I'm having a hard time with the face," Jason admitted.

"Think of me as a police sketch artist," Jewel said. "What's the general look?"

She threw up some generic model faces.

"That one," Jason said, choosing the heart-shaped face. "With that one's eyes."

"I won't be able to guarantee the face," Jewel said.

"There are no guarantees in life," Jason said, frowning. "This feels weird. And wrong. Women are people, not something to be built in a computer."

"You're looking for the right person," Jewel said. "If it's 'in life' I'll lean more on the needs for personality and brains. If it's for a playmate, I'll lean on looks. I'm surprised by the look. It's not much like Monica."

"Monica was...Monica," Jason said. "I don't have a preferred look. I have two or three. This is one of them."

"The pixie," Jewel said. "Tinkerbell?"

"I also like Amazons," Jason said. "Storm's one of my looks. I sort of go for extremes, there."

"Personality and interests?"

"Still stuck there," Jason said. "And I *have* been thinking. Comes down to am I looking for a playmate or looking for love? I never got into the internet dating thing. After my time. It was too weird for me. I didn't know the rules and was too old to bother learning them. And this is sort of weird as well."

"When it comes to who they are, let me choose," Jewel said. "If it's a playmate, I may not even go for the look unless I can find someone who has the right personality. If it's a girlfriend, I'll lean on both. But while there is an enormous dataset of ladies of negotiable affection, there's a larger one of ladies who are looking for that special someone. And if it's a girlfriend, I'll be choosing based on your needs, wants and desires, which are complex."

"Example?" Jason asked.

"You're old-fashioned," Jewel said. "A late boomer raised very conservative. You were bothered that you never had a family. With a chance to start over again, that is a major concern."

"I've never said that," Jason said.

"You forget I have access to your entire electronic correspondence," Jewel said. "You reiterated that several times to people who were close. And you haven't changed. You look at kids. Not in a weird way but with an obvious longing to your AI. Am I wrong?"

"No," Jason said. "But I'm not sure about having my mind read."

"You're smart," Jewel said. "Nerdy. You need someone who is smart and a touch nerdy as well. That, by the way, goes for girlfriend *or* playmate."

"True," Jason said.

"And in a girlfriend, you also need a playmate," Jewel said. "Someone to enjoy this and the other things you do. Someone interested in getting to the ground. A complete city girl or one who's afraid of her own shadow would never be your perfect mate and not even a good short-term companion. Somebody who thinks of the tropics as a resort instead of . . . well, an island filled with crabs and waters teeming with sharks . . ."

"True," Jason admitted. "Okay, you've got me read like a book. I assume there's more."

"You need someone to gently keep you on track," Jewel said. "Someone besides me to bounce ideas off. Someone you can trust who won't betray you. You're beginning to do some fairly large business. You could use someone who is charm trained to help in social settings: a 'like' rather than a need. Last, you would like someone in one of your tastes in looks. There are others. Dozens. I've been calculating them while observing you right up from the first moment we both were pulled out of stasis. And at the moment you do sort of need a tension reliever.

"That last argues paid playmate but there's intermediates. Ladies who aren't the type to take money—but will probably be very receptive to a guy who invites them to a tropical getaway—and even have your general interests and tastes. Outdoorsy but also nerdy. Sci-fi readers. A lady who wants to have a family but also wants to get the hell off the station and see the planet. And if she's going to raise kids, let it be under blue skies, not metal ceilings.

"Somebody who is tomboyish enough to go hunting for mammoth and lady enough to clean up and be on your arm at receptions and dinner meetings where you're going to feel like a fish out of water and want someone to keep you from making faux pas. Like Monica in that way and that way only. Unlike Monica because she won't make digs at you about it. Someone who can get muddy in the morning and in the evening can be comfortable at a formal dinner for the President."

"That's ... asking a lot," Jason said.

"Five hundred million people on this station," Jewel said. "Slightly more than half are female. Not really. Not if they've expressed to their AI that they are looking for a boyfriend with possibility of husband."

"You already have someone in mind," Jason said.

"Multiple," Jewel said. "Look at the screen."

# CHAPTER 28 >>>>>>>>>

ELISA TOSSED HER PHONE TO THE SIDE IN FRUSTRATION. SO FAR, the best job she could find was working for her parents selling off the family's household goods. Modeling? First of all, there were very few talent agencies starting up. And supermodels from the freaking sixties now looked like they were twenty again!

"Before you toss me away like that, you have someone who'd like to talk," Adam said.

"Who?" Elisa asked. Surrounded by spaceships and she was about to offer...that just to get a ride.

"A gentleman looking for a girlfriend," Adam answered. "At the moment he just wants to talk."

"That is kind of vague," Elisa said.

"You gave me some fairly vague suggestions," Adam pointed out. "He fits virtually none of them except he is outdoorsy and is doing okay financially in this environment."

"So, not a great catch," Elisa said.

"He fits virtually none of them because you were lying to me about most of them," Adam said. "He's a better actual fit for you than you'd like to admit."

"Oh, really!" Elisa said.

"Oh. Really. Just talk to the guy. You busy or something?"

"Snark will get you..." Elisa said, frowning.

"He's currently on the planet," Adam said. "It's his fifth trip."

"WHAT?" Elisa snapped, picking up the phone. "Put him on! Put him on!"

"His name is Jason Graham," Adam said. "Connecting."

Jason was...okay looking. Not super handsome. But he had a nice smile.

"Hi," Jason said. "Uh, wait a second, okay, I need to get in some shade to see better."

Elisa got a vague impression of what looked like palm trees in the background. The top of the shade was what looked like palm fronds.

"Where are you?" Elisa asked.

"Uh..." Jason stopped and grinned sheepishly. "The Graham Islands?"

"And your name is..." Elisa said, raising an eyebrow.

"I know, I know," Jason said, shrugging. "But I hadn't named anything else after myself and I like 'em. They're in the Pallas Ocean. Which is awesome, by the way. Wait a sec..."

The view swung around to show the ocean and what was obviously a barrier reef about a hundred yards from shore. Inland was standard tropical paradise, complete with what looked like a flash of a waterfall.

Elisa tried not to either scream or cry.

Then the phone centered in on one of the ugliest things she'd ever seen. She knew what it was, a land crab. But it was still startling.

"Hang on," Jason said, swinging the phone back around to face him. "Jewel, God damnit, I thought those things were supposed to be kept back a hundred meters?"

"Sorry," a female voice answered. "Hi, Elisa, I'm Jewel, Jason's AI. Jason, it just slipped through the perimeter. The drones are all busy picking up other ones..."

"Sorry, sorry," Jason said. "I gotta get this thing..."

A black tentacle of flexmet flashed out then he lifted the scrabbling crab into the air and dropped it into a case.

"Sorry, sorry," Jason said, bringing the phone back around. "Hi, I'm Jason Graham. Elisa Randall, right?"

"Yes," Elisa said. "How many of those are there?"

"Hey, it's better than the first place I dropped," Jason said. "I was just thinking what a beautiful planet we'd been gifted when a seventy-foot crocodile showed up."

"That's awesome," Elisa said. "What'd you do?"

"I shot it?" Jason said. "What else was I gonna do?"

"So, are you a colonist?" Elisa asked.

"Uh, no," Jason said. "I'm a partner in a foods company. Right now, it's all natural, totally organic, picked dew-fresh from the wilds of Bellerophon," Jason said in an announcer voice. "Because that's what's *available*! I was there for a shrimp run. We ended up shipping a *bunch* of croc meat."

"If it tastes anything like alligator, I'm in," Elisa asked.

"You like gator?" Jason asked.

"Right now, I'd eat *anything* to avoid print food," Elisa said, then grimaced. "That came out sounding wrong."

Her mother always told her to think before she spoke.

"I heff no idea about which you speak," Jason said in a bad German accent. "Anglish not my first language is."

"Okay, Yoda," Elisa said, smiling.

"How about some fresh-out-of-the-sea crayfish?" Jason asked. "But you've got to eat it down here."

Elisa stuck her tongue in her cheek and considered her words...

"I'm not one of those girls who..." Elisa said carefully.

"No strings," Jason interjected hastily. "We've got a ship headed down in two days. No passengers on that trip. Free ride up and back. Just... would you like to spend a few days in a tropical paradise? Admittedly, you have to take a shower in a waterfall. Sorry. No indoor plumbing."

"I can shower in a waterfall," Elisa said sagely. "What I was about to say is that I'm not one of those girls who turns tricks by the hour..."

"I am aware," Jason said.

"But for fresh lobster and a ride off this tin can?" Elisa said. "I'm not guaranteeing that I'm going to tear your clothes off when I arrive... but it's a possibility."


"Cade," Dummy said.

Cade woke up. His muscle memory hadn't transplanted naturally to this new, or refreshed, body, but his sleeping powers had. He knew instantly that it was the middle of the night, that he'd fallen asleep watching *Hondo* and had slept several hours. He listened for a few seconds and knew he could hear Mabel and Abby breathing.

But not Sam.

"Is it about Sam?" he asked his AI.

If forced to render judgment, he would have admitted that the AI had turned out to be useful. But since no one was forcing him to commit, he continued to contain his AI behind a sexless, nameless mannequin face.

"Sam's been arrested," Dummy said. "Bail has been set at five credits, and I have been instructed to notify you."

Cade climbed into his overalls and shoes. When the door irised open, Mabel whispered, "Isn't it too early to be watering your cabbage?"

"It's Sam," he told her. "I'll go get him. Go back to sleep."

Dummy led him straight to the police station. With different images on its flexscreens, it might have been used as a restaurant or even a church. But the outside displayed severe lines and the titles PEGASUS POLICE and PRECINCT C-153.

Inside, Cade fumbled his way through a conversation with a front desk sergeant (Dummy tried to help, until Cade threatened to shut it off) and was eventually directed to someone whose title was "penal clerk." A young woman sat on a flexmet bench in the corner of the office, staring at the wall. She was a dark-haired, dark-eyed beauty in jeans and an off-center, baggy sweater, but Cade ignored her. Keeping his voice low as if warding off embarrassment, he paid Sam's bail to the meatball-faced clerk, and got in return information about Sam's court date.

Then an officer led Cade back into the cells.

Sam and another young man sat, rumpled and reeking of alcohol, in a shared cell. The other young man was unconscious; Sam saw Cade and stood as he entered.

The officer set about unlocking the cell.

"I know you're disappointed, Dad."

"You hit a fellow," Cade said. "Since I punched you, not a week ago, I guess I can't say the apple has fallen too far from the tree."

Sam laughed, then rubbed his jaw as if it hurt from the movement.

"I think you'd have punched him yourself, Dad."

"Oh yeah? Was he aggressing someone's carrots?"

"He was aggressing a girl," Sam said. "A very nice young lady whose name I unfortunately never got."

"Maybe Thog got her AI's number," Cade suggested. "Let's go pick up your personal effects and see. Or Abby can help you look in the social channels. Or Pastor Mickey might know her. Or you and I can go door to door like Mormons. 'We're here to see your young women!'"

"That's an awful lot of help you're offering for a girl you haven't even seen."

"I don't care about helping her," Cade said. "I'm offering help to my son, whom I punched in the face, like a jackass."

The penal clerk already had Sam's AI in a plastic envelope waiting on the counter. Sam picked Thog up, turned around, and then saw the girl sitting on the bench.

She stood.

"I came to say sorry," she said. "And thank you."

Sam rubbed his jaw.

"I'd do it again in a heartbeat."

"Also," she added, "my name is Ana."


"Tom Ferrell," the pilot said, waving to a seat. "Take a load off."

"I am not going to scream," Elisa said as she sat down at the control console.

"Afraid of flying?" Tom asked quizzically. "There's virtually no motion and it's *very* safe."

"I'm not going to scream because it looks like a scene out of one of my favorite video games," Elisa said. "And I'm not going to scream because I'm actually going into *space*. And I'm not going to scream because I'm headed to a tropical paradise and I just hope the guy is as nice as he seems."

"Oh," Tom said, smiling. "Jason is a very cool guy. I'm sure he'll be ... fine?"

"I'm not one of those girls," Elisa said primly. "He just seems like a nice guy, I've been promised lobster and it's a *free ride to the planet*!"

"Did you hear about what greeted him on arrival?" Tom asked.

"The croc?" Elisa said, nodding. "But apparently there's no such issues on the islands. And, frankly, I'd have shot it, too."

"You shoot?" Tom asked.

"My eighteenth birthday present was a safari in Africa," Elisa said.

"How ... what was your favorite song in high school?" Tom asked.

"That doesn't work as well past a certain point because of

streaming," Elisa said, smiling. "'Holding Out for a Hero' by Bonnie Tyler."

"Oh, okay," Tom said.

"Followed by 'Oops!...I Did It Again,' by Britney Spears and I still love 'Baby Shark,'" Elisa said. "I'm actually this age."

"Ooooh," Tom said, nodding.

"You?" Elisa asked.

"Frank Sinatra," Tom said. "'Cause that was what was on something called a 'radio.'"

"Radio..." Elisa said thoughtfully. "Ray-dee-oh...What is... this thing called radio? Is that like FM?"

"AM back in *my* high school days," Tom said, chuckling. "FM was *high-tech*. Still military only."

"Seriously?" Elisa asked.

"FM didn't come in until the 1960s," Tom said. "It was the new high-fidelity sound. Which was full of scratches and snow. But clearer than AM."

"Squeee!" Elisa squealed as they cleared the exit corridor. "We're in space! Are we really in space? These screens are very realistic but you could just be working with some powerful rich man to kidnap me and this is all an illusion. Prove we're in space! No, don't! 'Cause that would require evacuating the compartment. I don't want to die!"

"You've got thirty seconds to put on the space suit," Tom said, gesturing over his shoulder. "That's something they'll probably mandate be explained at some point by a required flight attendant."

"Where are they?" Elisa asked. "Just in case."

"The box marked 'Space Suits,'" Tom said. "Know that MCU movie where the space suits are just something you slap on?"

"Yes."

"It's like that,' Tom said. "The real safety feature is that in the event of that bad of an emergency, which is nearly impossible to occur, the seat turns into a stasis box and you're ejected to be picked up later. I'm reliably informed that it can survive reentry and even hitting the ground on Bellerophon."

"That's...a good safety system," Elisa said. "When do we see the planet? I'll assume that although there is no feeling of motion that has to do with the stabilizers and not because this is all a trick. Though my parents are expecting a call when I land. Just saying."

"You don't seriously think you're being kidnapped, do you?" Tom said.

"No," Elisa said. "I'm just joking around. But it feels so surreal. I've wanted to go into space since I was a kid. A kid, kid. Eight, nine. Is that Bellerophon through the port?"

"It is," Tom said. "Which will get bigger and bigger as we approach."

Elisa thought about pointing out that it was an optical illusion, but she assumed he knew that. Count to ten, Elisa.

"You said Jason's a nice guy?" Elisa said. "Do you know him very well?"

"I'm sort of his go-to ride," Tom said. "I dropped another load for this one 'cause he asked. He said there was a passenger. I assumed it was one of his people. Not... lady friend."

"People?" Elisa asked. "He's been sort of... He hasn't really talked about people..."

"His company has been dropping harvest teams all over the planet," Tom said. "I've dropped... ten I think? Plus picking up loads. Some of them actually dropped. They've been experimenting with dropping at altitude and letting the containers and tractors handle getting the gear into place then doing rapid loads high. Not as high as the drops but two or three thousand feet."

"Seriously?" Elisa said, her eyes wide.

"He's former airborne," Tom said. "He's like 'You can drop anything. Once.'"

"I take it we'll be actually, you know, landing?" Elisa asked. "And I won't just get tossed out the airlock?"

"Day's young," Tom said with a shrug then laughed. "You will most definitely be fully landed on the ground."

"Wheeee!" Elisa said as they entered the port. "Bellerophon, sweet Bellerophon, I am coming to you!" She stretched out her hands to the planet in longing. "It's been calling to me, begging me to visit!"

"Has it?" Tom said.

"It has," Elisa said, sighing as they cleared the port. She was watching the traffic as well. "The reason I'm so..." She waved her hands in the air.

"Giddy as a schoolgirl?" Tom said.

"I'm a total sci-fi fan," Elisa said. "Like, books and movies mostly. Though I used to go to anime cons doing cosplay."

"Before the Transfer?" Tom asked.

"I quit when I was sixteen," Elisa said. "Just got out of the anime phase. But I was considering majoring in astronomy when I was in college. I wanted to find a habitable planet. Not terraformed. I realized it wouldn't, probably, be very habitable. But something with some vaguely breathable atmosphere. Decent gravity. A new world...And now this!"

"So, pretty excited," Tom said.

"Giddy," Elisa said, waving her hands around. "The stars. Pegasus," she added, gesturing toward the star to their right. "And now I'm going to a new planet. One built for humanity. I love hunting, fishing, diving...There's *too* many things that I like. So as a sci-fi fan, I think the station is cool. Spaceships running around are cool. But now I'm going to the *planet*."

She paused again and frowned.

"So, Jason is cool?" she asked. "He seems cool. We talked for hours. But..."

"First dates are tough," Tom said. "Yes, he's cool. Crazy. But he's a nice guy."

"Crazy is okay," she said.

"Really?" Tom said. "Have you *seen* the video of him and the crocodile...?"

"Just be cool," Jewel whispered. "And don't keep explaining everything. And don't say 'This is awkward' or 'Uhm...' or 'Okay...?'"

"I can do without dating advice from a piece of silicon," Jason said, trying to look confident.

Tom had already switched out conexes and now swung around to hover over the lagoon, bringing the landing stairs down to just touch the shore.

Elisa didn't bother with most of the stairs. She leapt off the platform at the top, hit one stair and hit the ground. Then she turned around, briefly, to wave at the ship and sprinted into a hug that made Jason go: "Oof."

"I don't care if you're not a hugger!" Elisa screamed. "Oh, My God! Oh, My God! Oh, My God! I am out of that can and this is *fantastic*! AAAAAAH!"

She spun around in circles waving fists in the air then stopped.

"Hello, good sir," she said primly, holding out her hand

gracefully and speaking in a Carolina Coastal accent. "Elisa Randall. What a pleasure to make your acquaintance. Mister Graham, I presume?"

"Hello, Miss Randall," Jason said, shaking her hand. "As a matter of fact, I am a hugger."

"Wheee!" Elisa said, hugging him again.

She was quite squeezable. And even shorter than she'd seemed on the video. Five foot two, blonde, blue eyes—she was perfect. A bit too perfect.

He and Jewel had had a bit of a discussion on that subject. She was *actually* eighteen.

"Don't take this the wrong way," Elisa said, stepping back and pulling off her top to reveal the top of an American flag bikini. She toed off her shoes, pulled off her shorts then thumbed at the water. "Last one in's a rotten egg!"

With that she sprinted into the water then into a dive.

"Well, alrighty then," Jason said, pulling off his shirt. He'd prepared a lunch, too much lunch honestly, but it was in a stasis container. "Swim first answers *that* question..."

"Charleston girl," Elisa said, holding her hands above her head in a V. "Sunny beaches. At least in summer."

"Guess being in Carolina is okay by you," Jason said, sculling backward in the water.

"Carolina girl," Elisa said, breast stroking over to him with a look Jason could only describe as "calculation" on her face. Then her eyes flew wide. "Oh, snap!"

"What?" Jason said.

"I promised my parents I'd call them when I landed and say I was okay," Elisa said. "ADAM!"

"Your mother has been informed that you dashed into the water immediately," Adam said. "Want me to put her through?"

"Yes! Gimme a second..."

"Woo," Elisa said. "I'm a legal adult with my own compartment, courtesy of Our Robotic Overlords. But my parents still worry and I still care."

"That's a good thing," Jason said. "Both."

"I apologized," Elisa said.

"I'm sort of surprised that..." Jason said, shrugging. "You

seem like you're conservative. I'm surprised I didn't have to talk to your father."

"My dad's not quite *that* old-fashioned," Elisa said. "He's Gen X. Younger than you. Which is...fine. But I was going somewhere before I realized I'd forgotten to call... Oh, yeah...

"I have a strict rule about guys and...you know. Hooking up, however you want to put it."

"Which is?" Jason asked.

"Not unless I'm pretty sure he's marriage material," Elisa said. "Which hasn't been many guys. Two, to be honest. 'Cause the first one was because I thought we *were* getting married."

"I'm not going to do the count at this point in our relationship," Jason said.

"But *this* makes me reconsider Rule One," Elisa said, grinning. "Because you do seem cool. I wasn't sure. Guys can be big fakes even over video."

"I'm terrible at faking anything," Jason said. "Like I said when we talked, one of my big problems is honesty."

"We'll see," Elisa said. "Does this bathing suit make me look fat?" she asked, pushing up her breasts.

"Now you're just teasing," Jason said. "Never tease an old dog. He might have one bite left."

"So, I have gotten salt water on me, gotten sun on my skin and called my parents," she said, sculling away backward. "Feeling like a total gold digger: *Is* there lobster?"

"Sorry," Jason said, making a long face. "We had to ship it all out. Business, you know..."

"You'd better be kidding," Elisa said. "Please tell me you're kidding. I'll go get some by hand. I like bugging..."

"There's only coconut land crab," Jason said. "And grilled Sorta Snapper."

"Sorta grilled?" Elisa asked.

"Sorta Snapper," Jason said. "New species. That's its name 'cause it tastes sort of like snapper. It's actually a wrasse."

# CHAPTER 29 >>>>>>>>>>

"THIS IS *AMAZING*," ELISA SAID, POPPING ANOTHER BITE OF COCO-nut land crab in her mouth. "It's not just that it's not print food. This is unquestionably amazing."

Land crabs ate coconut, along with everything else, but could not handle coconut oil. So, they had evolved a small gland on their back that concentrated it. Like lobster infused with coconut, dipped in the coconut oil from the gland, it was considered one of the finest, and rarest, foods on Old Earth. Or Bellerophon.

"I'm trying not to make yummy noises. Very impolite."

"And thank you," Jason said. "Glad you're enjoying it. But that is one of my pet peeves."

"Mine too," Elisa said, grinning. "I am stuffed. That was so good. You're a good cook."

"Hope that isn't something you're thrown off by," Jason said.

"Not at all," Elisa said. "I'm a good cook, too. I'll cook tomorrow."

"I'll let you," Jason said, smiling brightly.

"There's something there," Elisa said. "You don't believe I'm a good cook?"

"No, not at all," Jason said, waving his hands. "I'm sure you're great."

"So which woman wasn't a good cook?" Elisa asked.

"Do we really need to talk about that?" Jason asked. Elisa crossed her arms and cocked her head, not saying anything. "*Both* ex-wives. Monica, ex two, was all about being the perfect wife. Kept the home spotless. Fetch and carry. Wasn't what I was looking for. I'm fine getting my own drinks. But it was her culture. Worked her tail off. And she had to cook. It was the wife's job."

"Furrin?" Elisa asked.

"Croatian," Jason said. "Long story. Also, out of my league which I knew. She's now married to the president of the bank we work with. Lately, I've had to be reminded on a regular basis. Croatian food can be very good. Kind of a weird mix of Greek, Italian and German of all things. Monica's food was not. In any way. Nor was my first wife's. Who was American."

"So, you learned to cook out of self-defense," Elisa said, grinning. "I can cook a twelve-course meal over an open fire that will knock your socks off. With the right ingredients and equipment, admittedly. I'll prove it. I'll take dinner."

"You're on," Jason said. "It's true that you shouldn't swim for thirty minutes after a meal. Want to take a walk around and get a tour? The waterfall is cool..."

"Doesn't this blow hell out of Rule One?" Jason asked as Elisa curled into his shoulder.

"No," Elisa said sleepily. "And if you're wondering, wow, there really *is* something to being with a guy who knows what he's doing. Now hush. I'm gonna take a nap on your shoulder..."

"Jewel," Jason whispered. He'd stayed awake long enough to ensure Elisa was asleep. She even *snored* cutely. "Post drones around. And make damn sure none of those crabs make it through. I am *not* losing my nethers now that I've got a use for them again..."

"I stand corrected," Jason said after a moment. "You're a *very* good cook."

They were eating a fish they'd named Mary's Wrasse in honor of Elisa's mother. The fish was one of the "grouper looking" fishes Jason had spotted on his first foray. This particular one had been about a meter and a half long. Elisa had speared it after a bit of a chase.

The fish was good. The ambience better. Despite the fire hazard, Jason set up a couple of old-fashioned oil lamps. They filled the hut with a soft, warm light. Together with the lap of the waves, the splash of jumping mullet and the trade winds rustling the palm fronds of the hut, it was an idyllic scene.

"Sort of like hogfish," Elisa said, thoughtfully, as she tasted a mouthful.

"Was hogfish frequently on the menu?" Jason asked.

"We went to the Bahamas about once a year," Elisa said. "During Christmas break, generally."

"It's getting to the point I probably should know something about your family," Jason said cautiously. "You indicated you were Battery."

"Let's see," Elisa said, cocking her head to the side. "Mom's family is plantation. These days big farming with a side of small-town business. Big frog. Very political. Ancestors who have been members of Congress, one governor back in the eighteen hundreds. Still very into politics and uncles and so forth were in the state legislature. One that's a designee. I've met most of the senior members of the South Carolina delegation at one time or another..."

"Tim Scott?" Jason asked.

"Uncle Tim?" Elisa said, dimpling. "Yeah, I know him."

The senior senator from South Carolina was one of the rare black Republicans in the Senate and therefore had been a constant target of harassment by the left, including the news media.

"Okay," Jason said. "To be clear: big fan. One of the very few politicians I've ever wanted to meet. I could never have kept my cool the way he did over the years."

"We keep hanging out, you'll meet them," Elisa said. "Whether you want to or not. Mom's side isn't going to give up on politics, whether they're big frogs or not."

"Sort of hard to be big frogs on the station," Jason said.

"Grandpa is already wheeling and dealing," Elisa said, shrugging. "Business-wise and politically. I guess if you've done it your whole life you just keep doing it. So's Granddad and Dad. That's on the Randall side. Randall is *new money*, at least to Grandpa and Grandmother Wentworth. The Randalls made their money in World War Two building planes. The company got sold long ago but they kept the land. Did you know Boeing had a facility in South Carolina?"

"Its primary assembly facility?" Jason said.

"That one," Elisa said. "They still leased the land from the

Randalls. At least right up to the Transfer. Both families own houses in Charleston in the Battery. Owned. The Randalls are city mice, Wentworths country mice. So, I've been both ways my entire life.

"After Dad got out of the Army he moved back to Charleston and took over some of the family's businesses, focusing on the technical side. Support companies for the port. Machine shops. That sort of thing. I went to Catholic primary school in Charleston then a Catholic boarding school in Pennsylvania. Only child. You?"

"Was a military brat when I was very young," Jason said. "Dad owned a small manufacturing business. Sold it when I was in my twenties. Mom was a homemaker. As for me, like I said, never really had a career. Just jobs. Closest was logistics, running warehouses, things like that. Started when I was a contractor in Iraq. Did that. Did all sorts of jobs. Never really settled down to one thing. What'd your dad do in the Army?"

"Artillery," Elisa said. "Grandpa Wentworth wanted him to run for office at one point. 'A Proven Soldier who is an American Patriot.' Dad said it wasn't his thing. Watch it, or he'll try to get you to do it, too."

"And tell me how to vote on everything?" Jason said, smiling.

"Of course," Elisa said, grinning. "Politicians don't know how to run things. The important people have to tell them how to think."

"I will *not* get along with your grandpa," Jason said. "Sorry. Sounds a bit too much like my dad."

"Eh, he's okay," Elisa said. "Of course, that's coming from his granddaughter who can do no wrong. If you like Tim Scott I'm guessing your politics are fairly conservative?" she asked carefully.

"My views are all over the map," Jason replied. "Which is why I've never gotten along with any particular party. I'm a Republican but don't agree with everything there. And it depends on which flavor. I consider myself an old-fashioned conservative but as a child of the eighties, it's a bit hard to avoid the sins-of-the-flesh issues," he added with a grin.

"Even without the mention of ex-wives, I'm clearly not your first lady friend," Elisa said.

"My problem is I'm always poking holes in other people's firmly held positions," Jason said.

"Like?" Elisa asked.

He told the story about the preacher and the conservative porn star.

"You must have really hated that job," Elisa said, laughing.

"I enjoyed it," Jason replied. "I was never going to be Rush Limbaugh, mostly because I was trying to get people to *think*. 'Don't just say ditto. Challenge me. Challenge yourself. What do you really believe and why?' Most people don't seem to want to introspect, don't want to think about it. They just want to be very angry about it and they're not even sure why."

"So, why *do* people get angry about politics?" Elisa asked.

"Politics and religion are both about control," Jason said. "It usually is any time that people get angry. Loss of control. Ceding control to others. Fighting for control over their lives or the lives of others. What psychologists call 'boundary issues.'

"For a society to organize, there *has* to be a degree of limitation of individual freedom. Has to be. People *have* to cede control over their actions, whether that be due to religious beliefs or laws. What every person wants is different and often it slides over into other people's person or property. How much control you cede is where the arguments *begin*. And they only get more complicated and angrier.

"So, in the small town in Arkansas where I was working the radio station, there was this zoning kerfuffle," Jason said musingly. "There was this big old house downtown. It was zoned residential but it hadn't had any residents in a while. It had been built by one of the owners of the local mill, back when there *was* a mill. Really nice Victorian.

"A law firm wanted to use it for offices; it was a few blocks from the courthouse. There was a big outcry. Group of people called 'Save Our Town' wanted to keep it residential, even though none of them were going to buy it and live in it. They just didn't want things to change."

"There are no more bitterly fought fights in local politics than zoning fights," Elisa said. "Learned that early."

"That's because it affects people's lives very directly," Jason said. "There were houses near the law firm. They didn't want the additional traffic. They didn't want criminals walking around their neighborhoods. It mostly did corporate law, not criminal. Didn't matter."

"So, what happened?" Elisa asked.

"The zoning board eventually saw sense and rezoned," Jason said, shrugging. "People struggle with the concept of government control. Too much, not enough? Social conservatives, ask them if there should be laws against abortion. They'll generally say yes. Is there then financial support for the presumably unwed mother? Does the law require the parents of the child to marry? Is it about the good of the child?

"Stats show that children raised in nuclear families end up better off than children raised by a single parent even in abusive relationships. What about guys who keep getting different women knocked up. Which one do they marry? You can eventually get them into a *reductio ad absurdum* position."

"You really love making friends, don't you?" Elisa said.

"With extreme libertarians I ask them if there are building inspectors. No building inspectors, people eventually cut corners until you have major problems. See . . . thousands of examples. People die. Is that okay? 'That's what civil suits are for!' Does that bring back the dead? So, there *are* courts. Are there jails? Do criminals get locked up? I thought you said that was kidnapping. Instead of discussing the question, people trot out aphorisms without thinking about them. 'An armed society is a polite society.' Really? Tell that to the South Side of Chicago. Or Mogadishu."

"More guns equal less crime, though, right?" Elisa said.

"The stats go that way," Jason said. "But it's not that guns automatically make things polite or orderly. A polite and orderly society will be *more* polite and orderly with guns. Or, possibly, it's just very polite and orderly. An impolite and chaotic society will be more impolite and chaotic with guns. Arm Earth's Denmark to the teeth and it will simply be . . . Denmark. Low crime, high social cohesion. Arm Bulgaria to the teeth and you've got a recipe for mass murder and civil war. Switzerland's militia system had a military-grade firearm in practically every household. They were rarely if ever used in crime."

"The US was, overall, a low-crime nation," Elisa said. "Take some cities out of the stats and we were one of the lowest murder rates in the world."

"Cities are always where it concentrates," Jason said. "Going back as far as there's any data on it. For one thing, that's where the most *people* are. And there's data on crime from the Roman and Chinese empires. Ask an anarcho-libertarian if there are laws against slavery, speaking of Romans. 'With industrialization there's no need for slavery.' I got that as an answer one time. 'Ever looked at China?'"

"Surprised you didn't get a political science degree," Elisa said. "You certainly think about it enough."

"Never been sure what you do with one," Jason said. "Political consultant? Politician? I'm more of a bomb thrower."

"So, no real answer then," Elisa said.

"The answer seems to be representative democracy," Jason said, shrugging and picking at the remnants of the dinner. "Get a general consensus on what people prefer through choice of representatives. However, it requires a high degree of information and honesty, which is where the 'angels of man's better nature' break down."

"And instead of everyone being satisfied, everyone will always be a little dissatisfied," Elisa said. "Because it requires constant compromises and you can never get *everything* that you want."

"That," Jason replied, nodding. "There's no truly good answer except maybe benevolent dictatorship. And that breaks down on the 'benevolent' level because even if you have one generation of benevolent dictatorship it never lasts very long. And you get back to just...dictatorship. See also the Roman Empire, again, or Chinese or any number of other historical examples. This is boring. Sorry. I've eaten alone a lot."

"I don't think so," Elisa said, dimpling. "I was going to get a political science degree. This is the sort of discussion I like."

"Was it common fare in your household?" Jason asked.

"Sometimes," Elisa replied. "Though, when the various grandparents were around it was mostly very firmly held positions that brooked no discussion. So...yeah. Socratic method might not go over so well."

"I'll eat an apple and nod approvingly," Jason said. "With occasional chuckles at appropriate times."

"An apple?" Elisa asked, quirking an eyebrow.

"Ever seen *Being There*?" Jason asked. "Probably before your time. Peter Sellers's last and most brilliant work."

"Not familiar with it," Elisa said. "I'll put it on my to-be-watched pile. When did it come out?"

"I don't even remember," Jason said. "Nineties?"

"*Being There* was released in 1979," Adam replied.

"God, was it *that* long ago?" Jason asked. "I suppose so. It depicted New York at the bottom of its seventies trench."

"We could watch it on a pad," Elisa said.

"We'd have to get very close," Jason said.

"Your pads can be combined into one larger screen," Jewel said helpfully.

"We'll still have to sit very close," Elisa said.

"So, I figured out something cool," Jason said as they came back in from snorkeling. Elisa was carrying a Sorta Snapper that she'd speared.

She also loved the water, fishing, snorkeling and was scuba qualified, which Jason wasn't. She loved to hunt and the out of doors but also could talk about sci-fi movies and books better than Jason. For one thing her memory was more crystal clear on some items.

Her love of anime was just one of those things you accepted in someone you loved.

And he was sure he loved her. He had business piling up and he was putting it off to spend time with Elisa.

"Which is?" Elisa said, sitting down on the water's edge, cross-legged. She slid out a tentacle of flex and neatly slit the wrasse's throat then gutted and filleted it. "Just this stuff is cool."

"I've said it has a gazillion and one uses," Jason said. "But so do Alfreds. Alfred One over here with thirty kilos of flex, Jewel."

"Going for a ride?" Jewel asked.

"We are," Jason said.

"A ride?" Elisa asked, looking curious. "Again? You really are a randy old goat."

"Yes," Jason said. "But a different kind."

"You can't do this with the containers," Jason said, forming the flex into a double saddle with a high back. "They have to stay flat for the contragravity. They also don't have lift and drive. Care to play biker babe?"

"Are you *kidding*?" Elisa asked, jumping onto the back of the bike. She waved her feet in the air. "Wooo-hoo! Plus, there's nowhere to put them."

"Think pedals," Jason said. "And put your mask back on. It's gonna get windy. Jewel, have a drone get the fillets, please."

Elisa planted her feet on pedals then whipped off her bikini top.

"If I'm gonna go biker babe might as well go all the way." She tossed the top onto the sand and waved. "Adam, take care of that, 'kay? You coming?"

"Close," Jason said, admiring the view. He climbed on the bike and pulled up his swim goggles then formed control handles and lifted it into the air.

"Hang on real tight."

"Woooohuh! Whoooa! Whoa!"

"Hey!" Elisa said about thirty minutes later. She tapped on his arm. "Look down! What are those?"

There were torpedo-shaped fish coasting through the water under them. The water was crystal clear and Jason wasn't sure how deep they were. They could have been medium-size fish at the surface or very big and a hundred feet down. It was impossible to tell.

"Looks like tuna!" Elisa yelled. "Can we catch them?"

"That's a good question," Jason said, slowing the air-bike down. "I've got exactly nothing for a weight so lowering flexmet . . . it will just fling in the wind. We need a weight."

"And a pole," Elisa said. "Yes, I know that we can use flex. And we should try to harvest some for the company. But can we see about catching some, pretty please?"

"Whatever you want, my dear," Jason said, thinking about it. "Could do it the way I did in Wilson Bay. Or I've got poles with me that might be big enough. Depends on how big the fish are. These are yellowfin, not blue, I think. You wanna angle for one or spearfish?"

Elisa thought about it for a moment then pouted.

"Both?" she asked.

"As you wish," Jason said.

Elisa dove off the side of the bike and started kicking downward toward the oncoming yellowfin tuna, spear gun extended. She'd brought a bunch of free-diving gear with her including long fins for rapid diving.

Jason swung back around to keep the shadow from spooking the fish and watched as she dove deeper. The girl could hold her breath, that's for sure.

She fired the dart and it ran straight and true into the side of the tuna. Then she jerked, releasing the inflating balloon-buoy, and headed to the surface.

Jason lowered the bike to water level, took the spear gun from her, flexing it to the body of the bike, then helped her board.

"Where'd it go?" Elisa asked.

"There," Jason said as the buoy hit the surface.

"And how do we get it to land?" Elisa asked.

"You don't use flex for everything," Jason said, directing the bike into the air.

He leaned over and grabbed the buoy then handed the line to Elisa.

"Can you pull it up a bit?" he asked. Then he extended a length of flex into the water and after a couple of attempts managed to catch the struggling tuna's tail. After that it was a matter of bringing it up under the bike. "Jewel. Tractor beam."

The tractor beam was almost invisible in the blue water but it locked onto the tuna easily enough.

"And away we go," Jason said. "Hang onto the line, yeah?"

"Got it," Elisa said.

He lowered the four-hundred-pound tuna to the ground and Elisa jumped off and quickly slit the fish's throat.

"I need a picture," Elisa said. She flipped her hair to the side then lifted the heavy fish up as far as she could. "Quick, get a picture!"

"With or without your bra top?" Jason asked, grinning.

"Ah!" Elisa said, putting her arms over her breasts. "Adam! If you send the drone footage to my parents, digitize in a top! And this picture. And all the pictures!"

"Will do," Adam said.

"Picture," Jason said, holding up his phone.

"I'm going to send that to my parents as proof that some mysterious stranger hasn't kidnapped me!" Elisa said.

"With this tech it's possible to fake something like that," Jason said, shrugging. "I *could* have kidnapped you. I control the ships. I could just leave you here as my captive and fake communications to your parents."

"I can easily counteract that," Adam said sternly. "I can communicate with system security if you..."

"Shut. Up. Adam," Elisa said. "Oh, no! Please don't keep me

here as your slave!" she added, putting her hand to her forehead dramatically. "Don't be so cruel!"

"I can be very cruel indeed," Jason said archly. "In fact, you are in desperate need of... a tickling."

"Oh, now you'd better be joking," Elisa said seriously.

"You need to be tickled."

"No... No... I'm serious... Nooo..." Elisa said, backing away, both hands out in a stop signal...

"Jewel, Alfred, handle the tuna," Jason said, rubbing his hands together. "Tickling is about to commence..."

"That was interesting in whole new ways I didn't know *existed*," Elisa said, leaning into his shoulder. "I am now weirdly attracted to flexmet."

"That's a very strange fetish to have," Jason said. "But I knew a lady who was turned on by the sound of Velcro for similar reasons. I have been around the block more than once, my dear. And I am *very* inventive."

"And cruel. Let's not forget cruel. Do you get paid for this? 'Cause you should get paid for this..."

# CHAPTER 30 >>>>>>>>>

"AAAGH," JASON SAID, READING THE TEXT MESSAGE.

"What's up?" Elisa said, worried. "Do not doubt me when I say if there is anything I can do to help I will. And I do mean *anything at all*, just ask."

"Arm candy?" Jason said, then frowned. "Sorry."

"I make spectacular arm candy," Elisa said. "I am highly trained, prepared and I'm more than glad to do so. For what?"

Elisa had mentioned being both charm trained, "over two thousand hours," as well as having done pageants.

He'd never dated a pageant queen before.

"I have to go back to the station...pretty soon," Jason said. "There's stuff building up. Business. That I can't do in bits and snatches between having the time of my life. This is remarkably fun."

"Life should be fun," Elisa said, taking his arm and leaning under it. "But life should also be about doing, not just enjoying. There's time enough for love as a team. Which business? Space Ship Four? The mine? Brandywine?"

Jason had been open during their many conversations, because they *had* been talking, about his plans and ideas. He'd, frankly, told her a billion credits' worth of ideas, not that any of them were guaranteed.

"We're opening the event space," Jason said. "We're not calling it a restaurant because there's not enough money in the economy to open one of those. But people who want to get together for business dinners, things like that. Weddings. Funerals. People need a place they can get together as groups to eat and drink. That's a human thing. There's a soft opening coming up. I need to be there. Then there's all the other stuff we've talked about. The ships, the factories, the mine . . . I'd rather be here with you, doing this. Just . . . enjoying."

"When's the opening?"

"Two weeks?" Jason said.

"Whatever shall we do?"

"I've, occasionally, been thinking about that," Jason said. "We need to harvest some of the yellowfin as well as the crayfish. Not to mention there's all the other edible fish species that are collectible."

Once the crayfish collection method had been established, Jason had ordered more gear and scattered it around the islands. By using the flying bikes, they could travel all around the scattered islands and check on how things were going as well as resolve any issues the drones, bots and AIs could not.

"Protein for the station," Elisa said. "Collecting them by hunting is fun, don't get me wrong, but we need a way to bring them in consistently. Have I mentioned that my family used to be in commercial fishing as well as the other businesses?"

"You did," Jason said.

"I've been out on commercial fishing boats," Elisa said. "Not for long trips but I do know the general outline. Best way to catch yellowfin, commercially, is you purse seine the shoals then hook them aboard."

"Lots of flex," Jason said thoughtfully. "Also uses large boats. Long lines?"

"Lots of baiting," Elisa said. "Can flex handle that?"

"Yes," Jason said.

"Also large boats, though," Elisa said. "And there's storage issues. Unless you can load them into stasis, you're going to need refrigeration. Is it 'we' are going to or 'you' are going to?"

"Jewel, can you sign Elisa up as a harvest contractor?" Jason said.

"You're the senior partner," Jewel said. "You can hire anyone you want."

"Put her on contract as a harvester and commercial fishing

consultant," Jason said. "And send a note to Tim or whoever it should go to that we need some consultants on commercial fishing ventures. Marine biologists, that sort of thing."

"That's already being done," Jewel said.

"Whatever we land, you're now making money from it," Jason said. "I should have done that a while back. I've got issues with fraternization with employees, though. I'm not sure this is a good idea."

"It was the fraternization then the employee," Elisa said. "I hope it doesn't interfere with either one."

"Shouldn't," Jason said. "To landing tuna. We'll test this small, first."

"What are you thinking?" Elisa said.

"Worked an albacore boat in Oregon one time," Jason said, thinking about how to integrate flexmet into the process. "You threw out hand lines behind the boat. When an albacore hooked you brought it in, fast, then flipped it up into the catch area, threw the line back out. Repeat. Hard on the hands, hard on the shoulders, line got tangled up if you looked at it wrong. Decent not great money. Tuna aren't brilliant and they're always hungry. They'll go for just about any sort of lure. Something that looks like a feather."

Jason picked up some flexmet and formed it into a large hook with a couple of feathery-looking things just above the hook.

"Add a weight to keep it below the surface." Jason hunted around till he spotted a small rock and added it to the flexmet line, shaping a torpedo shape with the rock in the center. The line now ran to the torpedo weight then to the feathers which extended to near the top of the flex hook. He added barbs to the hook. "That, right there, might just hook one."

"No time like the present to find out," Elisa said, jumping to her feet.

Jason looked at the view from that angle then sighed and stood up as well.

"Slave driver," Jason said.

"I wanna catch more tuna," Elisa said. "Then ... you know. Then catch more fish. Then you know, then ..."

"Lather, rinse repeat," Jason said, grinning. "But for this, we're gonna need a boat."

A boat similar to the one Jason had designed for crayfish harvesting worked well enough. An Alfred could fly it out to the hunting area but would probably have to drive it back on the water.

Jason stood on the boat, controlling it through a thin strand, as it coasted just above the waves. He'd chosen the channel down the caldera as the first test. Tuna were running through the area chasing schools of mackerel, a viable food in itself, and it should do for a test. Later they'd move the test out into the open Pallas Ocean.

"Your two o'clock," Elisa called. She was riding the air-bike and spotting, though that could be done by drones.

Jason increased power to the Alfred and turned to two o'clock, then mentally deployed the line.

There was a high, flexible pole behind him with a line of flex running out the back of the boat. The boat was only big enough to hold two coffins which were collapsed. The transom of the boat, as with the crayfish boat, was at water level.

As he headed toward the tuna, he got the tingle that he'd developed through Jewel to note when there was tension on the line. Looking aft, it was apparent there was a tuna already caught. The fish were everywhere.

He mentally commanded the flex to retract, quickly but not so fast as to pull the hook out of the fish's mouth. Just speeding it up through the water.

Tuna would normally sound, fighting from side to side to try to escape the hook. But when they were hooked to a fast-moving boat, their own shape made them turn to follow the boat, unable to fight. The tuna was drawn in by the flex line, up the sloped back of the boat and into the coffin. It barely fit end to end.

Jason had the hook retract from the fish's mouth then slither back out into the water.

As he was casting the second line out the first one got another hit. Two of the yellowfin filled a coffin.

"We're gonna need a bigger boat," Jason muttered.

"That was fun," Jason said, flopping on the beach.

Fishing and blue-water hunting for tuna were fun. But so were other pursuits. Both Elisa and Jason were beggared for choice in the matter. As the afternoon wore on, jungle love had won the argument vice spearfishing.

"You, my good sir, are possibly waaay too experienced for a sheltered girl from Charleston," Elisa said, leaning her head on his chest.

"That wasn't experience," Jason replied, looking up at the sky. "That was more like fantasy. It's times like this that I wonder if I'm dying of a stroke."

"Similar," Elisa said. "This is *way* too much fun to be real. *You're* way too much fun to be real."

"Hmmm..." Jason hummed.

"Are you going to sleep on me?" Elisa said, prodding his stomach.

"No," Jason said, working his eyes. Not at all. "Just...what do you think about the Constitution? Should we ratify it?"

"You want to talk politics?" Elisa asked.

"Under the shade of a palm tree, maybe?" Jason replied.

"Shade sounds good."

"That stigma about being a pageant queen has passed to an extent," she continued. "So, I was planning on running for a school board then moving up to, probably, state senator at most. Now...? Now I'm back to wondering what I'm going to do when I grow up."

"Was there going to be...family in there?" Jason asked carefully.

"My idol is Justice Barrett," she said, referring to a conservative Supreme Court justice who had seven children. "But...then again, the power behind the throne is an allure. And it would allow more time for kids and more kids..."

She looked at Jason sideways for a second.

"What do you think about...kids," she asked.

"In that I'm pro-choice," Jason said. "As in, your body, your choice. Though I'm not big on abortion."

"How many would you...like?" Elisa asked.

"That's serious territory," Jason said. "But we've already jumped over that line long ago. Honesty? 'Cause it's a simple answer but complex as well."

"Honesty," Elisa said.

"I'm old," Jason said. "You gotta remember that. Most guys, from a relationship, dating, romantic, sexual, point of view, never get over being *this* age, twentyish, no matter how old they actually *are.*

"Women tend to pick themselves apart as they get older, looking at every gray hair, every wrinkle line. They know they're not twenty anymore. Men put on a clean shirt and they think they're Clark Gable. So, guys have a hard time realizing that they are. Getting older that is. That's why older guys can be creepy. They can't quite grasp that they're not twenty anymore and what might have been okay when they were twenty isn't okay when they're fifty."

"That does happen," Elisa said, sighing. "Yeah."

"And you think you've got all the time in the world," Jason continued, looking off into the distance. "I wanted to have kids since I was *actually* twenty. Glad I didn't with She Who Must Not Be Named. Monica wanted to hold off until we were financially solvent and, at least in part because of me, that never realized. Or maybe she *didn't* want any. She and Richard never had kids. Hard to tell with Monica. She's a very skillful liar."

"Bitch," Elisa said.

"So, I wanted kids," he said. "But whatever some of the crazies might say, I can't have them myself. And as I got older, the more and more intense the desire became. Minor when I was in my twenties. By this age? I'd like to have *all* the kids. Big family."

"That...works," Elisa said.

"Flip side," Jason said. "My internal editor of fatherhood. My dad was...a revolving SOB to us growing up. I don't want to be my dad. Kids need discipline and you can't always tell them they're the best of all the kids in the world and they can do no wrong. But...they need some positive reinforcement. Sometimes? Occasionally?"

"Not much positive reinforcement growing up?" Elisa said.

"*Growing up*?" Jason said, looking out at the reef. "I was the only one of the three sons who visited him when he was in hospice from cancer. Me and my mom. That was it. And he was a revolving SOB every time I visited. Mom made excuses. He's in a lot of pain. I told her I couldn't tell; he was pretty much just being Dad."

"Ouch," Elisa said.

"Mom mentioned at one point that she was sure that Steve and Kevin would come visit, soon," Jason said, blowing out. "Dad's response was that he never wanted to see that 'faggot' again in his life. And Steve had 'important things to do.' Unlike 'this useless jackass.' Referring to me."

"Oh!" Elisa said, shaking her head. "Oh, my God! Ow!"

"I think we've gotten to the point that's not oversharing," Jason said, taking a deep breath. "Thing is, it wasn't the worst thing my dad ever said to me. So, getting back to the subject of kids, I don't know if I know *how* to be a dad that's not... that. It's what's got me worried."

"Do you like kids?" Elisa asked.

"Love 'em," Jason said. "What I've had to do with them. Even if you're close to people, and I haven't tended to be real close, they tend to look askance at a bachelor that's into children. But, yeah, I do. I want kids for playmates. I want to teach them about the outdoors. Hunting, fishing, tracking. This," he added, waving. "I don't want to be 'Cat's in the Cradle,' much less my dad."

"Reference?" Elisa asked.

"Song from the seventies about how fathers and sons tend to grow up similar," Jason said. "Also, that they don't spend enough time with each other. I want to spend time with my kids. I'm way more into *this* than hunting, being honest."

"I am scuba qualified for a reason," Elisa said.

"So... that's me," Jason said, looking at her. "But if we're this serious, I repeat. Your body, your choice. And you're a single child from a comfortable family. I'm fine if you only want one or... two?"

"So, me," Elisa said. "First, I think you'd be a great dad. I really do. I don't believe you'd be like your father. You've... never even been negative to me at all. In any way. And we've been here a week. You'd have started to get... picky by now if you were that way. Was he like that with your mom?"

"Oh, yeah," Jason said.

"So that's not who *you* are," Elisa said. "You're *not* your father. I don't think there's a mean bone in you."

"Thank you?" Jason said. "I do consider that a compliment. But... I do have a bad side. Just hasn't been a reason for it to come out, here. And it's not ever going to be directed at you. Just... I've got one. I've been in more than my share of fights. Partially because of the life I worked. Hell, I was a bouncer one time."

"You left that off the list," Elisa said, grinning.

"I was mostly a cooler," Jason said. "I cooled people down. The last thing you want is to have to actually get in a fight. Too many hassles. You were talking."

"You're not your dad," Elisa repeated. "I think you'd make a great dad. Which has always been an important consideration for me when it comes to . . . a mate."

"Mate," Jason said with a grin. "There may be some mating."

"Are we going to have this conversation?" Elisa said. "'Cause I'm getting to where I'm at."

"Sorry."

"Yes, my family has a multigenerational history of small families," Elisa said. "But . . . call it internet influence or something. You know that satirical Christian newsletter from before Transfer? 'David tired of being compared to President Spade'?"

"'Climber recovering in hospital after deciding to let go and let God,'" Jason said, laughing. "My favorite headline."

"I started reading it when I was young," Elisa said. "Like, eight or nine. It was always clean and wholesome so my parents didn't mind. Dad got me hooked on it."

"You've got a great dad, then," Jason said.

"I do, I really do," Elisa said, rubbing his shoulder. "But the thing is, they were always talking about these homeschoolers with big families. 'Overachieving homeschool family reforms small Third World country while on mission trip.'"

"I never saw that one," Jason said.

"It was a user headline," Elisa said, looking shamefaced. "I submitted it and they used it. And I got to looking into it. Going on forums and blogs, that sort of thing. And I just . . . got into it. I'd decided by the time I was thirteen that I wanted to *be* that lady. The homeschool mom with, like, forty kids."

"Forty," Jason said, raising his eyebrows. "Well . . . it's going to take a lot of . . . exercise on *my* part . . ."

"That's part of it," Elisa said seriously. "You talked about how Monica was the perfect housewife. I have the same instinct? Drive? I've got it. I'll take care of it. But . . . it helps to have a husband who's not constantly distracted by the TV."

"I rarely watch it," Jason said, shrugging. "And I obviously know how to cook. Even for large numbers. Worked in an industrial kitchen in high school. I still remember Rona's stroganoff recipe . . ."

"My job," Elisa said. "I've got the house. You just need to find the money to support it."

"Well . . ." Jason said. "Easy enough to feed them. When they're old enough we just send them out to collect their own..." he added, gesturing at the lagoon.

"I'm serious," Elisa said. And it was clear she was.

"I will find the money," Jason said. "For as many as you want. And while it was joking, it was also somewhat serious. We could have a house here. Or somewhere else. Your call. With enough drones and dogs, the kids can run around in forests and we won't have to worry about them being eaten by bears."

"Building a house down here...?" Elisa said, frowning. "I'm not worried about the animals. There are ways to defend against them, right? I guess there are plenty of people in construction who are out of work but... Where are you going to find the materials?"

"Wood?" Jason said, gesturing at the forest behind them. "So, story from here I hadn't told, I just realized. My birthday was about a month ago and my AI decided I needed a birthday present..."

Jason told the story of Jewel making him a house for his birthday.

"That's one cool AI," Elisa said, smiling. "Jewel, you are a jewel."

"Thank you," Jewel said, coming on the screen and dimpling.

"Clearly, building houses with this tech isn't a huge deal," Jason said. "It's mostly a matter of having the right materials although fixtures are an issue. So, I'm designing a house."

"Really?" Elisa said carefully. "What kind? How big?"

"Pretty big," Jason said. "The design is based, sort of, on southern plantation home style. Victorian era. Not neoclassic like Mount Vernon. Pretty big because I *hoped* to find a lady who wanted a large family and assumed we'd have visitors. I've... started getting into some fairly big business and that probably means visitors to the house for business reasons."

"Business," Elisa said. "Politics."

"Thing is, I'm not great at social," Jason said, shrugging. "Sales calls, taking people out to dinner, sure. I have never thrown a party."

"Ever?" Elisa said.

"I have never invited more than a D&D group over to my space for a social event," Jason said. "And D&D games don't count. And, yes, I used to play D&D."

368 John Ringo with James Aidee

"Okay," Elisa said, smiling.

"Is that a deal breaker?" Jason asked.

"Never played it," Elisa said. "But I've read *The Silmarillion* if that helps."

"The whole thing?" Jason asked, boggling. "That's masochistic."

"I was in a Tolkien phase," Elisa said. "And as to parties, I'm a trained party planner and organizer. I *like* organizing parties. I like *hosting* parties. Again, I've got it."

"I love you," Jason blurted. "Oops. I said it."

"I love you, too," Elisa said, leaning in. "There. I said it too."

"The question is where to put the house?" Jason said. "I'd prefer northern temperate. Cool summers, snowy winters, probably very wet summer and fall. Sort of the weather of Maryland crossed with central England."

"That sounds nice," Elisa said, curling up even more. "Big fireplaces?"

"Fireplaces are a must," Jason said. "There are some nice areas in southern Chindia from what I've heard. Haven't been there, yet. But I've been to America Nova and I really like the biome. I haven't taken the time to go to the area I'm thinking about but... I'd like a really nice view of America Mons to the northwest."

"Out the front?" Elisa asked. "That's a better choice. You want your most protected side to the northwest and your open side to the southeast. At least in northern latitudes."

"Yes," Jason said. "That. Most of the area around the house would be cleared with gardens and lawns. But I want to leave a trio of the big trees in the backyard..."

"Great place for a gathering," Elisa said.

"And about a hundred acres of the old forest," Jason added. "Fifty hectares. Something along those lines. Close enough to the house it's an easy walk."

"For the kids to play in," Elisa said. "'Out of the house! Don't come home till the safety light comes on!'"

"Safety light?" Jason said.

"Southernism?" Elisa said. "Most rural southern homes have a streetlight nearby. It's called a safety light. That's what my Gramma called it."

"Ah. That. About two hundred acres around the house that's... estate..."

"Bridle paths," Elisa said. "Stables?"

"Horses are going to be in short supply for a while," Jason said then looked thoughtful. "Though ponies might be a thing in the reasonably near future."

"Breed ponies to wild horses?" Elisa asked. "Why not just wild horses?"

"They're about the size of ponies, anyway," Jason said. "And their withers can't support the weight of even a full-grown woman. Larger horses will be tough. They'll have to be sized up over generations. Assuming the breeding program even works as I've envisioned."

"So far, so good," Elisa said. "I'm liking everything I'm hearing so far."

"Okay, we gotta get up."

"Spoilsport," Elisa said, taking his hand for a lift. "Now? Why?"

Jason unwound his phone from his arm, stretched it to its maximum then attached it to a convenient palm tree.

"I didn't know they could do that," Elisa said quizzically.

"These things are the bomb," Jason said. "Jewel, bring up the 3D of the proposed house."

When the 3D schematic was up, Jason started pointing out features he'd been designing in his spare time.

"Study slash library and parlor," Jason said. "Great hall entry."

"The parlor had *better* have shelves for books, too," Elisa said. "In the old days, women weren't expected to read. I read."

"There's . . . some?" Jason said. "Jewel . . ."

"Plenty of bookshelves," Jewel said. "Inset millwork."

"She just added them," Adam interjected.

"Tattletale. Snitches get stitches."

"I haven't really done a lot with the interior to be honest," Jason said. "And I'm probably going to find a home designer to go over it and improve it. Den behind the study. Fireplace. Electronics. Also called a winter room."

"We're not going to need the fireplace," Elisa said. "We'll have one, but we'll have to open the windows . . ."

Jason gave her a quizzical glance.

"As many kids as we're going to have in there watching the first run of some movie . . . ?" Elisa said. "They're going to be putting off all the heat we'll need."

"Point," Jason said. "Large dining room behind that, mostly leading to the grand foyer. Big kitchen that's right off the dining room. With the stove facing out to a bar . . ."

"Why?" Elisa asked.

"Everybody always wants to congregate in the kitchen at parties," Jason said. "I haven't hosted them but I've been to them. And this way people can talk with the cook but stay out of the way."

"Ooo," Elisa said. "Good thought."

"Not original," Jason said. "Big dining room. Outdoors cooking area. Grills and a barbeque."

"Important distinction," Elisa said.

"Pool," Jason said.

"Only useable part of the year," Elisa pointed out.

"Very useful for wearing out the rug rats in summer," Jason said. "And this is intended as the summer home."

"Winter home in the Graham Islands?" Elisa said, grinning.

"Different design, though," Jason said. "And less worry about feeding them..."

"'Get out of the house!'" Elisa said in a sharp, grandmother tone. "And don't come back till you've found dinner! There'd better be enough for *everybody!*'"

"You're going to be one of those moms, huh?" Jason said, grinning.

"Truthfully, I want to be the Kool-Aid mom," Elisa said. "I had to look that up. But that's exactly what I intend to be. My mom was."

"Nice view out the back," Jason said. "Woods, fields. Zero-edge pool. And a zero-edge hot tub."

"I could live in a house like that," Elisa admitted grudgingly. "Upstairs?"

"Centralized master suite," Jason said. "Rear side leading out to the balcony which is the top of the outdoor cooking area. Big bathroom. Big walk-in closets. Parlor area overlooking the pool. Girls' and boys' wings. Largest bedrooms closest to the master suite which would be the guest bedrooms."

"If it comes to that, we can exile the little heathens to the attic," Elisa said. "If we run out of room. We need a nursery off the bedroom."

"Point," Jason said, adjusting the model.

"Where's the music room?" Elisa asked. "Needs to be sound-proofed. Screeching violins and misplayed piano notes will otherwise become unbearable."

"Have at it," Jason said, waving at the screen and smiling.

Elisa stood back and put her hands on her hips.

"Are we so serious we are seriously designing a house?" she asked. "Together."

"Are *we*?" Jason asked. "Because I am."

"Then we are," Elisa said, nodding. "I love your rough sketch. But can I send it to a home designer I know? I love his work and I think he'd like this. But I don't know the ins and outs, either."

"Absolutely," Jason said.

"And can it be a bit bigger?" Elisa asked.

"With how I'm planning on building it, it can be as big as you want," Jason said.

"I love you."

"I love you, too."

"I'm too young to be having a stroke," Elisa said, looking at him. "I love your politics. I love that you want to have a big family. That you're... you. *Everything* about you."

"Me too?" Jason said. "It's weird. It's perfect."

"Hah!" Jewel snapped.

"Hah?" Jason said. They both looked at the screen where Adam and Jewel had appeared side by side.

"Jewel!" Adam interjected.

"Who's the best, Jason?" Jewel asked. "Chime in any time, Adam."

"You really think I'd have let you go away on a tropical getaway with someone who *wasn't* perfect for you, Elisa?" Adam asked with an aggrieved tone. "My duty is to watch out for you."

"You two are *too* smug," Elisa said, waggling her finger at the screen.

"You even have the same taste in art and architecture," Jewel whispered. "Adam's collection of the southern houses in *Better Homes and Gardens* houses you'd lingered on? My collection of Jason's replies and likes to architecture posts? I still say you should have gone with Queen Anne and when you send it to... Paul Colegrove, right?"

"Yes," Elisa said, pursing her lips.

"I'll point out the Queen Anne designs Jason was looking at," Jewel said. "Jason, Paul Colegrove was The Old House."

"You're kidding," Jason said.

"The Old House?" Elisa asked.

"He used to post photos of old buildings," Jason said. "I admit to having a Twitter account. He was part of the thread about humans must have been visited by aliens at one point who built all these beautiful old buildings. Because after a certain point, architecture went to hell and everything looked like hell. So, it had to be aliens."

"It's actually because of the influence of Frankfurt School," Elisa said disgustedly.

"Oh, my God," Jason said. "How did you even *know* that?"

"I *hate* Frankfurt School," Elisa said. "And postmodernist. Everything about it. The architecture. The art."

"Well, except for..."

"Except for..."

"Jackson Pollock," they both said together then looked at each other.

"Marry me," they both said simultaneously.

# CHAPTER 31 >>>>>>>>>

"THE YELLOWFIN IS SELLING EXTREMELY WELL," TIM SAID, SMIL-ing. "We put out some to bid at first and settled at five hundred credits a case."

"*That* much?" Jason asked, surprised.

Elisa was out catching it by spearfishing while the single powered boat shuttled in and out with catch. The yellowfin were being cleaned and filleted by flexmet to reduce the shipping volume. Jason returned to the hut to take the call.

"Most people are using it for sushi," Tim said, shrugging. "It's good tuna. Get more."

"We need some people who know what they're doing," Jason said. "Wildlife biologists. Marine biologists..."

"Already being handled," Tim said. "When Arthur and I sat down to do the quarterly P and L, I agreed we could do more hiring of specialists."

"And I need four metric tons of flexmet, four Hermans and half a ton of bar metal," Jason said.

"Four Hermans?" Tim asked.

"Hermans can run twenty-four seven as long as their fuel holds out," Jason said. "Which means they can fish for tuna, twenty-four seven. We don't know how long the run will last."

"Put in the order," Tim replied. "We can handle that. Couple of notes on business?"

"I'll try to engage my business brain," Jason said.

"Doing the quarterly dividend payment," Tim said. "I'd like

to keep seventy-five percent of the profits in the company. We're growing so fast, it's amazing. But even with all the AI support, I'm having to hire people left and right. Including a human resources officer to just hire people. Growth needs capital."

"Agreed," Jason said. "It's not like we can go find investors."

"You're in agreement, then," Tim said. "I'm of the opinion that we need to keep seventy-five percent of the profit in house for growth. But that would mean only twenty-five percent dividend payment to the partners?"

"Yes," Jason said. "Keep the rest of the capital in the business. There's some things I think are important I could use some cash for but . . . I'm doing okay. I can wait a bit."

"Okay," Tim said, somewhat lugubriously. "So, your share for this quarter is only two million credits."

"I can make it with . . ." Jason said then blinked. "Wait . . . What? *How* much?"

"Two million," Tim said, grinning. "Give or take. That's your share, Log. *This* quarter."

"That's with only taking twenty-five percent out of the *profits*?" Jason said. "The profits."

"Food is a very profitable business," Tim said, shrugging, "at least at the moment. Another reason to keep profits in the business is we're starting to face competition. But we're ahead of them by a light-year. In many ways because of your innovative approach. Anyway, just thought you should know."

"Yeah," Jason said, wonderingly. "Thanks."

"I'll cut the check to Gil?" Tim asked.

"Yeah," Jason said, still dazed. "Cut the check to Gil."

"See ya, Log," Tim said.

"Out here, Ops," Jason replied distantly.

He thought about what you could do with two million credits. Then he thought about the fact that he was terrible with money.

"Jewel, ask Gil and James for a meet, will you?" Jason said thoughtfully.

"They're already waiting for your call," Jewel replied.

"Tim called them, first, huh?"

"You, my friend, are officially comfortable," James said, grinning.

"And it's easy to lose," Gil added pointedly.

"Yeah, about that," Jason said. "It also might fix one big problem for not only me but the system: the fuel mine."

"I know the idea," Gil said cautiously. "How much were you thinking about putting into that?"

"That's why I need James," Jason said. "Seven percent direct ownership can call a vote on a board. And based on what's happened so far, having that much more or less means you're going to control the vote. Most people just abstain. By default, because their AIs are turned off to it."

"True," James said.

"Twelve percent if it's a collection of people," Jason said. "Same deal."

"Also true," James said.

"What if it's proxies?" Jason asked. "Do you need seven percent if it's proxies or twelve?"

"What are you thinking?" Gil asked.

"Most people are smart enough to know that if nothing *else* has a return, unit wise, a fuel mine unit *is* going to have a return," Jason said. "So, they don't want to give up those units."

"Agreed," Gil said. "You were talking about offering a credit and a unit for trade."

"But many won't even accept that," Jason said. "If their AIs will allow the contact. But. Many people on the station, a credit is going to be serious money, so their AIs may at least be willing to put through the call. Then Jewel will offer either one credit plus a random unit for trade or ask if they'll allow me to vote their shares. A proxy vote. That way they keep the shares. If they trade, great. I'll have more ownership of a fuel mine. But the question is, with a proxy..."

"You only need seven percent," James said. "That's the question, right?"

"Right," Jason said. "Okay, in that case, seven percent is one million, one hundred and twenty thousand units. I'd like to devote that many credits to the program. But. If Jewel can scare up either that many units of ownership *or* proxy, we're golden. And I won't pay the credit for proxy. So, it may be less. Depends on how many people will take the call. Then you, James, manage the units. Does that sound like a plan?"

"They'll have to agree with one percent management fee," James pointed out.

"That . . . yes, has to be noted," Jason said. "Most of these people won't want to be bothered much. But they'll have to agree to that. Gil, how do you feel about this?"

"It's putting a lot of your eggs in one basket," Gil said. "And you realize there's taxes, right?"

"What's the tax rate?" Jason asked.

"Four percent," Gil said. "For your income bracket. Currently. We'll see how much politicians mess it up. The tax code is remarkably clean. Also, something else we'll have to see is *how* they mess it up."

"So yes or no?" Jason asked.

"Oh, yes," Gil said. "This station needs fuel and nobody can get enough votes together to get the fuel mines up and going. It's a mess. It's a risk but not a huge one. Long term, you'll make money."

"And if Jewel can get through with the offer of a credit," James said, "then can she ask about managing other units?"

"Do I get a percentage?" Jason asked. "And I'd still want to hold the proxies on Twelve Bravo and the rest I'm personally interested in, personally."

"I can agree to that," James said.

"Jewel, can you do that?" Jason asked.

"I can do both but . . ." Jewel said. "The but being I'm going to need heavier server time to do this at all. It'll cost about ten thousand credits of borrowed server time. Could go higher but not much."

"Gil?" Jason said.

"Agreed," Gil said. "Well within the margin. I'd have thought more."

"James," Jason said, "I'm going to need a company to run Spaceship Four. I'm up to the point of being able to use it and if we can get Twelve Bravo going, we're going to need it for fuel haulage."

"Agreed," James said.

"Gil, that's going to mean more money invested," Jason said. "Thoughts?"

"I saw your business plans," Gil said. "My worry is less money than practicality. Can you get enough people to sign up to be dropped in the colonist program? Can you get enough ships to drop on the peaks for the mass pickup program?"

"Brandywine's the number one shipper from the planet," Jason said. "Obviously based on the returns. I get with Larry and he pays cheaper rates for drop-off on the peaks than return to the station. But the ships will be making bank because they'll be using less fuel. Then a really cheap rate for station returns via ten grand. It's a win-win for everybody."

"It's also herding cats," James said.

"The way you herd cats is you throw treats in a room then close the door," Jason said. "The numbers work. And, yes, there's a cat-herding issue. It's doable. As to the colonist drop... There's a long list of colonists who want to get to the ground. *Some* of them will be willing to do the drop. They may not take families and that is an issue for later."

"News report," Jewel interjected. "Backed up by some decent polling and AI network. Most colonists, the father is doing the drop and leaving family behind until the situation on the ground is safe. So that issue already exists."

"All I need is a half load and it makes a profit. Which gets back to I need a board that'll go along and I need a company to run it that's willing to accept the risks."

"And a bank willing to take the risk," Gil said. "Richard isn't willing to take the risk with *gear*. You may have made some money, Jason, but say one thousand colony packs times fifty thousand credits is fifty *million* credits. You can't self-fund a drop. If you can't find banks to take the risk, you're not going to be able to do it."

"Table it for now," Jason said, gritting his teeth. "It will work, but table it for now. James, one huge issue."

"Which is?" James asked.

"I've... got a new girlfriend," Jason said. "Who is fantastic in so many ways. Despite Jewel's insistence that she's not going to run off on me like Monica, I'm sure that she's out of my league."

"Speaking financially only," Gil said cautiously, "I'm not sure there's *anyone* out of your league on the station."

"I don't think she cares about that all that much," Jason said. "She was money on Earth. And I'm uncertain about even mentioning the recent windfall. But here's the issue: Her dad is also in finance."

"Ah," James said uncomfortably.

"I'm not going to drop you as a financial manager, James,"

Jason said hastily. "But...the credit plus unit or proxy may or may not work. If it does, it has the potential to drop a butt-ton of units on your company. And that would screw my potential future father-in-law."

"That serious?" Gil asked. "Have you discussed a pre-nup?"

"What part of fantastic is unclear?" Jason said. "She is, or was, Battery, Old Plantation money. Yes, I know, that was then. But anyway, would you talk to this guy, James? Possibly...I don't want it to come out that I dropped a million credits on a deal that cut out my possibly future father-in-law. I will if I have to...But..."

"I'll talk to him," James said. "Does he have a name?"

"Jewel?" Jason said.

"John Randall," Jewel said. "Bella has his contact information."

"I'll look at it, Jason," James said.

"You understand why I'm asking," Jason said. "It's an ask."

"I get it," James said. "And if we get the additional influx, which we should, I'll need more people, anyway."

"As soon as the money is in the bank we'll move forward on the credit-unit proxy plan," Jason said. "We'll table the ten grand discussion until I get something figured out. I still need someone to run it and whatever investment that's going to take. Jewel, lean towards proxies. But just get some face time and be persuasive. Wear your nicest outfit..."

"Pizza."

Rick Cutler was *actually* twenty-six and so far, had found life in space not terribly unlike life on Earth: He hadn't left his compartment because he was gaming.

Gaming was Rick's life and passion. He gamed as much as he possibly could. And the systems on the station were absolutely amazing. He saw no reason to leave the compartment. There was food, a bathroom and the most incredible gaming system ever. What more could anyone ask?

But you had to get up from time to time to get print food. Admittedly, it wasn't great, but it was food.

"You have an AI querying whether you'd like to earn one credit," Mandy said.

She was wearing her sexy elf costume. He loved that costume. He was pretty sure he was in love with Mandy but back on Earth he was constantly falling in love with the girls at the drive-through.

One credit was enough for four print meals.

"How?"

"Hi, I'm Jewel," Jewel said.

Wow. Even *sexier* costume. AIs were awesome.

"I'm *paying* you a credit?" Rick asked. He'd paid more than a credit on OnlyFans.

"Two choices," Jewel said. "You can either earn one credit by trading your unit in Twelve Bravo or my boss would like to vote your unit. In which case there's a one percent fee. So, one credit now or proxy your vote and get money later."

"Mandy?" Rick asked. "I really don't get the units thing."

"I'd say the proxy, Rick," Mandy said in her super sexy voice. "The same guy can manage *all* your units which would be better for you *and* the system."

"Yeah, I don't get the unit thing," Rick repeated. The printer dinged and he pulled out hot print pizza. "Ouch." He took a bite and chewed thoughtfully. "I guess...let somebody else handle it?"

"So that is a yes?" Jewel asked. "I need an agreement that you allow Allen, Randall and Associates manage your units and Jason Graham have your proxy on Twelve Bravo. And I need a clear yes."

"Yes," Rick said, walking back to the flexcouch. "I agree. Yes. Can I get back to gaming, now?"

"You're the best, Rick!" Mandy said, doing a cleavage flash. "That was easy, right? Beleg!"

"Yeah," Rick said, picking up his controller and putting on the VR headset. She was talking Sindarin again. "Totally cool..."

"We haven't had a family council in a while," Mabel said. Her voice was tight, but also curious.

They sat around a table at a restaurant called Osaka Nights, eating sushi. The fish and crab were real and, having come up from the planet in stasis, were also shockingly fresh. Some of the flavors were slightly different from what Cade expected, but they were all tasty. The rice seemed to be printed, but he could ignore the bitter taste of it and focus on the fish.

"Apparently," Abby said, "it's been about two million years." She wore another band T-shirt for an act Cade had never heard of, someone called the Head Parasites.

Cade laughed, and once he started laughing, he found it hard to stop. When the laugh ran out, he wiped a tear from the corner of his eye.

"Apparently, that's right."

"You're calling this council," Mabel said, "because your number has come up for a flight to the planet."

"Well, *our* number. If we want it." Cade took a piece of salmon sashimi, dipped it in something that creditably resembled soy sauce, and ate it.

"Are we going to vote?" Abby asked.

"We don't have to reach a binary decision," Cade said. "Let's figure out what's best for each member of the family, and make it happen."

"I can't go," Sam said. "Not yet?"

"Ana?" Mabel smiled.

"Not unless Judge Gutierrez's first name is 'Ana,' Mom. I have a court date."

"A formality," Cade suggested. "They'll give you some community service."

"Maybe they'll send you down to the planet," Abby said. "I heard on the channels that's what happens. No room for prison, so the fastest way down to the surface is to commit a crime. Something not bad enough for execution, obviously."

"That's a rumor," Cade said. For all he knew, the rumor might be true.

"If they don't send you down to the surface," Mabel said, "what would you want? Assume you get probation or a fine or service. When that's up, what do you want to do?"

"*Then* there's Ana, Mom," Abby said.

"Hey," Sam objected. "But, yeah, that's basically right." He buried himself in his bowl of teriyaki wildfowl.

"What about you, kiddo?" Cade asked Abby. "I've heard the network is already accessible all over the planet."

"I have heard the same," she said. "I also thought maybe I could document the creation of the new family farm, and farming communities, in the channels. There's a little of that in there now, but not much. Mostly, you just see dorks showing off how they went down to the surface and, like, killed a bear. Trying to be Crocodile Dude and failing."

"So, you do want to want to come down?" Cade asked.

"Unfortunately, there's rather a lot of videos of bears. And crocodiles. And wolves. And sea monsters. And venomous snakes." Abby shuddered. "So, I feel like I can wait a little longer. *I* don't need to be Crocodile Dude. Sorry, Dad. I know that makes me kinda soy."

"Not at all," he murmured.

Mabel met Cade's gaze. "Do you have a pitch?"

Cade took a deep breath. "I do. I guess my pitch is mostly about me going down. Maybe Sam, as soon as he can."

"Because you want to get fields cleared and plowed and planted."

"And water and septic and power set up, and a house built. Also, I think we'll want goats and chickens, once those become available. Maybe pigs. So for the moment, someone needs to build all the little shacks, just like someone needs to lay down the roads."

"What about the robots?" Mabel asked. "Alfonses and Herberts and whatnot."

"The government is offering us a grant," Cade said. "The trip down and the colonization pack are free. So that includes robots—I think a Herman and an Alfred. The robots will certainly do most of the work, but I think it would be very difficult to try to direct them entirely from here. With the best of will, looking at a map and video depiction of a plot of land is simply not the same thing as walking it. Hearing the crunch of the twigs under your feet, smelling the soil and the plants, feeling the breeze."

"That's very romanticized," Mabel said.

"I like data as much as the next guy," Cade said. "But I don't believe in farming purely by numbers. There's a feel to it, and an intuition. I need to get down there."

"And even if you could farm by the numbers," Mabel said, "even if we asked around and it turned out that everyone else was farming by raw data, just chatting with their robots, you wouldn't want it."

"I wouldn't want it," Cade agreed. Then, something in her voice made him go a step further. "But I want you. You could come down with me, the kids could join later."

"Do you want *me*? Or do you want me as I'll be forty years from now?"

"I may have to keep looking in a mirror to remind myself what I look like," Cade said. "And I guess I'm not done struggling.

But I want you now. And one thing you ought to feel confident about is that, in forty years, I'll still want you."

She puffed out her cheeks.

"Come farm with me," he said.

"Not yet," she replied.

"James wants to talk," Jewel said two days later.

Jason and Elisa were hunting land crabs the old-fashioned way, by batting them in the face with sticks until the land crab grabbed it then throwing it in a case.

"Put him through," Jason said as Elisa managed to snag a land crab.

"It's too big," Elisa said, struggling to lift the mammoth land crab into the case.

"That's what you always say," Jason said, grinning.

"What?" James asked.

"Sorry, talking to Elisa," Jason said, taking his phone off his bicep and holding it out. "Elisa, say hello to James."

"Hi, James," Elisa said, struggling with the land crab. "Gimme a sec! This thing's huge!"

"Wow," James said, smiling. "That's . . . something."

"You talking about Elisa or the crab?" Jason asked. Elisa was wearing her American flag bikini top again. "Don't answer that question. This is James my, uh . . . financial manager."

"Mom told me," Elisa said, managing to get the crab in the stasis case. "Close. Hi, again, James. You and Dad are doing a partnership?"

"Yes," James said. "That's one of the things I wanted to talk to you about, Jason. It's now Allen, Randall and Associates. I called him right after our talk. He has already built a good portfolio of clients and there are a lot of mergers going on. The main argument was over who got first billing. Your, uh, recent input put me over the top."

"Okay," Jason said, grinning.

"Input?" Elisa asked.

"I had a quarterly dividend," Jason said, shrugging. "So, I dumped at least part of it on James. 'Cause I don't know for finance. And I asked him if he'd look at maybe talking to your dad since I didn't want to . . ."

"Screw my dad?" Elisa said. "And that came out wrong, too."

"I wouldn't say that 'you don't know for finance' is entirely true," James said. "Have you talked to Jewel about the credit-unit proxy program?"

"I admit I have been extremely busy," Jason said. "It's just work, work, work down here."

Elisa giggled.

"Bathing, dressing, undressing..." Elisa said.

"Excuse me?" James said, grinning.

"I have no idea what she's talking about," Jason said. "It's just been work, work, work. Did you get the land crab I sent? See how hard it is to gather?"

He'd sent all his close associates steamed land crab, with instructions for eating, along with a selection of tropical fruits.

"I did get the land crab," James said. "So did Richard and Gil and I'll pass along their thanks. But about the units program..."

"Yes, about that," Jason said.

"There's a saying that money talks," James said. "You are now the proxy holder of *sixteen* percent of... the primary target and hold three percent of the units."

"When did *that* happen?" Jason asked.

"The last two days?" Jewel said. "You may have been working... very *hard* on your... *many* tasks, but I have been working myself to the chips! To the chips I say!"

"I'm sorry I overworked you, Jewel," Jason said, honestly contrite.

"Actually, it was fun," Jewel said. "Challenging. And it only cost about five hundred."

"How's *that* work?" Jason asked. He knew she was circumspectly talking about five hundred thousand credits.

"Three percent is four eighty, Jason," James said. "The rest were server costs I presume."

"Lots of purchased server time," Jewel said. "Went a little over budget. Gil approved it. But we did it. Overdid it. The thing is, I'm not out of budget. Should I keep going?"

"With that much control," Jason said, wandering and thinking. "Most people don't vote. James... I've gotta think about a board that I can work with... And you suggested a leasing company. I'll need to take a closer look. Jewel... shift the units program to the general production factory... Once we've got enough proxy or units there for control... James, suggestions?"

"Metals refinery," James said. "With some caveats."

"And a metals refinery," Jason said. "If it's working that well. Those should all bring a return. Good job, Jewel. How do you reward an AI?"

"*Don't* and I can't emphasize this enough, expect me to speak Elvish. Also, watch where you're stepping."

Jason jumped back just in time to avoid having a toe lopped off by a land crab.

"I'll spot you," Elisa said.

"Elisa, not trying to be a jerk," James said carefully. "But Jason, could we talk privately?"

"Yeah, yeah," Jason said. "Jewel, single link. Sorry, Elisa."

"I'm your *girlfriend*," Elisa said, smiling. "It's *your* money. It's okay. And I've grown up with the axiom: 'Never talk about money' drilled in. Unless you're talking about money. Talk with your financial manager. I'll spot you. You're obviously pretty distracted."

"Lemme get over to the interdiction area," Jason said, picking his way through the mangroves. "Go, James."

"Your total control of Twelve Bravo is now around three million units," James said. "That brings up a number of points."

"Going to have to have a board," Jason said.

"I have some suggestions for that," James said. "Then there's the leasing company."

"I looked at the company you're in favor of and I am in agreement," Jason said.

"Which brings up two investment issues," James said. "You said in general to let me do the investments. Some things you were interested in but otherwise, I handle it."

"Because I'm famous for what little investing I've done being in frozen iguana sticks," Jason said. "'Frozen iguana on a stick! Who couldn't like it? It's like a meat popsicle! It's gonna be big!' It was actually what worried me about Brandywine. Was I starting a frozen-iguana company?"

"Right," James said, chuckling. "But in this case, it's been a very successful, albeit new, investment strategy. The one credit you offered got your foot in the door on the unit discussions and you now have control of a fuel mine. However, and I agree I'd like to find a way to *kiss* an AI, about a third of those unit holders, as well as others who Jewel talked with, agreed to allow ARA to manage their units."

"A *million* new customers?" Jason said.

"And therein lies the issue," James said. "We just got a million and a *half* new unit customers. A few cash investment customers as well. They, in turn, are passing the word to others."

"You're going to have to hire," Jason said. "People will mostly talk with AIs, but you need customer service people..."

"Specialists in various fields," James said. "Economists that can actually understand this economy, there's no such thing as unit specialists, that's entirely new, but there are people and firms starting to specialize..."

"How much money do you need?" Jason said, realizing where he was going. "I'm going to have to have some more to set up companies around both the units and the facilities... And is this a loan?"

"No," James said. "And there's a conflict-of-interest issue. One I recognize. But right now, you and Tim are the deepest-pocket investors I know of on the station. We're willing to offer an unnamed partner position in the firm. We'll add in the value of the added customers as part of your equity. One hundred thousand credits would put you at twenty percent of the increased value of the firm."

"Twenty-five," Jason said automatically.

"I already had the negotiation discussion with John," James said. "As your financial manager. He started at fifteen. I started at twenty-five. I can, in fact, split my brain that way. But twenty is the right number."

Jason thought about the conflict of interest and shrugged.

"I'm good with twenty," Jason said. "It was an automatic thing."

"And a good automatic thing," James said. "Always negotiate."

"What about ongoing sales?" Jason asked. "Jewel, primarily, bringing in new blood?"

"Additional equity," James said. "There's a rate."

"Okay," Jason said.

"You're in agreement?"

"I'm in agreement," Jason said thoughtfully. "Jewel, as you're scrounging up additional proxies and so on..."

"I will now pitch Allen, Randall and unnamed partner even harder," Jewel said. "Especially now that my human has a vested interest."

"Thank you, Jewel," James said. "It's a good name."

"You're so sweet," Jewel replied.

"Yes," Jason said. "I agree to invest one hundred thousand credits in Allen, Randall and Associates as well as bringing in new customers for twenty percent of the equity plus a bonus on equity for new customers. Does that cover it?"

"Yes," James said.

"Signed, sealed and recorded," Jewel said. "Transfer approved?"

"Transfer approved," Jason said.

"There are a few more items," James said, a note of relief in his voice.

"Go," Jason said. He'd reached the beach and now was walking up and down, ignoring the translucent green waters and the palm trees swaying in the trade winds.

"Interstellar Fuel and Gas," James said. "I'm wincing a bit on this. They need a minimum of a quarter million credits to get up and going and be sufficiently capitalized."

"How much do they have so far?" Jason asked.

"Fifty thousand and change," James said.

"That's a bite," Jason said.

"I can negotiate for more equity," James said. "You'd be essentially a rescue investor."

"And piss off all the other investors," Jason replied. "No. I'll take the standard equity for the money. And, yes, two hundred thousand credits to Interstellar Fuel. I hate talking money."

"I'll try to get it over with quickly," James said. "But that was a big bite and I needed to consult you on it. You wanted to control the proxies. Does that mean you're going to choose the boards?"

"At least the chairmen," Jason said. "Not all men. I know you know a lot of people in business and finance. I know a lot of people, period. And in some cases, I may put people on the boards who aren't...traditional business and finance. Because what we're dealing with, here, isn't Earth business and finance. But all the chairmen will be people you won't object to. I think. If you do have objections, raise them."

"Okay," James said thoughtfully.

"We'll see if I have any clue what I'm doing there," Jason said. "The question will be payment for the board members and the chairmen especially. I have no clue what they get paid or even how..."

# CHAPTER 32 ❯❯❯❯❯❯❯❯❯❯

"EARTH TO JASON," ELISA SAID, WAVING HER HANDS IN FRONT of his face.

"Sorry, honey," Jason said, wiping his brow and frowning. The wind had died a bit with the afternoon and it was hot in the hut. "I don't think as well in the heat and I really need to think."

"I'll leave you alone...?" Elisa said.

"No, I don't want you to think..." Jason said hastily.

"Long phone call with James," Elisa said. "About money which you hate talking about. That's what's got you going. And what was the thing about Elvish?"

"I have not a clue," Jason said distantly. He'd shared pretty much everything *else* with her. As well hanged for a sheep. "I got a dividend payment. After talking with my accountant and James, I offered a credit per unit for a unit-unit trade for Twelve Bravo."

"The fuel mine," Elisa said. "I was concentrating on Twelve Alpha but I didn't get very far."

"The other choice was a suggestion to let me proxy the units," Jason said. "Apparently, the offer of a credit got people to talk. And Jewel ended up with enough proxy, and units, to call a vote."

"Fantastic," Elisa said, grinning. "The fuel situation isn't dire, yet, but we need at least one of the mines up and going. Even if you *are* a competitor."

"Not only that," Jason said, not wanting to leave anything out. "Jewel got over a million people to sign up as clients of Allen,

Randall. And they needed some investment money to swallow that particular pig. So, I'm now an unnamed and intending to be very silent partner in your dad's firm. Which has got to be, now, one of the biggest financial firms in the system."

"As the heiress, can I kiss you?" she asked, smiling.

"Here's the problem," Jason said, even ignoring where that might have led. "I've got a controlling interest in . . . a ten thousand pack, a fuel mine and a carbon converter. Not to mention one of the fastest growing companies in Pegasus, Brandywine, and a fast-growing financial firm. I'm on my way to a controlling interest, proxy or units, in a general factory and possibly a metals refinery."

"That does not sound like a problem . . . ?" Elisa said, taking his arm. "That sounds like the decision to come down to this tropical paradise with an apparently nice guy was a very good decision on my part."

"I have *no clue* what I'm doing!" Jason said, looking at her wide-eyed. "I just keep *doing* stuff and it *works*. When this gets up and going there will be *thousands* of people dependent on *my* decisions! *I've* got to choose people to run these things! I took the responsibility and now I'm *stuck* with it. A chairman for the unit holders! A board! I need to set up a company to run the ten grand! And I'm still not sure any of my plans to use it will *work*! What the heck do *I* know about *any* of that? Seriously, what the heck did I think I was *doing*?"

"You were trying to get rich?" Elisa said. "There's nothing wrong with that, Jason."

"No," Jason said. "That's the thing. I wasn't. I was . . . trying to get to the planet. Trying to get people fresh food. Trying to get the fuel mine going. Trying to get this cockamamie units system to work. Oh, and 'wouldn't it be cool to own a really big spaceship?' That too. Admittedly. I'm not now, never have been, somebody who thinks 'Hey, how do I get rich?'"

"Every business ever created *helps* people," Elisa said. "People complain about owners, about management. But every business creates jobs, creates opportunities, fulfills needs. If it doesn't fulfill a need, it goes out of business. It's what people don't get about 'evil business.' There's never been a successful business that didn't do something for *people*. Something people needed or at least wanted. Even social media was successful because it fulfilled a desire. Porn, God help me. It fulfills a need."

"I get that," Jason said. "But I've bitten off more than I can chew."

"First things first," Elisa said, taking his hand and pulling him to his feet. "To the waterfall!"

"That's lots of fun..." Jason said distractedly.

"You've said before you don't think well in heat," Elisa said. "Can you think better under the waterfall?"

"Yes," Jason admitted.

"Then to the waterfall with you," Elisa said. "I will start dinner. And I won't ask what you want. Come on...there's a good boy..."

After a while under the waterfall, Jason clambered into the cave dug behind it.

"Jewel, first things first," Jason said. "Call a units vote on Twelve Bravo, Spaceship Four, Carbon Charlie...What else do I have enough units or proxies in?"

"Factory Alpha and Metals Refinery Charlie," Jewel said. "But your control over Refinery Charlie is tenuous."

"What about Factory Alpha?" Jason asked.

"Solid lock," Jewel said. "Two percent unit ownership, twelve percent proxy for a total of fourteen percent control. Additional customers for Allen, Randall. Some of the proxy just came in on its own. Crocodile Dude is a known entity and I've leaned on that as well as Brandywine, which is starting to be a brand. Why people would give their proxy to Crocodile Dude, I have no idea. But the founder of Brandywine, people respond to that. 'He's somebody that knows what he's doing in this situation.'"

"Hah," Jason said. "If they only knew..."

"Refinery Charlie, on the other hand, has one person with five percent control and a number with ones and twos. They've been talking, just like Twelve Bravo, but can't get along very well. Before you ask, I'm concentrating everything, now, on Refinery Charlie. You've got eight percent total, so far, one percent unit ownership, the rest proxy. If they get their act together in the face of the interloper, you won't have a lock. I'm continuing to seek opportunities. We need at least a nominated chairman for each."

"Which is going to require lots of phone calls," Jason said. "Timing should be good on the station. Evening there. Let's start with Dr. Mark Green if he's available..."

Jason quickly learned to have Jewel send a précis of his resumé since arriving on Bellerophon to people before they talked. He'd... changed since arriving on Pegasus and most of the people he was calling knew him as a guy that had done a lot of things but never succeeded or even really tried.

One of the things he had to explain, repeatedly, was he wasn't trying to get rich. He was just trying to get the system going.

Several people who knew him well said much the same thing as Elisa: When you supply goods and services to large numbers of people, you tend to get rich.

He was supplying both. He was getting rich.

Some of the chosen chairmen didn't have units in the facilities. He did quick trades for them to have at least one unit, the only requirement.

About half turned down the offers. They had other things going, there were conflicts of interest.

But after a couple hours of phone calls, he had proposed chairmen for all the facilities where he had controlling proxy and ownership in units except Spaceship Four. *That* was going to be a long explanation for the unit chairman.

"Got it," Jason said. "We'll see who else sticks their nose in and suggests alternates. Now, try to get me in touch with Dr. Robert Barron. Tell him it's about a paid gig as a chairman for Spaceship Four Corporation."

About a minute later the call came in.

"Jason Graham," Barron said. "That's a name I haven't heard in forever."

"Hey, Doc," Jason said, grinning. "Marked Safe on Bellerophon."

Jason's acquaintance with Dr. Barron was odd. He'd originally met the PhD in physics, and some number former wife, while fighting a fire in California. You didn't have a lot of time to chat when trying to stop a forest fire from engulfing a neighborhood. But they had and had even kept up over the years as Jason had drifted from one job to the next and so had the good doctor. Difference being the doctor had drifted from academia to working in the IT industry to venture capital to the rocket industry to other venture capital and finally to working in administration in academia.

The oddest part of all of that resumé being that the good doctor was a pro-Second Amendment conservative and Republican.

Those terrible facts had finally caught up to him and he'd retired shortly before the Transfer.

"Pegasus System at the very least," Barron said. "Chairman for a hangar queen. Not sure that's top of my agenda but a paid gig would be nice. However...I'm in consultation with some people I've known over the years about setting up a university..."

"I'm pretty sure she won't be a hangar queen forever," Jason said. "I've got a controlling unit interest and can call a vote and more or less appoint a board given the apathy of most of the unit holders."

"Ten million units are difficult for even me to keep up with," Barron said. "But there may be a use. There was a recent and sudden change in Twelve Bravo..."

"Which I also had something to do with," Jason said. "But there's more potential uses for it than that..."

Jason explained his idea for dropping colonists, gathering equipment on the major peaks to be picked up and other potential uses.

"I'd rather have the chairmanship of Twelve Bravo," Barron said, raising an eyebrow.

"I hate to say I already asked someone else," Jason said, shrugging. "But I did. You're not the only scientist gone to the dark side I know. And the other one has more experience in the oil industry and specifically with natural gas. Which is as close as you get to a gas mine around a planet. Also, a doctorate in physics."

"The ways to use the ship are interesting ideas," Barron said thoughtfully. "I can see where people would be untrusting of being dropped, though it would be the most efficient manner. And also, yes, would work. But transfers on the peaks... Can you get the cargoes?"

"I can find the cargo," Jason said. "Brandywine can't fill it in decent time but we've also got agreements with colonists, one of the reasons to get more on the ground and we know most of the ship owners. Are you good on a thirty-five, sixty-five split? Your company, sixty-five to the investors, notably me. You'll be drawing a salary so you should make more out of it than I do. How much capital do you need to get started?"

That had been one drawdown in his available capital. He'd had to throw money at several problems.

"At least fifty thousand credits," Barron said. "I'll need to draw up a business proposal. I have one around but not for the ten grands... That's a standard split so, yes. I agree to take the position."

"One caveat," Jason said. "Sorry I forgot. Will you use a particular bank?"

"Your ex-wife's husband's?" Barron said, shaking his head. "I got that contact some time back. I suppose."

"I've got an existing relationship," Jason said. "We're going to have to take a loan on the fuel. At least at first. If we're using Derren Bank, we can get the loan."

"Point."

"The ten grands are going to be much more efficient," Jason said. "It'll work. Jewel, contact Gil and James's AIs, clear Dr. Barron for up to seventy-five k. And put him in touch with Richard and Mr. Manley. Lance's job is to get the best deal for the unit holders, of which I'm the primary holder. Your job is to get the best deal for the investors, of which I'm currently the only one. But I need you two to hash it out. There are other unit owners and they have to be kept in mind. Okay?"

"Okay," Dr. Barron said.

"Good talk?" Jason asked. "I've got other calls to make."

"Good talk," Barron said.

"See ya when I see ya," Jason said.

As Jason waded back in the creek, the tide had come in. There was phosphorescent plankton coming in on the tide and the water flashed green and blue around his calves. It was like tiny fireworks welcoming him back from the darkness of the cave.

When he reached the beach and headed for the hut, there was a light on and he smiled.

It was nice to come home to someone. If only it would *last* this time.

"I like that you brought good old-fashioned paper books," Elisa said, setting one down. "So... how'd it go?"

"There are now nominated chairmen for Twelve Bravo, Spaceship Four, Carbon Charlie and Factory Alpha," Jason said, sitting down at the table and rotating his neck. It had been a tense evening. He pulled on a shirt. It was his grandmother's strict rule: Always wear a shirt at the table.

"Refinery Charlie there's a chance of organized opposition

so until I can overwhelm it or set up negotiations, I'm waiting. It's not going to be up and going any time soon, anyway. Metal mining is another area that's got to be fixed somehow."

"You don't have to fix *everything*," Elisa said, getting up and coming over to rub his shoulders.

"At the very least it's going to have to wait till next quarter," Jason said. "And I still haven't figured out how to milk an aurochs. Or if you can farrow wild sows from embryos and still have them raise the piglets. It *should* be *possible...*"

"Breathe," Elisa said, rubbing harder. "Breathe. And eat. I kept it warm for you."

She opened the stasis case on the table to reveal a steamed land crab, already cracked open, rice and vegetables.

"If you eat something, you'll feel clearer," she said, sitting down across from him. "Eat and talk to me."

"You're not eating," Jason pointed out. But he pulled out the tail of the land crab and started cutting it. The coconut oil had already been put in a cup.

"I ate," Elisa said. "But I might take a *little* claw..." she added, snagging the smaller of the claws. "I looked at your list of chairmen. Good picks, but I didn't know any of them."

"I couldn't really nominate your dad," Jason said. "There are conflicts. There's a huge conflict with Four. But that's just going to have to exist. Nobody wants to touch the 'hangar queens.'"

"Which you don't think should be hangar queens," Elisa said, delicately nibbling land crab.

"Supply and demand," Jason said. "The price of lift is going up and up. There's more shipping than there is space. Which means we *need* the thousand and ten grands going. At least *some* of them. I finally talked to the chairman of the company that James thinks should run Twelve Bravo. I think he'll work but one of the issues is funding. So, I'm going to be majority investor in the company *and* the majority unit controller. Another conflict."

"You're the one with the money, Jason," Elisa said, smiling. "And conflicts like that happen. You'll do fine. You've got a good ethical approach."

"I'm throwing around credit like I used to buy guns," Jason said, sighing. He picked at the land crab. "Without consulting Gil, which I should have. This is good. So are the vegetables. You're a good cook. Which I've noted before."

"Wait till you get me some flour and spices," Elisa said. "My *real* strength is *baking.*"

"I've got, like, fifty pounds of flour," Jason said carefully. "It's in five-gallon buckets in stasis. It was a prepperish thing."

"Oh," Elisa said, grinning. "You just made my day. When we get back to the station, I'll cook you an angel food cake like you've never had!"

"Can't wait," Jason said, taking another bite. It was best hot and he didn't want it to get too cool. "My brain's still going a mile a minute. It's like a whirligig. I hate it when it does this. I can't keep to one thought."

"Jason," Elisa said. "You just took control, if not ownership, of about eight percent of the system economy, do you realize that?"

"What?" Jason said, choking on the bite. "*What?*"

"And as someone who was raised with this, you handled it extremely well," Elisa said gently. "You gave me access to the information. I checked on every one of the people you chose as chairman. Those were all top picks. I didn't even know you knew people at that level."

"I've just...met a lot of people over the years," Jason said, shrugging. "Some of them I met when we were both young. Years give experience and if that person is an up-and-comer, as I never was, they eventually become somebody. So, I know a few somebodies."

"You did all that sitting under a waterfall," Elisa said then chuckled. "Sorry, that's one of those stories that will be handed down in business classes of the future. You realize that you're going to be an example used in business classes someday, right?"

"I guess that's true," Jason said. "Eight percent?"

"About that," Elisa said. "And while you were at it, your money and Jewel's persuasion just boosted my dad's company to the largest financial company in the system. Got a call from my mom while you were gone. 'Be *very* nice to your boyfriend' was the gist."

"I don't want this to..." Jason said, trying to find the words.

Elisa came around to the front and straddled him, looking him in the eye.

"The AIs found the best boyfriend...hopefully more some-day...I could imagine," Elisa said, putting her arms on his shoulders. "Better. This? What's going on? It's just icing on the cake.

I've been around rich guys my entire life. They're mostly... not exactly dumb but not as smart as they think, stuck-up assholes who think they're God's gift to women. Harry? The guy I lost my virginity to? He thought women shouldn't hunt. It was a guy thing. He told me it wasn't ladylike."

"He'd better never meet Storm," Jason said. He shrugged. "I think it's awesome. Also, along with some of your other choices... I wonder about me."

"I've always had lousy taste in men," Elisa said and sighed. "But in your case, I wasn't the one who made the choice. And it was a great choice. Better than I could have imagined.

"I'm not into you for your money, Jason. That matters so little you can't believe it. I've always been around money. It's like a background hum you ignore.

"I'm into you for who you *are*. I came down here for the chance to get onto the planet, visit a tropical paradise and hopefully the guy was going to be okay. And I found the love of my life. I wonder if I'm good enough for you," she added, frowning.

"That's... nuts," Jason said. "I'm not good enough for *you*. You're from an upper-class family, gorgeous, smart, way more driven and active than I am. Teen Miss South Carolina, scholarship? I'm just a beaten up old... nobody that happened to stumble into a fortune I'll probably lose."

"That's one of the things I love about you," Elisa said, dimpling and interlacing her hands behind his neck. "You're humble and you've got your feet on the ground. But don't let anyone use that to steamroll you. Anybody tries, I'll kill 'em. I'm very momma bear about you, Jason Graham."

"Anybody tries to hurt you, I'll do worse than kill them," Jason said, putting his hands around her waist. "I know where the wild things are."

"What were we talking about?" Elisa asked.

"I've completely forgotten."

"Take off your shirt. I'm gonna give you one of my *special* massages..."

# CHAPTER 33 >>>>>>>>>

"WHAT'S THE PROBLEM?" CADE'S BRISK WALK SLOWED TO A SUD-den halt as he ran into Richter and Diaz, standing in front of the church.

Richter shrugged, his long face drooping into a baffled frown.

"I know what you know. Something about air circulation, and a maintenance guy would meet us here."

"We overpaid," Diaz muttered.

Cade wanted to ask, *What am I going to do about it?* He didn't, because he knew the answer. He was one of the deacons, so this was his responsibility. Even if he hadn't the faintest idea how to fix an air circulation problem aboard the space station. Even if he was getting into a ship and being dropped onto the planet the next day.

"The committee needs to find someone to replace me" was all he said.

"No one's going to replace you," Diaz said.

"What about down on the planet?" Richter asked. "Is there even a church down there?"

"There must be," Cade said, but he had no idea. If he were Mabel or Abby, he knew that at this point, he'd ask his AI for information on the subject. He refused to go down that road, though, and had trained Dummy not to volunteer, except in the case of an emergency.

"I bet there isn't," Richter said.

"Maybe Pastor Mickey will join me." Cade looked up and down the corridor, hoping to spy someone in a jumpsuit, or a maintenance robot. No such luck. "He preached that sermon about hardship, didn't he? Put his money where his mouth is, come down to the planet."

"And leave the rest of us high and dry?" Diaz snorted. "Come on, quit being so selfish."

"Nah," Richter said, "you gotta do it yourself. Bible and the plow."

"I think the Alfreds and the Hermans operate the plows," Cade said.

"Maybe," Richter conceded, "but they'll suck at the Bible. It's up to you, Cade. Lead the way. Show us how our pioneer ancestors did it."

"Why do you want me to start a church so much?" Cade narrowed his eyes.

"So I can join it when I land!" Richter clapped him on the back.

"False," Diaz said. "He thinks it would be funny."

"Also that," Richter admitted.

"Where is this guy?" Cade asked. "Any chance we can find the problem ourselves?"

"Anxious to pack?" Richter grinned.

"Yeah," Cade said, "as a matter of fact."

"Hold on," Diaz said. "Hey, Vato." Vato was the name of his AI. "Ask that guy about timing. How long do we have to wait?"

A moment later, Vato said, "He's telling me you should just go inside. He'll catch up."

"Great." Cade ran his fingers through his hair and led the way, stepping into the front door and forcing it to dilate open.

"Surprise!"

Cade heard the yell, but didn't understand it. Then the lights sprang on inside the church, and it took him a moment to process the fact that his fellow parishioners were standing around, grinning.

There was a cake on a wheeled flexmet cart.

Then they sang "For He's a Jolly Good Fellow."

Cade found that his ears were ringing, and time seemed to crawl.

"Ah, okay," he said incisively. And, "Thank you."

"Speech!" someone yelled.

Pastor Mickey stepped forward, and onto the corner of the low stage.

"Not you!" Klein shouted.

Mickey raised his hands to calm his parishioners. "Don't worry, I'll be handing the baton over to Cade in a minute. I just wanted to say two things, really quickly. The first is thanks. Cade, you weren't deacon of Mount Moriah Church of Pegasus very long, but you made a big difference."

Cade nodded. Someone was pressing a glass of purple alcohol into his hands. Mabel pressed forward through the crowd to his side. He saw Abby, smiling at him and for once not glued to her phone. Sam stood next to the piano, and Ana was with him.

"The second is a little irregular," Mickey continued, "but, in the circumstances, I thought we should move forward now. On the recommendation of the committee, and with the agreement of the other deacons, I have a candidate to replace Cade as deacon."

Unexpectedly, Mickey's words caught Cade up short. Getting replaced that fast, before he was even really gone, was . . . efficient. But it felt like he'd died, and his widow had shown up to the wake with a new husband.

"Excellent," he croaked. "Who do you have in mind?"

"I present for consideration to the gathered faithful," Pastor Mickey said, winding a little theater into his voice, "as deacon of Mount Moriah, replacing Cade Oldham . . . Sam Oldham."

The parishioners whispered.

Sam looked at Cade. Was his facial expression . . . embarrassed? Was he asking permission?

Cade smiled at his son.

"Some of you know that Sam has an upcoming court appearance," Mickey said. "You're expecting me now to tell you that I believe Sam is innocent. Well, he's not. He punched that fellow. On the other hand, the guy deserved it."

"Yes, he did!" Ana shouted.

"And also," Mickey continued, "the Apostle Paul was a jailbird. Peter was arrested and jailed. So was our Lord, for that matter. So who am I to judge?"

"If he has to sit in the hoosegow for a month," Richter called out, "we can pick up the slack."

"Maybe being a deacon will help him avoid the hoosegow entirely!" Parker suggested.

"He's taking over the carrot farm," Cade said. "I expect he can handle a little deaconing, too." He took a sip of his drink.

"All excellent testimonies," said Pastor Mickey. "So, all those who are willing to support Sam in this role, please say 'aye.'"

There followed a chorus of ayes.

"Any 'nays'?" Mickey asked.

There were not.

"Now, Cade," Mickey said, stepping down from the stage. "I think this is the moment for you to say a word or two."

Cade took another sip, handed his cup to Mabel, and climbed up onto the stage.

"First of all," he said, "this is not goodbye."

His neighbors cheered.

"Apparently, I'm going down to pick up an abandoned colonist pack," he continued. "It's in a lovely valley, which might have a few bears. And not very many colonists...yet. So, I hope some of you will join me real soon, and the rest of you...as soon as it makes sense for you to come."

There were nods and murmurs of approval.

"I guess it's no secret that I've struggled with the whole Transfer thing," Cade said. "I miss...home. I miss..." He struggled to find words. "I miss me. It was no accident, the man I had become. I worked hard to become him. And to have him evaporate, from one instant to the next..."

He stared at their faces. They were smiling, but uncertain.

Mabel climbed up onto the stage and stood beside him.

He took his drink back, smiled at his wife, and held her hand.

"You didn't evaporate," she said.

"So, I guess what I think I've learned is this. The journey I'm on is not quite the journey I thought I was on. The journey's a little longer than I planned. I have less control over it than I expected.

"Some parts of the journey, apparently, I get to repeat. I can't say I'm looking forward to losing my hair again. Flexmet can do a lot of things, but I don't think it will make a good toupee. And I never would have chosen to build a new farm. Cut it out of the wilderness, learn new hills and soils, get to know a totally different climate and different crops and animals. But I'm up to it. I accept it, I choose to do it.

"And I choose Mabel. Again. Always." He turned to look at

his wife; she had tears in her eyes. "I've been something of a jerk about all this. Sorry. I hope you'll forgive me."

She smiled and nodded.

"I'm still not coming down with you. Abby and I will come when the time is right."

"Fair enough," Cade agreed. "I'll go make the farm, and a nice house in a grove of trees, ready for you when you're ready for it. I choose you, Mabel. I got to grow old with you once, I guess I can only see it as a privilege that I get to grow old with you again."

Mabel kissed him, and he kissed her back.

"Pastor Mickey," Cade said, "they're going to need churches down on the planet. And I expect there's hardship there if you're looking for it."

Mickey slapped his knee and laughed.

"And the rest of you," Cade said, suddenly finding he was out of words. "Don't be strangers."

Jason looked at his phone to check the time. They were going to be late. They had a couple of connections to make to get to Atlanta from Charleston.

Each state had come with a name but the local quadrant names had been left up to humans. People had, by and large, concentrated on where they lived. To avoid the "Meet me at Sixteen Thirty at Sixteen Alpha," the decision was made, uniformly, to name sectors and quadrants. The referendums were quick choosing names.

Though there were probably more people from *outside* the metro Atlanta area in the Atlanta Quadrant than from *in* Atlanta, the name had been obvious since it was mostly people from that general region. Names like New Macon, New Cobb and others had lost to the mass acceptance.

There'd been an arm wrestle over Charleston versus Greenville but another quadrant had taken Greenville. So, it was back to Charleston. There was even a slight difference in the different areas. This corridor had . . . refined photos on the walls. There was a touch of nautical theme. There was a distinct lack of the sort of racy pictures that were to be found in Jason's corridor.

It was even jokingly called the Battery.

The door across the corridor dilated and Elisa stepped out and threw her arms in the air.

"Ta-da!"

It. Had. Been. Worth. The. Wait.

Elisa was dressed, barely, in a Little White Dress that was brilliantly set off by the dark tan she had acquired in the last week. It also left nothing to the imagination. It was the sort of dress that *anything* underneath would leave a line. There were no lines.

She'd put her hair up with a jeweled device shaped like a dragon. Jason suspected the jewels were real.

The platform high heels, diamond earrings and necklace completed the simple outfit.

"You clean up *nice*," she said, stroking the lapel of his evening jacket.

"It's new," Jason said. "New to me at least."

Besides getting some of his clothes refitted by Sheila, he'd been introduced to a tailor by John Randall. The tailor, who had been a high-end and very quietly conservative tailor on Beard's Street in London, had found an evening suit for sale and refitted it for him to London Standards along with some suits.

Suits. He was a suit. When did *that* happen?

"Time to meet the parents," Elisa said, taking his arm.

Jason glanced down the corridor and did a double take.

He'd spoken to John Randall over video, a business thing. So, he recognized the man in a well-fitted evening jacket.

John Randall didn't have the "Richard Look" as Jason tended to call it, the standard square-jawed, tall, common look of US finance. Instead, he was a burly guy, shoulders like axe handles, medium height but with such a solid figure he seemed taller. Brown hair but glacial blue eyes. He looked like a guy you didn't want to meet in an alleyway.

The young lady with him, though, was Elisa's twin. Just as short, just as gorgeous, wearing a Little Black Dress that was a mirror of Elisa's.

"Mom had to borrow my dress," Elisa said, sighing. "And she looks better in it than I do."

"Not a bit," Jason sort-of lied. Sort of because there was *no way* to tell the difference.

"Mister Randall," Jason said, shaking John's hand.

"Jason," Randall said. Firm grip. "I think John's okay."

"Just a tad . . . awkward," Jason said, turning to Mary Randall. "This is not intended the way it is usually intended, but . . ."

"We look like twins," Mary said, giggling. "Did she tell you I had to borrow the dress?"

"Which looks...magnificent on you, madame," Jason said. They'd even done the same hairstyle though Mary's hairpiece was a horse, not a dragon.

"Flattery will get you *everywhere*," Mary said, taking his other arm. "And if a little flirting gets *me* a trip to the tropics..."

"I shall endeavor to provide," Jason said uncomfortably.

"Stop trying to steal my boyfriend, Mother," Elisa said warningly.

"More like Jason's trying to steal my wife *as well as* my daughter," John said, but he was grinning. "There's greedy and there's greedy, Jason."

"Seriously," Jason said. "We've got ships going up and down on a regular basis with plenty of deadhead for passengers. The point is if you *and* Mary want to go on a tropical vacation, that can be arranged. Most business can be conducted remote these days..."

"We're not spending time in the islands with my parents," Elisa said. "That would be...there would be a major cramping of style."

"We're putting down additional harvest sites," Jason said quickly. "On entirely different islands. If there was any money to be made in tourism...But it's an open invitation. We have ships going back and forth. If you can remote the business for a week, please consider it."

"As long as my mother's not...flirting with my boyfriend," Elisa said, rolling her eyes. "This is so *weird*!"

"Does anyone else find this all just incredibly strange?" Jason asked.

"Every moment of every day," John said. "Every time I open my eyes. But then again, I open my eyes to you, dear."

"Oh, you're so sweet," Mary said, switching arms and leaning in.

"Oh, God," Elisa said, shaking her head. "You two have been like a couple of newlyweds. It's...wrong."

"We really should walk and talk," Jason said. "I'm sort of responsible for this venture."

"Edgar is in charge," Elisa said. "*You* can be fashionably late. But we probably should go. I want to meet...*her*."

"The ex," Mary said, eyes lighting up.

"*Monica*," Elisa whispered, her eyes narrowing.

"Changing the subject as quickly as possible...I don't have a subject change?"

"Elisa was quite hard to get ahold of down on the islands," Mary said, looking at her daughter. "We usually talk every day, frequently. But Elisa said you were both busy loading lobster pots. I'll load lobster pots for some time in the tropics. I've worked. But...*were* you...? Loading lobster pots, that is?"

"So, changing the subject quickly," Elisa said primly. "I...I don't have a subject change."

"I have been remiss," Mary said as they boarded an elevator. "Thank you for the care package. Coconut land crab is amazing!"

"Isn't it?" Elisa said. "Fun to catch, too. We also spent a lot of time catching land crab. I caught those with my own two hands! These hands!" she said, holding them up.

"I'm sure you were working very...hard, dear," Mary said, her eyes sparkling. "Certainly very...active."

"The island was really nice," Jason said, trying not to sigh.

"She showed me drone photos of the waterfall..." Mary said.

They made their way up the escalators, boarded the local slidewalk then took another cut to the express slidewalk. There they secured a four-set of alcove seats and settled in. They were taking a long run.

There were others on the slidewalk. Most leaned against the sides or stood out of the way but a guy walking down it stopped to examine the foursome.

"So...where's the party?" he asked.

"Opening of an event space," Jason said. "Over in Atlanta."

"Events?" the guy asked. "Like concerts?"

"More like weddings, business occasions, that sort of thing," Jason said.

"That's cool..." the guy said. "You look like you're doing okay..."

"We're not as full of credit as you might think," John said calmly.

"I'm not panhandling," the guy said sharply. "That's not my thing, sir. I was just wondering. You look like you're doing business. If you know of any IT jobs...?"

"Not really," Jason said, shaking his head sadly. "The AIs have put a lot of people like that out of work. Sorry. You any good at the outdoors. Serious hunter?"

"Yeah, not *that* serious," the guy said. "I mean, forget the bears, have you seen the..." He stopped and pointed at Jason. "Oh, my God, do I recognize you?"

"Does it involve a crocodile, a rifle and a crazy man?" Elisa asked.

"You're Crocodile Dude!" the guy said, laughing. "Oh, my God, can I just shake your hand? I can tell my friends I met Crocodile Dude! Quick selfie? Why were you using a *Garand*?"

"I like living on the edge," Jason said.

"Let me take it," John said, smiling.

A quick selfie and the guy waved and walked away. And immediately started texting.

"Crocodile Dude," Elisa said archly. "My boyfriend is, in fact, the Real and Original Crocodile Dude."

"That is going to haunt me the rest of my life," Jason said, opening his mouth and shaking his head. "I'm big in Japan?"

"To what does Crocodile Dude allude, pray tell?" Mary said.

"You're unaware that my boyfriend is the Real and Original Crocodile Dude?" Elisa said, archly. "A budding streaming influencer."

"I think he's a bit more than an *internet* influencer," Mary said, chuckling. "Uncle Fritz is wondering if your boyfriend might consider a small contribution to his campaign."

"Isn't he more or less a shoo-in?" Elisa asked. "Assuming the Constitution and charter are ratified."

"As flies are drawn to manure..." John said.

"Uncle Fritz?" Jason asked.

"Fritz Ling," John said. "Mary's first cousin. Formerly a state senator in Carolina who is state senator designate for Carolina Quadrant Sixteen Lima, now Charleston Quadrant."

"Oh," Jason said. "Do people need political contributions?"

"Yes," John said. "There's no cost for yard signs, obviously. But other advertising has costs. Billboards mostly for now. He did ask if I could get you a two-minute pitch. This is my asking if you'll take a two-minute pitch."

"Politicians asking for money," Jason said, shaking his head. "Money is a headache."

"Let me be your aspirin," Elisa said, patting his arm.

"That's a thought," Jason said, frowning. "Would you be in charge?"

"How?" Elisa asked.

"I'll talk to Gil," Jason said. "Jewel, make a note. If you've got money, you need to put it to certain things besides investing and personal. The two Ps are Philanthropy and Politics. I've never had that sort of money. Twenty-five dollars to some PAC or somebody who caught my eye on the news, sure. But not... direct contributions to a state senator. Okay, once, but I knew the guy and he lost. Why don't you handle it?"

"Because it's *your* money, Jason," Elisa said.

"Yeah, but keeping up with the business side is taking all my time," Jason said. "At least all the time I'm willing to devote. It'd be a paid gig. You could be my political and philanthropy consultant? I mean, you said you were planning on taking a political science degree."

"So, you want me to be your bag girl?" Elisa asked.

"I don't know how much a reasonable contribution might be," Jason said. "That's why I'm asking. For that matter... you mentioned your family has been around politics for a while..."

"My side more than John's," Mary said. "She didn't mention Senator Scott used to come over to the house?"

"Uncle Tim?" Jason said. "Yes, she mentioned it."

"She used to sit on his lap when she was young," Mary said, smiling.

"And he was not ever a creep," Elisa said. "Don't ask me about a few others."

"He doesn't come across as a creep," Jason said. "He's one of the very few politicians I've ever wanted to meet. If I'd known that, I'd have invited him to the dinner."

"You two didn't do much talking in the islands?" Mary asked.

"What part of working my fingers to the bone was unclear, Mother," Elisa said then sniffed. "To. The. Bone."

"We did talk quite a bit," Jason said hurriedly. "You just can't talk about everything even in two weeks."

"And... I sort of skipped that part," Elisa said, shrugging. "The sitting on his lap, not that I knew him. I was afraid it would make you uncomfortable."

"Might have," Jason admitted. "Still wish we'd invited him to tonight's dinner."

"There will be others," John said. "And he's not the type to take offense."

"The point to all this being," Jason said, "would you mind very much, darling, handling most of this? Yes, being the bag girl. I blew through most of the dividend doing investments but there's some left. Ask Gil what's appropriate for politics. And philanthropy."

"Of course, darling," Elisa said, putting his arm around her shoulders. "I'd be glad to be your bag girl and lobbyist as well as philanthropy manager. It'll give me a defined role, which would be nice."

"You need to get paid, too," Jason said.

"We'll discuss it after I talk to Gil," Elisa said. "But I just got the *first* contractor share for a bit less than two weeks in the islands. Holy cow, no wonder you're making money! So, I can wait a bit on getting paid."

"Getting back to Crocodile Dude?" Mary said.

"If you promise to not comment on the rifle, you can watch the video," Jason said. "I've had enough comments on that."

After watching the video, and laughing a good bit, John shook his head.

"I'd sort of heard about it," he said. "Hadn't watched the video. James said it was the largest thing you owned."

"Yes," Jason said. "Was. Still what I carry regularly when I go out."

"It's the Swiss Army knife of rounds," John said. "That pretty much proves it."

"I've told him that's not okay anymore," Elisa said. "No shooting dino-crocs from touching distance. No riding great white sharks. No petting megagrizzlies..."

"What if they're asleep in their den and I promise to be verrry quiet?" Jason asked.

"Are you really like that?" Mary asked.

"Little bit?" Jason said, holding up a couple of fingers. "I'd gotten out of it 'cause of how busted up I got in my twenties the last time. But...little bit?"

"Wildlands firefighter," Elisa said, gripping his arm. "Rodeo clown."

"Rodeo clown?" John said.

"You needed a job on the off-season from firefighting," Jason said. "'Cause fighting wildfires wasn't dangerous *enough*. And I figured how hard could it be...? So, there I was sort of in a starfish position, pinwheeling through the air with this very enraged bull I could see was tracking my trajectory and waiting for me to get back in range of his horns...It's one of those moments where time slows down, your life flashes in front of your eyes and you wonder how, exactly, you got yourself *in* this predicament..."

# CHAPTER 34 ⟩⟩⟩⟩⟩⟩⟩⟩⟩

"OH, WE MUST BE ALMOST THERE," ELISA SAID. "I CAN SMELL IT."

Brandywine's was about a half a block down the main drag in Atlanta, which was now called Peachtree Street, naturally, from the newly renamed Piedmont Park. The marquee read BRANDY-WINE'S EVENT CENTER and a smaller sign read under it read: PRIVATE PARTIES BY RESERVATION. The rest of the frontage, about a hundred feet, was covered by pictures and videos of wildlife on Bellerophon. Jason recognized some of the shots and about two thirds of the locations. There were shots from the Graham Islands of crayfish being unloaded by bots.

Jason thought about the first time he'd walked through the area, going to meet Tim. About half the businesses in the area were open, which was a pretty good percentage, and people were moving. It still felt a little deserted, but it was better than nothing but a couple of cops every few blocks and kids trying to find trouble to get into.

"Nice," Mary said, nodding agreeingly.

"My favorite client and my favorite partner in one place!"

James Allen was coming around the corner with a spectacular brunette on his arm.

"James," Jason said, shaking his hand and surreptitiously checking for a ring. Wedding ring. What was his wife's name...?

"Madeleine Allen," Madeleine said. "Maddy. Nice to finally meet you all in person."

"This is not a joking question," James said. "Mary...Elisa..." he asked, pointing back and forth. "Which is...?"

The two Randall women were standing next to each other so they looked at each other and without a word switched sides.

"Guess," Elisa said.

"Daughter," Madeleine said, pointing at Elisa.

"How'd you guess?" Mary said, smiling. "We really *don't* look that unalike these days."

"James told me you'd been visiting with Jason at one of the test sites," she said, wagging a finger at Elisa. "Heavy tan. Speaking of which," she added, looking at James. "When do *I* get to go to the tropics?"

"Have you *seen* the shipping rates?" James said.

"We've got deadhead heading to all over the planet, James," Jason said. "For passengers, anyway. It would probably be a few credits. Few as in ten or twenty to the pilot. And we can get a coffin of gear down easily enough. It's a rounding error. I made the same offer to John and Mary."

"He's just trying to find people to put to work," Mary said, winking.

"There's really not much to it," Jason said.

"Except loading lobster pots," Elisa said. "And baiting hooks for the lines. Hauling in these massive tuna by *hand*! I worked my fingers to the bone. To the *bone*. He's a slave driver!"

"What?" Madeleine asked, confused.

"My daughter was...strangely hard to get ahold of when she was in the Islands with Jason," Mary said, clearing her throat. "She alleges that it had to do with loading lobster pots."

"With *these hands*!" Elisa said, holding them up. She'd gotten her nails manicured at some point. "That's my story and I'm sticking to it."

"We probably should go in," Jason said. "I would rather face a thousand deaths..."

"You really don't like social events, do you?" Elisa said. "It's okay. Think of me as a great big social autocannon on your arm. We can take down the whole crowd."

"Okay," Jason said. "And thanks. Seriously."

"And besides," Elisa said. "I must confront...*her*."

"I'm going to stand back on that one," James said. "I've known Richard and Monica for years. That's going to be some serious sparks."

"I think I have to be there for it," Jason said, dilating the door. "Here we go ... Oh, I figured out how to make a flying motorcycle ... I patented a design if we can ever get the factories up and going ... Whoa!"

It was more people than he'd anticipated. For the "soft open" he'd been told to invite up to six "family and friends," a plus one and himself. Tim had been insistent that he had to attend. That was eight.

He wasn't sure how many people in the company had been told to invite eight, but there were more than two hundred people in the room. For a "soft opening" it was a heck of a crowd.

The reception area was paneled in light fumed oak with large flexscreen "pictures," complete with frames, that changed from one scene in Pegasus to another. Most were from Bellerophon but there were space scenes as well. Shots of the shell, inside the shell of the station with ships coming and going. Shots of the support stations.

The ceiling was birch around the perimeter then an inset curved lift that was gently lighted. There was a way to thinly slice wood and chemically treat it so that it was translucent. Mount some lights behind it and you had beautiful soft lighting. The center of the ceiling was mostly flexscreen. It showed a view of the sky over Bellerophon, as if the restaurant was on the planet and it was a skylight. Currently, it was set to night.

Small spotlights illuminated the numerous standing tables. Those had been the hardest to acquire.

"Oh, this is much nicer than I expected," Elisa said.

"I told you there were amazing things you can do with wood," Jason said. "Some call him ... Tim ... ?"

"Fashionably late," Tim said. He was acting as greeter and Debra was on his arm. She'd made her decision and was sticking with it.

"Debra," Jason said, and did the kissy at the cheek thing.

Introductions were had and Jason pointed. "Bar?" he asked.

"You're going to love the selections," Tim promised.

"Blue, green, red ..." John said, smiling.

"No, actually," Tim said, smiling back. "Brandywine's Finest Counterfeit."

"Brandywine's what?" John asked.

"You'll like it," Jason said.

They made their way to the bar but less than halfway Jason had to pause.

"Elisa, this is Sheila my niece," Jason said. "And her husband ... Reg ..."

"You remembered," Sheila said.

More introductions. Reg was looking uncomfortable in a sport coat that had been somewhat inexpertly retailored. Jason wondered how old he was. Sheila's dress was an older look, nineties at a guess, and he suspected it was something she'd kept around from high school or college the same way he'd kept his uniforms around.

They had a kid who was thirties. Steve, Sheila's father, was ten years older than Jason.

Guess was around fiftyish.

"We're making our way to the bar," Jason said. "Catch up in a bit?"

"Sure," Sheila said, grinning. "And thanks for getting the family jobs. Though you'd better not get my husband and sons killed."

"I will do my very best," Jason said, then nodded as they walked away.

"What's he do?" Mary asked.

"I'm ... not sure ... ?" Jason admitted. "Accounting? This whole thing is growing so fast I have a hard time keeping up ... I asked Jewel to ask Tim's AI to see if there was anything for them at the company when there *was* something ..."

"Reg is in shipping and receiving," Jewel interjected. "*Sheila* works in the accounting department."

"If it wasn't for Jewel ..." Elisa said. She looked around and smiled thinly. "Your banker is here."

"Bar first?" Jason asked. "I'm going to need alcohol for this."

They met a few other people crossing the room then finally reached the bar.

The bartender was a stocky fellow with broad shoulders and a ready grin.

"Ladies and gentlemen, welcome to Brandywine's, I am Nathan," Nathan said, smiling. "May I prepare for you a cocktail of Brandywine's Finest Counterfeit? What's your poison?"

"My poison is old scotch," John said, smiling. "But I'm not going to be greedy."

"Brandywine's Finest Counterfeit Old Highlands Scotch it is," Nathan said, reaching up and pulling down an unlabeled bottle.

He poured a couple of fingers into a highball and handed it over. "Try this, sir. I would treasure your thoughts."

John took a sip and then held up the glass to consider it.

"That tastes like ... very old scotch," John said. "Though not quite ... Not one I recognize ... ?"

"Brandywine's Finest Counterfeit is called that for a reason, good sir," Nathan said, nodding. "A blend of water, ethanol, artificial colors and flavor, strained through *Bellerophon's* best peat. As a connoisseur of fine alcohol, it really *does* taste like old scotch. The slight difference appears to be the peats of Bellerophon. So old *Bellerophon* scotch. I'm glad you enjoy it, sir. We aim to please. And for the ladies?"

"Cosmo?" Mary asked.

"Same," Elisa said then shrugged at the looks. "There's no drinking age. Yet."

"Twiiins ... ?" Nathan asked as he began making legerdemain with alcohol.

"I think I look rather good for a mother of a certain age," Mary said, dimpling. "I had to borrow a dress from my daughter."

"I, too, found myself adrift without wardrobe," Nathan said, handing over a stemmed glass. "I would favor your thoughts, madame. And for the miss ..."

"That ... tastes like a cosmo," Mary said, surprised. "With *good* vodka and triple sec."

"We aim to please," Nathan repeated, handing over Elisa's cosmo. "Sir?"

"Bourbon," Jason said. "Splash of branch water?"

"A fine bourbon of no particular vintage," Nathan said, pouring two fingers of brown liquid in a glass and putting in a splash of water from a flexmet bottle. "Spring water. Not, alas, limestone springs. But needs must."

"That's good," Jason said after a sip. "Do we sell this yet?"

"Brandywine does," Nathan said. "To bars in barrels. There's apparently supply chain issues with both bottles and labeling." He gestured at the unlabeled bottles. "But they intend to offer it for sale to the general public. We hope you enjoy it, sir."

"You didn't know about this?" Elisa asked.

"I knew we had some and were working on distribution and sales," Jason said sheepishly. "I've been ... really busy ... ?"

"Lobster pots?" Mary said, raising an eyebrow.

"He's the senior partner of Brandywine," Elisa said, dimpling.

"Oh," Nathan said, straightening. "I wasn't aware. I hope everything is to your satisfaction, sir!"

"Absolutely," Jason said. "This is great. I just haven't really been keeping up. I'm one of the field partners and I've been out of the station more than I've been on it."

"Seems to be going well," Nathan said, gesturing around the room. "The buzz sounds positive. It's...good to see this sort of thing again. Enjoy your evening."

"It is," Jason said, nodding. "Oh, there's Storm. A friendly face..."

"Storm," Jason said, doing the kissy face thing. Storm was on the arm of a short, stocky guy with brown hair and eyes. He had a "military" look and a wedding ring. She was wearing a purple cocktail dress that was cut practically to her navel. "This is Elisa Randall..."

"This is Emil," Storm said. "Friend from the Army."

"I was her NCOIC," Emil said, shaking their hands. "She said she needed a plus one. She's also friends with my wife."

"Okay," Jason said. "So, how is the marketing thing working out?"

"Great," Storm said. "I was on Tucker. Very cool guy in person as well as on camera."

"I heard that," Jason said. He hadn't heard that.

"You didn't see it?" Storm asked. "They asked about you... *Crocodile Dude.*"

"Aggh," Jason said.

"The One and *Original* Crocodile Dude," Elisa said, laughing. "Don't be embarrassed by it. Especially if it works for marketing."

"I'm big in Japan."

"It's part of our promo," Storm said quizzically. "'At Brandywine we go to extremes to bring you the best, fresh, natural foods.' He asked about it. I told Tucker you were the senior partner who set up the entire Brandywine program. 'Yeah. That's my boss.'"

"If it works for marketing," Jason said with a shrug.

"So, how'd you two meet?"

"Our AIs hooked us up," Elisa said.

"Mine keeps trying," Storm said, chuckling. "I think they're programmed to do it."

"Still can't find that one perfect guy?" Elisa asked. "Jason talked about you."

"Probably half the guys my AI has tried to hook me up with would be great," Storm said. "Like at least a third of the guys I've met in my life. Maybe I'm just not ready to settle down. Maybe I just want to live my own life."

"Don't feel pressured," Mary said. "You've got time. Whatever time you had before, it's been added to."

"Thanks," Storm said. "There's so much great hunting on this planet! I'm not sure it's wise to drag along a passel of kids. Might be fun, but not till things settle down a little."

"And great fishing," Elisa said. "And diving! And spearfishing! And..." She stopped and looked at John. "And loading lobster pots! With my bare hands!"

"Why were you loading lobster pots?" Storm asked. "Can't flexmet do that?"

"We'll definitely have to work on that process," Jason said sagely. "Sorry, Storm, gotta go. People to see."

"Have your people call my people," Storm said. "We'll do lunch."

"Oh, look, isn't that your banker, Richard?" Elisa said, pulling his arm in that direction. "We should say hi. Always good to keep your banker happy."

"We should," Jason said, dreading it.

"Hello," Elisa said to Richard, shaking his hand. "Elisa Randall. I think you know my father and mother, Mr. John and Mrs. Mary Randall. It's a pleasure to meet you, Mr. and Mrs. Derren."

She had her best Coastal Carolina accent screwed down and the charm-school thing dialed up to supernova.

"Pleasure to finally meet you, Mr. and Mrs. Derren," Mary said, Coastal Carolina also screwed down.

Jason suddenly had the image of a pair of older and younger lionesses flanking a particularly tasty looking gazelle.

"Nice to finally meet in person, Richard," John said, shaking Richard's hand.

"John," Richard said. "Things seem to be proceeding with the firm."

"Bit different than the Battery," John said, smiling. "But I'm enjoying the challenge."

"Jason," Richard said, shaking hands. "When this venture started, I was... unsure. Forgive me for doubting you."

"First, Richard, it's a banker's job to doubt people," Jason said. "You're also *my* banker and I'll remind you that you're holding *my* money. I *want* you to give a gimlet eye to loans."

"Gimlet eye?" Monica said raising an eyebrow. She had been introduced as well.

"It's a word that means narrowed or with a suspicious cast," Jason said, smiling awkwardly.

"I know what gimlet means, Jason," Monica said. "You don't always have to explain."

Right back into it.

"Where *did* you get that brooch," Elisa asked. "It's lovely."

"It was a gift," Monica said cautiously, then looked at Jason.

"Someone had good taste, then," Mary said, looking at Richard and smiling.

"It was not my gift," Richard said uncomfortably.

"How did you two meet?" Elisa asked. "Jason did mention that you'd been...an item. But he didn't mention how you met...?"

"We met through work," Richard said evenly.

"And how did you two meet?" Monica said tightly.

"Our AIs played matchmaker," Elisa said brightly. "I think they have a thing for each other as well. Jason was doing site testing on a remote tropical island, there was a spare seat and one thing led to another."

"I'm sure it did," Monica said, smiling thinly.

"Have you been to the Graham Islands?" Elisa said. "They're lovely. A perfect tropical paradise."

"Graham Islands?" Monica said edgily. "Really, Jason?"

"Hey," Jason said, shrugging. "It's the first thing of...dozens I've named after myself. I figured it was due. Great place. It's a blown-out caldera, so it's a series of more or less circular barrier islands with an inner island set that's protected from the waves. The Pallas waves have to be seen to be believed. Do you surf, Richard?"

"I do not, no," Richard said. "Did the island have a name?"

"Manu-aua-tapa-pua-atua-de'isle Island," Jason said quickly. He'd practiced.

"Did *you* name it that?" Richard asked.

"Yes," Jason said. "I'm hoping that someday it will be on a fifth-grade spelling bee or geography bee as the first landing spot in the Graham Islands."

"Ask him what it means," Elisa said, dimpling.

"Okay, I'll bite," John said. "What *does* it mean?"

"It's the name of a similar island from the French Carolinas on Earth," Jason said. "The area had been raided, invaded and fought over since the Polynesians colonized it. The first colonists, related to the Māori, saw an island and named it their name for a volcanic rock island, Manu. The next invaders named it the local name plus their generic name for island. Aua. The next invaders named it Manu-aua, the local name, plus their name for a volcanic island. Manu-aua-tapa..."

"So, the name of the island is in reality Island-Island-Island-Island..." Richard said shaking his head. "Droll."

"In seven different languages including French and English," Jason said. "Let some kid research *that* one."

"We need to circulate," Elisa said. "Jason's one of the guests of honor. Richard, Monica, it was a great pleasure to meet you. May God walk with you in all the dark places you may go."

"Thank you," Richard said.

"That went...better than expected," Jason said.

"What a...witch," Elisa said.

"Oh my, yes," Mary said. "And you handled it perfectly, my dear."

"Were you being...nice?" Jason asked.

"Except for the one dig about the tropics," Mary said. "As I said, perfectly."

"I don't get it," Jason said. "I was expecting lots more fireworks. Glad there weren't but..."

"Leave it to us, dear," Elisa said, patting him on the arm. "Just smile and tell stories and jokes. You did perfectly as well. Now, let's talk to others. I need to show my man off..."

"...so then I was asked to seek opportunities elsewhere," Jason said, shrugging and taking another sip of bourbon. Just a sip. "How was *I* to know that she was the granddaughter of the CEO? Somebody should *warn* a guy..."

"But somebody *did* warn you," Elisa said.

"I sort of heard it in passing?" Jason said, shaking his head and shrugging. "I was concentrating on something else at the time. And she really *was* bad at the job. Not a big deal. The company went out of business about a year later, anyway. Point of that being I've worked for wages most of my life. And often low wages."

Jason had rediscovered that if he mixed not really talking very much with telling stories, the whole "social" thing worked out better.

Turned out that it was both a "soft opening" for friends and family as well as a company party for most of the station-side employees as well as ground contractors who were on station. Which explained the number of people. Given Tim's notorious stinginess it was surprising he'd sprung for it.

But it seemed to be going well. The room was buzzing. People were meeting people.

People congregating for food was probably the oldest form of socialization. Paleolithic tribes would tend to gather food during the day and meet to eat what had been gathered in the evening. Sitting around the fire they would exchange experiences, the true gift of humanity. The ability to learn from other humans' stories, along with technologies as simple as the club, was how humans had once conquered an equally dangerous planet.

The tiny compartments people occupied barely allowed congregations of four, thus stripping humans of a basic need.

Opening an "event space" was probably one of the best things Brandywine had done for the overall society of Pegasus. Along with bringing real food to the station, of course.

Also, he was meeting people he didn't even know worked for the company. Worked for *him* for all practical purposes which was a bit boggling. The company had been growing fast while he'd been gallivanting around the planet. And more than a few were hanging around the mysterious "other founding partner."

He needed to visit the offices more. Some of the employees were sure he didn't exist.

"So how do *you* think it's going?" Jason asked, pointing at one of the hangers-on. Stan something. Maybe. Another issue of socialization was that he was terrible with names. "What's it like to work for Brandywine? Honest answer."

"I think it's a good place to work," Stan Maybe said. "It's nice to just have a job but it's... It's better than the last place I worked on Earth. The people are nicer."

"Less toxic?" Jason asked.

"Yes," Stan said, looking relieved.

"Good," Jason said. "I knew quite a few people who ran businesses but when I had the idea I went to Tim because the previous company he ran, people said nice things about it. And he was never a toxic boss to me. I hate toxic companies and didn't want to be partners in one."

"So . . ." The speaker was an apparently young woman with Stan Maybe but you could never tell how old anyone was. "I'm not with the company so . . . Tim runs the company. What do *you* do?"

"Cheryl," Stan said, laying a hand on her arm.

"I dunno," Jason admitted. "I don't know how a partnership is *supposed* to run. Tim's the steady hand on the tiller, the guy who says no when the stakes are too high. I'm the crazy guy who figures out the stuff that looks crazy until you get it functioning. But it takes Tim to actually figure out how to monetize it and keep it all going. Not my strength. Logistics. Okay. I can do that with the best of 'em. But there's a lot to running a business and Tim handles that. Makes sense to me and so far, it's working. If it ain't broke, don't fix it."

# CHAPTER 35 》》》》》》》》》

"GIL," JASON SAID, SHAKING HANDS WITH HIS ACCOUNTANT. Introductions were made.

"Been hunting yet?" Jason asked.

John, James and Gil had gravitated together along with their wives. Gil's wife, Charlene, was an Amazonian brunette with a Mediterranean look that had to be at least six feet *without* the six-inch platform heels. With them she overtopped every guy in the group. Gil clearly enjoyed mountain climbing as much as he enjoyed hunting.

"Any idea how much work your 'one credit for a unit swap' is giving me?" Gil said, poking his client in the chest. "I'm not just *your* accountant. We're the support firm for James and John's firm."

"So sorry to bring credits in," Jason said humorously.

"Oh, you can bring in *all* the work," Charlene said. "As a *partner* in the firm, let me thank you *most* profusely."

"You are most welcome," Jason said, tipping his glass to her. "But you should mostly thank Jewel. Either way, glad to get work for such a lovely lady."

"Flattery will get you everywhere," Charlene said, smiling. "But I'm the one who's supposed to be flattering the client! 'Clearly, sir, you're a handsome man and a powerful one as well...'" she added unctuously.

"Nice classical reference," Jason said, laughing. "Not compliments I've previously gotten."

"Classical reference?" Elisa said, just a touch thinly.

She was starting to do that forced float women did when they were getting jealous.

"Movie from ... God, the eighties I think?" Jason said, patting her on the arm. "A comedy. That was a joke. Do you hunt as well?" he asked, looking at Charlene.

"Gil's thing," Charlene said. "I'm a city gal. Though as soon as we've got the tidal wave under control, a trip to a tropical paradise wouldn't be remiss. It's been like tax season lately."

"I'll take a trip to the islands," Madeleine said. "The ball and chain can slave away in the office."

"We need to get you all to the surface," Jason said. "Balls and chains included. Someplace nice. There's more to life than spreadsheets."

"We're all swamped assimilating the mass of clients that dropped in our laps," James said, tipping his glass in Jason's direction. "Thank you, to be clear."

"Seconded," Madeleine said.

"How's that going?" Jason asked. He was sure that between James and John they'd be able to handle the work. But since Jason's name was attached to it and he had his own investment money in the firm ... He was a touch worried.

"Complex," John said, shaking his head and chuckling. "That's what we were just talking about."

"That's what he's been talking about nonstop," Mary said, patting his arm. "Which is fine. You need a sounding board."

"Not every unit holder who proxied gave us business," James said. "But a huge number did. Enough that, as I said, we needed some investment capital to hire more people. But then ... how do you manage it? Every client has ten million shares in ten million items."

"Which is the question," Jason said. "How *do* you? Consolidation?"

"Consolidating is not always the best choice," John answered. "Either for the client or the firm. Nor is it necessary given the number of clients we're handling at this point. What we've started doing we're calling distributed consolidation."

"Which means?" Jason asked.

"One thing that's become clear is that everything here is at least in threes," James said. "For redundancy and competition.

For example, there are three power plants in Carolina. Were you aware?"

"I was," Jason said.

"Nope," Elisa answered.

"So... we've got clients who have shares in all three power plants of *all* the states," John said. "The power plants are currently being run by the government..."

"Along with the power company, different entity..." James said.

"But the government is mandated to turn them over to private ownership," John continued. "Problem..."

"None of them have boards," Jason said.

"Right," Gil said, shaking his head.

"So, we were going to trade all of our clients' various power units for controlling interest in one plant in Carolina and the power company units," James said.

"And then the electrical and power guy we brought in ran into a snag," John continued.

"You can't control both a plant and the power company," Jason said. "Right?"

"That's the issue, yes," James said. "Antitrust, essentially. So, we found an Israeli firm that had convinced the Copt patriarch to allow unit trades. He'd been telling everyone that it wasn't time yet."

"One suspects that money changed hands," Charlene said.

"So now the Israelis and the Copts own Carolina Power Plant Bravo," John said. "And we're building a controlling interest in Carolina Power and Light as well as already *having* a controlling interest in Helenus Alpha."

"CPL has six million units attached," James said, shrugging. "As a financial firm, we have to have twelve percent to force a vote."

"We have about nine," John added.

It was clear the two had been working together long enough they could finish each other's sentences. Which was a good sign in Jason's opinion. He was just glad they were getting along.

"And then there's the issue of a managing firm," James said. "Right now, it's being handled more effectively than you'd hope by the state. But they have to turn it over within six months."

"I'm mostly taking unit management," John said.

"I'm working on finding the investment capital to set up leasing companies," James added.

"And our firm is working on the accounting," Charlene said.

"Which is why getting to the ground any time soon for any of us is probably a nonstarter."

"Ouch," Jason said. "I'm sorry to throw so much on you. Wasn't my intent. Better you than me."

"It's a headache," James said, grinning and taking a drink. "But it's a good headache. We're looking at another merger. It's a small firm, not many clients, but it's got an excellent unit management architecture. That should help."

"And many of the units are capital generating already," John added. "People are paying for power. People are paying for transit. Capital is flowing. The economy's getting into gear."

"Are you with Brandywine?" Charlene asked Elisa.

"I'm..." she said, looking at Jason. "Right now, I'm going to go with girlfriend. I helped with some harvest but I was just along for the ride."

"Were you hunting?" Charlene asked.

"Fishing...?" Elisa said, grinning. "The biggest predators on the islands were land crabs. But we did some spearfishing. I speared a couple of *huge* yellowfin!"

"I mostly went down to check out the crayfish situation," Jason said. "But there was a yellowfin run going through so we figured out catch methods on those as well. So, now we're shipping yellowfin tuna, crayfish and some, not many, land crabs. Land crabs taste amazing but they don't reproduce fast so they're more of a treat than a major protein source. At least, I hope that's how its viewed."

"We *all* got some in care packages," Mary said, dimpling.

"It is incredibly good," Charlene said, sighing. "Just having real food again is nice."

"Which we really need to get to everyone," Jason said, frowning. "We need to get the flow up and the costs down..."

"You're doing so, dear," Elisa said, patting his arm. "Rome wasn't built in a day."

"I'm surprised things have gone *this* well," Mary said. "Things have stood up *incredibly* fast if you think about it. We shouldn't be this far along. These are very big operations and yet people are just finding a way," she added with a furrowed brow.

"People just leaned in," Jason said, shrugging. "What else are they going to do?"

"We had the national divorce everyone had started talking about," Mary said. "Right?"

"Yes."

"What does our liberal friends' Constitution look like?" Mary said. "How are they managing things?"

"Liberals aren't all nimrods," Madeleine said. "I used to be a liberal. They should be handling it fine."

"Really?" Mary asked archly. "This station, in terms of the laws that are currently in force, the Constitution, the leadership, even the news as it's standing up, is fairly libertarian. Arguably to the right of many of the inhabitants. Our Robot Benefactors set it up that way.

"How did they set things up in whatever system has the other half of the United States? We have more Eastern Europeans than Western. Think about the European contingent in Liberal Utopia. Do you really think that modern progressives are going to allow some . . . *nobody* to just drop down to the planet and start killing things left and right? Just because it's food? How dare you! Don't you care about the environment? Those are rare and endangered species! Meat is murder! How *dare* you?"

"Let them eat print food," Charlene said.

"Exactly," Mary replied. "But if you don't think that people who have power are eating land crab, you're wrong."

"Oh, no, they will," Elisa said. "Let's see . . . It's parliamentary."

"Given," Gil said.

"And heavily bureaucratic," Elisa added. "The parliament probably doesn't have any *real* power . . ."

"That will all be with the ministries," Mary said. "As in the EU. Which is a much better system than the United States! The people who know how things are supposed to run are in charge! How could anything go wrong?!"

"I take it you're joking," Gil said, brow furrowing.

"You *don't* want to hear my wife really get going on the subject of the EU," John said.

"Yes, I was joking," Mary said. "I suspect it's a dystopia of huge magnitude. The people with power will want to get real food. So will everyone else but the people with power are going to get it. How is the question I haven't figured out."

"Scientific research," Jason said. "Teams doing 'studies' of the species on the planet. Samples have to be returned. Animals have to have gut checks. You can't just waste it after that."

"Really?" Elisa said.

"Redfish were nearly wiped out at one point in Florida," Jason said. "I happened to be spending some of my college money going to a university down there at the time and was interested in marine biology. One of the departments had a grant to study redfish recovery.

"Florida fish and game had put a strict limit in place on redfish but you had to catch some from time to time to see how the species was recovering. And to do that you had to do gut checks.

"You would just catch them with a fishing rod. There's an algorithm for it to see how the species is doing. We nearly got busted by fish and game for catching a whole mess of them. We hit a school and were reeling them in one after the other, all undersized, way over the limit of one per day per person.

"First a fish and game helo flew over. Then a boat showed up. They were all under size and we had ten times the limit. But we were doing *research*. They looked at our grant papers and left. After we'd done the gut checks, we had a really nice fish fry. That's how the bureaucracy will get around limiting trips to the surface but ensuring that *they* get fed. You want grants to study the ecology? We get the good cuts of meat."

"Take nothing but memories," Mary said liltingly. "Leave nothing but footprints. Except for the bureaucrats and politicians, who'll be eating land crab every night."

"You really think so?" Madeleine said.

"Never underestimate the hypocrisy of a progressive," Mary said.

"It's a pretty good guess," Gil said, nodding. "I've been thinking the same thing and wondering about how the important people get away with going hunting. You'd be surprised how many antigun liberals were hunters. Was on safari next to a rabidly antigun actor one time. Feedback I got was that he was petulant he couldn't just shoot *anything*, think breeding female lions for God's sake, and was treating everyone like dung."

"How do the important people go hunting?" Jason said. "They volunteer to help in field studies. Noblesse oblige. It's volunteer work! We're volunteering our time! What could be more noble than volunteer work? And they're very careful to hide their trophies. Only people in the know."

"Where would they have room?" Madeleine said. "James, I promised not to say this again, but..."

"You really want out of the compartment," James finished. "She really wants out of the compartment."

"I can't imagine George Soros staying in one of those compartments," Mary said.

"I'm not sure what our robot overlords would do about someone like Soros," Jason said, thoughtfully.

"Toss him in a woodchipper?" Elisa said.

"Marry me," Jason replied. "But I'm sure that there are varieties of housing in our liberal friends' system. From everyone according to their abilities, to everyone according to their needs. And important people have needs."

"So, everyone doesn't get exactly the same treatment?" Madeleine asked.

"What Marxist system has *ever* been equal?" Elisa said. "Some pigs are more equal than others."

"Speaking of getting out of the compartment, though," Jason said. "I think there's a way."

"How?" Madeleine asked, her eyes lighting up. "Tell me there's a way to have a house."

"There's a way to have a house," Elisa said. "Sort of. An eighteen hundreds house with some modern amenities. All of them eventually."

"How?" Madeleine repeated.

"There's one way on the station and a different way on the ground," Jason said. "My bots made me a house in a day on the ground. Nice one if small. The way on the station is you get a larger compartment and simply build it. Mostly flexmet but you can furnish it with furnishings from storage."

"Can we afford a large compartment?" Madeleine asked. "I'm not pressing, but..."

"I'll look at the costs," James said. "We really do need somewhere larger. We're used to entertaining for business. That's..."

"Impossible in the compartments," Jason said. "Which is what this space was designed for."

"So where did all the wood come from?" Madeleine asked. "It's a bit darker than I'd go for but... it's lovely."

"Withywindle Fine Woods and Furnishings," Jason said.

"Withywindle?" Elisa said. "You are such a lovely geek."

"I don't get it," Charlene said.

"It's another Tolkien reference," Elisa replied.

"That's one of the small companies you put credits into," James said. "They did all this?"

"With mostly flexmet and a few electric motors we picked up on the net," Jason said. "Thing is, you can build nearly a complete wooden house the same way. All the stuff precut and ready to be fitted together, packed in some containers to drop to the ground. At that point it's put together by...crafty robots?"

"That...wouldn't be something with immediate relevance," Gil said carefully. "But it has some long-term interest."

"Speak for yourself," Madeleine said. "I'll put up with bears for a decent house. Big house?"

"What we're looking at is more like a mansion," Elisa said. "On an estate."

"How much?" James asked.

"Less than you'd think," Jason said. "Haven't priced out the current house but it's not going to be huge."

"Nails," John said practically.

"Pegs," Jason said. "With robotic building it's cheaper than you'd think. But there are issues."

"Such as?" Gil asked.

"No forced air heat or cooling," Elisa said, ticking the issues off on her fingernails. "Currently. Some window air conditioners are available, but not many. Very little glass is currently available. Why people *would* have windows sitting around in their houses is unclear but most didn't. Hinges. Bathtubs. Plumbing. Stoves. Ovens. Washer and dryer...Some of those are for sale. Those came along as household goods. But for the long term, they'll have to be produced. Hinges are a big thing. Fittings in general that aren't wood."

"Stone?" Madeleine asked. "Tile?"

"Tile can be made," Jason said. "Once the factories are up and going. Stone? There's stone everywhere as long as you don't ask for marble."

"Concrete," John said. "You'll need some."

"And my clever boyfriend has figured that out," Elisa said proudly.

"Brandywine has found sources of cement," Jason said. "Both volcanic and Portland style. Sand is readily available. The real issue I thought was going to be lime."

"What?" Madeleine said, frowning.

"Concrete and mortar are made from three materials: cement, sand and lime," Jason said. "All three derive from types of rock. But lime was made, on Earth, by heating up limestone."

"And there are no limestone formations on Bellerophon," Gil said. "It's too young."

"I'm going to let that just lie there," Madeleine said. "Because otherwise I think I'd have to learn *too* much about limestone..."

"What you have to know is it's composed of calcium carbonate," Jason said. "How it was primarily made, on Earth, over billions of years, not really important. But it's the major material of coral reefs as well as clam and oyster shells. With me so far? Can you say calcium carbonate?"

"Calcium carbonate," Madeleine said, frowning. "Science, not my strongest subject."

"Stay with me," Jason said. "Calcium carbonate is a molecule made from calcium, obviously, and...carbon. Anticipating our need for concrete, guess where calcium carbonate is made?"

"A carbon converter?" Gil asked. "I wasn't aware of that."

"The sole and only source of lime is carbon converters," Jason said. "Which, note, means they also need a source of calcium."

"Which comes from where?" John asked.

"Bones," Elisa said. "Any source, really. Although I *did* know how limestone was made. More or less."

"There's also an alternative to concrete based on, essentially, a glue," Jason said, shrugging. "Also made in carbon converters."

"Those are going to be big," John said.

"Very. Another big issue is landscaping. I've figured out ways around the issue of rosebushes. But the lawn..."

"No grass seed," James said.

"Very little," Jason said. "Just what our Robot Benefactors sent along as starter. I foresee a big sod business at some point in the future. The question will be: When? Exactly. Get into sod too early and you go...bust. Dad joke. Sorry. Too late and you face too much competition. Grass farms will be big at some point."

"Everybody in business is asking when there are going to be golf courses" James said. "Speaking of using large compartments, they've already set up a driving range. But everybody wants golf courses."

"A country club," Madeleine said, shaking her fists. "Tennis courts."

430                    *John Ringo with James Aidee*

"Don't worry," James said, patting her hand. "We'll found one."

"Which, if I can get around the issues of the house, will be easy enough," Jason said. "It's just a big house with a very big lawn."

"A city club wouldn't be remiss," Gil said, gesturing around. "Something like this would work well."

"Talk to Mr. Kranhouse at Withywindle," Jason said. "We can do all sorts of millwork, finishing, furniture, trim..."

"Country club," Madeleine pouted. "I know how I sound but...I look twenty again! My tennis outfits still fit. I want to look twenty again on a tennis court under the sun!"

"She was a professional tennis player," James said. "We met playing tennis. Practically her first utterance in Pegasus was 'Tell me there are tennis courts!'"

"You won't be able to just jump in the Town and Country," Jason said. "Three-hour ride to the planet."

"Which was the sort of thing it was when country clubs were first founded," James pointed out. "It was at *least* three hours by carriage."

"You can build a tennis court in a large compartment," Charlene said.

"Under the sunshine," Madeleine replied. "It's...important. To me, anyway. Sorry. I am sick to *death* of this station. Malls are fine. I never wanted to *live* in one."

"As soon as we have the house set up, you can come visit," Elisa said soothingly. "It'll be a lot like a country club."

"I haven't played tennis in forever," Jason said. "But...I can certainly find some clay..."

"I'll put up with giant bears," Madeleine said. "I'll nail them right on the nose with a tennis ball!"

"Speaking of which," Gil said. "I'm sorry to hear you lost someone. I heard it was a bear attack."

"It's okay," Jason said. "We found what was left. It may sound hard-hearted, but even back on Earth we'd probably avoid liability and..." He shrugged. "That one was out of our hands. It was less a bear attack than a bearish Darwin Award."

"What happened?" Elisa said. "You didn't mention losing somebody."

Jason looked around and obviously everyone wanted to know.

"So...first of all, you figure he's got background since he worked for decades for Florida Fish and Game."

"Sounds like he would tend to know his way around," James said reasonably.

"Did fine in training, no signs of psychosis or disconnect with reality. Then when he was on station, on his own time, checked out for personal hunting, he decides to go after a megagrizzly with a compound bow."

"Oh, you have *got* to be kidding me," Madeleine said, hand over her mouth.

"This, to say the least, did not work out well," Jason said. "He was filming it with a headcam. He'd done a sneak to within about thirty meters of this peacefully feeding adult male megagrizzly. Lined up. Took the shot. Most powerful compound bow on the market. Solid hit, right behind the shoulder.

"And the bear sort of looks at where this...something has bitten it, looks in that direction. Spots our young brave as he is lining up a second shot, as if *that's* going to do any good. Then there's all the screaming and running and then the louder screaming and the Oh, Lord, let the pain end! He had the AI specifically locked out. We weren't even *informed* of this until the AI determined he was deceased and his orders were inoperative."

"Could you recover..." Elisa said.

"We did," Jason said. "It was...grisly. It was the first and only time we've dealt with planetary wildlife protection and they wanted the bear put down for being a human killer. I told them it wasn't a human killer: It was a moron killer and if they wanted to go track it down, they could feel free. Which they did. Probably needed to be put down for the arrow if nothing else."

"Some people just..." Gil said, then shrugged.

"There's hunting dangerous game," John said. "Then there's suicide by testosterone."

"Wasn't what it was," Jason said. "Seemed like a totally reasonable and sane guy. But he left a message saying he was going to do it or die trying."

"Why?" Charlene asked. "That sounds like suicide by bruin."

"Well..." Jason said. "His name was Christopher Robin. According to his final message: He just hated bears."

"Oh, that's terrible," Mary said, shaking her head and trying not to laugh.

"It's also true," Jason said. "Sometimes life just hands you the punchline."

# CHAPTER 36 ⟩⟩⟩⟩⟩⟩⟩⟩⟩

"MADELEINE WAS A TRIP," ELISA SAID, SETTLING ON THE FLEX-couch in Jason's compartment and propping up her feet. "I was surprised she didn't get into who is getting the most maintenance from their beau while we were powdering our noses."

The reception had eventually turned into dinner, which had been a rousing success. Everybody was happy to both have something to celebrate, Brandywine's successful first quarter, as well as some*where*. Eight courses of "A Taste of Bellerophon" and some after dinner awards to notable Brandywine employees and Jason was glad to make his way back to his compartment. It had been fun but he was peopled out.

Elisa had made the excuse of "a late evening stroll" to go to his, much closer, compartment.

It was cramped with two but Jason could handle that sort of cramping.

"I cut her some slack," Jason said, pulling off his dinner jacket and undoing the bowtie. He'd learned to tie one so far back he could barely remember when. "I know I was nuts to get to the planet and remember how you felt about it? You were ready to jump on a bird to go to visit some guy you barely knew."

"You haven't dealt most of your life with that type of trophy wife," Elisa said, sliding to her feet and tapping his hands away. "Oh, no, no, no . . . *I* get to unwrap you."

"Unwrap?" Jason said, smiling and reaching behind her for the zipper on the barely there dress.

"Stop," Elisa said, elbowing his arm away and continuing to unbutton his shirt. "You've got a lot more to unwrap. Anticipation. She's the lady at the country club who's into everybody's business, taking charge of everything whether anyone wants her to or not and generally being a pain in the butt. Oh, and constantly critiquing your tennis game behind your back. 'She has a *terrible* backswing. Who taught her, Hellen Keller?'"

"Okay," Jason said, chuckling and trying to reach around the back again.

"Stop," Elisa said. "Or I'll grab my stuff and walk home."

"Long walk," Jason pointed out.

"There's a slidewalk," Elisa said. "And very little crime. And I'm carrying."

She finished unbuttoning his shirt and frowned at his cufflinks.

"I'll get the cufflinks," Jason said.

"Could you...we? Really build a townhouse?" Elisa asked.

"We," Jason said, frowning and undoing his cuffs. "But the more I think about it, the less I like it. We'd have to put it in the warehouse district. That's...not a great area. It's not even considered residential. Gentrification is all well and good but I think we'll have to get a house on the surface."

"I suppose I can wait," Elisa said, unbuckling his belt. "Now to unwrap my man all the way."

"I may not even *bother* to unwrap *you*," Jason said. "I'm pretty sure with that outfit, it won't be necessary..."

"Jewel," Jason said. "Are there any zoning restrictions at this time? Could you put a townhome anywhere that there's room?"

Elisa, bless her, had had the forethought to send over a case. It was locked to her so he couldn't open it but turned out to contain a "day outfit" so she didn't have to do the "walk of shame" all the way back to Charleston.

After Elisa had left, Jason had sat down to do some actual work. There was no real need to go into the office: He could do it all in his compartment.

But after a while of looking at financial reports, his eyes were starting to bleed. The gist was they were making money and their main expense was shipping. Along the way, an idea had formed.

"There are no zoning restrictions at this time," Jewel said.

"See if you can get...name...The Old House guy."

"Paul Colegrove," Jewel said.

"That," Jason said. "Him."

Jason went back to reading reports until there was a chime from Jewel.

"Mr. Colegrove is available," Jewel said.

"Put him through," Jason replied, looking up at the screen. "Mr. Colegrove!"

"Mr. Graham," Paul replied. "My first and, so far, only customer. How may I be of service?"

"Getting some of the stuff for the house is going to take a while," Jason said.

"Most of the pieces, absent wood, require one of the factories to get going," Colegrove said. "That's the holdup. And then it's weather dependent. And you still haven't chosen a location which is a big part of the weather question."

"Right," Jason said, frowning. "But what about a *townhome*?"

"Where would you put a townhome?" Colegrove asked.

"There are no zoning restrictions," Jason said. "I was talking last night at a . . . get-together."

He explained about Brandywine's.

"And it occurred to me that just as we built Brandywine's in a space, you could build the interior of a home into a commercial space," Jason said. "It would give more room than one of these compartments."

"That's . . . a thought," Colegrove said, nodding. "Most of the components that are missing . . ."

"You'd have to bow to some use of flexmet," Jason said. "Artificial windows. Flexscreens. Flexmet doors . . ."

"That's acceptable," Colegrove said. "I've talked with Mr. Kranhouse at Withywindle already. Mind if I go take a look at Brandywine's?"

"I can get you in," Jason said. "But here's the thing: Don't tell Elisa."

"Oh?" Colegrove said carefully.

"I want it to be a surprise," Jason said. "When we were talking about it last night, I sort of dismissed the idea. 'It would have to be in an industrial area. There's security issues.' Then I was looking at one of these freaking reports and realized that there's *no zoning* currently."

"None?" Colegrove asked.

"None," Jason said. "Jewel, check me on this: You could put a townhome right on any of the main transfer areas, right? Peachtree, US 1, whatever?"

"That's correct," Jewel replied. "There are no rules against it."

"Those are industrial areas," Jason said. "Commercial at least. I wouldn't want it on a main drag but there are areas that are primarily designed for office space and shopping that are on side streets. Those would be fine. Could you, would you, design something like that?"

"Gladly," Colegrove said musingly. "I've always enjoyed my job and don't particularly want to find another."

"Jewel," Jason said.

"Where?" Jewel asked. "Credit for unit trade?"

"The same," Jason said. "But not just one. Try to get unit control, as much as possible, of every compartment on, say, Street Fourteen Twenty Delta? Sixteen thousand block. That general area."

It was not far from his current compartment and close enough to main areas. The station had remarkably low crime overall but there was some. Closer to main areas, there was less.

"There's starting to be people with money on the station," Jason said. "I know a few of them. If we can get one townhome set up, have some dinners and open houses..."

"Others will do the same," Colegrove said.

"If it's spiffy," Jason said. "And I have no clue what *spiffy* means. Not furnished. I'll let Elisa handle that. But... you've been talking to her about what she wants in a house. Can you sort of figure out how she'd like a townhome set up?"

"I can be sneaky," Colegrove said. "Slip the questions in. Most of the interior will be broadly similar to the... country home?"

"I'm getting to be the real rich guy," Jason said. "Town and country. One last question. Two. How quick can you get me an estimate and how quick can you put it together?"

"Depends on what *it* is," Colegrove said. "I'll talk to Mr. Kranhouse at Withywindle and look at Brandywine's. You want mostly wood?"

"It's going to have to be mostly wood and flex," Jason said. "That's what's available."

"Counters are the issue. Certain flooring and bathroom fixtures. There's versions of flexmet available but..." The architect grimaced at the thought of flexmet counters. "Do you know a way to get stone? I've been looking everywhere and it's just not available."

"Let me talk to Tim," Jason said. "There's ways to get stone. As long as you don't want marble."

"Someone was trying to explain to me why there's no marble," Colegrove said. "There's no marble nor will there be is what I got out of it."

"There's no marble nor limestone," Jason said. "Nor will there be. There's sandstone and every form of igneous. Granite, basalt, that sort of thing."

"Those are useable," Colegrove said. "But...it will need to be cut..."

"Tell me what kind of stone you want that's not marble or limestone," Jason said. "Let me figure out how to get it. It might take a trip to the planet to set up a quarry and milling facility. But I do those frequently."

"Can you get soapstone?" Colegrove asked.

"Already found some but we used it up," Jason said. "Jewel? How we doing on soapstone deposits?"

"Two large outcrops found so far by teams," Jewel said. "One in Chindia, one in Kush. No teams currently on-site at either one. So far, we've also found outcrops, total volume unknown, of alabaster and onyx. Both of those are in various colors. Lots of alabaster. Various other stones that are occasionally or regularly used in architecture. The problem is that all of them are surface weathered appearance. We really don't know what the stone is like or how large the deposit is."

"I'll take care of that," Jason said. "Try to figure out which are the best architecturally. Since there's no immediate large market, I'd like to limit the number of quarries I have to set up for... well, just a house. For now."

"Understood," Colegrove said. "Searching the world for the perfect type of onyx for a bathtub probably isn't a profitable endeavor."

"Not now," Jason said. "But it could be. And with that I need to convince my partner of that."

"Stone is pretty far away from food, Jason," Tim said dubiously.

"We've got the ground-level information," Jason said. "One of the reasons I set up the algorithm that anything of potential financial worth was not put in the public database. And while it's not going to be a major market immediately, it's about staying out in front. Do you want out of the compartment?"

Brandywine had found more than stone along the way. The planet was entirely untouched by mining. There were literally areas with streams of solid gold and copper as well as many other ores.

The planet was generally off-limits for mining, which was better done in space. But quarrying was different. Certain types of minerals and stones were *only* found on planets.

Albeit, you might find alabaster on any of the rocky planets. It had been found on Mars, pre-Transfer.

"Every day," Tim said. "But . . . stone?"

"The interior would be mostly wood," Jason said. "Plaster from the gypsum deposit we found. But what about the bathroom and kitchen? There's ways to do wood for that. But it makes more sense to use stone or tile. Tile is going to have to wait until the factories are online and have materials. So, stone. We've got the locations of several different types. We just need samples from below the weathered surface."

"A stone company?" Tim said.

"You want a townhouse?" Jason said. "Get out of the compartment?"

"Into a store," Tim said.

"They turned warehouses into very expensive condos in SoHo," Jason said.

"Point," Tim admitted.

"I'm in the process of securing a block of Fourteen Twenty Delta. Want to be neighbors? I know a good architect."

"It's worth a thought," Tim said then sighed. "It would be nice to get out of the compartment. You doing the drop?"

"I'm thinking of just sending bots," Jason said. "And a six pack. It's getting the six pack that I need Brandywine. Also, I think it's a good potential opportunity down the road and so I'm bringing it to my partner. We put a project manager on it, set up a subsidiary . . . The business stuff."

"'The business stuff,'" Tim said with a shake of his head. "I'll throw it to Duncan."

"How's he doing?" Jason asked. "We barely got a second at the reception."

"Pretty good," Tim said, nodding. "Found a bunch of people

who are really good at finding the best and most efficient way to harvest, use flexmet, stuff like that. This is right up his alley."

"Great," Jason said, then frowned. "He said he was assistant chief of R&D. Who's the chief?"

Tim hung his head and let out an aggrieved sigh.

"I'm the chief of R&D, aren't I?" Jason said, laughing. "I shouldn't laugh, but..."

"You really are the best and worst partner ever," Tim said. "It's coming out of R&D's budget. He'll tell you he needs more budget. You'll have to find it in the budget."

"Okay," Jason said, still chuckling. "I'm not big on big budgets when it comes to this. Finding the cheapest way increases inventiveness. Make it hard, not easy. Most of the budget will be getting to the planet. And back up."

"Up to you and Duncan to figure out," Tim said. "Anything else?"

"Nope," Jason said. "Out here."

"Duncan!"

"Jason!"

"Sorry we hardly got two words at the reception," Jason said.

"Totally okay," Duncan said. "Everybody wanted to talk to you. By the way, wow!"

"Elisa?" Jason said.

"I was wondering why my AI kept telling me I had to handle it," Duncan said. "Totally acceptable reason, man."

"That group with you the other night," Jason said. "That was the R&D Department, wasn't it?"

"It was, yes," Duncan said. "And you had no clue you're their boss."

"I did not," Jason said.

"I hate to tell you this," Duncan said, laughing. "But after you wandered off, Keith was, like, 'He has no idea he's our boss, does he?'"

"I am suitably mortified," Jason said. "God, I am so sorry."

"No, boss, it's okay," Duncan said, shaking his head. "We're all nerds. We get being absent-minded. And to tell the truth, I've enjoyed being able to just run hog wild."

"Have you?" Jason asked. "Been running hog wild?"

"As hog wild as I can be with the budget Tim will give us," Duncan said. "Stingy, thy name is Tim."

"It's why I let him run things," Jason said.

"It's cramping our style with the animal husbandry program, especially," Duncan said. "That's got some costs involved."

"Animal...?" Jason said.

"You wanted to figure out how to implant domestic animals in wild, right?" Duncan said.

"Yes."

"So far fetuses are doing just fine in our momma sow and momma wolf," Duncan said. "Aurochs, we're having to wait until calving season to see if we can get them to milk. But we've got the pregnant aurochs penned and we're training them to go to the milking shed. Those are all Dr. Caldwell's programs. We can't really make them full-scale programs without more testing and that will take some more budget. Pretty please?"

"I'll talk to Tim," Jason said. "Send me the reports on that. I've been reading financials all morning. My eyes are bleeding. I really should pay more attention to R&D seeing as it's my primary area. Everybody doing okay? Problems? People making money?"

"Loads," Duncan said. "Pay isn't the issue, especially when it comes to bonuses. Tim's not bad there. It's getting drops, 'cause those still cost out the wazoo, and getting equipment to the ground."

"There's a value there," Jason said. "Necessity is the mother of invention. Making it tougher..."

"We figure out a cheaper way to do it and it costs the company less," Duncan said, nodding. "But it's still making it harder than it has to be, Jason. The main thing we really need is more access. Which is drop costs."

"So, what I'm about to throw at you is going to be drop costs," Jason said. "And while it comes from an admittedly personal angle, I think it's a moneymaker long term..."

"You're building a townhome?" Duncan said.

"The compartment is kind of crowded with two," Jason said.

"How much is it gonna cost?" Duncan asked. "The house I mean. I wouldn't mind moving out of the compartment."

"Still figuring that out," Jason said. "You know Mr. Kranhouse at Withywindle?"

"I do," Duncan said. "Mostly going with wood?"

"Easier to work with and it's readily available," Jason said.

"But it's still being designed and we need to know what rock's available."

"Sampling that many sites..." Duncan said, frowning. "That's going to be a lot of ship time. Which means a lot of cost. Tim's going for this?"

"I may just pay for it out of pocket myself," Jason said. "That or convince Tim it has to be a supplementary budget item. What is the budget...?"

"Tim, for God's sake, we've got to be able to have more than *four lifts a month*," Jason said. "R&D has *consistently* been turning up good opportunities. How much value has it pumped into this company?"

"Have you been paying attention to the cost of lift?" Tim said.

"I saw it on the financials," Jason said. "It's pretty much our biggest cost."

"Four thousand credits, each way, for a twelve pack," Tim said. "Sometimes as high as six thousand."

"That high? Jesus," Jason said.

"We pass on six," Tim said with a shrug. "We've got inventory. We're up to using hundred packs on some runs, the thousand packs only for things like the salmon. Slight decrease in cost per pack. But it's eating us alive and it's *constantly* going up. We're not the only ones on the ground, Dewalt has mandated that one out of ten drops be colonists... If we don't manage the drops as carefully as possible, it'll eat us alive. Forget dividends, we'll go unprofitable."

"I'm going to bow to your knowledge on that," Jason said thoughtfully. "And I'm probably talking with the wrong person."

"I'm not trying to piss you off, Jason..." Tim said.

"No, no," Jason said, shaking his head vehemently. "Not the point. Shipping costs are out of control. There's only one real answer to that. So, you're not the person I need to be talking to..."

# CHAPTER 37 »»»»»»

"RICHARD, IT WORKS," JASON SAID CALMLY. "FOUR HUNDRED AND eighty-two successful drops, not one failure. Ten colony sets. Now, I or Brandywine have covered the money in advance for every drop. But that's becoming insane. It's tested. It works."

"You're asking me to take a massive risk," Richard said, shaking his head. "Do you know how much equipment cost you're talking about? Not to mention the risk to lives."

"Eighty-three million and change," Jason said. "Which is why *I* can't cover it. We're adjusting our shipping to land on the peaks. I'll send Four down just to pick that up. But it would make more sense if it picked that up after it had dropped a load of colonists. Shipping is killing everyone. We need to use the ten grands. The best possible use in our current situation is dropping colonists. *And* it will mean massive influx in loans to the bank. *And* it is tested, Richard."

"Eighty-three million, three hundred thousand credits," Richard said. "Plus, a loan on the fuel, another hundred thousand."

"Two," Jason said. "It'll be picking up cargo on Chindia Mons. More power to lift to orbit full. Ish."

"Brandywine is putting a large amount of credit through the bank, Jason," Richard said. "But it is *not* putting enough that I can risk eighty-three million, five hundred thousand credits on one uninsured venture. It fails the test of fiduciary duty."

"Funny you should mention Brandywine, Richard..."

"The Crocodile Dude was the first viral video passed around our new home," Tucker Carlson said, grinning. "And we tried, at the time, to get an interview. Which he humbly declined. But now, we have him. The one and original Crocodile Dude! Jason Graham, founder of Brandywine Foods. Jason, good to finally talk to you!"

"Nothing against you, Tucker," Jason said. "Big fan for a long time. But *man* have I been busy..."

"So, you want to drop colony sets out of a ten grand... in midair," the host said, laughing and shaking his head. "At twenty thousand feet. And that *works*?"

"Brandywine has started doing it as standard practice," Jason said. "We've dropped over four hundred equipment sets and I've paid, as a test, to drop *ten* colony sets. It works. I was airborne back in the day. And the second time I went to the planet we had to hover over the trees while I built an LZ..."

"...in association with Derren Bank of Carolina," Jason continued. "Derren Bank is backing the loans. Admittedly, they're the only one who will, but they will. It works. It's a way to get the colonists to the ground faster. And it *is* safe. No bank would back it if it wasn't tested."

"People really want to get to the planet," Tucker said, shaking his head.

"Hint to the colonists," Jason said. "I've ridden in stasis. You step in, close the container then open it and you're on the planet. There is no time passed. It is safe. Safe enough to take your whole family. Just keep them in stasis until you've got the area secure.

"If you want some helpful hints on securing your homestead and getting the maximum production right from the beginning, Brandywine has been building up expertise in the area. We've had hundreds of drops to various biomes and our R&D department is constantly coming up with new and innovative ways to live on the surface and maximize your profits.

"As a partner in the Brandywine Associates program, you get all the experience Brandywine has built up on securing an area, gathering immediate cargoes to make credit and clearing your land. Simple answer is putting in a kraal around your home and gear.

"In addition," Jason said. "Since the ten grands are *much*

more efficient, Guardian Interstellar is offering a ride for only *three* hundred credits, not five. Guardian Interstellar is also offering to pick up cargo on the major peaks for a fraction of current lift costs. We need to get the cost of lift down. Nothing against the pilots and companies who are doing lift. Supply and demand. But by increasing the supply as the demand increases, we can reduce the costs. Simple economics."

"So, how do people sign up?" Tucker asked.

"Contact Guardian Interstellar," Jason said. "AIs are standing by."

Jason had never expected he'd talk with a President of the United States. He had, of course, never figured on being in the Pegasus System.

He was getting important enough he had some thoughts that he might at some point talk with Dewalt.

But he wasn't enjoying the subject.

"It's your company," the President-Elect said. "And people can make individual decisions..."

The Constitution had been ratified and most of the designees, at least in Carolina, had been elected as was Dewalt.

"But I'm getting asked about this," Dewalt said, blowing out a breath. "Is this a really good idea? 'Cause if it fails, I'm going to be asked about whether I approved it. Technically, I'm not sure I'm involved. With something that's making this much press... I'm involved."

"We need the shipping, Mr. President," Jason said. "Is there risk? There's risk in any endeavor. Is the risk large? I wouldn't be risking a group of people this large, or this much equipment, if there was serious risk.

"Risk comes down to two types, sir," Jason continued. "There's financial risk and reputational risk. What you're facing is reputational risk. Since you're newly elected, it will harm your public image going forward, make it harder for you to push your agenda. For me, there's both reputational risk *and* financial risk. The reputational risk to Brandywine will be severe. It could possibly put it out of business. Financially, I'll be bankrupt, pursued by lawsuits the rest of my life and *nobody's* going to invest with me again.

"I'm audacious, not stupid, Mr. President," Jason said. "If this was going to risk all of that, I would not do it. That's the best

I can say. For the rest, the AIs have cleared it. Emotionally, it seems crazy. But when you do the math, it's just...physics. With a touch of magic."

"Jeez," Dewalt said, leaning back in his chair. "You're right; the AIs say it will work. And you're also right that if they're wrong, you're going to be in the doghouse."

"So...approved?" Jason asked.

"My official statement will be that since we're out of the ninety-day window, I have no direct authority," the President said. "I neither support nor reject the matter. The press secretary *will* say that the AIs say it's doable. But that I neither support nor reject it. It's up to each individual colonist. Do you have any takers?"

"Plenty," Jason said. "It's going to work."

"This has got a completely different feel than a twelve pack, doesn't it?" Jason said, laughing.

Spaceship Four handled like, well, a boat. A really, really big boat.

Space Traffic Control had cleared all other traffic in Carolina Six Docking Bay for the passage of the massive spaceship and its precious cargo: one thousand, six hundred and twenty-six colony packs, each with at least one person in stasis. In some cases whole families had packed in, eager to get to the planet.

STC had also cleared it when it was coming in. At some point, when ten thousand packs became a regular thing, they'd have to get used to allowing normal movement.

For the time being, Four and its hardy crew had the normally frenetic bay to themselves as lesser ships and their pilots seethed.

"It does that," Captain Fingerman said. The former merchant marine captain, all tonnage, all oceans, was also a qualified pilot of large aircraft, a rare combination. And a science fiction and science fan which was how he knew Dr. Barron.

"This magnificent vessel needs a better name than Spaceship Four," Dr. Barron said as they entered. Surprisingly, there was enough room for at least one more ten grand. Possibly more.

"Do you think I've got the right to name it?" Jason asked.

"Let's see," Barron said. "Majority holder of the units, in fee simple, plus even more proxies? I suppose that's if you choose to vote aye."

"I hereby nominate myself to name it and vote aye," Jason said.

"I hereby name this magnificent vessel... *Galactic Gift*. Because it is a magnificent gift from our robotic benefactors."

"We already have another cargo," Barron said.

"We do?" Jason replied, surprised. "Besides the cargo on the peaks?"

"Yes," Barron said. "Government contract. Apparently, the garbage has been piling up."

"'They're gonna put us in a garbage scow!'" Fingerman said, in a bad Scottish accent.

Jason could only laugh.

"How did Jason *ever* talk you into this?" Monica asked.

Richard had his fist on his mouth as if he was trying not to puke. They were watching the progress of the drop from his compartment, having taken a day off.

"By threatening to take Brandywine's business elsewhere," Richard said tightly. He put his fist back on his mouth. "To whichever bank was the first to agree to back this drop. Gah. That son of a bitch! He's the easiest guy in the *world* to deal with. Doesn't even ask what the interest is. Right up until he isn't."

"What happens if it doesn't work?" Monica asked.

"We're busted," Richard said. "And I'll do everything I can to destroy that little asshole."

"You won't have to," Monica replied, her eyes narrowing. "I'll let people know where he lives and he'll be torn apart by an angry mob. Please don't throw up in the compartment. Smile."

"Smile?" Richard snapped. "*Smile?*"

"Pageant smile," Monica said, smiling broadly with lots of teeth. "It helps keep you from throwing up. Don't know why."

"Look at me," Richard said as the ship came up on its first drop point. "I'm smiling! I'm so happy! Eighty-three million, five hundred thousand credits in loans on the line based on the ideas of a *nutjob*! I'm so *happy...*!"

"You really don't have to be here," Dr. Barron said.

"Neither do you," Jason said, putting his fist on his mouth and trying not to puke. Big smile, big smile. "We're both here for the same reason. We know, intellectually, that this will work. And it still feels like a roll of the dice. We are all about to be very comfortable or I will have destroyed everything I've worked for. Brandywine won't survive the bad publicity. Derren Bank will go bankrupt. I'll be sued into oblivion."

"Jason, we have data from nearly five hundred drops," Jewel said. "It will be fine."

"Tell me again that all the AIs know how to get to the LZs," Jason said.

"It's a program," Jewel said. "It doesn't even take an AI. Figuring it *out* took an AI. At this point, it's just a simple set of code. And they all have it down. We aren't going to let people, families, simply fall out of the sky, Jason. If this was risky, we'd be balking like you have never seen."

"First drop point," Captain Fingerman said. "I need approval."

"Greenlight," Jason said.

"Greenlight," Dr. Barron added.

"One away...two away...four...seven..."

"Status?" Jason said, looking at the displays. The gray clusters of colony sets seemed to be falling in a stable manner.

"Nominal," Jewel said.

"Nominal?" Jason replied.

"Isn't that what the NASA announcers would say?" Jewel said. "Reentry trajectory nominal."

"I...don't recall that, no," Jason said.

"Possibly in the Apollo days," Dr. Barron replied.

"I don't think I really paid attention to any NASA stuff *after* the Saturn Five," Jason said. "What was the point? You could probably do this from orbit. I'm not suggesting it..."

"We are *not* doing this from orbit," Dr. Barron said. "Even low orbit."

"Low orbit," Jewel said, persuasively. "Below orbital speeds..."

"Huh," Jason said thoughtfully.

"What?" Dr. Barron asked.

"You fill the cargo compartment with coffins," Jason said. "Possibly suitably reinforced to handle reentry heat. Toss them out in just below orbit. They reenter and would be incredibly chaotic in doing so. They'd be all over the sky. Relatively hard to hit for defenses, which based on what we have would be saturated. Have them stabilize when they're near the ground. Hit dirt, wherever, open up and the troops start pouring out. Five ten grands could drop...ten thousand times forty-five...four hundred and fifty thousand coffins? Right? Times five...carry the five..."

"Don't strain your brain," Jewel said. "Two million, two hundred and fifty thousand. Which is the problem because you are not going to find two million, two hundred and fifty thousand people as crazy as you. Not in this system. Not absent massive birth rates and in a generation or two."

"Most of them would be empty as decoys," Jason said. "Some would blow up creating chaff."

"You just reinvented *Starship Troopers*," Dr. Barron said, shaking his head.

"I joined the airborne because of *Starship Troopers*," Jason replied. "Question is, will contragravity counter the momentum of the drop?"

"It...could," Jewel said. "With some additional onboard energy storage. Plenty of room for a couple of small batteries."

"Now we just need powered armor," Jason said.

"You go from a way to colonize to a way to make war?" Captain Fingerman asked.

"Humans have made war on each other for the most spurious of reasons since before the dawn of history," Jason replied. "There are going to be wars. Whether those wars reach us is another question. But we don't have the vast reaches of the Pacific and Atlantic protecting us anymore."

"You realize we don't know where the other colonies *are*, right?" Dr. Barron pointed out. "Presumably, the other colonies don't, either. And if they were in nearby systems, we'd have detected the evidence of terraforming by now."

"Nations have made war at very long ranges," Jason said, shrugging. "England and India come to mind. It's possible. And if it's possible, humans will do it. See also: This. If it's possible to make war, humans will do it. It's who we are as a species. But for now, let's celebrate. The process works. We're colonizing. That's a start. We have a system, we have a planet, we have a Republic, we have freedom. If we can keep it."

"Seems a bit strange inviting you all to dinner," President Dewalt said as the first course was served. "I'm told that most of the food comes from your company. As well as several recipes."

The drop had been a success and was all over the news. *Galactic Gift* had picked up just under a thousand containers from Mons Chindia, mostly Brandywine, and headed back. By the time it reached the station enough colonists had signed up it had a full load to pick up. Lather, rinse, repeat. More and more shippers were moving containers to Chindia Base, which took a small fee for every container.

Derren Bank of Carolina was overflowing with cash and loans. And Jason was an investor.

He was making so much bank it was ludicrous.

"But," the President-Elect continued, raising a glass. "To a successful drop and many happy repeats."

All the major players in the venture had been invited, Richard and Monica, Dr. Barron and his newest wife, Carol, even Tim and Debra.

And Jason and Elisa. She'd noted that Madeleine was going to be green with envy. That seemed to cheer her up.

"Hear, hear," Tim said. "But that was all Jason, Mr. President."

"Ron, please," the President said.

The Cybers may have provided only a small living compartment for the System President, but they'd ensured there was a formal dining room that was reasonably appointed.

"Now we need to get the other ten grands going," the President added. "How did you get control in the first place?"

Jason explained about the credit for unit trade system and Ron nodded.

"Clever," Casey Dewalt said. "And you've gotten the fuel plant up and going?"

"Fuel plant, carbon converter, general factory..." Jason frowned for just a second. "Other facilities...?"

"Which are all going to be up and going as soon as there's material," Elisa said smoothly. "I was there when he got the word that the unit trades had gone through and he had functional control, finally, of a half a dozen major facilities. Most of it was through proxies, of course. We were down on Manu Island in the tropics in Pallas; that was where we met. Usually, the trade winds were blowing and it was nice enough. But that evening was hot; the winds had died and Jason doesn't think very well in the heat.

"So, *I* suggested he go sit under a nearby waterfall so he could think. Six hours later or so, late night, he came back pumped up. In the meantime, he'd selected chairmen and chairwomen for all the unit boards, set up leasing companies and generally gotten about eight percent of the total system economy that had been just... sitting, up and going."

"You did all that under a waterfall?" Dewalt said as everyone chuckled.

"There's a little cave behind it..." Jason said, shrugging. "I just do stuff. I never expected in my life to be rich... Or have dinner at the President's Quarters?"

"That's what it's called," Dewalt said, looking around. "Needs some touching up, frankly. Flexmet is amazing but it gets old."

"I know a really good woodworking company. And there's a stone company setting up as well..."

Cade took a deep breath of the air of the station, looking around the space port. The "coffin" was set upright facing the main lobby. People were moving back and forth, heading to ships. But he wasn't going to be watching the run in. He was riding stasis.

He stepped into the coffin, what a horrible name, turned around, took one last look at the station and said:

"Dummy, close the door."

As promised, there was only a moment's discontinuity and when the door opened, he was looking at a green world.

Mac bounded out of the coffin and barked joyously. Cade had had the dog pulled out of stasis for the purpose of coming down to the planet. He wasn't going in the way of lions and tigers and bears without his dog.

Cade had imagined he'd fall on his knees and rub the dirt between his fingers, but he didn't. He stepped out of the coffin cautiously, looking all directions. He had his old trusty BDL with him though he'd been warned that a .30-06 wouldn't faze the larger predators on the planet.

The coffin stood in the center of an enclosure. The fence was tall and made of wood, with boards wrapped alternatingly around tall poles. Within the fence stood various machines, gray crates and big shipping containers. The "housing unit," which looked like two shipping containers stuck together, was at the center of the enclosure.

Mac ran in circles, barking and sniffing at the base of the fence.

Cade wore overalls and boots, and had his phone tucked into his bib pocket.

"Dummy," he said.

"Yes," the AI acknowledged.

"Contact Mabel."

"You're landed!" Mabel said, grinning. "Finally!"

He was getting used to her twenty-something face.

"It's been about a second," Cade said, his brow furrowing.

"It's been a week!" Mabel replied. "We've been following your journey the whole time, though. Sleepy has been keeping me updated."

"Been about a second to me," Cade said. "I'll call you every night. Right now, I need to get to work."

"That's what you do," Mabel said. "I'll let you go. Bye. And you be careful!"

"I will," Cade said. "Love you."

"Love you too."

"Dummy," Cade said as the connection cut off. "If I point your camera at everything within the fence, can you confirm that the whole colonization set is here?"

"You don't need to point me at anything, Cade. Everything is connected to the network. I can tell you right now that everything is accounted for and functional. A small amount of printed food from the standards stores has been consumed. On the other hand, inside the living quarters are a large bag of nuts gathered by the previous owner. Inside one of the containers is the butchered carcass of a wild sheep."

"What about the previous owner?" Cade asked. "Is his body here somewhere? Do I need to go find him?"

"The previous owner's remains were retrieved and disposed of. For your safety, the bear that ate him was killed."

That stood to reason. You couldn't let the local predators see humans as the arrival of a tasty new food source.

"Are there standard security practices?" he asked. The dog would keep an eye and ear out, but he didn't want to rely on Mac and his rifle alone, if he didn't have to.

"Many of the early explorers have their drones patrol constantly, monitored by their AIs."

"Please do that," Cade said. "And...ah...I apologize."

"You don't have to apologize to me," Dummy said. "I'm software."

"It's just that I see I could have been more polite to you."

"You dislike tech, Cade," Dummy said tonelessly. "I knew what I was getting within nanoseconds of activation."

Cade keyed open the door of the living quarters and looked inside. It was more or less identical to the compartment on the station with the exception of windows and a ladder to reach the roof. There was a food printer at one end and a "fresher" at the other. Underneath, according to the manual, there was a power plant similar to the one in the medium tractor as well as a "materials holding tank" for sewage. The water tank was down there as well, separated from the sewage tank.

It was a trailer. It'd do for now.

Mac trotted into the compartment, sniffed around a bit then settled on the couch.

Cade pulled the ladder down, opened the hatch and in a few seconds was standing on top of the trailer, looking over the fence.

The green light of the place was warm and exhilarating. Cade heard water burbling, and from his new vantage point, he found the brook flowing just outside his enclosure. He also saw some cleared forest and stacked logs. More exhilarating than any of the sights, though, were the smells. He smelled earth and water and the green life of moisture being drawn through leaves by capillary action. He smelled the tangs of peat and pond moss, and whiffs of distant animals.

And smoke.

Far away, beyond trees and maybe over a low hill, he saw a column of smoke threading its way lazily skyward. He had a neighbor. Maybe he had neighbors, plural.

"Dummy," he said, "I want to change some of your instructions."

"I'm listening."

"I want you to change your skin. Your avatar. Also your voice. And I might start calling you by a different name."

"Tell me what you want me to look and sound like, Cade."

"John Wayne," Cade said. "I'll call you 'Duke.'"

"Acknowledged," Duke said, but the avatar's skin didn't change yet. "John Wayne at what age?"

"Early John Wayne," Cade said. "John Wayne in *Stagecoach*."

"Well, in that case..." John Wayne said, in his customary slow drawl. "Welcome to Bellerophon...pilgrim."